Welcome to Effham Falls Copy

Small Town Tales

Moorhead Friends Writing Group

Copyright © 2023 by Moorhead Friends Writing Group

All rights reserved.

No portion of this book may be reproduced in any form without written permission from the publisher or author, except as permitted by U.S. copyright law.

This is a work of fiction. Names, characters, places, and incidents either are the product of the author's imagination or are used fictitiously. Any resemblance to actual persons, living or dead, events, or locales is entirely coincidental.

First Paperback Edition April 2023

Edited by Robin Pope Cain

Cover Design & Wrap by Tiffany Fier

Cover Photo by W. Scott Olson

Contents

Introduction Thomas Maltman	1
Where is Effham Falls? People & Places of the Arrowhead Region Eileen C. Tronnes Nelson	5
Four Corners Matthew R. Clark	13
The Top Prize Neal Romriell	29
House Hunting Michele R. Willman	47
Two Arrowheads William R. Bartlett	57
Doppelgänger Jason Bursack	79
The Carnival Comes To Town Scott Dyson	91
The Card Dan McKay	105
One Small Cloud in the Sky Alexander Vayle	119

Dolls Chris Stenson	139
The Meter Reader Daniel Haynes	167
The Guest Susette Quinn	179
Heart's Desire T.J. Fier	199
The Nudi Alibi Tina Holland	209
I Don't Know You Silvia Villalobos	229
The Come Hither Donna R. Wood	247
The Family Graveyard Shift Sarah Nour	259
Choices Barbara Bustamante	273
It Came From The Woods Sadie Mendenhall-Cariveau	283
Final Wish Robin Cain	299
Thank You	318

Introduction

Thomas Maltman

When did you last visit Winesburg, Ohio, spend time in Staggerford, Minnesota, or listen in on the gossiping residents of Little Wing, Wisconsin? None of these places can be found on any map or atlas, and yet for readers of Sherwood Anderson, Jon Hassler, or Nikolas Butler, these fictional Midwestern small towns are just as real as those you might travel to by car. You only need to lift the book off the shelf to be transported once more.

Those who love speculative fiction may fondly recall spending time in Ray Bradbury's Green Town, Illinois, or visiting the haunted regions of Stephen King's Castle Rock, Maine. "It was a small town by a small river and a small lake in a small northern part of a Midwest state," begins Ray Bradbury's "The Halloween Tree," which opens by describing an ordinary place in every way until sunset when "night came out under each tree and spread," ushering the reader into the world of the strange.

Readers can now add a new town on the map of imaginary places. With this publication, prepare to travel to Effham Falls, Minnesota, a small town where reality and the supernatural coexist.

Before you do, stop for a moment and consider. Why do these small towns endure in the imagination long after the authors have finished their work? What is it about the lesser-traveled backroads of America that fires the imagination of readers and writers alike?

Before my wife and I moved to Morgan, Minnesota, home to some nine-hundred souls, I had never before lived in a small town. Yet here I was in Little House on the Prairie territory, a mere forty miles away from Plum Creek, Minnesota, where the Ingalls family once purchased a sod home dug from the earth. Small town life proved to be a revelation for me. "You can live here for twenty-five years and still be counted a stranger," one long-time resident confided to me.

As the husband of the town's young new Lutheran pastor, and as a teacher at the local high school with a graduating class of twenty-six students, I wasn't used to people knowing my name as soon as I set foot in the town grocery store. Life in this fishbowl required some adjustment. Another pastor who moved to a small town in Nebraska described how she was walking across her living room one day when she tripped. A moment later the phone rang. "Are you okay?" said the voice on the other end.

Surely, as Norm from the show *Cheers* might assure us, there is comfort in living in a place where "everybody knows your name." At a high school basketball game, I watched as a teacher passed her newborn baby around the stands, the bundled child moving from hand to hand. There was such beautiful trust in the moment, as if the baby belonged to them all. This longing to know others and to be known is a central part of our human existence, and small towns provide this comfort.

Yet, small towns also compel our attention for their dark side. "A man went on a journey or a stranger came to town" are the two most basic story patterns found in fiction. The stranger who enters the story? You better believe that when he or she shows up that the ingrained traditions of this small town are about to be exposed and called to question. I had only lived in Morgan for less than a year when another teacher told me the town secret, a story of murder and suicide that would one day become the spark for my second novel, *Little Wolves*.

One of the first things I teach my intro to creative writing students is how to trap their characters. Put your characters in an enclosed space—a locked room, an elevator that quits working, a car stranded by the side of the road—and see not only what happens, but what your characters are made of and what is revealed by their choices. Small towns can also sometimes feel like a trap, especially for those who don't fit in.

Ultimately, small towns offer a microcosm of the human experience, all that is light and dark within us brought into sharper focus by geographic limitation. This is one reason authors are drawn to such spaces, since they provide a clear backdrop for the timeless dramas of our existence.

So, prepare yourself now for Effham Falls, Minnesota. The stories that follow traverse a terrain that includes both the literary and the supernatural, but no matter the genre, the characters here in this place face hard choices. How can a woman dispose of the ashes of a man who mistreated her in life? What mystery lies behind the discovery of a ring with a finger still attached? What mission brings a stranger from distant St. Paul? Demons and doppelgangers and antique dolls capable of possession await in these pages. Both books and bookstores may become doorways to magic. How far will the characters go to find fortune, even if it means resorting to robbery, cheating, or braving a curse? The only thing certain in Effham Falls, is that nothing will quite be the same again.

Welcome to Effham Falls, Reader. May you enjoy your stay here and come again.

THOMAS MALTMAN is the author of *The Night Birds*, *Little Wolves*, and *The Land*.

Where is Effham Falls? People & Places of the Arrowhead Region

Eileen C. Tronnes Nelson

The Arrowhead Region is in Northeast Minnesota and gets its name from the pointed shape of a Native American arrowhead. The Arrowhead Region consists of seven counties in the northeastern part of the state, which stretches across the Boundary Waters Canoe Area Wilderness and Voyageurs National Park in the north to the western edge of Lake Superior in the south and extends westward into the counties in the heart of Minnesota's Northwoods. Primarily rural region, the major industries include mining and lumbering companies. (*See* the maps from Norman K. Risjord (2005), *A Popular History of Minnesota*. MN: Minnesota Historical Society Press.):

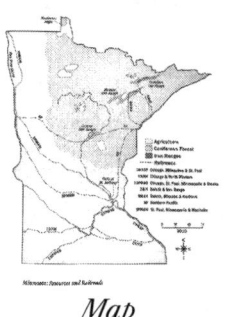

Map

Description automatically generated

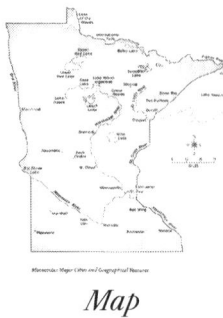

Map

Description automatically generated

Three Iron Ranges and Four Tribal Lands

Contained in this Arrowhead Region are three Iron Ranges: Cuyuna, Mesabi, and Vermilion ("The Range"), and four Tribal lands: Mille Lacs, Fond du Lac, Leech Lake, and Bois Forte.

The Top Ten Communities by Population

Duluth, Quad Cities (Eveleth, Gilbert, Mountain Iron, Virginia), Hibbing, Cloquet, Grand Rapids, Hermantown, International Falls, Chisholm, Rice Lake, Two Harbors, and Ely. (Retrieved September 23, 2022, from https://www.northlandconnection.com.)

Lumber Industry

The lumbering industry "Stump Jumpers" played an important part in the early economy but declined rapidly after 1900 because the pine forests were depleted, and the natural regrowth of aspen and birch had limited commercial value. In the latter half of the 20th century, however, Minnesota's forest industry was revitalized with the growth of the wood pulp and waferboard industries. ("Minnesota - Economy | Britannica"). Pine, balsam, and spruce are harvested for pulpwood, while aspen -- once considered a weed tree -- became the preferred species for waferboard manufacturing and accounts for about seven-tenths of the commercially harvested wood in Minnesota.

Iron Ore Industry

Commercial iron ore production began in Minnesota in 1884 at Soudan, on the Vermilion Range. After the huge iron reserves of the Mesabi Range were discovered at Mountain Iron in 1890, large-scale production ensued.

Hibbing, the largest open-pit iron mine in the world, is three miles wide and 500 feet deep. A person senses the ghosts of previous miners and cyclical boom and bust of their fortunes. A young Bob Dylan wrote and recorded "North Country Blues," a song about the desperate plight of an iron miner's wife left to care for three children after a mine shutdown. ("North Country Blues." Retrieved September 24, 2022, from https://m.youtube.com/watch?v=r5GjjUppig8.)

Hibbing, Minnesota, former home to:

Bob Dylan, aka Robert Zimmerman, grew up in Hibbing. To understand Bob Dylan, visiting Hibbing offers insights into the desolation and snowy emptiness shaping the Nobel Laureate's inner space and artistic obsession. Growing up in the north, in an isolated place like Hibbing, with long winters, Dylan must have acquired a way of looking at the world he might never have had if he had grown up in a place like sunny San Diego. Hibbing shaped an ordinary teenager and helped turn him into the Shakespeare of our age.

Vincent Bugliosi (Deputy District Attorney in California, successfully prosecuted Charles Manson and other defendants accused of the Tate-LaBianca, seven murders that took place between August 9-10, 1969. Bugliosi is credited especially with gaining conviction of Manson, who was not directly involved in the murders. Bugliosi is the author of *Helter Skelter, And the Sea Will Tell, Reclaiming History: The Assassination of President John F. Kennedy,* and *The Prosecution of George W. Bush for Murder.*).

Dick Garmaker (Minnesota Lakers and New York Knicks basketball player.).

Roger Maris (New York Yankee baseball player, broke Babe Ruth's single season home run record hitting sixty-one in 1961. Roger Maris died of cancer at age 51. The famous Sanford Roger Maris Cancer Center in Fargo, North Dakota, is one of the top cancer centers -- named in honor of Roger Maris. (My son, Douglas A. Nelson, is receiving cancer treatment at the Roger Maris Cancer Center for prostate cancer that has metastasized to his spine.)

Kevin McHale (Boston Celtics basketball player and coach of the Minnesota Timberwolves.).

Rudy Perpich (Governor of Minnesota for ten years, December 29, 1976 to January 4, 1979, and again from January 3, 1983 to January 7, 1991).

Luigino "Jeno" Paulucci (an American food industry magnate, founder of seventy companies. A pioneer of ready-made ethnic foods, such as Chinese Chun King, Italian Jeno's Inc. which was a pizza company that sold frozen pizzas.).

Gary Puckett (born in Hibbing, raised in Yakima, Washington. Gary Puckett and *The Union Gap*, an American pop rock group. Grammy for Best New Artist, mainly popular for his song, *"Woman, Woman"*). (Gary Puckett and *The Union Gap*. Retrieved September 25, 2022, from https://music.youtube.com/watch?v=i-utzhbHv7Q.)

Eveleth, Minnesota, First Sexual Harassment Class Action Lawsuit

Lois Jenson and her coworkers, Patricia S. Kosmach and Kathleen Anderson, filed the first ever sexual harassment class action lawsuit tried in the United States federal court. *Jenson v. Eveleth Taconite Co.*, 130 F.3d 1287 (8th Cir. 1997). The female miners endured a range of abuse while working in the Eveleth Taconite Company mines. A movie, *North County* (2005), starring Charlize Theron, Frances McDormand, and Woody Harrelson, inspired by the true story, based on the first major successful class action sexual harassment case in the United States, *Jenson vs. Eveleth Taconite Co*. (E. Tronnes Nelson, Personal knowledge).

Grand Rapids, Minnesota, former home of:

Judy Garland, aka Frances Ethel Gumm, was born in Grand Rapids, Minnesota on June 10, 1922. The birthplace is now a museum dedicated to her life and career. Judy is a famous American actress and singer. Among her numerous roles, she is known world-wide for playing Dorothy Gale in *The Wizard of Oz* (1939). (E. Tronnes Nelson, Personal visit to Garland Museum).

Duluth, Minnesota, Glensheen Congdon Estate

Glensheen, the Congdon estate in Duluth, Minnesota, is on the National Register of Historic Places and was donated to the University of Minnesota Duluth, which operates Glensheen. Aside from its architectural significance, Glensheen is known for the murders of Elisabeth Congdon and her nurse, Velma Pietila, on June 27, 1977. Roger Caldwell, the second husband of Elisabeth's adopted daughter, Marjorie Congdon, LeRoy Caldwell Hagen, was convicted of two counts of first-degree murder and received two life sentences. Marjorie was charged with aiding and abetting and conspiracy to commit murder but was acquitted on all charges. (E. Tronnes Nelson, Personal visit to Glensheen.)

Edmund Fitzgerald Iron Ore Freighter

The *Edmund Fitzgerald*, a 729-foot iron ore freighter sank in Lake Superior on November 10, 1975. *Edmund Fitzgerald* was the largest ship on North America's Great Lakes. There were 26,000 tons of taconite iron ore onboard. There was a severe ice and windstorm with thirty-five foot waves and 80 mph hurricane west winds. Twenty-nine sailors perished when the Edmund Fitzgerald sank in water 530 feet deep. Gordon Lightfoot wrote the haunting song, "The Wreck of The Edmund Fitzgerald," and donated the profits to the families of the victims. (*See* "The Wreck of the Edmund Fitzgerald" (w/lyrics) by Gordon Lightfoot. Retrieved September 23, 2022, from https://www.youtube.com/watch?v=lE2LOhs5jaE.)

Split Rock Lighthouse

Split Rock Lighthouse State Park, North of Two Harbors, Minnesota, is on the North Shore of Lake Superior. In 1905, a November storm claimed twenty-nine vessels, killing seventy-eight seamen, within a dozen miles of the Split Rock River. After the tragic sinking of the ships Split Rock Lighthouse was built in response to the storm of 1905, with a fog signal building completed in 1909. For fifty-nine years, lighthouse keepers operated the candlepower beacon at Split Rock Lighthouse, warning ships away from the rock and the waters of the treacherous North Shore.)

Because technology is now on ships, the Split Rock Lighthouse beacon is no longer operational. In 1971, the federal government deeded the lighthouse station to the State of Minnesota to be operated as a historic site. (E. Tronnes Nelson, Personal visit to Split Rock Lighthouse.)

Moose Lake, Minnesota, Sex Offender Facility

Moose Lake is twenty-five miles southwest of Cloquet, Minnesota. The Minnesota Correctional Facility-Moose Lake is one of two state-run facilities for treatment of adult sex offenders. As of September 29, 2022, Moose Lake is housing 992 sex offenders. The sex offenders are held under the "Civil

Commitment" law. This means that after the sex offenders' sentence is complete, the state can deem them an on-going threat and keep them locked up indefinitely under the law. (Minnesota Department of Corrections Facility – Moose Lake Inmate Profile 9/29/2022. Retrieved September 29, 2022, from https://coms.doc.state.mn.us/tourreport/06MFacilityInmateProfile.pdf.)

Nopeming Sanatorium, Duluth, Minnesota

The Nopeming Sanatorium Children's Building was built to house children who contracted tuberculosis. Nopeming is an Ojibwe name, translated to "In the Woods." The sanatorium was opened in 1912 on the southern outskirts of Duluth. The secluded wooded area allowed quarantining of tuberculosis patients. Nopeming housed fifty tuberculosis patients at first, eventually increasing to three hundred.

Medication developed for tuberculosis treatment allowed for patients to remain at home. Thus, in 1971, Nopeming became a nursing home. In 2002, the decision was made to close the facility. Nopeming was purchased by a non-profit group, that then ran tours to raise funds to upgrade the building. In 2019, all tours were shut down due to fire code violations.

There are stories of using the boiler room to burn the bodies of those who died of tuberculosis, and stories of ghosts haunting the building. The Travel Channel's "Ghost Adventure" show in 2015 featuring Nopeming, increasing the number of people fascinated with the paranormal activity to investigate. (Trisha Taurinskas (2022, September 20), Stranger than fiction: Nopeming Sanatorium's history of tuberculosis, ghost hunts and ownership scandals, *Grand Forks Herald*, Retrieved September 27, 2022, from https://www.grandforksherald.com/news/the-vault/stranger-than-fiction-nopeming-sanatoriums-history-of-tuberculosis-ghost-hunts-and-ownership-scandals.)

Eveleth, Minnesota, United States Hockey Hall of Fame

Hockey is popular sport in Minnesota and North Dakota. The United States Hockey Hall of Fame Museum in Eveleth was established in 1973 to preserve the history of ice hockey in the United States and was dedicated to America's high school and college hockey champions. The Hockey Hall honors and recognizes outstanding coaches, players, builders, and administrators who contribute to the success and promotion of American Hockey.

"Steve Cash, **Jim Johannson, Jocelyne Lamoureux-Davidson, Monique Lamoureux-Morando,** and **Ryan Miller** were formally enshrined into the United States Hockey Hall of Fame as the Class of 2022, on November 30, 2022, at the RiverCentre in St. Paul, Minnesota." (Retrieved September 27, 2022, from https://ushockeyhalloffame.com/news_article/show/1238391.)

Jocelyne Lamoureux-Davidson and **Monique Lamoureux-Morando** are identical twins raised in Grand Forks, North Dakota. Linda Lamoureux, mother of the twins, had six babies in five years. The twins are the youngest and have four older hockey-playing brothers: Jean-Philippe, Jacques, Pierre-Paul, and Mario. Linda is a marathon runner including a five-time Boston Marathon participant. Jean-Pierre, father of the six hockey children, is a goalie on the University of North Dakota Hockey team.

During the Olympics in Pyeongchang, South Korea, Monique scored the tying goal with six minutes, twenty-one seconds left in regulation, and Jocelyn put away the decisive goal in the shootout to beat Canada, 3-2, to win the Gold Medals in the Olympics-February 2018. (Lamoureux twins selected to U.S. Hockey Hall of Fame. Brad Elliott Schlossman (2022, September 8), Lamoureux-twins selected to US Hockey Hall of Fame, *Grand Forks Herald*. Retrieved September 27, 2022, from https://grandforksherald.com/sports/und-hockey/lamoureux-twins-selected-to-u-s-hockey-hall-of-fame.)

Jocelyne and Monique made a tremendous positive impact on women's hockey in America. They made countless contributions to the game throughout their impressive careers—twenty International Medals, six World Championships, two Olympic Silver Medals, and one Olympic Gold Medal.

Monique and Jocelyne both now have children: Mickey, born December 2018, and Nelson, born January 2019, respectively. Monique and Jocelyn also received the North Dakota Theodore Roosevelt Rough Rider Award, the highest commendation that a citizen of North Dakota can receive. Roger Maris became the youngest recipient of the North Dakota Roosevelt Rough Rider Award, though, edging out the twins by one year.

Throughout their hockey years, marriages, and having babies, both obtained graduate degrees at the University of North Dakota. Additionally, Jocelyne and Monique are authors of, *Dare to Make History: Chasing a Dream and Fighting for Equity* (2021) (NY: Radius Book Group).

EILEEN C. TRONNES NELSON lives in Grand Forks and is a graduate of the University of North Dakota and Moorhead State University. Certified Paralegal National Association of Legal Assistants, retired after serving nearly forty years at Central Legal Research, School of Law, UND, Grand Forks, ND. She enjoys spending time with her two sons, two daughters, six grandchildren, three bonus grandchildren, three great-grandsons, and in-laws: daughter-, son-, three grandsons-, two granddaughters-. She is researching Scandinavian genealogy and writing her historical non-fiction *Settlers in America* series of six books on how she found her Swedish and Norwegian ancestors. This includes the brutal murder of Marie Wick; asphyxiation of Eleanor Thompson; documents of Johnson & Tronnes property; and in 2018, traveling in Sweden and Norway with her granddaughter. Additionally, she is writing non-fiction books about the murder of Dianne Bill; Flood of 1997; Covid-19; Domestic Abuse; Genealogy of Living Family; Greed; & UND. She can be reached at AuthorEileenTronnesNelson@gmail.com

Four Corners
Matthew R. Clark

The night was dark, darker than the pit of the coal mine, and if there was one thing Tanner Cullen hated, it was walking alone in the dark. It wasn't because he was afraid or anything, but that he couldn't see. It was an annoyance, like a chore his mother made him do after he got home from work.

He looked down at the useless lantern in his hand, the handle making a metallic click against the iron cage that held the glass in place. He had forgotten his box of matches back at the mine, and Forman Cory wouldn't allow him back in to get them. Those matches would be gone by the morning, stolen by some opportunistic asshole, and he would be out almost a full day's pay. He would have to get up early tomorrow to get a new box. He let out a sigh. It was just another thing to add to his bad luck.

He glanced up at the dark blanket of clouds that covered the stars of the Minnesota sky. The darkness wouldn't stop him from his nightly ritual.

Tanner often spent this walk wondering what other twelve-year-old boys around the world were doing. He imagined them playing in lavish gardens, in warm wool clothes, waiting for their fathers to come home before enjoying a nice family dinner.

This was such a contrast from his life, of his circumstances, of his luck. Tanner used to be like the boys he imagined. Sure, he never had a lavish garden, or expensive clothes, but he had a father.

The thought of his father quickened his pace and snapped him out of his daydream.

He was on Thirty-First Street, a dirt road that led up to the only saloon in town open at this time of night, The Rusty Nail.

When he first arrived, the owner of the saloon, Mr. Talsen, thought the great town of Effham Falls was some hidden jewel of a town meant to be a great city. But as the months dragged on, Tanner saw poor Mr. Talsen become just as hungry as the miners. He was broke and barely making ends meet.

The dirt road began to light up dimly as the Rusty Nail's swinging doors came into view. Tanner fumbled around in his right pants pocket and rubbed two five-cent pieces together. He would have to buy matches in the morning, so he could only limit himself to one ale tonight.

As he got closer, he noticed flat earth running across Thirty-First Street, alongside the saloon. He stopped in the center of the intersecting dirt paths. Something felt weird. His hair stood up. His chest felt cold. A plume of white smoke left his mouth. His body started to shiver. Just outside the cone of light coming from the Rusty Nail, in the thick darkness, came a deep gurgling laugh.

Tanner bolted for the saloon entrance. The doors swung violently as he barreled inside. He slammed face first into the gut of Father Harry Ilks.

"Whoa, boy," the father said. "What are you doing running in here like that? The consumption got a hold of your soul that bad that you must run like the devil is at your back?"

Tanner glanced back at the doors, waiting for whatever that was to creep inside. But nothing ever came.

He caught his breath and composed himself. He was just hearing things, that's all. He couldn't act like a scared child now. The saloon's patrons were sparse, but word traveled fast in Effham Falls. He was in the presence of men and he couldn't let them see his fear. If they saw him crying like he had the first day at the mine, the torment would start all over again.

He looked up at the priest. "I'm just thirsty, Father."

At almost seven feet tall, Ilks was a mountain of a man with thick black hair, a goatee, and ice-like blue eyes. Tanner feared him, not because of his size but because of his constant preaching of hellfire and brimstone.

"What are you doing here?" Tanner asked.

Ilks eyed him for a while but then smiled and ruffled Tanner's dirty hair. "Keeping track of the comings and goings, boy." He surveyed all the patrons lined up at the bar. "Heathens don't usually indulge so much when God is watching them."

"Aye. Don't put that kinda fear into the boy, Father," a woman from behind the bar said.

A smile spread across Tanner's face when he saw Mrs. Talsen cleaning a glass mug, and giving Father Ilks her dagger eyes, as she would say.

For as mean as Mr. Talsen came off, his wife was the opposite. She was warm and loving. After Tanner's father died, the couple took a protector-like role over him. He still needed to pay for his drink, but they made sure he was taken care of in terms of clothes and food.

She turned her attention to him and gave him a warm smile. "You want something to eat, Tan? I have some leftover beef stew I can warm up for ya."

Tanner nodded eagerly. He didn't realize how hungry he was until food was mentioned. His stomach was roaring. "Yes, ma'am. I don't know if my mother made anything before leaving for work. Thank you."

Mrs. Talsen gave him a sad smile and hurried off to the kitchen.

Father Ilks took a deep breath and smiled. "Mrs. Talsen is a true servant of God." A frown replaced his smile. "Even though she owns a business that is offensive to our Lord."

"Oy! Piss off, Harry," someone with a thick Irish accent yelled from the back of the saloon. Tanner knew that could only be Clancy Cordon, the only Irish immigrant in all of Minnesota – or so Clancy claimed.

"Is that how you'll answer the Lord when he comes knocking on your door, Mr. Cordon?" Ilks replied. "What will you say to God when He comes to give you your reward for doing His good work?"

"The Lord doesn't concern himself with the likes of us, Father," Clancy said as he got up from his table. "He doesn't care what happens to us." He pointed a wobbly finger towards Tanner. "The Lord let the mine eat his pa, didn't he? He made that little boy work the same mine and forced his ma into the whore house. Is that what you call the Lord's reward?"

Tanner's face burned hot. Everyone in town knew the rotten luck his family had endured the past year. But that didn't lessen the sting of it being said out loud.

Tanner's grip on the useless lantern tightened and before he knew it, it was flying. The glass and iron crashed against the saloon wall, mere inches from Clancy's head. Shards of glass fell to the floor and oil oozed down the wall.

"What business is it of yours, Clancy?" Tanner shouted. "Piss off, you bogtrotter."

The Irish man flipped his table over, only adding more glass to the floor. "Alright, you little bastard. You think you've got enough hair on your chest to come at me, do ya, boy?"

At their right, someone cleared their throat rather loudly. There was the sound of metal sliding over wood.

Mr. Talsen stood behind the bar, a wheel gun resting menacingly in front of him. "That's enough," he said, his tone like a coiled whip, full of power but restrained. "I think it's time you left, Mr. Cordon."

Clancy looked at the bartender, the gun, then Tanner. He held a finger to one nostril and snorted. A black blob of coal-infused snot shot out and splattered on Mr. Talsen's clean wooden floor. "I won't forget this, boy," Clancy said with a scowl. "Maybe I'll pay a visit to the whore house before going home. I know a gal there who could really use the money."

Father Ilk stood behind Tanner and put two bear-like hands on his shoulders. "I believe Mr. Talsen told you to leave, Clancy."

Clancy shrugged and headed for the door, a sinister smile on his coal covered face. "Aye. That he did."

Tanner watched the Irishman walk through the swinging doors, out into the cool dark night. He hoped that whatever tried to get him on the road would get Clancy.

"Here ya go, Tan," Mrs. Talsen called out as she brought a bowl of steaming stew to the bar. "I had to warm it back up over the fire. It's a little hot so be careful."

"Thank you," Tanner said, sitting down in front of the bubbling stew. The steam rose and caressed his face. His stomach roared and he couldn't deny himself any longer. He dunked a piece of bread into the stew and ate.

Mr. Talsen nudged his wife and pointed towards the shards of glass and broken lantern near the back wall of the saloon. "We had a little accident. Can you sweep up that mess, dear?"

With that, she was off again.

Mr. Talsen watched Tanner as he ate, his eyes full of pity. It was enough to make Tanner want to leave. He swallowed his bite of bread, pulled one of the five-cent pieces from his pocket and slid it across the bar, "Can I get an ale, sir?"

Mr. Talsen looked down at the coin, his graying eyebrows furrowed. "Why don't you save that, boy?" He nodded towards his wife who was meticulously sweeping up the glass. "You're going to need to buy a new lantern."

"Nonsense," Father Ilks said as he sat down on the stool beside Tanner. "I have an extra one in the cart I can give you, boy. Don't worry about that. Have you an ale, son." The father slid a five-cent piece towards the bartender. "And one for me too, sir."

"Deciding to dine with the sinners tonight, Father?" Mr. Talsen said as he poured the two of them large mugs of beer. "The Lord won't punish ya for having a sip, I take it."

Ilks laughed when the bartender slid the mugs towards them. "The Holy Son broke bread with murderers and whores. I am just having a drink with the good people of Effham Falls." He picked up the mug and took a sip. "Besides, the Lord says to not overindulge. One ale won't subject me to His wrath." He gave Tanner a wink.

Tanner took his last piece of bread and wiped the bowl clean. Full and ready to start on his drink, he lifted the heavy mug and drank deeply. The golden liquid drizzled out from the side of his mouth. He wiped his face with a dirty sleeve. His body finally warm after the dreadful cold he felt on the road, he was satisfied.

"Mr. Talsen," Tanner said after another sip. "Are they making another road? I saw the flat dirt crossing Thirty-First Street beside the saloon."

Mr. Talsen nodded. "You are correct. I believe it's going to lead up to St. Barbara's. Is that right, Father?"

Father Ilks gave a shallow nod of his own. "I believe so." He took another sip of beer. "But I need to consecrate that crossroad before they continue. I would have brought the relics tonight if I knew about it."

A fog slowly seeped in around Tanner's mind. The beer was strong tonight. "Why do you need to do that, Father? Does a road need to be blessed before leading to the church?"

"It's a crossroad," Ilks replied. "It's a demon's place of business unless it has been blessed by the Lord."

Tanner leaned in. "A demon?" A chill ran up his spine and his body went cold like it had on the road.

"That's right." Ilks eyed him, a hard look in his eye. "They skulk around the four corners, waiting for a desperate soul to make a deal."

"Deal?" Tanner asked. "What do you mean?"

"Wealth, power, women, anything your heart desires, they can make happen." He snorted. "But the price is your eternal soul, an eternity in darkness and fire." He looked around at the sparse number of people still in the Rusty Nail. "And half of these people would sacrifice their children for a taste of gold." He let out a tired sigh then drained his beer. "It's sad how desperate this world makes people. They're so willing to give up the eternal gift that God has given them for worldly possessions." He gave Tanner a weak smile. "I should do the blessing tonight before a demon finds it."

Tanner knew the crossroads had already been claimed. It had to be a demon that he felt on the road. He could make a deal with it. He could get his father back. "What if a demon is already at the crossroad?"

The father laughed. "I doubt it. They just cut that groove this morning." He paused, looking deep within his mug. "But if there is one, I will need to exorcise it. A long process that I will probably need a bishop for." He got up from his stool and ruffled Tanner's hair. "So I better bless it now before it comes to that. Be a good boy, Tanner. God will reward you at the end of your trials and tribulations." He nodded towards Mr. Talsen and walked out the door.

Tanner's mind swam with possibilities. The father's warning didn't worry him. What good was his soul if he couldn't eat? See his mother? Be with his dad? He could have it all back. He could be like the other children around the world.

"A deal with a demon, huh?" Mr. Talsen said as he cleaned the mug the father had used. "I should have done that a long time ago." He chuckled.

"What deal would you make, Mr. Talsen?" Tanner asked.

The older man smiled at him. "I'd ask for some luck."

"Luck?"

The man nodded. "I just need a little luck. With it, I could turn this town around. I could really make it something special."

Tanner eyed him as he nursed the last half of his ale. "Do you ever think of moving back to New York?"

A sad smile spread across Mr. Talsen's face. "I do. Constantly. But there's something about this place. I know it can grow into a rose, that it can shine as bright as a diamond. I would hate to leave it behind and watch it grow from afar. I want to be here, I want to see it become what I know it can be."

Tanner gave Mr. Talsen's words some thought as he drained his beer. He then told the couple goodnight and headed for the door. He was going to make a deal.

The night seemed darker, and the air felt colder than before. A low fog had settled in around the street and became thicker near the new crossroad. Tanner, head swimming with alcohol and the possibility of having his father back, marched forward, fist clenched. His legs shook with each step. His teeth chattered. He stood in the center of the street, in the exact spot where he had heard the laughter. Ilks hadn't told him how to summon the demon, but that didn't seem to matter. Tanner could sense something watching him.

"Hello?" he squeaked out. "Anyone out here?"

A lantern suddenly lit up, the yellow light cutting through the darkness. "Well, well, well," a figure in the fog cooed. The sound was soft and tender like his mother's. "I thought I had scared you off, little one."

Tanner froze when the dark shape glided through the fog as if it were levitating. "Were you the one laughing?"

"I was." The figure came into full view, the light almost blinding Tanner.

She was tall and garbed in a long black robe with a deep hood. Tanner couldn't make out her features at all, even in the light of the lantern. The only thing he could see were the blazing orange eyes that peered out from the inky blackness of her hood.

"Are you a demon?"

The figure shrugged. "If that's what you want to call me. My name is Aragorda, servant of Mammon, Lord of Wealth. What brings you to seek me out tonight?" She let the hood slip off, revealing her features.

Even in the limited light of the lantern, Tanner could see her beauty. She had long flowing red hair, a sharp nose with a full face. Freckles ran across the bridge of her nose and under her strange blazing eyes. She smiled at him, revealing impossibly-white teeth behind her plump lips.

Tanner was gob smacked. This was a demon? "I want to make a deal," he whispered, then cleared his throat. "I want my dad back."

Aragorda clicked her tongue and waved a finger at him. "I cannot resurrect the dead, little one."

Tanner felt as if a lightning bolt had struck his chest. He stared at her, wondering if this was some sort of prank. Father Ilk said they could do anything for a price, yet they couldn't bring back his father? His bad luck had struck again. "Why can't you?"

"His soul is beyond our grasp to claim. Even if we could, his body is too deteriorated to host it. Besides, we are not in the business of returning souls to the mortal plane. Ask something else of me and it shall be yours."

Tanner felt a soothing hand glide along his back, a comforting arm wrap around his shoulder, and the warmth of Aragorda's body on him. Tanner gritted his teeth, trying in vain to fight back the tears. "I just wanted my dad back."

"I am sorry, little one. I cannot grant that." She seemed so motherly now, far from the sinister figure that laughed in the darkness. She raised his face to hers with the tip of her finger under his chin. "But what I can promise you is wealth, power, and good fortune."

"Good fortune?" Tanner repeated. He remembered what Mr. Talsen had said he would ask. "Can you give me good luck?"

Her smile widened, eyes blazed bright. "Why, yes, I can. Is that what you wish?"

What else could Tanner do? He could ask for wealth, but Mr. Talsen was wealthy before coming to Effham Falls and now he was barely scraping by. He could ask for power, but what good was power when you had no wealth? Maybe with a little bit of luck, he could have it all.

"That is what I want. I want good luck."

Aragorda stood up quickly. Her eyes outshone the lantern she carried. A flaming halo appeared above her head, and wings of ash spread behind her back. She was an angel of fire, an image of a goddess of flame and shadow. The crossroads erupted in an inferno and Tanner thought that the whole town would sink into the very pits of hell.

As quickly as the blaze came, it faded away. The night was still and quiet, the fog rolled back in, and Aragorda was gone.

Tanner panicked. "Aragorda?" he shouted. "Aragorda, where are you?"

Lantern light appeared in the thick of the fog.

"Tanner? I was hoping you were still here." Father Ilks' massive frame came trudging out from the darkness towards him.

Tanner felt as if he had just been caught. If Ilks he had seen those flames, he would know about his dealings with the demon. "I thought you left for the church, Father?"

"I did. I was halfway down the road when I remembered that I was supposed to give you this." He pulled out a lantern from the satchel hanging over his shoulder and handed it and a box of matches to Tanner. "Here are some matches too. I'm sure you could always use an extra box."

Tanner was speechless. He didn't know if his was fear or gratitude. "Thank you, Father."

Ilks patted him on the shoulder and led him to his one-horse cart. "Think nothing of it, boy. Let's get you home. I still need to consecrate this crossroad tonight."

Tanner hopped in the wagon, his mind preoccupied with Aragorda and where she had gone. Did he get his deal? How was he supposed to know? When did he have to pay?

"Father Ilks, what happens if someone makes a deal with a demon?"

Ilks climbed into the driver's side of the cart and lightly whipped the donkey with the reins. The donkey yee'd and haw'd before slowly trotting down the foggy road.

"Well, what I was taught was that the deal itself is like a door. Once someone makes a deal, the door opens. You have allowed them to cross to the other side, our side." He let out a disgusted growl and shook his head. "That kind of evil is like an infestation. It spreads. It brings a blight onto the land. The people become slaves to their sins. The land becomes less fruitful, full of death. A black pit that mars the perfect green creation of the Holy Father."

Tanner could see the priest was worked up. His jaw slid from side to side, his eyebrows furrowed, black shadows covered the lines in his face. What exactly had he done?

"What about the person who makes the deal?"

Ilks scowled. "They become soulless husks. They are dragged to hell to suffer for eternity where only the tears of God will give them a moment's peace."

Tanner sat silent in the cart, the realization of what he had done slowly dawning on him.

The outside of Tanner's house was dark. His mother hadn't left a candle lit for him, probably presuming that he had his lantern. He waved goodbye to the priest and walked inside. The air in the home was familiar and welcoming but there was another smell he barely recognized.

He struck one of the matches Ilks had given him and lit a candle. Orange light flooded the small home, exposing the ratty couch, dirty rug, and the feet of both beds that were against the back wall. In the kitchen immediately to his left, the small wood stove still glowed with hot ashes.

A plate full of sweet cakes on the table beside the stove drew his attention. As he picked up his first slice, he saw a handwritten note under the plate. He pulled the note free as he took a bite. The cake was surprisingly still warm, and the rich taste of honey filled his mouth.

He held the note beside the flickering candle flame and read.

Good evening, Tan.

I hope work was well. I'm off for the night and shall return by morning. I made you some sweet cakes, try not to eat them all in one sitting. I'll see you tomorrow.

Love,
Mum.
Postscript,
Payment will be due in twenty-four years.

Tanner let the note drop to the floor. Aragorda had accepted the deal.

Tanner Cullen watched Mrs. Talsen's old wrinkly hands tremble as she signed the deed. Her signature finalized his purchase of the Rusty Nail Saloon.

Tanner snatched the deed from the table and quickly folded it down the center. He placed it in an envelope and stamped it, trying to keep his eyes off the document. He knew how much time he had left. He didn't need to be reminded. "Thank you, Mrs. Talsen. I will get this to the bank, and you can retire in peace."

Mrs. Talsen scowled at him. "I have half a mind to burn this place down."

Tanner couldn't help but laugh. "At least try to keep this civil, Beth. Don't you see? I can make Charles' vision of this place, of Effham Falls, a reality. A jewel of the Midwest. That's what he thought this place could become."

"Aye," she said, looking down at the old bar her husband used to haunt. She sat in silence for a long time. Tanner was about to leave when she glared at him, giving him her dagger eyes. "A jewel, that's what he thought it could be. But you have covered it in crimson. No one likes blood diamonds, boy. What you are making those children do is—"

Tanner didn't have time to discuss morality with the old hag all morning. He was literally running out of it. "What I do with my workers, my coal mine, and my diamonds are none of your concern, Beth. Just be thankful I bought this trash heap and didn't tear it down." He forced a smile. "Good day, Mrs. Talsen."

The truth of the matter was that Tanner wanted that saloon for Mr. Talsen's sake. He was the one with the vision, the one who gave him the idea for this deal, and his life was all the better for it. He wanted to honor the man and make his dream a reality. No matter the cost.

The morning sun shone dimly behind the smog from the mines. Tanner took out his hanky from the front pocket of his suit and covered his mouth. The smell was horrible this early in the morning.

Three black birds flew overhead as he walked down Thirty-First Street towards the crossroad where he had made his deal. The birds perched on the street sign and watched Tanner when he stopped on the corner.

The crossing street had been named Serpent's Lane. Tanner had spent a lot of money to make this crossroad the heart of Effham Falls. He had paid for sidewalks, benches, iron electric lamps, and even the holly bushes. It was the place where his luck first started to turn, and he wanted it to be remembered as such, even though he was the only one who knew the significance.

"Mr. Cullen," an old gruff voice said. "How are we this morning?"

Tanner turned on his heels to see old Father Ilks limping down the sidewalk.

The years hadn't been kind to the priest. St. Barbara Catholic church was looking a little rundown and hardly anyone attended. They were too enamored with the prospect of finding diamonds in the mine like Tanner had. This drove the father to visit the Nail quite often, until he was nothing more than a drunk.

Tanner plastered on his smile, removed his top hat, and bowed to the shamed priest. "We are quite well this morning, Father." He straightened and carefully placed his hat back on his head. "And how are you? On your way to the Rusty Nail?"

The father laughed. "Aye, son. That I am." He ran a dirty hand through the last strands of his graying hair. His once bright blue eyes that peered into the soul were now dull and cloudy. "But while I have you, I was hoping to see you at service tonight. I would like to talk to you about renovation."

"Father, I—"

"Please, Tan. Just hear me out. The church could use some upkeep, needs the coffers filled, if you get my meaning." He waved a hand over the immaculate crossroad. "You did all this with the diamonds you found. Why not do something for the Lord and his people?"

Tanner scoffed. "You have people? The last time I walked inside that church, the crucifix was leaning on the pulpit, Father. But if it's a handout you're looking for..." Tanner fumbled around his jacket pocket and pulled out a roll of bills. He thumbed out five twenty-dollar bills and tossed them at the priest with such force that it caused the black birds to fly away. "Here's your tithe. Spend it in good health, you miserable drunk."

When Tanner walked inside, the bank accountant, Daniel, called him back to his office. Tanner kept his head down to avoid seeing the amount of time he had left.

"Mr. Cullen, is that the deed to the Talsen's saloon?" Daniel asked when he sat down behind his desk.

Tanner tossed the envelope on the desk. "Indeed."

They both forced a light chuckle.

"Can we speed this along, Daniel? I have somewhere to be, and I don't want to be late."

Daniel nodded and slid on his spectacles. "I'll have you out of here in no time, sir." He cut open the envelope with a letter opener and pulled out the deed. He looked it over and put a red approval stamp on the bottom. He handed the deed back to Tanner with a smile. "The Rusty Nail is yours, sir. I'll be sure to put the money in Mrs. Talsen's estate."

Tanner took the paper from Daniel, making sure to keep his eyes locked with the man. "Thank you, my friend." He stood up but, by chance, caught sight of the reflection in Daniel's mirror of the deed in his hand. At the bottom of the document, near the stamp, was the countdown: Zero years, zero months, zero days, twelve hours, thirty minutes, and seventeen seconds.

A cold sweat formed on Tanner's brow, ran down his back, and turned his spine to ice.

"Are you alright, Mr. Cullen?" Daniel asked.

Tanner forced his eyes away from the mirror. "Quite alright." He put on his mask -- a warm smile. "I just can't wait to see what the future holds for Effham Falls."

The hours passed like sand flowing through an hourglass. Tanner sat in his mother's lavish living room, a room with couches stuffed with fine cotton and wrapped in dyed white horsehair. Flecks of gold were carefully inlaid into the amber wood to create a stunning ornate piece. He had gotten the couches for her birthday. The red center rug covering the pine floors was immaculate. Even as the fireplace roared with orange flame, the rug showed no degradation.

Tanner took it all in. The golden picture frames, the silk curtains, the amber whiskey in a near fogless crystal glass by his chair. Did he make the right choice? Was this worth the cost of his soul?

He looked at the ripped piece of paper in his hand. Zero years, zero months, zero days, two hours, eleven minutes, twenty-eight seconds.

He took a sip of whiskey from his crystal glass. Clancy Cordon walked in with a long pipe in his mouth. He puffed on it, trying to get the tobacco to take to the coal. As a plume of white smoke escaped his lips, he turned to Tanner.

"Hey-o, son," he said, a sad smile on his face. He sat down on the opposite couch. "I didn't know you were visiting tonight, boy. I would have had the maid cook us up some coffee and cake or something."

Clancy had visited Tanner's mother in the whore house the night Tanner had stuck his deal. But instead of debauchery, lust, and violence as the Irishman hinted, the two of them had fallen in love. A few months later, Clancy proposed. He had bought her a brilliant ring that held one of Tanner's diamonds. It was rough going at first but, after a while, Clancy became a sort of role model for Tanner. Clancy wasn't a hardworking man, nothing like his father, but he was a cutthroat and used shortcuts to get ahead, a skill Tanner readily adopted to buy his property and businesses.

Tanner waved him off. "No need, Da. I'm fine with my drink."

Clancy puffed on his pipe and shrugged. "Well, I be hungry, boy-o. That maid has your mother's sweet bread recipe down to a T. It almost tastes exactly how your mother makes them." His smile showed off his yellow teeth.

Tanner forced a smile as well then took another sip of his drink. "How is Mother, Clancy?"

The Irishman let out a long sigh mixed with smoke. "Lacy isn't good, boy. She's come down with something awful." He took another puff off his pipe. "She is hot to the touch, can barely breathe." He shook his head. "Her skin is pale and clammy. The doc says to stay away from her until he figures out what is wrong with her."

Tanner's heart dropped. He hoped to leave his mother the town before his payment was due, but it seemed she wasn't going to be far behind him. It would all go to Clancy. "Well, I shan't disturb her." He pulled out the letter he had written earlier in the evening and handed it to his stepfather. "Please give this to my mother when she feels up to it."

Clancy reluctantly took the letter and examined it. He gave Tanner a confused look. "Why not give it to her yourself?"

"It's just estate paperwork," he lied. "Just be sure she reads them."

Clancy nodded and stuffed the letter in his robe. "I reckon I can do that, boy-o."

The mansion known as Cullen Manor stood on a freshly deforested hilltop. Tanner looked up at the large brick house, examining each brick and bush. He walked through the black iron gate and entered the lavish garden he had spent years cultivating.

Although it was night, the electric lamps illuminated the blooming flowers and ripening apples on the apple trees. He picked a bright red apple and took a bite. The fruit was sweet and crisp, the acid foaming in his mouth as he chewed.

"One last walk through the garden, little one?"

Tanner almost choked on his bite of apple. He turned to face Aragorda and his heart dropped. She was as intimidating and beautiful as she was when he was a boy. Dread coiled around his spine like ice. This was it. His final moments on this earth.

Had he made Mr. Talsen proud? Did he make his vision a reality? All these thoughts flooded his mind when the representation of eternal damnation smiled at him. His time was finally up. He felt like the little boy walking up Thirty-First Street with a useless lantern once again.

He held out his hand. "Care to take a stroll, my lady?"

Aragorda smiled and took his hand. She was warm to the touch, but distant and emotionally cold. She had done this countless times and he was just the next payment to collect. But to him, she was the last person with whom he would spend his last moments. She had given him this life after all.

The two walked in silence for a time as they admired the blooming flowers of the Japanese maples and bright berries of the holly bushes.

"Only two minutes left, little one," she cooed as she gently plucked a ripe red apple from a tree.

Tanner took in one last deep breath in the garden and thought back on his life. The diamonds, the riches, the lavish lifestyle, his family, and Mr. Talsen.

"I am ready." He smiled at Aragorda. "I dare say, I would be the envy of any twelve-year-old boy." He looked up at the bright stars of the Minnesota sky one last time. "Who wouldn't want a life such as this? Who wouldn't give their soul to be remembered in history as the man who put Effham Falls on the map?" Turning to the demon, he gave a shallow nod. "Effham Falls will be a gem one day because of us."

Aragorda offered a tender smile and placed a hand on his shoulder "A gem indeed, little one."

Suddenly, everything went dark.

MATTHEW R. CLARK is from South Carolina where he resides with his wife and daughter. After reading *The Lord of the Rings* trilogy in middle school, he dabbled in writing fan fiction of his favorite series. This love of fantasy and writing has followed him since. He is currently working on publishing his debut novel and hopes to have it released by 2024.

The Top Prize
Neal Romriell

A bead of sweat rolled down the side of Oscar's face, momentarily breaking his concentration. He'd been on too good a run today for things to go badly now. He rhythmically tapped his foot to the electronic beats of a pop song he didn't know, letting the momentum build up. Barely blinking, pupils focused on the glowing pink ninety-nine, Oscar fell into what he liked to think of as 'the trance'.

Three...

A girl at the Pac-Man machine sneezed.

Two...

Al opened his office door.

One...

Now!

Muscle memory took over as Oscar slammed his hand down on the plunger. The familiar sticky blue pad sunk with the pressure, sending a pulse of lights towards the giant wheel of numbers spinning endlessly in the cabinet.

The final light in the chain lit just as the ninety-nine panel swooped in front of it, changing the pink to blue and setting off the warbly *You're a Winner* voice.

"Gotcha!"

Oscar turned when he heard the ticket wheel within the machine start to spin. The other kids who'd gathered around to watch him looked on in awe as ticket after ticket spewed from the cabinet.

"Holy hell, Oscar, you never lose."

He turned to Bill Miller, the youngest of the onlookers, and flashed a smirk. "Twenty-three days, twenty-three jackpots."

"Al must hate you." Kyle, Bill's older brother, kept his eyes glued to the stream of tickets as he spoke.

Oscar looked in the direction of the office, the door of which was now closed, and smiled. "He knows what I want, and he knows I'm going to get it."

The group turned as one towards the front counter of Quarters Arcade. There, barely five feet behind the main register, stood the wall of fabulous prizes. Shiny disks, stuffed animals, joke gum, whoopie cushions, and Quarters Arcade clothing all hung there, beckoning the children of Effham Falls. Each and every prize was worth spending a few bucks, just for the chance to win enough tickets, and Oscar didn't care about any of them.

No, he had eyes for only one prize. A prize so special, requiring so many tickets to purchase that it wasn't relegated to the wall of common prizes. Oscar was after the top prize, located in a special padlocked glass container next to the popcorn machine.

For the princely sum of ten thousand tickets, you could purchase the bowling-ball-sized, acrylic—not cheap plastic—Magic 8 Ball. The thing supposedly weighed six pounds or more and was completely impractical. This made Oscar covet it even more.

"I'm getting that Magic 8 Ball, no matter what."

His audience all nodded their approval.

With a practiced motion, Kyle reached down and pulled an extra ticket from the spool. He began compiling the bundle into a nice neat stack to add to the collection. "How many tickets do you have now?"

Oscar pulled out his little notepad, flipping to the correct page. After jotting down a fresh one hundred tickets, he added the numbers up in his head. "4,071."

Bill let out a low whistle. "That's still a long ways from ten thousand."

"That it is, Bill." He pulled a folded piece of paper from his back pocket. "Good thing Al's bringing back his Fourth of July contest." He opened the flyer towards the other boys. "Twenty-five hundred tickets to the winner. Enough to buy a decent prize or..." he shoved the flyer back in his pocket, "a quarter of the tickets needed for the top prize."

They all glanced towards the front of the arcade where a sign with previous winners of the contest hung gathering dust.

Carter, Nick, Brandon, and Allie had each won. Now, after a year's absence, Al was bringing the contest back.

Oscar heard the office door open again, and knew Al was probably watching him. He didn't give the owner the pleasure of being acknowledged.

"Guys, I'll have that Magic 8 Ball before Labor Day. You can count on it."

The next day, Oscar arrived at the arcade only moments after it opened, fully intending to rip down the replacement flyer as he had the previous several days. Only this time, it seemed Al had gotten wise to him. The arcade was peppered with flyers about the Fourth of July contest. Nearly every game cabinet had at least one paper on it, and the bulletin board was covered in them. Oscar hadn't presumed that removing the flyer each day would completely eliminate his competition, but he'd hoped it would lessen their numbers.

Removing all of these would be a bit too obvious. He looked for Al as he headed towards the quarter exchanger but couldn't see him. The only employee currently visible was Martin, and he was watching Oscar closely.

No matter. Oscar had a feeling about the goal he'd set. Something deep within him knew the top prize was going to be his. He just had to stick to the plan. Eat a big breakfast each day, then spend the five bucks his mother and father gave him for lunch at the arcade. Eat a big dinner, go to bed full, and be a few hundred tickets closer to the goal.

As he put the first of his dollar bills into the machine, he got a good look at the flyer taped to the front of it. At a glance, it looked like all of the other flyers he'd torn down. But the longer he stared at it, he noticed a subtle difference.

At the bottom of the paper, in very small print, a new line had been added.

Warning: If you attempt to cheat, you will be sorry.

Oscar looked at another flyer attached to a nearby pinball machine. Sure enough, the line was on that page as well.

If you attempt to cheat? The contest was very straightforward. Each entrant would play one game of Skee-Ball, one timed game of Ms. Pac-Man, and a game of Whack-A-Mole. The person with the highest combined score would win.

Oscar knew he was great at the first test, better than average at the arcade game, and passable at whacking moles. His main reason for wanting fewer competitors was to, hopefully, avoid some of the older boys who were quick with a mallet, or the real aces at the arcade portion of the competition. He wondered if Al had added the line because of his tear down campaign.

"I'll just have to do better than everyone else," Oscar mumbled as he cashed in another bill. With the quarters firmly secured in his pocket, he headed for his first machine of the day and began working on his quota.

"I saw Craig Smith looking at the flyers last night!" The words practically flew out of Kyle's mouth as soon as he saw Oscar the next afternoon. "He's got the high score on both Ms. Pac-Man cabinets."

Oscar winced but forced himself to look unsurprised. "Yeah, I kind of figured he'd enter."

Bill scratched his head. "Are you sure? The older kids don't really seem to care about the prize wall."

Oscar shook his head. "Nah, Craig wouldn't do it for the tickets. He'd do it just to show off to the other guys."

Kyle nodded. "You might actually be able to ask him for the tickets if he wins."

Oscar felt his muscles tighten. "I won't have to ask him for the tickets, because I'm going to *win* the contest."

"But what if you don't?" Bill asked.

Oscar brushed off the question. Craig Smith, or any of the other people that frequented the arcade, for that matter, didn't have the drive, didn't have the goal he did. Could he earn the Magic 8 Ball without winning the contest? Possibly. But would it be a whole lot easier with those tickets? Absolutely.

He kicked a loose stone at his feet. "Each contestant only gets five minutes on the arcade machine, so I have to be more efficient than him for those five minutes. He can keep the high score."

"Oh, cool," Kyle replied.

Oscar smiled. "I can't wait to see Al's face when he has to unlock that case. He probably thought the number would never be reached," he said, kicking another rock, hoping his nerves weren't showing.

Bill nodded. "You think he'll give you that one? I figured he had one in a box in the back or something."

"Maybe, but I hope not. That ball has been under the case for years at this point, and I want to be the one who gets it."

Earning the top prize was as much about everybody knowing you'd won it as it was getting the prize itself. Oscar craved seeing the faces of the other kids when Al handed it over.

"Come on, I need to go earn my tickets for the day."

Oscar stared at the wooden ball in his hand, then looked at the scoreboard to be sure. The score read 1,250. A good score. Actually, a great score. But the problem wasn't the score, it was the ball. This was his ninth ball.

Normally in Skee-Ball, you get eight balls to roll up the ramp. There were rings marked twenty-five, fifty, seventy-five and one hundred. The higher the number, the smaller the ring. While these were all straight forward and in a line, near the top right and left were special tubes, barely big enough for the balls to fit through. These two were worth two hundred each, making sixteen hundred points the best possible score one could achieve. And yet here, in his hand, he held a ninth ball, practically insuring he'd tie his best score ever.

Oscar looked around, but no one was watching. After a moment, he rolled the ball, unsure if the machine would even acknowledge the points. The ball went straight up the ramp and into the one hundred slot, and up went his score. He looked at the tickets sitting on the floor and pondered the actions he'd taken. He plunked another quarter into the machine and watched as the eight balls rolled down. You could just barely see the edge of the top ball, but that was it. There were only eight in the machine, meaning one had evidently been recycled during his previous game.

"How did it get through the peg?" He spoke the words aloud, as though the machine would respond.

With a sigh, Oscar launched the first ball. It rolled straight up and into the one-hundred-point hole, barely touching the plastic ring. The familiar *click* sounded when the used ball collided with the peg that held it back until the next game.

Muscle memory took over and Oscar scooped up the next ball. He had a pattern for his rolls, and after starting with the easy one hundred, his next target was the two hundred tube on the right. He pulled back his arm to throw but stopped mid-motion.

One of the tricks he'd learned for hitting the high point holes was attacking them straight on was harder than making what he thought of as a chip shot. By putting a bit of spin on the ball and bouncing it off one side or the other, the odds your shot would fall went up. Being right-handed, he normally hit the ball off the left side bumper, deflecting it towards the right-side hole. Except last time he'd done it differently.

A crowd of older boys had walked by, heedless of those around them. Their proximity caused him to move to the side, and he'd launched the ball into the opposite bumper, banking it into the *left* hole. A bit sloppy, but it had gotten the job done. He stared at the ball now in his hand and wondered if maybe it had done more than get the job done.

He quickly made a few calculations, then repeated the motion he thought he'd taken the previous round. The ball hit the bumper, ricocheted, went up the ramp, and just missed going in the left-side two hundred slot. He pulled the next ball. The stack came down and left a gap behind the last ball.

Again, he threw the ball right, putting a bit of a different spin on it. Again, it bounced off the rail, up the ramp, and missed the hole. The motion, the angle, something was off. Oscar realized he was thinking too much, something his father complained about when golfing. "*You're in your own head, Frank!*"

Picking up the next ball, Oscar cleared his mind, letting the sounds of the arcade blend together as he entered 'the trance'.

Three...

Someone started playing Centipede.

Two...

One of the pinball machine's tilt alarms went off.

One...

Throw!

Oscar released the ball, twisting his wrist to gain the proper spin. The ball bounced off the bumper and—

He heard the ball drop, saw the lights flash indicating a two-hundred-point score, but he didn't pay attention to those. He paid attention to the ball that came rolling down the chute, a ball that should still be stuck behind the pin, awaiting the next game.

"Woah."

After a fast look around, he tried again and, while this ball didn't fall in the hole, it did free yet another wooden orb which came rolling down.

Oscar looked up at the score. This game was already a bust, so he fired off all the remaining balls, not bothering to take any trick shots. He looked down the line of Skee-Ball machines and saw one of those announcement posters with the little *If you cheat you'll be sorry* notes at the bottom.

Triggering and extra ball halfway into the game wouldn't be practical, but if he did so on his second shot, he'd get one extra ball without creating a gap in the chute. An extra ball would mean extra points and, if he did it without looking suspicious or nervous, chances were pretty good he'd guarantee himself the high score for the Skee-Ball portion of the competition.

A tinge of excitement coursed through him as he dropped in his next quarter. He was going to get that top prize for sure.

The night of July third, Oscar barely ate any supper. His mother and father both admonished him for leaving so much food on his plate, but he waved them off as he headed to his room. He'd spent the previous few days perfecting the Skee-Ball trick and making sure it worked on all the lanes. It did, and he was confident it could be pulled off without being noticed. At least he'd been until that afternoon.

Bill and Kyle accompanied him to Quarters, primarily because he'd offered them each a dollar to come along. Without telling them what he was doing, he asked them to observe his Skee-Ball game, explaining he needed to practice in front of a crowd.

With the two boys watching him, he'd triggered the extra ball. Neither said a word. As far as he could tell they hadn't noticed anything out of the ordinary. He gathered his tickets, smiling the entire time, but as he went to scribble down the addition in his notebook, someone bumped into him. When he looked up, he came face-to-face with Al. The owner of Quarters was wearing his usual dull brown apron, and his hair was as unkept and greasy as ever. Something about his eyes, however, startled Oscar. They seemed to glow, as if from an inner light.

"Oh, Oscar, sorry about that. How do you think you'll do in the contest tomorrow?"

Oscar wasn't sure if the malice in Al's voice was his imagination or real but, either way, the look and question unnerved him.

"I—I think I'll do okay."

Al nodded, sniffing back a great glob of snot as he did. "Just okay? I don't know about that. Feels to me like you might win the whole thing."

With that, Al continued towards the front of the arcade.

Oscar and the others watched him go, then Bill asked, "What was that all about?"

Hours later, Oscar still couldn't shake the feeling of dread that the look in Al's eyes had given him.

Once upon a time, Oscar's reason for wanting the top prize was pride and the recognition that earning it would bring him. Now, he wanted to get it so that he'd never have to set foot in Quarters again.

Sleep came in fits that night; his dreams invaded by a terrifying image of Al, with his exaggerated limbs and fanged teeth, chasing him through Quarters. The whole time, Oscar carried the Magic 8 Ball as Al screamed wicked threats towards him and his family.

By the time the first light of dawn began creeping into his bedroom, Oscar's anxiety had peaked. The stress and worry of the previous night were slowly replaced by hope and excitement for the contest.

After eating a huge breakfast, he hurried out the door. The only thing on his mind was his impending victory.

Oscar couldn't believe the number of people crowded around the arcade's entrance when he arrived. Dozens of kids were waiting for the doors to open. Any hope of there being only a few contestants went right out the window.

Minutes before ten o'clock, the front doors opened, and the crowd began to filter in a few at a time. Oscar was about to enter when he heard his name being called. Upon turning, he spotted Bill and Kyle approaching.

"Hey guys."

"Hey, Oscar. You ready to win those tickets?"

Oscar looked up at the neon sign hanging over the entrance and a shiver ran down his body when he remembered the previous night's dreams. "Yeah, I think so."

Bill wrapped an arm around his shoulder. "Then what are we waiting for?"

Inside, a large yellow sign directed contest participants to check in at the front desk. Oscar left Bill and Kyle behind and joined a short line of youths, most of whom were older than him.

Al was personally checking in the entrants, confirming they'd paid their fee and making each a white name tag.

Someone stepped on the heel of Oscar's shoe.

"Hey!" Oscar turned and found Craig Smith standing over him. The older boy was wearing a red shirt with a lightning bolt on it and a blue green checked hat.

"Oh, sorry dude."

Oscar scowled but said nothing more as he fixed his shoe. There wasn't any way to tell whether it had been an accident, or intentional on the part of the older boy, and he didn't need to dwell on it when he had a competition to win.

After an exaggerated cough, Al called, "Next."

Oscar stepped to the counter.

Al adjusted his glasses and gave him a big, toothy grin. "Good morning, Oscar. Looks like you're all set." He peeled a name tag off a half empty page of them. "Here you are. Go join the others by the basketball hoops and we'll get started shortly."

Oscar placed the name tag on his shirt and stepped away from the counter.

Al's voice rang out over the din of the arcade. "Oh, and good luck."

The words were normal enough, but Oscar detected the same malice he'd felt the day before when he'd noticed the odd glint in Al's eyes. Did he know what Oscar was planning to do? How could he?

A chalkboard on wheels had been parked near the middle of the arcade. All fourteen of the day's participants were listed, along with a graph to display their scores in each of the games.

Once all the contestants were done checking in, Al picked up a microphone and a loud burst of feedback rang through the building. Al tapped the mic a few times, creating more feedback and eliciting several shrieks and groans from the assembled youth.

"Happy Fourth of July, everyone." Al's voice boomed through the speakers. "I have to admit, I didn't think my little competition would garner such a response." He pointed towards the chalkboard. "I almost ran out of room on the board!"

Standing among the others, waiting for Al to stop his rambling, Oscar began to feel his trepidation flow away. The moment was at hand, and he needed to concentrate on the goal—the top prize.

Oscar was grouped with three other kids as the first ones at the Whack-A-Mole machine. The key was to hit the moles quickly. The higher they rose, the less you scored, but mindlessly whacking at the table didn't really do much good. The machine would sometimes try and trick you by moving moles up only slightly before pulling them back down. These moles didn't score you points even if you hit them cleanly.

Oscar thought this was common knowledge, but the first three youth proceeded to hammer at the table relentlessly. While none of their scores were terrible by Whack-A-Mole standards, Oscar was sure he could beat them.

Mallet at the ready, he concentrated on the motion of the mole hats and sound of the pistons before striking. Moles that fully extended made a wee bit more noise than the fake outs, and when the buzzer sounded, he'd easily beaten the current best score by 175 points.

Stepping back, he noticed the other kids shaking their heads, clearly jealous of his skill. He glanced towards the front of the arcade but couldn't see the Magic 8 Ball. He knew it was there though, waiting for him.

Their group shifted to Mrs. Pac-Man next. Normally, the arcade featured two cabinets but, today, one of the Galaga units had been repurposed into a third playable Mrs. Pac-Man game. The imposter cabinet was a bad omen. Anyone playing on it would likely post a worse score simply by virtue of the stick not moving up or down normally. As luck would have it, he didn't get assigned to Galaga, instead getting his favorite of the two true cabinets.

He did about as good as he'd expected, earning a decent score in his five minutes while still only ranking second amongst his group. He felt pretty good about everything—until he spotted the chalkboard. Craig Smith had evidently played the Skee-Ball game of his life, posting a shocking score of 1,350, tying Oscar's own personal best. Suddenly, triggering the extra ball wasn't a matter of practicality. It was a matter of necessity. He turned his gaze towards the Skee-Ball alley and froze.

Al was standing at the front of the lanes, backed by half a dozen kids waiting to see the next group, which was Oscar's group. Al's eyes seemed to be glowing again, and his withering gaze was focused directly on Oscar. Al smiled, chapped lips pulling back to reveal crooked, mismatched teeth. A shudder coursed through Oscar, and he felt a very strong need to use the bathroom.

The call went out for the final rotations. Al blinked and turned away. Oscar rubbed his head, feeling clammy sweat, which he wiped away with the shoulder of his shirt.

Oscar looked to his left and found Craig standing over him again. The older boy nodded towards the scoreboard. "Seems to me, as long as I don't bite the big one playing that stupid mole whacking game, those tickets will be mine."

"Maybe." An utterly ridiculous response by Oscar, which slipped out as if another person had said it.

Oscar saw where the scores stood, and Craig was right. Oscar needed a minimum of 1,450 points to put his score entirely out of reach for Craig but considering that would be a cool one hundred points more than his personal record, even using the secret bonus ball might not guarantee a win.

With slumped shoulders, Oscar walked to the Skee-Ball alley, and saw Bill and Kyle standing with the other onlookers. Bill gave him an enthusiastic thumbs up, which Oscar responded to with a shrug. He could still pull this off. He just needed to concentrate.

They were each assigned a lane and, by strange coincidence, Oscar's was where he'd originally discovered the cheat. It happened to be the easiest lane to perform the trick. The blocks had fallen into place, and he was ready.

Al walked by, using a special key to trigger the balls for each lane. "Contestants, prepare to throw."

Oscar stepped up to the lane and picked up his first ball. The familiar weight of the wooden orb was comforting. He bounced the ball in his palm, feeling the knicks and dents created over years of use.

"Begin throwing!" Al's voice cut through the din of the arcade.

Looking down the line of contestants, Oscar saw Al staring at him with those eerily glowing eyes. He turned his attention back to the ramp, which seemed to be as long as a bowling lane. The scoring chutes were a hundred feet away.

All around him, the other participants threw ball after ball, yet he hadn't thrown his first.

You're in your own head, Frank!

His father's words rang through his head, giving him something to focus on. Closing his eyes, he pictured the giant eight ball. "I've got this."

With eyes still closed, Oscar launched his first ball. When he heard the ringing as his ball entered the chute, he opened his eyes. He'd scored one hundred points. Impressed with himself, he picked up his next ball. Flipping it over in his hand, he prepared to pull off the trick that would ensure him an extra ball.

After a quick glance towards the scoreboard, he launched the second ball. One bounce, a second, up the ramp, over the bump and clank, into the back of the machine. The ball fell into the twenty-five-point hole.

Oscar's heart sank, and not just because of the score. He'd launched the ball wrong. Without even pulling up the next ball he already knew the cheat hadn't triggered. Not only was he not going to get an extra ball, without a miracle, he had no chance of coming close to a record score.

Oscar glanced back down the line of contestants and saw Al, who was smiling and looking more jovial and welcoming than Oscar had ever seen him.

For some reason, at a moment he knew he should be terribly disappointed, Oscar felt an odd sense of relief. He turned and saw Bill and Kyle both cheering him on. He gave them a thumbs up, then returned to rolling Skee-balls.

It was the worst game Oscar played in over a year. Two other competitors in his heat beat him and, yet, he was happy. He couldn't explain it. The day should have felt like a disaster, but he felt light, free.

Even with the retched Skee-Ball performance, Oscar still finished third on the day, picking up five hundred tickets for his efforts. Craig won, of course, and immediately used his tickets to buy a ridiculous, oversized cowboy hat.

Such a waste, Oscar thought. Not that he cared what Craig did with his winnings. Oscar would still get the top prize before summer was over.

Oscar spent the next week playing the big-ticket games at a furious pace, merging the daily stipend his parents gave him with some of his own money earned from selling a few baseball cards, and left-over birthday money. The infusion of tickets brought him well within reach of his goal.

As he left Quarters on the afternoon of July 11th, he relished that, soon, the Magic 8 Ball would be his. Oscar was so wrapped up in the thought of holding the top prize, he barely noticed the first police car to go whizzing by. The second one, its sirens wailing, snapped him out of his revelry.

When a third car went screaming by, Oscar knew something was wrong. The Effham Falls police rarely behaved like the cops in the movies, all lights flashing and guns waving. Only a real emergency would bring out this many squad cars, lit up like they were leading the Christmas parade.

Oscar's pace quickened as he followed the direction he'd seen the last car go. After only a few blocks, he spotted what was likely every police officer in Effham lining 7th Street. The largest concentration of cars were parked in front of a house about halfway down the block. It only took checking off a few landmarks to realize which house it was.

Craig Smith's.

Barricades were being erected to block off the street, and a crowd was gathering. Oscar approached, a knot tightening in his gut.

Warning: If you attempt to cheat, you will be sorry.

The statement played through his mind suddenly, but why? He hadn't cheated, though he'd fully intended to. In the end, chance, dumb luck, or his own conscious had gotten the best of him.

"Sorry."

The word sounded as though it came from far away, but he looked up and saw an officer holding out his hand. Oscar had walked through the crowd on instinct and now stood directly in front of the barrier.

"You can't come any closer, son."

Oscar nodded and took his place with the other citizens attempting to catch a glimpse of what was happening on 7th Street.

All around him, people murmured, speculating and gossiping. Oscar didn't join them. Unexplainably, Oscar knew something terrible had happened to Craig Smith. And Al was somehow behind it.

For two days, the town buzzed with whispered suspicions. Everybody had heard *something*, usually from a nameless police source. Regardless of how the rumors framed it—blood-soaked walls, a mysteriously torn baseball glove, or a forlorn note left to his parents—the troubling reality was that Craig Smith had disappeared from his home while his entire family was there.

Most of the kids in Effham were kept home by anxious parents, locked indoors for those two days out of worry that another disappearance might occur.

On the morning of the third day, Craig Smith's body was found along County Road 8, about six miles from town.

"Marty went to the funeral. He said everybody was crying and saying what a sweet boy Craig was," Bill said.

Oscar, Kyle, and Bill were sitting under the high school bleachers, trying to avoid the midday sun. A seven o'clock curfew had been ordered by the city's police, which meant hanging out in the afternoon heat.

Oscar wasn't sure about how sweet Craig was, but he believed that everybody at the funeral had been crying. Thankfully, his parents hadn't drug him to the proceedings.

Kyle traced a few lines in the dirt with his finger. "The cops still don't know why he was out there all alone."

Oscar looked through the slats of the bleachers, studying the empty football field and its fading lumberjack painted on the center line. "Remember two summers ago, when Allie Reynolds disappeared?"

Bill nodded. "Yeah. She was found out in the woods by the old Rambus farm."

Kyle looked up nervously, but nobody spoke. The fact that two kids had gone missing, only to later be found dead outside town wasn't something they, or anybody for that matter, wanted to think about.

The thought that Al had something to do with Craig's death still clung to Oscar's mind, but the rational part of him argued against it fiercely. All the odd stuff—the glowing eyes, the menacing voice—had simply been caused by Oscar's own self-induced stress about winning the contest and earning the top prize.

He stuffed a hand in his pocket, feeling the notepad where he kept his ticket tally. Pulling it out, he flipped to the page with his total: 9,362. So close, except that he hadn't been back to Quarters since the day of Craig's disappearance.

Warning: If you attempt to cheat, you will be sorry.

Craig hadn't cheated, or probably hadn't cheated, but even if he had, Al hadn't killed him for doing so. Stuff like that didn't happen. At least Oscar didn't think it happened.

He shoved the notepad back in his pocket, next to the wad of bills he'd saved by not going to the arcade.

On the morning of July 31st, at ten twenty-two, Oscar, Bill, and Kyle walked into Quarters Arcade. Each carried a shoebox full of tickets, totaling 10,016 between them.

Al must have known this would be the day, as he was behind the counter waiting for the group when they arrived.

"Good morning, Oscar."

"Good morning, sir. I've got some tickets I'd like to cash in."

"Oh, well then, what will it be?" Al turned his attention to the prize wall. "A new shirt, or maybe that kaleidoscope?"

Oscar wasn't exactly in a mood to play games with Al. "No, sir, I've got ten thousand tickets, and I'll be spending them all on one prize."

Al turned back towards the boys, his lips crooked up in a mischievous half smile. "Well then, you'll be wanting the top prize, won't you?"

"Yes, sir."

Though no crowd stood gathered in anticipation, Oscar felt satisfaction as Al fumbled around with his keys before finally inserting one into the padlock. After a prolonged struggle with the lock, Al finally pulled the plastic box up, freeing the top prize from its confinement.

The owner of Quarters let out a long, low whistle. "Ten thousand. Never thought I'd see a kid with enough patience to reach that number." He picked up the Magic 8 Ball box and placed it on the counter.

Oscar, Kyle, and Bill each placed their shoebox on the counter.

Al looked at the boxes for a moment, then pushed the Magic 8 Ball's box towards Oscar. "No need to count them, eh? They're all there, all 10,016."

Oscar blinked and froze mid-reach. How did Al know the *exact* number of tickets? "Ye—yes sir."

"Good, good. Have fun, boys." With that, Al picked up the three boxes, walked out from behind the counter, and headed towards the back of the arcade.

Oscar watched him for a moment before grabbing the box, which did weigh a considerable amount. He took time to admire the packaging, an all-black background with bright neon letters and images. It looked like a top prize and felt like a top prize.

He was about to turn towards the exit when something in the glass display case caught his eye. Sitting next to a pop cap gun were three plush figures, each wearing a red shirt with a lightning bolt, and a blue and green checkered hat. His gaze shifted, as though guided by invisible hands, until he was staring at another set of plush dolls. These bore pig tails and a brightly colored dress. He knew immediately that Allie Reynolds had looked exactly the same on the day she won the competition. Terror grew inside him, twisting his guts and blurring his vision.

"Oscar, are you okay?" Kyle's voice was far away, warbly.

A hand touched Oscar's shoulder and he jumped, almost dropping the Magic 8 Ball box. The hand belonged to Bill.

"What's wrong?" Bill asked him.

Oscar's vision refocused as he took in a gasping breath. "No—nothing, I'm fine." He looked past Bill and Kyle and spotted Al standing near the back of the arcade, boxes still in hand. The owner's eyes glowed brightly, and he was smiling so big and grotesque that Oscar could see it from all the way across the room.

Oscar nodded towards the arcade's entrance. "Come on, let's get out of here."

Magic 8 Ball in hand, Kyle and Bill by his side, Oscar McKinley walked out of Quarters Arcade and never came back.

Ever.

NEAL ROMRIELL was born and raised in Idaho where he honed his storytelling skills while spending evenings around the campfire with his family. After graduating high school, Neal moved to the east coast, where he still lives with his wife and three daughters. Neal's debut novel *Site Alpha* was published in June of 2022. He is currently working on a sequel to *Site Alpha*, as well as a fantasy series. He hopes the first book in that series will release in 2024.

House Hunting

Michele R. Willman

"Bentley? Bentley." Olive stopped, one hand on the knob of the half-open door, the other clutching a second-hand Kate Spade bag.

A grunt erupted from the blue calico recliner that engulfed Olive's slender husband.

"I'm going. I'm meeting Karna. Remember?" Olive tapped her foot and glanced around the narrow entryway, giving him another moment. "We're sharing a bottle of wine, so I'll probably be late. After ten, maybe eleven." She resisted an impulse to step back into the living room and confirm that he was listening, that he understood.

As an "uh-huh" emerged from the depths of the chair, Olive turned away and grabbed her eggplant shawl from the coat rack.

"Bye, then." She threw the shawl around her shoulders and across her sagging middle to keep out the September chill as she stepped out the door. Pointing the keys at the Thunderbird, she mimed clicking to unlock the driver's door. When no beep-beep responded, she trudged over and fitted Bentley's key into the lock of the aging vehicle.

Twenty-five years. Twenty-five years ago that day, Olive had married Bentley in the park down the block from her parents' two-story on Seventh Street in Effham Falls, Minnesota. After an early cold snap, the fall weather had turned unseasonably warm and she'd sweated through her full-length, satin gown. The once puffed sleeves had hung off her shoulders like deflated balloons. Despite the dampness pooling under her arms and the bangs clinging to her forehead, she had felt beautiful, fresh, hopeful. The guests had complimented her dewy appearance.

Although she'd stopped perming her hair before the wedding, her sister, Everly, had helped her curl it all the way around with a hot iron so that it bounced pleasantly when she tucked it behind her ears. Everly had even placed a stray chrysanthemum, orange tinged with yellow, that had dislodged itself from some unfortunate bridesmaid's bouquet, into Olive's hair.

That day, the sun had reflected off her gown. The sequins had twinkled and shimmered when she swung her hips from side to side. The smiling relatives, and even her cousin, Doreen, had seemed happy for her. Bentley had leaned down, shaking hands with the guests, his face handsome and sun-kissed. His DiCaprio bangs swung becomingly along his brow. Olive had stood on tiptoes to kiss ruddy cheeks as friends and family moved along the receiving line. Bentley and Olive had glowed with pride and potential, flanked by their parents.

Twenty-five years. A quarter of a century. Half her life.

Olive pushed a wilting hair from her face as she twirled the key in the lock of the Thunderbird. She hunkered down and squeezed into the driver's seat, ratcheting it forward until she could reach the pedals. *Damned Thunderbird.* Her Honda was in for repairs, and she was stuck with this monstrosity for now. She made a mental note to move the seat back when she returned or Bentley would moan about it come Monday morning.

The entire receiving line, except for her and Bentley, were all gone now. His mom, Estella, had just had time to impart some of the McKinley wisdom before succumbing to cancer three months after the wedding. Estella had loved to share the story of Bentley's unusual name with Olive and anyone who would listen, explaining how a boy with such promise should have a classic name from a classic story. Bentley had "great expectations," she'd assured everyone, and her new daughter-in-law was lucky to have caught his fancy. Olive hadn't had the heart to correct the frail woman's misreading of a novel that Olive had read three times over. She'd sat by Estella's bedside, stroking her hand, and mopping her face with a cool cloth.

 Rumbling down residential streets into downtown, Olive fumbled with her iPhone as she pulled to a stop at a red light, tapping Karna's number before the light turned green and the driver behind her got impatient.

"Karna?" She switched to speakerphone and tossed the phone on the passenger seat. Of course, the Thunderbird didn't have Bluetooth.

"Olive?" Karna spoke over a background of shuffling feet and indistinct voices. "Where are you?"

"Karna? Oh shoot. Are you there already? I'm running behind. I mean...I'll just be a little late—"

"I know I'm early again." Karna interrupted. "Sorry. I came straight from work. Are you sure you want to go out tonight?"

"Don't be sorr—Ope! Wait a second. Damn slow driver." Olive tapped her brakes to avoid sneaking up too close to the car that crept down the residential street like it was waiting for a parade. "Just a sec."

Glancing in her rear-view mirror and seeing no one, Olive edged around the Buick. She grimaced at the driver as the slower car dropped behind her. The white-haired occupant, dwarfed by the steering wheel, leaned forward with two hands parked at 9 and 3. *Figures.* "Ok. I'm good," she assured Karna. Olive accelerated and slid back into her lane before reaching Main Street, then slammed on her brakes at another red light.

If it had been darker, if it had been winter, if it wasn't the least little bit of rush hour that Effham Falls had, she'd have gone straight through it. No one would see. No one would know it was her. But she didn't want to draw attention to herself. Not now. It had been enough to pass old Mrs. who-knows-what with her white hair and steady pace.

Olive tapped her foot on the gas impatiently, like a drag racer primed for the tree to light up. The Buick with its elderly occupant crept up behind her and slowed to a stop a good car-length behind. Olive waited.

"Olive?" a tentative voice rose from the empty passenger seat. "About tonight...?"

"Yeah. I'm still here. Stupid old lady drivers. That's all."

"Well, are you really going to be late if you're in the car already?"

Olive fidgeted and re-adjusted the too-tall seatbelt that chafed her neck. "I need...to pick up something for Bentley. I've got his car. Mine's in the shop."

"Still?"

"I should get it back tomorrow if Bentley can drive me over."

The light turned green and, after a delicate honk from the old lady who'd edged up behind her nearly nose-to-bumper, Olive shot across the bright intersection into another residential area and turned onto a side street just past First United Methodist

Church. The street was unfamiliar though the neighborhood wasn't too far from her usual haunts.

"What are you picking up? I mean, what part of town?" Karna persisted.

"Uh, pharmacy run. You know. Forgot to pick it up on lunch."

Inching further down the street, Olive scanned the addresses on a row of brown, nondescript townhouses. The tiny numbers rising above the identical doors were hard to make out. Every other building staggered back behind its partner. She hadn't had a chance to investigate this recent construction yet and she craned her neck, peering at both sides of the street to get the lay of the land. Older homes flanked the cluster of newer buildings, and she could still hear the light traffic from Main Street just a few blocks away.

"Well then. I'll just order the wine and get started." Karna's giggle wafted again from the passenger seat.

Olive cringed. Karna was just too old to try to sound coy. She must be trying to impress the other waiting patrons, probably all young and able to hold their liquor. But, Olive reminded herself, she and her friends had chosen La Piazza even though it catered to Millennials. Their pizza was the best in town, and they had half-priced wine at happy hour. Were they even called Millennials anymore or were they called Gen Z now? Olive could never quite keep it straight. It was early for the youngsters to be out. She expected they'd still be styling their hair and shimmying into their thin-strapped dresses. Or maybe into those hideous jumpers. What decade did they think it was? They looked like they were wearing baby rompers.

"Don't be late or you don't know what's going to happen." Another giggle from Karna. "See you soon then? As long as you're sure. A half-hour or so?" she queried.

"Yeah. Half-hour or so. Bye." Olive slowed and ended the call.

Twenty-five years. Twenty-five years this night.

Olive pulled a U-turn at the end of Oak Court Road and trolled back down the street, checking the addresses on the other side.

1801-1805-1809. M*ust be one of the damn buildings in the back.*

Turning from the nearly vacant street into what looked like a converted alley, Olive was thankful for the extra hours of daylight the northern sun afforded as she squinted to see the house numbers. Why couldn't they just push all the buildings up against the street instead of trying to crowd these extra ones in-between?

While Olive scrutinized addresses, Bentley, propped in his Lazy-Boy, hoped that Olive was being easy on the 'Bird. He gingerly adjusted his lean frame to take the pressure from his left shoulder and winced, reaching up to rub the tendon lightly. He should have asked Olive to bring him the rest of last night's pizza still in the box on the table where they'd left it after dinner the previous night. It always tasted good warmed in the toaster oven the next day, although Olive rarely bothered to heat it up for him. He liked when the crust crisped up again just like when it was delivered.

Bentley grabbed another Miller Lite from the six-pack at his feet, hoping it would make him feel full. The game was at a lull, and he didn't feel like watching the Vikings lose again so he switched over to *CSI*. Maybe Olive would bring him some leftovers so that he could eat before he went to bed. Maybe she'd even order him a burger to go like she used to when she went out with the girls back when they were first married. He hadn't received a to-go box for a while. He sipped his beer and focused on the T.V.

Back on Oak Court Road, Olive uttered a small sound of exasperation, wishing once again she'd updated her eyeglass prescription the last time she'd been to see Dr. Brown. But the lenses would have been $75, even with the same outdated frames that she'd settled on years ago. They'd never looked good on her. Why had she been convinced by the perky, blonde optical specialist to go rimless? The slight frames made it look like she was wearing two monocles propped in her eyes. A female Colonel Mustard, times two.

"How do you like my new glasses?" she'd asked Bentley as soon as he came through the front door, the new frames perched on her pert nose. She'd pursed her lips. She'd promised herself that she'd wait for him to notice.

"Just a minute. Just a minute." Bentley had pulled off his boots and set them in the boot tray next to the door. He'd hung up his wool, winter dress coat and set his keys and wallet in the basket on the hall table. "Now, let me see." He'd put one hand on each of Olive's shoulders, looking down as she tilted her face up toward his.

She waved her head from side-to-side to give him the best view.

"Stop doing that. I can't see what I'm looking at." Bentley had gripped her shoulders more tightly. "Who picked these out?"

"I did."

"Well, then you don't know your own face. You should have gotten bigger ones. That's what's popular now. And they'd sit better."

"Oh." Olive put on a cheerful face. "Yeah, it was hard to pick."

Bentley dropped his hands from her shoulders and kissed her just where her hair parted down the middle, like he always did. A few shimmers of gray peeked through the roots.

"You can get better ones next time." Bentley edged past her to the kitchen, pulled a Miller from the fridge, and popped the top. "What's for dinner?"

Shrugging off the memory, Olive pulled into the parking area of the townhouses and drove around number 1809 to check the numbers on the buildings set back from the street. She passed 1813, then found 1819, the last building on the left. Now that she was closer, she could see the neat block letters above the doors, the no-nonsense front steps and matching screen doors. The letters A and B stood prominently on the front of 1819. C must be on the back side. Olive hesitated before pulling into an empty space in front of 1819A. Most of the time, these spots were reserved for residents, but there didn't appear to be parking on the other side of the building, nor was there a sign for guest parking. She preferred visiting single-family dwellings where it was clear that both residents and guests should just park in the drive. And attached garages were much better than the row of detached doors standing to the side like a row of identical quadruplets. She sighed and turned off the car.

The bell on the door of La Piazza jangled again and yet another couple entered. Karna, almost through her first glass of the house red, startled as the host approached.

"Ma'am, your table is ready," he said.

Karna hesitated, then downed the glass and set it on the bar. With no elegant way off her perch on the barstool, she gripped her A-line skirt and edged to one side, tipping to the ground. The skirt rode up, displaying one fleshy knee without hose and the terrain of cellulite gently folding over it.

The host smiled, keeping his eyes on her face, as he held up two menus. "And there will be two of you?"

Karna ran her hands over her outfit and nodded, wishing they'd taken longer to clear the table, or that the smartly-dressed young couple—she swore the man looked like he was twelve—had lingered over their desserts and drinks.

The host led her to the center of the crowded warehouse-style open dining area and motioned to a table, pulling out a chair. It was one thing to perch on a stool, scroll through her phone, and sip her glass of wine at the bar. It was another to be at the table alone—and she was hesitant to order a bottle without consulting Olive. The women always deferred to Olive for the wine selection despite her habit of rushing in fifteen minutes late without apologies.

On their regular girls' nights, Olive would arrive, shake out her limp hair, and tuck her coat or scarf over her arm. As Olive leaned on the bar, Karna, Suzanne, and sometimes Mary, would finish their first glasses of wine and catch her up on the can't-wait gossip. Then, they'd all traipse to the table and Olive would peruse the wine menu, selecting their first bottle. But Suzanne had taken that job in Reno, and Mary had family in town, and it was just too awkward to wait for Olive, drinkless, seated at this exposed table recently vacated by the handsome couple.

"Wait. Excuse me." Karna's fingers stopped an inch from tapping the young man on the shoulder as he turned away. "Could we have a booth?"

As Karna surveilled the echoing space from the safety of the unfamiliar corner booth, Olive detached the seatbelt which retracted with a sharp ripping sound and rubbed against her neck, almost catching the open-weave fibers of her new shawl. She massaged the shawl, checking for snags, then pulled it around her and looped the ends together. Inspecting her face in the rear-view mirror, she pushed the browning waves behind her ears, and fussed at the shine of the fine, gray hairs in her part before reaching for her extra lipstick in the console. *Damn. It's still in the Honda.* She sighed again and dabbed on some cherry ChapStick from her purse, smacking her lips together. *Here we go.*

With no car on the driver's side, she pushed the door wide, gripped the top of the window frame and hauled herself from the low seat. Olive half-expected the little old lady from the stoplight to witness her unsteady clamber from the car, but there was no one. Only two green minivans and a smart, red Volkswagen.

Families. Carpools. Noise. Fuss.

Trailing around the sidewalk to C on the other side of the building, Olive passed a Greenley Realty sign that read: Open House 4-6 pm. She appreciated having the option to come later in the day. So many of these open houses were at one or two o'clock when there was little reason to go out except for shopping. She had been pleased to find that this one fit her schedule. And she was going out anyway.

A gray-haired, balding man in a pressed suit whom she didn't recognize lingered in the doorway. A slight breeze disturbed the few wisps of hair clinging to the top of his head. He gestured to the postage-stamp green space and established flower beds on either side of the concrete stairs as a man and woman— *probably Millennials*—retreated. Turning away from the waving realtor and passing by Olive, they smiled briefly in greeting. Olive continued past the small lawn, the bushes of four-o'clocks still shut tight against the late afternoon Minnesota sunlight, and nodded at the man in the doorway.

"You're here for the Open House, ma'am?" he said. "You're going to love it."

Olive gave no response, brushed past him through the open door, and stopped. Taking in the tidy open floorplan, the neutral shades, she frowned. Clearly staged and barren. As if it hadn't been lived in during its few short years, or months, of existence.

Twenty-five years. Twenty-five years, she'd been in the Cape Cod on Fisher Lane. Olive and Bentley.

She half-turned as the realtor jostled her, attempting to follow her into the dwelling. Instead of entering behind her, he was forced to teeter on the brink of the doorstep, unable to move into the room without pushing her aside. She pulled her shawl tighter around herself and stood, assessing the room before her.

He gestured at the modest living area, flapping his arm between Olive's rigid back and the door frame. "New construction. Single owner. Great for singles—or families. Families, too. Lots of space—"

"I'll think about it." She took a step back, nearly bumping into him in turn but he managed to dodge by taking a step down and leaning against the wrought-iron handrail. "I have to go," Olive said. "I have an appointment." She turned and walked back down the stairs, past the four o'clocks, and around the building. She fished the car key from her pocket and raised it to beep ineffectually at the Thunderbird, still parked neatly in front of 1819A, anticipating her return.

MICHELE R. WILLMAN is an instructor of English, a writer, and a mother of four girls. Current writing projects include a series of short stories and a novel about the lives and relationships of mothers and daughters. Her work has been published in *MidAmerica*, the *North Dakota Quarterly*, *Humanities ND Magazine*, and elsewhere. When not reading and writing, Michele enjoys crocheting, knitting, gardening, spending time with her family and dogs, and enjoying the outdoors.

Two Arrowheads

William R. Bartlett

A gust of wind blew the hat off my head the day I dug up the skeleton. My name's Pete Walsingham, and I own The Lawn Ranger, a landscaping and snow removal business. My operation is fairly well known here in Effham Falls where I handle most of the people who don't want to sweat on a hot, summer day or risk the ice during a winter blast. In addition to private landscaping, I have a contract with the city, so I'm doing all right.

Most of the time, I stay in the office, handling phone calls, making sure my crew is in the right place at the right time, and scheduling projects like this one. But this day, Ted, my backhoe operator, had taken the machine to Cariveau, a good two hours west, to excavate the grave for his great aunt. That left me without Ted or the backhoe, and I wanted to get started on this job for the mayor, Richard Talbot.

Hizzoner's wife had watched a home improvement program on cable and now she absolutely had to have a firepit. A fancy one. Not too close to the house, but not too far away, either. Our mayor was fairly easy to get along with, and Susan, his wife, liked being a big fish in a little pond. This meant entertaining, of course, with a few of the other dozen or so wives of the influential men who made this small town their home.

Some called him Mayor Dick behind his back, but not me. I always thought Talbot wasn't bad, an unassuming man who made a very good living in investment banking but looked like he'd be happier hanging out with the farmers at the Feed and Seed. He loved Susan to distraction, though, so I stood in a corner of his backyard with a line and transit, landscaping paint, along with a shovel and my gloves. Since I owned the company, my presence would have proven to Susan they were the important people she thought they were. But she couldn't see. Richard and Suzy weren't scheduled back from their Mediterranean cruise until the next day.

The Talbots had good soil, it was my job to make sure of that, so it surprised me when my shovel hit something hard about ten inches down. Most likely, a little gravel left over from when their house was built. I didn't think much of it.

Unlike the promotional ball caps from seed companies and implement dealers that most men wore, my hat had a flat, broad brim that protects my neck and ears. Unfortunately, it catches the wind easily. More often than not, I can catch it before it blows off, but this day, my hands were full of shovel, and I was too slow. I didn't mind. Work is never delayed by a chance to catch your breath. I reached for the hat wedged in the shallow trench I'd already dug, but a yellow glint caught my eye. Gold.

This was no job for a shovel, so I tossed it to one side and laid on the grass, like they'd taught us in college when I went on archeological digs. I parted the dirt with the care of a mother examining her newborn for the first time. A ring. No, a woman's ring, judging by the size, with a tree root growing through it. I parted the soil along the root, but the whole thing was only about an inch long. Dear God. I'd found a ring with a finger in it.

※

The sign above the door read, '*Effham Falls Gazette and North County Shopper*'. A smaller sign, '*JP*', nestled in the corner of the window, near the door. Bennett Davies, or Bennie, as everyone called her, had run the *Gazette* for as long as I could remember, the third generation, or more, of her family to do so.

As Justice of the Peace, she held the position of local law enforcement, not that she was needed. The county patrol, once in the morning and once in the afternoon, discouraged most criminal activity.

 Bennie usually wore an old, tie-dyed tee shirt and stained jeans, but a uniform blouse hung on the wall next to her desk, complete with a shield, a Smokey-the-Bear hat, and a gun belt so old, it held a revolver in the holster. I have no idea if the weapon was loaded. On the rare occurrences when after-hours law enforcement was needed, usually for some kids with beer or a spousal disagreement, she slid the shirt over her omnipresent tee, leaving a patch of tie-dye prominently displayed at the neck of official khaki.

Pushing open the door rang a bell that had probably been there for all three generations of the Davies clan who'd kept the town informed of mad dogs and farmers' markets.

Bennie looked up from her desk. "Well, Aldon Peter Ellis Fyffe-Walsingham. His own self. Come in to buy a bigger ad? Maybe one with a little truth enclosed, like, 'Pay me to haul off your grass clippings and leaves, then pay me again to buy and deliver first-rate compost.' You have quite a deal going there, don't you?"

"It's the American way." I grinned at the skinny, old hippie with her long, gray hair secured at the back of her neck in its customary leather strap and wooden pin. "I can't tell you how many sheets of your rag have found their way into my compost heaps. And I asked you not to broadcast my family pedigree. I don't want anybody's awe or pity. Only their checks in my mailbox." I leaned on the counter.

"Don't worry, youngster, I'll keep your secret safe. Nobody here but us chickens." She sat back in her chair. "If you're not upgrading your ad, how can I help you?"

"I might've found a woman today."

"Your wife know about this?"

"Not yet. It'll be OK, though. The lady I found was buried almost a foot deep, and she's old, judging by the soil composition. I have no clue how old without excavating, but she's still wearing a gold ring that might date back a century or more."

Bennie blanched. I hadn't expected that, not from a hard-bitten, old journalist. But she recovered before I could say anything.

"Aw, hell, Pete, you know how much I don't like putting on that shirt and all that goes with it." She gave an exasperated sigh and muttered, almost to herself. "I absolutely hate wearing a bra." The owner, editor, reporter, and copy rat bent over her computer. "I don't think we've ever had a murder here, and I haven't heard anything about missing females for a while. Let me log into the county's system and see what shows up."

I walked behind the counter, selected the State mug from her collection of unmatched cups, poured myself some coffee, and sat in her extra chair.

"C'mon in and take a load off," Bennie said, too wrapped up to notice I'd already done that. "I've got some coffee that's not even a couple hours old. This shouldn't take too long."

There are coffee gourmets, or so I've heard, but it all tastes the same to me, dark and bitter. However, I didn't have anything else to do and nothing else to drink, so I spent the time alternating between taking sips and resting my eyes while Bennie pored through the county files.

"I couldn't find any open missing persons cases in this area, and I went back to when they started keeping records."

"Should we call the sheriff?"

Bennie took the lid off an old glass jar, releasing a cucumber/sage aroma, dipped her fingertips in and rubbed the lotion into her hands. "Nah, they wouldn't be any help." She replaced the lid and cast a sour look toward her hanging uniform. "I guess I should take a look. No telling what's in that ring without checking. For all we know, it could be construction debris from when they built the mayor's house."

"You know my background, don't you." It wasn't a question. Part and parcel of being a small-town newspaper owner was being the local snoop. She knew damn good and well I'd studied archeology up at State but couldn't find a job after graduation. Eventually, I gave up and went back to the job that put me through college. Bennie was there when I'd had my business name stenciled on my first vehicle with a big write-up and picture of me beside the truck on the front page, above the fold. The honor position. "That was a finger bone inside that ring."

"Yeah, yeah. It's just that I really don't like wearing that shirt. We all despised uniforms when I was in school."

"Tell you what, then." I drained my coffee and took the mug back to the sink. "Don't wear it. Instead of going as the long arm of the law, you're just a small-town reporter, looking for a story. If you think we need to, we can always file the county's report later. I already have everything we need, so we can head straight there."

"Aw, hell. The paper doesn't have anybody to watch it while I'm gone."

"Bennie, nobody comes here, anyway. They do everything over the phone or on your website. Let's go."

She hemmed and hawed, but a few minutes later, she locked the door behind her and settled into my truck.

Within minutes, we stood at the edge of the little trench in the mayor's backyard. "I didn't want a crow or jay to get excited about the shiny thing, so I covered it up again. This'll just take me a minute." I dropped prone and moved the dirt with my fingers, a tiny bit at a time until I felt the cold metal. "Found it. Let me clear it out a bit."

"Hot damn." Bennie's voice came out soft and low, like she couldn't believe her eyes. She dropped to her knees, then laid herself flat, pulled out her phone and took several pictures, squirming to get different angles.

"What do you think now? Is that a root? I'll need a lab to be sure, but it may be the second or third proximal phalange, the bone closest to the palm, either the index or middle finger. The ring may have sheltered it from decomposition." I fished out some orange-painted nails from my pocket and stuck them into the ground, bracketing the finger and ring. "Are you ready?"

"Now or never."

This time, I used the dental pick, working it slowly under the bone, feeling for any obstruction. When the bone was free, I worked a sandwich bag under the finger until I had about the same amount showing on each side, then lifted it up, keeping smooth and even pressure until I set it on the ground beside the little trench.

"Seems like the back of the ring to me," Bennie said. "How's the other side look?"

"Let's find out." I put another sandwich bag on top of the finger and held the bone tightly between the two bags, then flipped it over, revealing a long oval, almost like a signet.

"What is that?" Bennie barely whispered.

I soaked a cotton swab in some water, slid it under the clear plastic and scrubbed until a design became visible. Two concentric circles, bisected by a long line, with two perpendicular crossbars, one above the circles and one below. A part of a third circle, like horns from a bull, topped off the long line. I frowned. *Where had I seen that before?*

"Put her back."

I'd never heard Bennie's voice quiver like that, and it startled me. "What?" I jerked my head up and stared at her, shivering like she'd just walked out of a cold shower.

"She doesn't deserve this. We're desecrating her grave. This isn't right." Her pallor reminded me of the momentary blanch back at the office.

"We don't even know when she died. Just because she's wearing an old ring doesn't mean she wasn't murdered some time more recent. This could be a real crime."

"I think she's First Nations, one of the eastern tribes. If she is, and the tribal council gets wind of this, there'll be hell to pay."

"OK, you've got a point. But let's at least see if we can find out how she died. Once we know, we'll be able to pass on more complete information when we call the county."

"All right, all right. But we have to go in from the side."

"Are you out of your mind? Remember, I know what I'm doing. I have all the tools needed to do it right, and I'm a trained professional... well, trained, anyway. The site has to be measured and meticulously recorded. Otherwise, it gets torn up for nothing. Nobody learns anything, and it's all a big waste."

"Listen to me, Pete. Exposing her to the sun and sky is the ultimate indignity. This is serious, and I'm about a half inch away from exercising my authority. You don't want me to do that any more than I do. Either you do a limited excavation, going in from the side, or I call the county."

"But I found it. Why should the county jump in and take all the credit?"

"If you want a chance at the credit, we do it my way."

"This is ridiculous, you know. Why are you so wound up about this?"

Bennie stood over the trench, her chin jutting and arms crossed. "You aren't fooling me, either. You want to do a proper dig, document it, publish it in peer-reviewed journals and get a good job in your field of study. Well, that isn't going to happen here. Don't forget, I'm the one who writes up the report."

I hate being read, especially when it's accurate. She didn't say it out loud, but I caught the veiled threat about even finding the skeleton. "All right. We'll do it your way. I'll come in from the side with a probe. If I find anything, I'll dig it out, one small grain at a time. If it's not too wet, I'll use my brush. Does that suit you?"

She took a deep breath and nodded. "According to my reading, most burials of First Nations peoples had their head in the west, facing east to see the sunrise on the last day. Where are you going to start?"

"The ring was upside down, so her hand probably slid off the body, pointing toward her feet, after she was placed in the grave. That would make our find close to her hips, maybe a little lower, and about the same level as her back. I'll start a bit higher and work my way up, toward her head. If we find any signs of a fatal wound, it would probably be around the thoracic cavity or the head."

The more time I spent prone on the grass, the more I enjoyed looking for the facts. Just like being back in college. I worked the slender probe into the side of the trench, about eight inches up from where we found the ring.

"I'm looking for some thoracic vertebrae. There may not be any left, but if she was murdered, the chest would be the best place to start a search for evidence."

Bennie said nothing, but paced around the short trench, circling like a turkey vulture riding a thermal. Her reaction had startled me. I hadn't done anything to make her upset, at least not intentionally, and her continued pacing clearly showed her agitation. But I had other things on my mind. My probe found something hard.

"Bingo."

She squatted beside me. "What is it?"

"Don't know yet. All I can say is I found something. Hand me some of those painted nails, and I'll mark it." I slid the nail into the ground and worked my way west, one centimeter at a time, marking each hit with another nail until I stopped, about eighteen inches later.

"This should be good for starters. I'd kill for some water."

She tossed me a bottle and looked down into the dirt. "Is that long enough?"

"I didn't try to get the whole back, just the thoracic vertebrae." I took another slug. "Are you OK? First, you don't want me to do this, now you're like a kid on Christmas Eve. What gives?"

"Aw, I'm sorry if I bit your nose off. This thing has me a little edgy, that's all." She stared at the orange nails, sticking out of the rich, black dirt. "How much longer you think we got?"

"Hard to tell. Maybe another half hour or so, give or take." I took the trowel and brush from the tool kit and laid back down. One obstruction wasn't as deep as the others, and it seemed the best place to start.

Bennie didn't pace this time. Instead, she laid on the ground and stared at the brush as I worked the soil away, crumbs at a time. I'd expected to find a rib, but I was wrong.

"See that?"

She grunted.

"A projectile point. An arrowhead. Don't touch it." I moved six inches toward where we thought the head would be, and started again, this time with the trowel, shaving thin layers off with each pass. After a few inches in with no results, I switched back to the brush. Just in time. "Well, well, well. What have we here?"

"I can't see anything."

"You don't know what to look for. Let me get some more dirt out of the way." After a few more minutes with the brush, I backed out of the trench.

Bennie's jaw dropped. "Is that another arrowhead? Stuck in the bone?"

"Yup. I'm no medical examiner, but it looks like the first one hit her close to or in the liver. The second one appears to have finished her off, possibly a *coup de gras*. If she was hit in the liver, she'd have bled out when the arrow was pulled, so either shot could have been fatal. The higher one would have gone through her sternum and penetrated her trachea before lodging in her spine, hitting her heart along the way. The blood from that wound alone would have drowned her."

"How do you know which hit first?"

"I don't. I was just going by the order I found them, but there wouldn't have been a need for a second shot if they'd gotten a good chest hit first. There may be more in her, too. We'll be able to tell when we get State out here for a complete excavation." I grinned at her. "Looks like you'll have to put on your other shirt."

She rose, crossed her arms, and stared into the trench. "Aw, hell. Maybe. Did you bring anything to cover her up?"

"I told you I already had everything I needed, didn't I? A couple of tarps and a four-by-eight sheet of OSB. That should be enough to keep things in order."

"All right, but before you do, I want her finger and ring back where you found them, exactly the way they were."

"Bennie, they're just going to dig that stuff up again. Why go to all that trouble? We can even send the finger to State for a carbon-fourteen dating."

"So... You're telling me you like the idea of a felony charge of interfering with a crime scene? Put it back, make it look undisturbed, and I won't mention it." She set her jaw but kept staring at the trench. "Come on, shake a leg. I have other things to do than play in the dirt."

Bennie unlocked the door to her shop and entered, holding it open for me.

"Have a seat and a cup of coffee, Pete. This may take a minute or two." She sat at her desk and opened her dedicated law enforcement computer, which played the Hawaii Five-0 theme song during the boot.

"Does that tune play every time you boot up that computer?"

"Yeah." Back in the office, Bennie sounded more and more like her old self. "Every damned time. I'd leave it up, but it has access to sensitive information, so I have to close it down whenever I go somewhere. At least I don't have to look at the actors' faces when I bring it back up."

"You're running low on clean cups." I took the same mug again and poured a cup, then sat in the chair I'd used earlier.

She grunted but said nothing.

"Hey, I just had an idea. You can write up your article in time for the next issue. Place yourself on the cover as a participant, too, in the place of honor. Local Journalist Discovers Dead Woman."

She turned away from her desk and gave me the dirtiest look I'd ever seen. "You don't have to hang around while I do this. If I need you, I'll call." Bennie started to turn back to the computer but stopped and faced me again. "And I don't want you talking about this with anyone, understand? Not your wife, your crew, and certainly not with Suzy Talbot. Nobody."

"You know the Talbots are due in from their cruise tomorrow morning. They'll have to be told why there's no work going on."

"If you absolutely have to, you can talk to the mayor. He has a politician's sense for what he should and shouldn't say. If he'd be willing to take a pay cut, I wouldn't be surprised to see him running for state treasurer someday. But don't tell another soul."

"I'll keep my mouth shut, but I don't want to expose myself to a felony charge sometime down the pike. You'd better make it clear that I came to you as soon as I found her."

Bennie had already returned her attention to her monitor and mumbled something I couldn't make out. I emptied the cup and placed it in the sink, but something on her desk caught my eye. A design printed on the left margin of her notepad. I'd never given it any thought whenever I'd seen it before, but my stomach dropped this time. The same design we'd found on that gold ring.

During the trip back home, two thoughts would not stop buzzing around my head. What was that design and why did Bennie act that way? But I pulled in just as Ted unhitched the trailer holding the backhoe and waved me over. My questions would have to wait.

I backed into the parking place where Michele, my belle, had driven a five-foot stake into the ground with a painted plaque, welded to the top: An old-fashioned facemask that covered only the eyes. She'd said that since I was THE Lawn Ranger, this marked the space as mine alone. Like I'd ever tell her to move her car, but she kept it open for me to use.

I cleared the truck bed just as Ted spoke. "Hey, Boss."

"Glad you're back. Everything straightened out for your great aunt?"

"Yeah, we got her laid in, nice and easy. Thanks for letting me use the backhoe. That part of the family doesn't have much money and this was a big help to them."

"Happy to. This was your grandfather's sister?"

"Yeah. Great Aunt Brenda Faye. You should have heard what they said about her when she was young. Quite a hellraiser. They said she had a reputation for swimming up in the Little Fork, but never liked shopping for bathing suits. That's not what I remember about her, though. She looked like a linebacker, but led the Ladies Bible Study Group, sang in the choir, and always brought a casserole with at least two pies for every church dinner. Funny, how some people change when they get older."

"Your great aunt? Skinny dipping?" Another image I didn't want in my head. "That's rich. It's hard to picture our grandparents as being hot teens with fresh hormones coursing through their veins, isn't it? I suppose it makes sense, but still."

He coughed. "We can't thank you enough for letting us use the company credit card." Ted pulled a bit of plastic and a receipt from his pocket and held them out to me.

"No problem. It's good having you work for me. Michele and I talked it over last night and we wanted to help. Did you leave a good tip?"

"Yeah. Twenty percent. Maybe a little better. Never was much good with numbers." He looked down at his boots. "I meant to let you know on Monday, but the backhoe needs greasing, and the hydraulics are getting loud again."

"What? And you're just now telling me?"

Ted looked miserable. "I meant to, but we don't always use it, so it just slipped my mind."

One damn' thing after another. I sighed. "OK, take it over to Coxswain's first thing in the morning. Stuff happens. I'm just glad it didn't break down while you were using it today."

He nodded and turned, but I stopped him before he took a step.

"Something's come up at the Talbot's and I need to speak to him before we do any more work. Don't, and I mean it, DO NOT go there until you hear from me. Got it?"

Ted squinted at me. "Yeah, sure, Pete. No problem."

"I can't tell you anything more about it. Not yet, at least. Hopefully, I'll be able to before your great nephews and nieces are burying me."

He smiled. "You bet, boss. Night."

"See you tomorrow."

My eyes burned from staring at the computer monitor, so I closed them and leaned back in my seat, stretching my arms over my head. I'd found the symbol used on the ring and Bennie's notepad in less than an hour. Mohican. Near

Stockbridge, Massachusetts. Unlike the Mohawk, they'd sided with the colonists during the Revolution and were forced out of the state after the war. They went west to Oneida, New York, then farther west to northeast Wisconsin. The rest of the time I spent trying to find out how this one symbol got here, but I'd had no luck.

"Pete?" Michele came into the room and wrapped her arms around me from behind. "I'm starving. You said you were going to feed me."

"I'm sorry, my love. Must have lost track of the time. What sounds good to you— steak or seafood?"

"Do you mean real steak, or fast-food burgers? Last time, I chose seafood and you took me to the VFW for their annual Fish 'n' Chips night."

"That was seafood."

"Barely. And it didn't come close to the cedar plank salmon I had my mouth set for."

"Tonight, real steak. I guarantee it— with chairs, cloth napkins, and you'll have to cut your meat with a knife."

She twirled me around in the chair to face her and planted a kiss on my lips. "That sounds wonderful, but it makes me suspicious, too. What's the occasion? Another business dinner?"

"A lot of my clients are members of that VFW, and it never hurts to make sure you're in good with the customer base. But, to answer your question, no. Just you and me, tonight." Keeping things from Michele has never felt right, so I guess this might have been a guilt date. Fortunately, she didn't pursue it. If she'd have asked, I'd have spilled my guts in a heartbeat, no matter what Bennie said.

The mayor pulled into his driveway about ten minutes after I did and parked beside me. I leaned on my hood and spoke when he got out. "Morning, Mr. Mayor. I hope you had a nice trip." I glanced toward the empty passenger seat. "Your better half OK?"

"Hiya, Pete. I've asked you to call me Rick. And, yes, she's fine. She and her friends wanted to stay a bit longer. Visit Zurich and Paris, maybe Vienna, too. How's Michele?"

A natural politician, always asking about others. "Great, but I have something I need to show you. I hate to get you before you even take your luggage inside, but this is important."

A look of curiosity crossed his face. "Sure. Lead on."

"It's around back." I walked beside him. "While I was doing some excavating for the fire ring foundation, I found something." I pulled the tarps and the OSB sheet out of the way, then kneeled beside the trench and moved some dirt away from the orange-painted nails until the ring and finger bone were visible.

"Is that gold?"

"Without a doubt. Probably close to twenty-four carat. And it's not on a stick. That's a finger bone, with the ring still on it. Judging by the size of the ring, a female last wore it."

Rick took a step backward. "Have you called the sheriff?"

"Not yet. I've been working with Bennie on it, but there's more. I did some excavating from the side of the trench, looking for what might have caused her death."

"What did you find?"

"It looks like she was killed, but a long time ago. I found two projectile points, flint arrowheads, inside her. Both appeared to come in from the front."

"Criminy." Talbot crossed his arms and stroked his mustache with his left hand. "Why didn't Bennie call the county?"

"The ring has an emblem on the other side, a sign of the Mohican people. She didn't want to get a tribal council involved, because they'd almost certainly want to block exhumation, plus they'd have ceremonies of their own to perform. It's possible we couldn't get this straightened out for a year or more."

"That's not what this town needs. Almost everyone who supports me wants to keep Effham Falls the way it is, and nobody is going to like the headlines. *'Small Town Mayor Fights Tribal Council on Ancient Remains'* would be one of the better ones."

"Do you know of anyone in this town who goes a long way back and might know something? A legend, a rumor, or just something they heard once? Anything?"

"My dad would have been your best bet about ten years ago. He was our town repository of local history. Some he researched himself and some, well, he simply kept his ears open and his mouth shut. Always said it was the best way to learn. Not any longer, though."

I blinked. "I'm sorry. I didn't know he'd passed."

"He hasn't, but he might as well have. He has dementia and is in a home, up in the county seat. Healthy as a horse, but his mind's like tuning an old-fashioned radio. Sometimes he's as sharp as both of us, but other times, he introduces himself to me. We had to put him in an institution for his own safety."

"Would you mind if I went for a visit?"

"Not a bit. He's at Blakewood, but I've got to warn you. Trying to get something out of him is like drawing to an inside straight. If you get it, you'll win bigtime, but the odds are against you."

"Thanks, Rick. I appreciate this."

Talbot groaned and ran his hand across his forehead. "Oh, crap. Susan was looking forward to having some of her friends over to sit around a fire when she gets back."

I grinned at him. "I've been thinking about that, too. How about an outdoor kitchen with a fireplace and chimney? Tailor made for entertaining and cooking out while keeping indoor facilities close. Plus, the chimney keeps the smoke out of people's faces and clothing. It might cost a bit, though."

He barked a short laugh, good-natured and nice to hear. "I shouldn't have any trouble selling her that. Can you email me some pictures?"

"No problem. I can think of a half a dozen without even trying." I reached down to a corner of the bottom tarp.

Rick grabbed another. "Let me give you a hand with that."

That's why he gets reelected. A first-rate guy.

With everything back in place, I pulled my truck out of the driveway, intent on the county seat. But first, I had to stop by the toy store.

Robert Talbot sat at the dining room table, even though lunch had finished a half hour earlier. I felt a little sorry for him, sitting all alone, but he didn't look lonely. Maybe I could make his day a little better.

"Mr. Talbot, my name's Pete, and this needs to be tested before I can give it away." I pulled a Frontier Lego set out of the bag and laid it on the table in front of him. "Think you could give me a hand?"

He studied the box for a moment but said nothing.

"Here," I said, "let me help." The lid took a little effort, but I slipped it off and slid the box top across the table, face down.

"No. I need to look at the picture."

"OK, let's empty everything out and see what we can build." I put the lid back on the box and stood it up where he could see. "How's that, Mr. Talbot?"

"Call me Robbie. That's fine." His fingers were quick and dexterous, putting things together almost without glancing at the colorful box.

My items took longer, but I didn't mind. If I could have gotten away with it, I'd have let him do it all. "I hear you know a lot about Effham Falls."

"Yep."

"Can you tell me something that almost no one knows?"

"Sure." He spoke without looking up, his fingers moving the blocks and fittings as he searched for a specific part. "My great-great granddad bought our land from the great-great granddad of Bennie Davies. She was cute when she was little."

I blinked. There had been some rumors about a connection between the families, but I had no idea this had happened. "How'd you know that?"

"Heard 'em talking. Ma had said there was an eclipse of the moon later that night and let me stay out in my treehouse to watch. I saw 'em coming and laid down flat, waiting to scare 'em when they got close, but they got mad at each other, so I kept quiet and listened."

A habit he'd kept all his life. "What did they say?"

After sundown but before full dark, the two old men trudged along the border of the field and stopped when they reached a dogwood tree.

"Thank you for finding the time to meet me here, Mr. Talbot."

"We're both busy men. You said there was something I should know before we formalize the purchase tomorrow?"

"I do not care what you do with the rest of the land, but you must not ever plow up the little piece around this tree."

"Mr. Davies, if I buy this land, I will use it as I see fit."

"Do what you wish with any other part, but you may not touch this. If you are unable to promise me, I shall not sell."

"You need my money to purchase your Washington Printing Press. If I cannot work all this land, I may not buy. To do so does not make sense, now, does it?"

"Look, Mr. Talbot, it is only a small spot. You cannot do much with this little parcel, anyway. And you know the rest of the land is good and rich."

"Why? Give me a good reason why I should not plow up my own land. My family is growing, and we need to eat and prosper. If God gives me the means, I would disrespect His gift if I did not use it productively. One reason is all I ask, only one reason."

"Because it is a grave, damn you!"

"What?"

"My mother was Mohican and wanted to return to her people with me. Pa refused to let her go, so she loaded our rifle and tried to shoot him, but it misfired. He shot her before she could try again. Ma died right around here and this is where she is buried."

Talbot stared at Davies. "Shot her? With what? Your pa never owned more than that one old flintlock, and you said your ma had it when she died."

"They both grew up in the same tribe. When Pa got older, he had to make his own arrows and bow. Every boy did it to show they were men and could support a family."

"How do you know this?"

"Pa must have felt guilty about what he had done, because he wrote everything down on a parchment. He never spoke of her death, but I found what he had written after he died."

Davies caressed a branch of the dogwood. "Her people did not like stone markers, but they felt this type of tree was special. They only live about forty years or so. Whenever one dies, we dig up a sapling and move it here. This one is my second planting."

"You should have told me earlier. I am no heathen, and I respect the dead."

"Now you know. Do I have your word that you will let my ma rest undisturbed?"

"Very well, Michael." Talbot held out his hand. "We will respect the grave of your mother."

"Thank you, Carter." Davies took the outstretched hand and shook. "That means a great deal to me."

Robbie snapped a piece of plastic into place and rolled the covered wagon toward me. "All done."

"What about those other pieces?"

The old man shrugged. "Extras. They're always good to keep. You know, just in case."

I nodded. "What would you like to do? Shall I leave it here, or disassemble everything and take it with me?"

"You'd go without it? Why?"

"You might want something to do tomorrow. You can take it all apart and have some fun with others. Besides, I had a good time, and it seemed like you did, too."

"Yeah, I get bored. Nobody comes to visit. If they do, they never stay long."

"Do you mind if I come back next week? Maybe I can find a different set."

Robbie flashed a shy smile. "That'd be nice. Richard hardly ever comes. Do you like pirates? I saw a ship in the directions."

"I'm not sure I can find one, but if I can it's yours. Who knows, I might even bring a friend." Maybe having Bennie spend a few hours once a week or so with him would help make her a little less sour.

The next afternoon, Bennie met me at Talbot's. "What do you need, Pete? I told you I had this under control."

"Look at you." I eyed her hat, uniform, and gun belt. "The very image of the law. Let's go around back. There's something I need to show you."

She caught up with me, and we strode toward the backyard.

"I know what happened, Bennie. Everything."

"No, you don't. You—" She stopped short and stared toward the area where her fourth great-grandmother rested. "You... You..."

"Yeah, how about that? Once I found out who she was, I cleaned everything up and put it back the way it was. She's still wearing her ring, too. In a week or so, nobody'll ever know I was here."

"But... Your dig. This could have been a way for you to get back into your career field."

"You know, I thought about that. Getting back in the trenches, seeing things people hadn't witnessed for hundreds, maybe thousands of years. But who wants to spend a lifetime among pompous, stuffy academics? Besides, I already have two things very few of them will ever get."

"OK, you won't get professional recognition. What'll they miss out on?"

"First, I own a business and directly contribute to the wellbeing of almost a dozen people. Second, I have a mortgage. While those poor schnooks are eating dust and plucking one parasite after another off their epidermis, I'm relaxing in air-conditioned comfort. Believe me when I say it's no skin off my nose." I nudged her along, the slightest of touches on her elbow. "C'mon, let's get closer."

"That's a dogwood, isn't it?"

"Of course. I put it in this morning. When I learned the Mohicans held that tree in high regard, doing the right thing was a no-brainer. I wanted to put a brass plaque with your family name just below the first branches but decided not to. Dogwoods don't live long enough to make it worthwhile. Instead of the plaque I got a one grafted pink and white, alternating branches."

"I remember the tree that used to be here."

"Rick said there'd been one. His dad brought him out to the tree, right before he went to college. Told him not to do anything near that dogwood but didn't say why. By the time our future mayor had finished college, built his career, and gotten married, the tree that used to be here had died. The contractor took it out when he built Rick's house."

Bennie stood in front of the tree, beside me. "There's more you don't know. Llewelyn Davies was fifteen years old and a British soldier from Shrewsbury, England during the Revolution.

When the regiment went into Stockbridge, Massachusetts, he got separated from his unit. Young and scared, he ran, and the Mohicans took him in. He married an English girl, Molly Jones, who was also adopted by the tribe after her parents had been killed by a band of Mohawks."

I kept my mouth shut. If she had more to say, I wasn't about to interrupt.

"Their son, Alan, waited until he was about forty before he married a young woman. Ayn-jahn-ee, the Algonquin equivalent of Angela, was her name, about sixteen or so. Apparently, she had an episode of some sort. Psychotic, schizophrenic, bipolar, whatever. Ayn-jahn-ee wanted to kill him and take their son, Michael, back to her people. Almost did, too. She had their only rifle loaded, but it didn't fire the first two times she pulled the trigger."

I glanced at Bennie, but she kept her eyes fixed on the freshly planted tree.

"Alan had a bow along with some arrows he'd made when he was a teen. His first arrow hit her right below her ribs on the right side, probably, as you said, in her liver, but that didn't put her down. She'd cocked the rifle and reset the frizzen a third time when he hit her with the second arrow, in the center of her chest. She was dead by the time he reached her."

"Holy cow, Bennie. I'm sorry. Even with what I learned... I had no idea."

"I wouldn't have, either, but Alan didn't like what he'd done and wrote it down on a sheepskin parchment. The family's been passing it down over the years, probably not even learning about it until they're settling an estate. But that's not the worst of it. When Alan reached Ayn-jahn-ee, he flipped the frizzen up and tried to empty the pan but couldn't."

Bennie turned toward me and grabbed both of my shoulders. "Pete, she'd never primed the lock. Ayn-jahn-ee could have cocked and pulled that trigger for years, and it still wouldn't have fired. He was never in any danger, and he killed her, thinking he was saving his own skin." Bennie released her grip and turned back, facing the tree.

"Oh, dear God. He took her life here, close to where we're standing. Then dug a grave and rolled her in." My knees had gone weak, but we had no chairs. A shot would have been nice, too, but I seldom drink and never during the day. "What do you think? Could he have murdered her and made up this story, just to keep from feeling guilty?"

"I'd wondered about that, too. But if he was trying to make himself look innocent, why would he have written about the empty pan? The rifle that was unable to fire wouldn't have been a good defense for him in front of a judge and jury. But one thing really seals it for me. When I reached the spot where he wrote about the empty pan, the ink was a little smeared. I talked a friend who works at the county's crime lab into letting me look at it under high magnification. There are tiny circles, watermarks, where his tears had hit the parchment. I think he loved her and never forgave himself." She took a deep breath and let it out. "One more tragedy in the long and bloody line."

"No wonder you looked like you'd seen a ghost when I showed the arrowheads to you. Why didn't you tell me then?"

"Aw, hell, Pete. Do you know anybody who looks forward to pulling their family skeletons out of the closet? Or ground? Or wherever? Then showing them to the whole world?" She shivered in the warm, afternoon sunlight. "No, thanks."

"Why did Alan bury her in such a shallow grave?"

"He didn't. The soil was deeper back then. Erosion over almost two centuries took its toll. Then, when the mayor built his house, the final grading almost uncovered her. I snuck over after the workers had left for the day and checked the whole damn' yard for any sign of her but couldn't find a thing. Not so much as a fingernail."

"I had to tell Rick. His memory lapse really embarrassed him. He was just eighteen when his dad told him about the tree but nothing about the grave. College and life away from Effham Falls, then bringing home a wife put a lot on his mind, and with the old tree gone when he came back, he never thought about what his father'd said. If you showed your parchment to him, he may set up an endowment that'll keep a dogwood here."

"I'm not mad at anyone for forgetting, but always having a tree for her would be nice. By the way, how were you able to learn as much as you did?"

"I had an eyewitness, or, rather, an ear-witness. Robbie was listening when Carter and Michael were discussing the land before the sale."

"Robbie? Richard's dad? I thought he was at Blakewood with dementia."

"He is. But I brought him some Legos to play with while we talked. The fine motor control along with the fact that they're toys opened synapses he hadn't used for years. When he spoke about this, he sounded just like an eight-year-old boy. Of course, he didn't have the detail you had, but you've confirmed everything Robbie said."

Bennie took my arm and strolled us back to the cars. "It's too early for something hard and too late for a pastry. How about we pop over to Emma Jean's for a cup of coffee?"

"I don't know. When I saw you armed and in uniform, I thought you were going to haul me off to the hoosegow."

"Aw, I never keep this old thing loaded, except when I have to go up to the county and qualify each month."

"Which means you're a dead shot, if I know anything about you. All right, after what you told me, I could use a little fortification. Besides, I think I know a way to get you a Pulitzer." I opened my truck door and climbed in. "I'll give you the details when we get there."

She pushed the door shut. "No, you have to tell me something to pique my interest right now. Otherwise, I may stand you up."

"Do you like pirates?"

WILLIAM R. BARTLETT has been writing the "Word from Dad" feature in *KC Parent Magazine* since April, 2009. He has a short story published in the Moorhead Friends Writing Group anthology, *Tales from the Frozen North*. His recently released book, *Nude, Light Housekeeping*, the story of a May/December relationship and the rather unconventional way it develops, is his first novel. A retired youngster of threescore and ten, Bill lives in the southern fringes of the Kansas City area, about six miles north of the oddly named city of Peculiar, Missouri with his Fayre and Gracious Wyffe, two sons, and an exceedingly pompous cat.

Doppelgänger

Jason Bursack

I might never have seen her for the first time if I hadn't gone up to the service counter with Daniel when he wanted his ticket changed. And then I might not have talked to her for the second time.

If it really was a second time. If it really was her.

"Yeah, I don't think it could have gone better," said Daniel, who is Greek, and thus talks with his hands.

We'd just finished a sales presentation that morning and it seemed a deal was imminent. We'd talked about it the whole drive to the airport, the whole wait through security, but we couldn't stop. The bonuses would be record-breaking. I chuckled and said, "They were practically, what's the word, at the demo."

"Like they were watching a thriller movie."

"Enrapt. That's the word."

"Tons of explosions."

"The first software demo ever produced by Michael Bay."

Daniel made a plosive noise and flung his arms out, generally not the best kind of gesture to make at an airport, but what actually got him in trouble was he smacked the woman in front of him in the back as he did this, hard enough to make her take a step forward to keep her balance. He turned, aghast. "So sorry!"

She veered around, looking surprised behind hipster glasses, traveling light with just an olive-green messenger bag slung over her left shoulder and a coffee thermos in her right hand. Her hair was long, blonde, her chin softly dimpled. She wore what was maybe a band t-shirt – my own musical tastes do not venture far into the twentieth century – with a blue flannel tied around her slim waist. She didn't say anything, just stared at Daniel and me with narrowing, intelligent eyes.

"I'm so sorry," repeated Daniel, reaching his hand out hesitantly toward her arm, clearly unsure if touching her would help or make the situation worse.

She frowned. Daniel's hand did not make contact. It occurred to me later that she was looking at us like some kind of larger routine had been shattered, a rule violated, as though Daniel and I had just casually walked in on her through a door marked Employees Only that she'd thought had been locked. "Oh, you're fine," she said, recovering. She smiled brightly, glanced down at her thermos. "Didn't even spill my coffee."

Eyeing the line ahead of us, I figured we could spend our time in worse ways than talking to this young woman. The topic of corporate triumph had in reality long been exhausted. I asked, "Light roast or dark?"

She took a step toward us, now standing in the same spot as she was when Daniel had hit her, indicating she was amiable to conversation. Later, I would suspect that she was playing a part. An actress in a play or movie, just one facet of a larger plan. "I'm a dark roast girl."

"Ah, we can trust you, then," I said, giving her a sly grin. "If you'd said light, I don't think we could be friends."

She laughed and looked back and forth at us. "So, what do you guys do? You look like businessmen."

Indeed. Daniel and I worked for a company that sold inventory management software to vintners. Daniel was the west coast territory manager. Me – I used to be a development engineer, because every good salesforce needs a person who actually knows what the product does.

"We're salesmen," said Daniel. "Our customers are wineries."

She laughed in a way that challenged us to not bore her. "What do you sell, grape seed?"

"Only the finest," I said. "My friend here and I pick and peel the grapes by hand, carefully split them using a patented method, and inspect the seeds under microscopes, assisted by high-powered diodes."

Daniel got on board with this. "We reject ninety percent of them, it's true. Our reputation for quality is world-wide."

The conversation went on like this for a while. I enjoyed the sound of her laugh, the way she sort of shrank into herself when she found a remark particularly amusing. She eventually told us that she was working on writing a book, had been in Sacramento for an interview. This was, of course, far more interesting than jokes about grape seed. I became intrigued. "Tell us more."

"I'm a reporter by trade. My partner in crime as it were, my coauthor, is a certain celebrity neurosurgeon."

"Celebrity? Who?" asked Daniel, now as interested as I was. He was a man obsessed with fame. He always hoped to run into Hollywood stars on every trip to California. I can't say I was immune to the phenomenon, especially on those nights we found ourselves in bars in certain areas of Los Angeles or visiting the most high-class wineries. Was the knockout who emerged from the private dining room for a moment to take a call Alisha Vikander, or simply a doppelgänger. I suppose our main difference is that he was infatuated with even minor levels of fame – b-list sports stars, second-string guitarists, aging character actors – these all got him excited.

It was her turn to smile, wryly. "Wouldn't you like to know? Maybe you can guess."

"What's the book about?" I asked, the names of precisely zero celebrity neurosurgeons coming to mind.

"I'm interviewing people who've had near-death experiences of the out-of-body type."

"Sounds interesting."

Daniel threw a wrench into the whole thing. "I've read," he said, eyes wide and hands out, "that near-death experiences are caused by a lack of oxygen to the brain. A sort of spasm of hallucination before you finally kick the bucket, but then you get revived and remember it."

She blinked, obviously trying to conceal an impulse to roll her eyes. "A woman in cardiac arrest in a Seattle hospital, while technically dead, saw a shoe on the roof. She revived and told the nurse. The nurse went and checked. It was there." As if to punctuate her remark, the counter opened up behind her, and she turned abruptly to go speak with the airport employee behind it. After a short exchange, she walked away, giving us no parting smile or even a brief wave. I watched her disappear into the throng, trying to keep an eye on her light head, to discern whether she was going to the bagel stand or continuing on toward some distant gate, but she was too short to keep track of in this manner for long.

I sighed. Daniel advanced to the counter to change his ticket.

It was ten in the morning, Pacific Standard Time, and the air temperature in Sacramento was seventy-three degrees.

※

I rarely make connections with people on airplanes, though there have been some memorable moments. Once, I spoke with an elderly couple who lived in Effham Falls, Minnesota, the town where I was born. My parents had whisked me away at the age of six, old enough to have vague memories of the place, and it produced a melancholy in my heart to hear their tales about its decline. Another time, a charmingly half-drunk woman somehow managed to arrange herself cross-legged in the seat next to me and talked my ear off while devouring a personal pizza from a cardboard box, before offering me the final slice. In the category of non-conversational bonding, once, a guy sitting next to me and I discovered we were both reading the same e-book on our phones, a subversive bestseller about how to get your life in order for young men. I'd felt I'd read it too late, somehow stumbled upon most of the advice in sundry other places, but it felt good in reading it to see my previous year before me, compactly arranged by a complete stranger. My new friend and I had simply exchanged knowing glances and continued to read.

On this particular flight, I sat next to a middle-aged couple that were mostly silent, occasionally speaking to each other in hushed voices as if they were afraid to wake the people around them, though it was early afternoon and I saw no one asleep. I was fine with this. I spent my flight time leaning against the side of the plane, head tilted toward the window, taking in the jagged ridges of the Rocky Mountains beneath a potent blue sky. I listened to Dvořák's New World Symphony through noise-canceling earbuds.

Upon landing, during the ritual phone-checking, I saw I had missed a call from the woman I was considering asking to marry me. Her name was Jennifer Bloom, always called Jen, and she was doing post-graduate work at an archaeological dig in southern Arizona. That she'd called me quickened my pulse. Jen, like any twenty-first century mobile-user, texted. A call from her must thus be an event on either side of a tremendous spectrum of meaning. It was either a butt-dial, as we still called them, or someone had died. I checked for a message and there was none, though I did not know if this made me feel better or worse. After deplaning, I called her from the terminal.

"Hey, sweetie," she said, sounding, to my relief, cheerful. I envisioned her sitting on her haunches in shorts atop some dusty rock under a hot sun, face shaded by a floppy hat, a glisten of sweat at the base of her pale throat, an obscure digging tool in her right hand as she held the phone in her left.

"Saw you called."

The music of her laugh was cut through with static. "Accident."

"Ah, good. I was afraid something bad happened."

"Sorry!"

"No worries."

"You in an airport?"

"Yeah, do I sound bad?"

"Terrible. Cutting in and out."

It was then I stopped walking, struck by a bizarre thought, perhaps spurred by a memory that had yet to consciously reveal itself. People shuffled and darted around me as I became completely motionless. I stood holding the staticky phone to my ear in this cool terminal, watching throngs of human beings swarm. A voice, impossible to understand, blared over a loudspeaker. I looked in people's eyes as they passed. They were tired, bored, sad, worried, anxious in a variety of ways, or, on rare occasion, joyful. I wondered how many people I was looking at, all at once. It must be close to two hundred, I thought.

A man in a sharp suit and tie scurried around a woman wearing a sundress, the breeze of his long, rushing legs fluttering her skirt.

A mother hustled toward the moving walkway flanked by twin girls, one of their small hands in each of hers, the girl on the left beginning to wail.

A woman who looked vaguely like my older sister leaned against a wall, scrolling on her phone, which was plugged into an outlet near her bare ankle.

A horn blared, and a small, uniformed man with gleaming eyes drove a cart full of hunched elderly travelers around my rudely positioned obstacle of a human body.

"Sam, you there?" crackled Jen.

I couldn't speak. Thinking inwardly, I became overwhelmed with the notion that I had just spent the last two hours in a metal container that hurtled through the sky at thirty-thousand feet, at hundreds of miles per hour, while listening to a symphonic performance of pristine quality, and was now speaking with my girlfriend half a continent away using an equally complex contraption that sent invisible signals that were either particles or waves but not both at the same time. And now, I was in a gigantic construct that blocked those signals, surrounded by hundreds, no – thousands, of complete strangers. The most overwhelming thing was that these strangers all had stories, just like me and Jen did. Their stories screamed at me to be told.

"Hey, sorry," is all I said.

A man with a slight limp and an unkempt beard made his way past me, hunched under the weight of a giant, dirty backpack. This man had a name, a history. A family, perhaps. A favorite time to eat dinner.

"You in Denver?"

"Yeah."

"I'll let you go, kay? Text me when you get home?"

I said the word yes, but I suspected she did not hear it, for I had lost the signal.

I texted her, knowing that she would enjoy the meta-nature of the words, texting about texting. "I'll text you when I get home."

She responded with a smiley face followed by an arrangement of parentheses and dots that were meant to resemble revealed breasts.

I spent the next three hours wandering the airport in an odd state of mind. I paid relentless attention to the strangers around me, desiring to know each of their stories. I'm sure my gaze made a number of them uncomfortable. I, myself, was uncomfortable. I was undergoing some kind of self-dissociation, perhaps like what people report having experienced after consuming psychedelic drugs. It is likely because of this state of mind that I saw her for the second time, seated at the bar of a cocktail lounge.

If it really was a second time. If it really was her.

She was reading a paperback, her messenger bag on the floor near her stool with the strap looped around her right ankle. I approached and stated a name I'd looked up before taking off from Sacramento, the only person I could fathom that could realistically be called a celebrity neurosurgeon.

She looked up at me, a mildly amused smile coming to her face. The name I'd mentioned was clearly masculine. "I'm sorry. My name is Eden."

I laughed. "Mine's Sam. But that wasn't what I meant. Isn't he the celebrity neurosurgeon?"

"The who? The what?"

"May I sit?"

She appraised me and then gave a small, precise nod.

I sat next to her and then asked, "So, is that your coauthor?"

"My coauthor?"

"For your book."

She blinked, peering into my eyes. "My book doesn't have a coauthor."

"You said before that it did."

"When? I've never seen you before in my life."

I was flummoxed. Was she toying with me? "You must have a twin, then. Who dresses exactly like you and has the same bag. We spoke in Sacramento, only hours ago."

She smiled and shook her head slowly. "I'll give you points for most original twist on the stalest of old pickup lines."

I felt myself flushing and almost denied this as my motivation, but, of course, regardless of the truth of the matter, denying that sort of thing can only make the situation worse. "So, wait, let's back up a moment. You are writing a book though?"

"I am."

"Is it about out-of-body near-death experiences?"

The head shaking continued. "No," she said, cutely drawing out the vowel. "It's a murder mystery set in Antarctica. I was writer-in-residence at McMurdo Station last year."

I laughed and was speechless. I found myself sinking back into the mental paralysis I'd experienced earlier. Eden's light eyes scrutinized mine. I did not understand the game we were playing, but it was clear that she'd won.

Until, that is, she suddenly took on an expression of shock. Her words became rapid, her voice high-pitched. "You really did talk to someone who looked just like me, didn't you? In another airport?"

"I'm afraid I did."

She leapt from her seat, sending the espresso she'd been sipping hurtling toward the bottom-shelf row of spirits and splattering them with foam, the small ceramic cup then ricocheting off the neck of a bottle of cheap gin and hitting the bartender, a young man with glazed eyes, in the leg. He turned, appearing only mildly concerned.

Eden, after having half-tripped over her messenger bag strap, hopping on one foot for a moment to keep from tumbling, swiped up the bag and sprinted from the bar, nearly colliding with a hostess. She bolted around one of those stands in the terminal hallways that sold a variety of watches, or it might have been some other kind of jewelry. I watched her disappear, and then turned back toward the bar. The customers stared at me, appalled, presumably wondering what I'd said to inspire her to take flight.

The bartender approached me wordlessly. He looked like a man who'd just been roused from a state of hibernation. I paid for Eden's espresso, added a ten-dollar tip, mouthed an apology to the bar as I rose from my seat, and departed the place.

It was shortly thereafter I was approached by three men in blue shirts, black slacks, and black ties. They wore hats with the logo of the airport, and an insignia on their lapels of a vaguely military nature.

All three of them looked exactly the same.

It must have been a year later. I was on a tram with Jen in Las Vegas, our honeymoon. We'd driven up from Mesa because after that day in Denver, I'd not flown again. I would never fly again. I even declined requests from good friends who wanted me to pick them up at the airport. "I don't do airports," I'd say, with no further explanation. Eventually, people stopped asking. Even Jen.

The tram came to a halt and its doors opened. People flooded the thing, packing us all together. I held a pole with my right hand and had my left arm around Jen's waist. She hugged my chest, and I gently nuzzled the top of her head with my stubbly chin.

As the tram lurched forward, that sensation of paralysis came over me once again. The crowd on the tram began to scream out to my mind. The people still up from the previous night's partying. The families who would just spend a half-day on the Strip so they could say they'd seen it before heading off to the real destination, the Grand Canyon. The hotel workers, the Elvis impersonators, the people who just plain lived there – they all invaded my psyche. Jen and I stood in the center of one car, and one couple in particular, near the end of the car, screamed at me the loudest. A young woman with neat, strawberry hair to her shoulders, accompanied by a man with short sandy hair that was messily flattened down on his head, as though he had just removed a hat, though he didn't seem to have one with him. They held hands tightly. In love but anxious, I thought.

"Hey, you okay?" whispered Jen. The feel of her warm breath against my ear jolted me back to physical reality.

"Yeah, fine," I said.

"I felt the baby kick," she said, pressing herself tighter to me.

And such a curious thing. The genesis of a human being. That the creature in Jen's womb was human life is logically unassailable. It is human and it is alive, so thus it is human life. But when does it become, as we say, its own person? How? Does a soul spring forth from nonexistence? Or was that soul present in the cosmic rafters, stored away on a shelf, sleepily in wait for some moment a few minutes or hours or days after my congress with Jen, ready to present itself to that egg? Or – did it wait until later? The billboards say, I have a heartbeat at so many months, I can smile at such and such a time, as though these markers of biological development might offer some clue, but I was never certain they did.

And if such a soul were indeed in this way to make itself manifest, had it at some point before inhabited a different body?

I had gone through my life, up to a certain point, unconcerned with these ideas. They were questions that never bothered me before I met Eden for a second time. The three strange men, though, insisted it was not her. It was not a second time.

One of them had said, "Perhaps these young women are twins separated at birth. Have you read twin studies?"

"Fascinating things," said another of the strange men.

The third continued, "Two guys meet for a twin study. They're middle-aged identical twins raised apart. They've never met."

The middle one spoke again. All three were to some extent friendly and relaxed, but there was a subtext. An agenda of high importance. Their voices were crisp and articulate. I just sat there in silence, listening. We were in a small room behind an unmarked door.

"They meet, for the first time, and they're wearing the same clothes. Like these women you met."

"These different women. Thoroughly different. Each her own person."

"Both these guys, they have startlingly similar stories. They got married the same year, for example."

"Both of them enjoy brown ales."

"Both their wives had mahogany hair and adorable chin dimples."

"These men decided to lose weight at age forty-one, and they both met their goals."

"In the same amount of time, actually. Down to the day."

"It's startling, you see, how similar twins are, even beyond the realm of appearance."

I wasn't sure how convinced I was. I had just wanted to get out of there. One of them gave me a voucher for a free car rental only after I agreed never to set foot in an airport again. He wouldn't explain why, yet I was in full, sincere agreement with their demand. The presence of these three identical men was overwhelming in ways I can't describe.

And now, on the tram, hugging my pregnant wife and looking at that distant couple, I felt similarly haunted.

"What you staring at?" asked Jen.

"Nothing," I said, looking down at her and trying to get lost in her eyes.

"Okay," she said, smiling.

At the next stop, my gaze was drawn up again. The couple in the far corner, still clutching hands, made their way to the door. My heart came to my throat. It was undeniable.

"Do those two look familiar to you?" I asked Jen.

She studied them. "Nope. She looks a little out of his league though, don't you think?"

I wasn't even thinking about that. My heart pounded in my chest.

I suggested to myself I'd seen them earlier in the day, just ran into them going one way on the Strip and now I was running into them going the other way. But I knew this wasn't true. The sight of them had roused something deep in my memory, an encounter from years ago.

Jen nuzzled my neck, the way a woman does when she wants you to forget everything in the world except for her. I swallowed, trying to still my mind and heart as the couple left the tram and wandered out onto the Strip. I wanted to dart after them, shout at them, get them to stop, ask them how I knew them.

Not that I really *knew* them.

But I had seen them before.

JASON BURSACK is a writer living in Fargo, North Dakota. His work has appeared in *Embark Literary Journal* and multiple anthologies.

The Carnival Comes To Town
Scott Dyson

"Hey, Audrey, look at this! We gotta go!" Janine exclaimed as she pointed at the brightly colored flier taped to the door of Mattson's Shell gas station on the corner of Eagle Avenue and Second Street. "The carnival hasn't been here in years!"

Audrey Lindstrom studied the flier. "Runs Thursday through Sunday." She grinned. "It might be fun."

A tall dark-skinned boy pushed the door open, forcing Janine and Audrey to jump backwards. "What are you nerds looking at?" he said before heading to the counter to pay for his gas.

"Look who's talking. Nerd." Audrey flipped the bird toward the boy's back.

"Right back atcha," he said without turning around.

She looked at Janine and made a surprised "O" with her mouth. "How did he know?" she mouthed soundlessly.

Janine widened her eyes and shrugged. They both stared at the older teenager as he paid for his gas with a credit card. "Totally hot," Janine whispered. Audrey nodded.

The boy turned around and walked toward them. His face was expressionless until he reached the door. "Seriously, what are you looking at?"

"Carnival," Audrey said, pointing to the flier. "It starts tomorrow."

He nodded. "I saw them setting up for it. Looks cool. You guys going?"

"Uh, maybe?" Audrey answered.

"Maybe?" Janine found her voice. "I'm definitely going."

"Cool. Me, too." He reached for the door then paused, stepping back. He looked from Janine to Audrey. "I'm Raj."

"We know," Janine said, too quickly.

"You do, huh?" Raj laughed. "I've seen you around the school," he said, gesturing toward Audrey. "Are you two freshmen at Effham Falls High?"

"Sophomores," Janine said.

"That's cool. Go Lumberjacks!" he said, grinning.

Raj studied both girls, but his gaze lingered on Audrey. He turned to leave, but then spun abruptly. "Hey, you wanna go with me and my friend Cam? Not like I'm asking you out, just...like, you know, I give you a ride to the carnival, maybe we hang out a little, or maybe we just do our own thing." He squinted and cocked his head as he studied Audrey's face, just long enough to make his intention obvious. Then he grinned and nodded. "Then I'll give you a ride home."

"I don't—" Audrey started.

"Yes! For sure!" Janine said.

"Cool." Raj held out his hand to Audrey. "Gimme your phone."

Audrey handed him the phone. Raj looked at it, then held it up to Audrey's face. He laughed, unlocked it, and punched the phone button. His thumbs flew over the screen, and his own phone began to ring. "Cool. You got my number, I got yours. Text me your address. Pick you guys up at seven tomorrow night?"

"I don't know," Audrey said. "It's a school night, you know. My parents are strict about going out on school nights."

Raj nodded. "Yeah, didn't think of that. Friday, then." He pushed open the door and strode out to his sporty white BMW. He opened the door, slid behind the steering wheel, and waved once as he drove off.

"Hello... Don't I even exist?" Janine shook her head.

"What are you talking about?"

"He barely looked at me. Couldn't tear his eyes off you."

"Come on," Audrey scoffed. "I'm a nobody."

"Well, he's not. He's Raj Priyanka. Doctor's son, rich as Bezos, and hotter than hell!"

Audrey cocked her head. "So why is he bothering with a couple of sophomores?"

"Ours is not to wonder why..." Janine quoted.

"Why am I getting *Carrie* vibes, then?"

"Oh, come on."

"I mean it. We're gonna end up covered in pig blood or something."

"Pig blood? Not a chance." Janine turned back to the carnival flier. "Though it is deer season..."

Audrey punched her lightly. "Don't even say that out loud!" She collected her Arizona Iced Tea and the Quest Bar she had purchased and pulled open the door. The pair exited into the parking lot where their bikes leaned against one of the outdoor ice chests. Audrey donned her backpack and mounted the bicycle, following Janine along the sidewalk until they reached their street.

"Who's picking you up?" Audrey's mother asked as Audrey descended the stairs toward the front door. Wearing her best jeans and a sweater featuring a character from her favorite Halloween film, *The Nightmare Before Christmas*, she had meticulously done her hair and makeup to look like it hadn't been done at all.

"Janine will be over in a minute," Audrey answered.

"That doesn't answer my question, young lady."

Audrey sighed. "Raj Priyanka. You know, Dr. Priyanka's son?"

"Hmm. And how do you know the boy?"

"School. Then Janine and I ran into him at the gas station on Second and Eagle. We were talking about the carnival, and he asked if we wanted to go with him and his friend. Not as a date. Just like to hang out, maybe go on some rides together." Audrey brushed a stray strand of hair out of her face. "We might not even hang out the whole evening, but Raj said he'll give us a ride home, too."

"Your father might not approve."

"Mom! What's not to approve? He's Dr. Priyanka's son, and he's really nice. Really smart, too. Like, he's taking calculus this year—as a junior."

"Hmm." Mom just stared at her.

A knock at the door saved her. Audrey opened it and found Janine standing there dressed in tight black yoga pants with a cute short skirt and a loose-fitting Wallows T-shirt. A jean jacket finished her ensemble, and Audrey was certain her friend had spent as much time as Audrey had in front of the mirror before coming over.

"Hi, Mrs. L!"

"Hello Janine. May I ask you a question?"

"Mom..."

"Do your parents approve of you going in a car with a young man they don't know?"

"Well, actually..." Janine smiled. "My mom has met Raj a few times. She does some freelance bookkeeping for Raj's father's practice. And she thinks Raj is just the nicest young man – her words, not mine."

Audrey watched her mother as Janine spoke and noticed that she relaxed visibly. Mrs. Lindstrom even smiled at the girls when a honk came from outside.

"Invite him in!" Audrey's mother suggested.

"Mom..." Audrey said. "Not tonight. This isn't a date. We're just going to a carnival with a couple of friends."

Audrey held her breath for a beat until her mother nodded. "Go then," she said. "Shoo. Oh, and have fun and, for God's sake, be careful!"

The two girls escaped out the front door and hurried down the walk toward Raj's BMW. Audrey could see the blond, blue-eyed Cam sitting in the passenger's seat. He opened the door as they approached.

"Hello, sophies," he greeted them. He flipped up the seat and Janine climbed in first. Audrey went to follow her, but Cam cut her off and joined Janine in the back seat.

Audrey slid into the passenger's seat and fastened her seatbelt. The leather seat felt warm against the back of her thighs and her lower back. "Wow! This is cool! I've never been in a Beemer before!" she said, smiling at Raj.

"Thank my father. Only the best for the fruit of his loins." Raj laughed.

"So you know Janine's mother," Audrey said.

"I do?"

Janine piped up. "Um, Audrey? I made that up. Cut through a lot of red tape, didn't it?"

Audrey looked over her shoulder at Janine sitting behind Raj, and Cam ignoring her, staring at his phone. She laughed.

"Believable lies. The best kind of lies," Raj said. "What did you say?"

"I told Audrey's mom that my mom has done some work for your father and thinks you are just the sweetest boy in the world. Or something like that."

Raj laughed. "Who knows? Maybe it's true." He looked over his shoulder. "Cam, get off your phone! We have guests with us!"

"Yeah, yeah." Cam's thumbs tapped the screen a few more times, then he clicked the device off and looked up from his lap. "What rides are you excited about?"

Janine piped up. "I've always liked the funhouse. But I like the Tilt-A-Whirl, too."

"Ferris Wheel," Audrey said. "I like seeing a long way."

"Ever been to the Mall of America?" Raj asked. "They have some pretty cool coasters there. Who likes coasters?"

"I'm a coaster guy," Cam said. "Not the lame ones like they have at these cheap little carnivals."

"I've never been on a big coaster," Audrey admitted.

"Oh, wow! I was on a bunch of them at this Six Flags theme park near Chicago. I almost puked when one of 'em was doing all these spins and stuff," Cam said.

"The Himalaya is fast," Raj said.

"Which one is that?" Cam asked.

"It's like a coaster that goes really fast in a circle. Feels like you're riding a snake or something because it goes up and down. A lot of carnivals have them."

"A snake?" Audrey asked. "Why a snake?"

"You'll see, if they have one."

"Will it make me puke?" Cam asked. "Because if it does, I'm in."

They all laughed, and Raj winked at Audrey.

She wondered about the wink for the rest of the ride to the carnival.

Raj parked his car near the back of the parking lot, about as far from other cars as he could get. Audrey noticed that he took up two spots between a couple of huge pick-up trucks.

"Last thing I need is to get the doors dinged. There are always a couple of these monsters parked like this in a lot, and I can kinda hide between them." Raj opened his door and stepped out. Audrey thought he whispered, "My dad would kill me if anything happens to it."

Audrey held the door as Janine climbed out of the back seat. "Tight squeeze," she said. She glanced back over her shoulder to see if Cam was following her. He wasn't.

Raj locked the car and they began the trek to the carnival's entrance, Raj and Cam walking ahead of Audrey and Janine. As they approached the ticket booths, Raj turned around and waited for the two girls.

"Hey, did you tell your mom that I was picking you up?" Raj asked Audrey when she joined them.

"Yes. I did," Audrey said.

"For a minute there, until I told her that little white lie, I didn't think she was gonna let you go," Janine said.

"Cool. Because she'd tell your dad," Raj said. "Right?"

"Maybe, if he calls. He's out of town on business at the moment."

"Hmm. Interesting." He turned back to Cam. "Hear that, Cam? The only person who knows we're with the girls here is Audrey's mother."

"What did you say?" Cam said. His phone was back in his hand, thumbs flying over the screen.

"I said that we could be serial killers, but her mom would know she's with me. So then I'd have to eliminate her, too."

"What?" Audrey said. This conversation was creeping her out. "Maybe we should just part company here."

Raj laughed. "Relax. I'm just being creepy. Halloween is coming, you know."

Audrey went along with it. "Oh, yeah. Just trying to scare me, right?" Her original plan seemed more and more like a bad idea. The new plan of ditching Raj and Cam seemed like a better solution.

"Sorry," Raj said. He seemed to sense he'd gone too far. His smile seemed less creepy, more genuine. "Let me treat everyone to some junk food. What do you all like?"

"How about a churro?" Janine suggested.

Audrey held up two fingers. "Me too."

"And a drink?" Raj asked.

"Sure! Diet cola, maybe," Audrey said.

"Got it. Two churros, two Diet Cokes." He walked away. Cam seemed to realize that Raj was gone and quickly followed.

"Well, that was weird," Audrey said. "Weird thing to say."

"He was just kidding," Janine said. "It was a joke."

"Yeah," Audrey agreed but it still creeped her out. "But, like, why are we here?"

"What do you mean? We wanted to go to the carnival and here we are."

"But why with Raj? And Cam? I mean, Cam is totally not interested. His eyes are all over every girl that walks by."

"That's because of me, probably," Janine said. "I know I'm not really pretty enough."

"And I am?" Audrey said. She shook her head and rolled her eyes.

"Let's be honest. I'm blond, blue-eyed, but I don't exactly have a cheerleader bod. You, on the other hand – you're tall and slim, and with that thick dark hair and dark brown eyes, you're a stunner."

"I'm not slim, I'm skinny," Audrey said. "No boobs."

"You're like a model. You just don't know it yet."

Raj appeared behind them, Cam in tow, holding up two churros and a cup. Cam held a bag of popcorn and another cup. "Figured we can share the drinks. Not enough hands to carry everything. Not like Kali."

"Who?" Janine asked.

"Kali. The Hindu goddess, you know? The one with the extra arms?"

"Are you Hindu?" Audrey asked.

"Well, my family is. Me, I don't know what I am, or what I'll be."

"I'm Lutheran," Audrey said, but immediately wondered why she'd said it.

"Like everyone else around here."

"Not me," Janine said. "I'm Roman Catholic."

"Is there a difference?"

The two girls looked at each other and shrugged. Audrey answered, "Not much, if I'm being real."

"Let's hit some rides," Raj said. "What's first?"

"Something tame. The Ferris Wheel?" Audrey suggested.

"Your favorite. Why not?" Raj pointed and led the way. "Cam, you're riding with Janine."

"Sure. Whatever," Cam said.

The line for the Ferris Wheel was short, and Raj joined Audrey in a red cart. The ride operator lowered the restraining bar in front of them and placed a locking pin. "Have fun," he said. The cart went up, then stopped as Janine and Cam boarded the next available seat.

"Cam's not much into this, is he?" Audrey asked.

"He's hot for Alyssa Pierson. You know, the cheerleader? He's kinda hoping she's not here. Doesn't want her to see him with me and two other girls."

"Why are you guys with us?" Audrey asked as the cart moved again.

Raj looked surprised. "You're pretty. And you seem really nice. We all wanted to go to the carnival, so here we are."

Audrey smiled. "Here we are."

"Is Audrey your first name?"

She was surprised by the question. "It's not. How did you know?"

"Just a feeling. I mean, you look like an 'Audrey' but something just seems off. What's your real first name?"

"Katherine. With a 'K.' But there were three other Katherines with a 'K' or with a 'C' in kindergarten, so I became Audrey."

The cart swung upward, and Raj said, "Katherine. That's so interesting. So is Audrey your middle name?"

"Yep."

"Katherine Audrey Lindstrom. K.A.L." Raj smiled as the cart rose to the very top and paused for more riders to load. He pulled out a flask from his jacket pocket and held it up. "Mind if I spike the drink? It's rum."

"Where did you get that?"

"The old man's liquor cabinet. Dad doesn't drink, except in private when he thinks no one knows. I just borrowed a little bit."

Audrey grinned. She unscrewed the cap and Raj poured some of the clear-colored liquid into the cup. "Stir it with the straw," he said, so she swirled it in the ice, replaced the lid, and handed it to Raj. She bit into what was left of the churro, then offered the rest to him.

Raj took a pull on the drink through the straw, then handed it back to Audrey. She sipped. Not terrible, she thought. It had a bite to it, but it wasn't unpleasant. She felt a warmth spread through her.

"Don't tell Cam. Or your friend."

Audrey grinned. She wondered if she was getting drunk.

"Nah," Raj said. "It's not that strong."

"Did I say that out loud?"

Raj laughed and nodded. "Maybe you *are* catching a buzz."

The wheel was spinning now, and so was Audrey's head. "I better stop," she said, handing the drink to Raj.

"I'll get you something else to eat. Did you have dinner?"

"No, I kinda skipped it."

"Ah. I'll get you a hot dog. Or a burger or something. You're probably hungry."

"Is this a date?"

"I don't know. Do you want it to be?"

"Yes," she said before she could stop herself.

Raj laughed. "Then it is."

Audrey wanted to lean into him. She wanted him to wrap his arm around her, or take her hand, but he made no moves at all. So she just looked around as they stopped near the top again, just past the highest point.

"Aw. It's over," Raj said. "What's next?"

"Funhouse?"

"I saw that they have a Himalaya ride, too. It's over there." He pointed at a circular building with a red and green roof.

"The Christmas-looking thing?"

"I guess it does look kinda Christmas-y."

"There's a Tilt-A-Whirl, too. I see it right there," Audrey said as the cart moved down.

"Your friend's favorite ride, right?"

"I think so."

"First, some food. Don't want you to get too tipsy." Raj laughed as the cart moved to the unloading platform and the attendant lifted the bar. When it came time to deboard, Raj helped Audrey out of the cart by taking her hand, but then immediately released it when they'd descended the stairs to the ground and waited for Cam and Janine.

Janine pointed through the booths and food stands. "Tilt-a-whirl is right there!"

"Okay, that's next," Raj said. "Want a bite to eat?"

"I'm good." Janine said.

"What do you want, Kali?"

Audrey, realizing Raj was referring to her initials, said, "Maybe a burger."

Raj nodded and went to the nearest food stand. Once again, Cam trailed after him.

"So, what happened?" Janine asked.

"Not much. We sipped a little rum," Audrey answered. "Oops. Wasn't supposed to tell you. My head's a little dizzy. That's why I have to eat something."

"Did he kiss you?"

"No, but he said it was a date!"

Janine just grinned when the boys returned. She leaned over and whispered in Audrey's ear. "Cam kissed me!"

"Really?"

Janine's eyes widened, and she mouthed, *Tell you later.*

Audrey wolfed down the burger. It tasted heavenly, although she knew it was probably the cheapest grade of meat the carnival could get, if it was even meat at all. Raj ate handfuls of the popcorn and cotton candy he'd bought. Cam was back to his disinterested self.

They made their way through a bunch of rides, going on the Tilt-A-Whirl, the Spider, a bumper car ride, and something called the Typhoon that rocked left and right until it reached its full height. Audrey felt her stomach drop when it left them feeling weightless for a few seconds at the end of each full swing.

When her phone rang, Audrey glanced at the caller identification. "My mom," she said, answering the phone.

"Yes...yeah, we're having a blast...very nice, yes. We had snacks and rode everything...yes, Mother, I know. One more ride and we'll leave." She hung up.

"What did your mom want?" Raj asked when Audrey turned back to him.

"She reminded me that I have to get home."

Raj smiled. "In that case, we better do the Himalaya now. They're getting ready to close up anyway. He took her hand and pulled her in the direction of the ride. But as they approached, the ride looked like it had already closed for the night.

"Oh, no. Your favorite," Audrey said.

"Let me talk to that guy," Raj said, pointing at the ride attendant. He jogged off, leaving the two girls with Cam.

Audrey saw him digging in his pocket, then something changed hands. Raj jogged back toward their group. "We can go."

"Just us?"

"Just us. Come on."

"Did you bribe him?" Audrey asked.

"I paid for a private ride. Let's get on."

As they approached, Audrey saw the picture of the many-armed goddess painted on the wall of the ride. "Who's that again?"

"Kali," Raj said. "But it's not right. Kali usually has four arms, not six. Although sometimes she has ten arms. That's her 'great' form."

"Kali,' Audrey repeated. *K-A-L-I...my initials.* She didn't know why she thought of it.

"Get on," the guy said to Raj.

"Let's sit over here. You two sit over there." Raj pointed to the far side of the ride's carts. Cam led Janine to the right, while Raj and Audrey moved to the left. They climbed into a cart, and Raj pulled down the safety bar. "Ready?" he asked Audrey.

"Hope I don't puke," she said.

The ride began to spin, undulating upward, downward, and always in a circle. Audrey felt the force of the air pressing against her face as it accelerated. Faster...faster...too fast?

"Isn't it going too fast?" she screamed to Raj, sitting to her left.

Raj's eyes were closed, and his lips were moving. The ride went faster and faster, and Audrey could barely see the walls or the opening as they spun.

And suddenly, the spinning stopped. She could still feel the force against her face, the motion in her stomach and inner ear, but the walls and center were stationary with respect to the ride vehicle. From her perspective, either the ride had come to a halt, or the entire building, including the loading platform and the walls, were spinning at the same rate as the Himalaya. Even the center...

No, the center was open. Audrey looked toward it and saw forever. She saw the stars, the galaxies, the void – and finally, the tentacles. Ten octopus-like arms extended from the central void. They reached for her as Raj watched, a small smile on his full lips.

Audrey screamed. The tentacles reached for her, touched her, encircled her, and lifted her easily from the ride. They drew her into the void and hugged her to the body from which they radiated. They showed her the true form of the goddess. And then she was engulfed.

The last words Audrey heard were from Raj. "Welcome back, Grandmother!"

*

The ride stopped. Cam and Janine approached Raj and Audrey from the left side of the ride as they walked unsteadily along the platform and down the stairs. Janine was a little dizzy, and she noticed that Raj was supporting Audrey as they stepped onto the dirt of the field where the carnival was set up. She couldn't wait to tell Audrey about Cam kissing her again.

"That was fun! So cool!" Janine exclaimed. Audrey's expression conveyed a seriousness that Janine wasn't used to.

"I truly enjoyed that experience," Audrey said. "Thank you, Rajesh. You have renewed me."

Janine studied her best friend, then said, "Are you okay, Audrey?"

"I am fine, Janine. Please. Call me by my initials. Kali."

"Kali? Like the goddess on the ride?"

"Exactly like the goddess."

"You're different."

"Perhaps." Audrey smiled her enigmatic smile again.

Janine knew *something* had happened; something had *changed* her friend. She wondered if Raji had done something.

As they climbed into his car, Janine observed the body language between her friend and Raj. Audrey sat straight up and so did Raj. Where she'd sensed a flirty interaction between the two earlier, she no longer saw one at all.

But they were friendly. Warm, even. Their actions were almost as if they were brother and sister, or cousins or something like that.

Raj dropped them off at Audrey's house, where Janine had earlier arranged to spend the night. Janine leaned in and said goodnight to Cam, who grunted something that may have been "See ya around." His eyes were on his phone. Raj hugged Audrey and whispered something in her ear. He placed his hands together and bowed.

Respectfully.

He pecked Audrey on the cheek and turned away, climbing into the Beemer and driving off slowly.

Audrey fumbled with the key, staring at it as if it was a foreign object before sliding it into the lock and turning it. She followed Janine inside the foyer and after the door was shut, she wrapped her arms around Janine and hugged her tenderly. "You remind me of Gauri, my golden one."

Janine cocked her head back and squinted, as if seeing her friend for the first time. "Yeah, I think maybe I'll go home."

Audrey smiled and Janine studied her eyes. They appeared to be green, rimmed with gold. She struggled to pull her gaze from her friend's eyes but failed.

"I think you should stay, Gauri."

"Who's this 'Gauri?' Why are you calling me that, Audrey?"

"I told you to call me Kali," Audrey said.

Audrey guided Janine into the house, her left firmly encircling Janine's shoulder, her eyes still holding Janine's gaze intently. Janine reached up to rub her eyes and saw a sword appear, as if by magic, in her friend's right hand. A blue flower seemed to bloom from the soft, tanned skin of Audrey's other arm.

Janine's mind cried out as Audrey shut the door to her room.

But her voice remained as silent as the void from which the goddess had emerged.

BY DAY, SCOTT DYSON works as a healthcare professional. He is also a husband and a father to two boys. In his spare time, he writes and self-publishes his tales of horror, mystery, and science fiction/fantasy. He has been writing since grade school, but it wasn't until the mid-1990's, when he was helping to host a book and writing forum on Delphi Internet Services called *The Book and Candle Pub*, that he got more serious about creating works of fiction. He has self-published three short story collections, four novellas, and a novel. He has had his fiction published in several anthologies, including *The Gates of Chaos*, for which he also served as the editor and publisher.

The Card
Dan McKay

David blared the horn and sped toward the men pummeling someone lying face down on the street. They scattered like roaches in the headlights. He screeched to a stop and rushed to the victim. Despite the blood, the man was alive.

"Go away," the man rasped. "They'll get you, too." David lifted the man under his arms and dragged him into the back seat.

"He's not a cop," someone down the street shouted.

"Get him!" another replied.

"Drive!" the beaten man urged.

A bottle shattered against David's car as the tires squealed. He took the corner hard, clinging to the steering wheel. The man in the back yelped as he rolled off the seat.

David looked over his shoulder. "Let's get you to the hospital." He passed back a stack of fast-food napkins for the man's bloody nose.

"No hospital. I'll be okay." He pulled himself up, clinging to the passenger seat headrest. "You saved my life. They'd just got started on me." He wadded up a napkin and staunched the blood flow.

"What happened?" David glanced in the rearview mirror. "Or do I want to know?"

The man shook his head. "You don't. It's a case of bad luck that's been a monkey on my back." His face brightened. "Hey, I'll pay you back."

"You don't owe me anything," David said. "Where can I take you?"

The man opened his wallet and paused for a moment. "The bus station. I need to leave town." They drove in silence, other than the man's occasional groans. David's hand quivered on the steering wheel. He'd risked enough already without getting tangled deeper. Could whoever had thrown the bottle have seen his license plate or recognized his car?

Ten minutes later, he pulled into the passenger drop-off area. "Can you make it from here?"

"Yeah, I can handle it. Thanks for the ride. I have something for you, after I get my ticket. Too hard to explain out here."

David weighed his options. The safest thing to do was to pass on the payment and drive off. A hand clasped his shoulder. "I know you're thinking of scooting as soon as I get out. Trust me, you want what I have for you."

"Is it legal?" The words left David's mouth before he could think about them. "I mean, something got you in trouble back there, and those guys didn't exactly look like law-abiding citizens." People had told him that was the wrong side of town to be on after dark and now he had first-hand proof.

The man coughed and clutched his ribs. "There's no law against it. You'll see." He dropped a five-dollar bill into David's lap. "Buy a deck of cards at the little store inside. Meet me in the passenger area."

David found the man in the far corner of the waiting area with his hat pulled low. In the light, he looked worried. He wasn't carrying any belongings, and that didn't appear to be an issue for him. "I don't even know your name. Mine's—"

The man held up his hand. "No names. It's better that way. I never met you; you never met me." He glanced around and pointed to the seat next to him. "I'll explain what I'm giving you, and you can be on your way."

David sat and waited, trying to contain his nervous energy.

"Do you play cards?" the man asked.

"Sometimes." David thought of the Friday lunch hour poker games with his coworkers. He wasn't as good as they were and rarely won anything.

"You'll want to play more after this." The man reached into his shirt pocket and pulled something out. "See this?"

"No. I don't see anything."

The man tapped his nose. "That's the point. What I have here can't be seen until you use it. Bring out those cards."

David stood. "I'm not sure what your angle is here, but I'm not playing cards tonight. I'd like to get back home and put this behind me." He turned and started to walk away.

"I hear you," the man said. "I'll try to make it quick. Thing is, I didn't get a good explanation when I got this thing. It took me months to learn how to use it properly. Otherwise, it's near worthless."

"What is it?" David asked over his shoulder.

"It's a trick card. Let me show you with one hand and then you can go."

"Card tricks." David returned and handed over the cards. "I'm in the downtown bus station surrounded by bums who pee in the bushes outside and you want to show me a card trick."

"They're just bums, same as anywhere." The man patted the seat. "Sit down." He fanned the five cards in his hand. "See these cards? What do we have? It's a new deck, never shuffled, so we have an ace, king, queen, jack, and ten. Suppose we want a pair of aces." He reached into his shirt pocket and mimed placing another card in his hand. "Now look." He fanned the cards. "Two aces, a king, queen, and jack."

"It's just a card trick."

"Not a card trick." He pointed. "Two aces, no ten. You take them." He handed them to David. "Now, tell me which cards you have."

"Same as you had. Two aces, king, queen, jack."

"Shuffle them in your hand and look again."

David went through the motions to shuffle. His eyebrows shot up. "Now I have a ten. Where did the other ace go?"

"It was never there." The man patted his shirt pocket. "Shuffling sends the trick card back to its owner. The original card, the ten, was always there. It just looked like an ace."

"I don't know about this," David said. "It's some sort of trick."

"You can do it, too. Let me give you the magic card." His face became serious. "Will you accept it and become its owner?"

David rolled his eyes. "Sure, I accept."

The man slid something into David's shirt pocket. "Now it's yours." He shuffled the deck and dealt five cards. "What a terrible poker hand. How would you fix this with one card?"

He examined the cards and wrinkled his nose. "Best you could do is a pair of sevens. If you had another seven."

The man nodded. "Add the trick card to your hand."

He picked up the cards and patted his shirt pocket. Something was actually there, although he couldn't see it, even when held up to the light. Was it even real? He slipped it in with the other cards and his jaw dropped as a three changed to a seven. "How'd it do that?"

"I have no earthly idea." He took the cards from David and shuffled them into the desk. A tired voice on the PA system announced the bus, and the man jumped to his feet wincing. "I've got to go. Good luck. Be subtle with it and don't ever tell anyone." He joined the group boarding the bus and disappeared.

David blinked. The man had taken the deck of cards. Where was the trick card? He patted his shirt pocket and found it. What had just happened? Somehow, he owned something magic. Actual magic!

Three months prior to meeting the man with the magic card, David Forschen had moved to Effham Falls to work as an accountant for the Fredrickson taconite mine. The Effham office handled the books for several mines, and his experience with multiple locations and intercompany reporting made for an easy interview. Only three people had applied for the job, and he suspected the others weren't CPAs.

When he received an offer the next day, David went back to sign employment papers. He mentioned he would need an apartment. The HR person recommended he check with the hardware store. "It's on *that* side of town," the HR rep said, "but I think it's pretty okay. It's cheap." David didn't mind cheap or "pretty okay" considering he wouldn't be getting big-city wages.

Two months later, David was updating a spreadsheet when Louis Dubois rapped on his cubicle wall. "Going to play poker with us today?" Louis was the only man in the office shorter than David. Many of the women were taller than both of them.

"Yeah, I'll be there." He saved the spreadsheet and pushed back from the desk. "I'll save this headache for later."

Dubois clicked his tongue and pointed a finger-gun at him. "Bring your money."

David trudged to the breakroom where his officemates sat around a table while Artie shuffled the deck. Texas Hold 'Em was the game of choice. Regular poker, draw or stud, seemed like a stuffy old-school game in comparison. Artie dealt blackjack out at the Rusty Nail on the weekends and liked to wear his green-tinted visor and a red garter on his bicep when they played. The cards sailed across the table, landing precisely in front of each player.

Half an hour later, David was down forty dollars. He would have lost more, but he'd learned to fold rather than hope for a miracle. Artie dealt another round. David had a king of spades and a three of hearts. The flop showed a four of hearts, a six of diamonds, and a ten of clubs. His best hope was high card or a miracle on the turn or river. He met the raise of a dollar, and the turn showed a queen of hearts. Betting continued, and David considered folding. He went in for another dollar and Artie flipped the river card over to show a seven of spades. David raised his cards to toss them.

Dubois rubbed his fists over his eyes. "*Tant pis!*"

David's two years of French in college were rusty, but he knew mocking when he heard it. *Tant pis*—tough luck. He clutched the cards to his chest while he pondered what to do. There was no way he would win with only a king. His hands brushed against his shirt pocket and froze. His pocket had been empty that morning when he put the shirt on. Could it be the trick card? Did it only show up when he was playing cards? He shifted his cards from his left hand to his right, masking when he slipped in the magic card. The king changed into a five of hearts. Why a five? He scanned the cards on the table. Three, four, five, six, seven—a straight. With no pairs on the table, there was no chance anyone had a full house or four of a kind. No chance anyone had a flush, either. His straight was the best possible hand.

It was wrong to cheat, but his dander was up. His Uncle Frank had told him if he didn't know who the mark was at the table, it was him. Years ago, after Uncle Frank had gone to prison, David had dismissed everything he had said. Now David had a moment of clarity. *Tant pis*, yourself, Louis. He tossed five dollars onto the table.

Dubois' grinned and chuckled. "You wish to donate to my hot date tonight? *Merci*." He tossed a five, likely one he'd gotten from David, into the pot and called. "Two pair," he crowed.

David flipped his cards over. "I have a straight."

The table fell silent for a moment. David relished the shocked look on Dubois' face. "Whoa, nerves of steel," Artie said. "You had nothing until the river." He gathered the cards and shuffled them. David felt a reassuring presence return to his shirt pocket. The game went on for another hour while he turned the tables and raked in two hundred and sixty-five dollars.

After work, David parked near the hardware store and walked through the alley. Since the recent end of Daylight Savings time, evenings were darker, and the fall weather had turned colder. Meager lights shined from back entrances to apartments in the other buildings nearby. While he could tell other people lived in the area, he seldom saw them.

He stopped to read a flyer titled "Is This Your Cat?" stapled to a power pole. Three color photos showed a gray cat on a porch, in a flower bed, and lounging beneath a bird bath next to scattered feathers. Below the photos it read: "Please keep your cat at home! It has been using my backyard for nefarious purposes! Thank you! Cindy Swanstrom"

"That's Wilbur," a voice said behind him. David whirled around. A lady he'd not seen before took the last drag of a cigarette and tossed the butt into the gravel. She wore a short black skirt over ripped black leggings and black combat-style boots. An unfastened motorcycle jacket over bare skin completed her ensemble. She pushed her hands into the jacket's side pockets and walked closer. "The cat."

"Oh."

She pulled her jacket open. Stunned, he gawped at her pale breasts.

Pain exploded on his jaw, and he crumpled to the ground. The woman's knee pressed his head into the gravel while deft fingers retrieved his wallet. Out of the corner of his eye, he spotted brass knuckles clasped in her fist, and then she was gone as quickly as it had started.

He sat dazed for a minute before staggering to his feet. It had been a lucky day, but had quickly turned sour. What a dope he'd been to fall for her trick.

On the way to his apartment, he spotted his wallet on the ground. The money was gone, but his ID and bank card remained. A tiny silver lining in a dark cloud. He climbed the metal steps one at a time, gripping the handrail.

Once inside, he examined the damage in his bathroom mirror. He picked bits of gravel off his face and wiggled a loose molar. His jawbone throbbed, and he heaped ice cubes onto a towel for an ice pack.

♣

David spent the next day in his apartment, popping ibuprofen, and refilling ice trays with water. By evening, the pain and swelling had subsided enough for him to venture out for food. At the Red Owl, he bought cans of soup so he wouldn't have to chew anything. Self-conscious of his bruise, he kept a hand on his cheek.

Was this karmic punishment for using the trick card? He couldn't bring himself to admit he had cheated. It was just a little help. Besides, Louis had goaded him into it.

On Sunday, David feigned sickness to avoid going out with his friends to the Rusty Nail to watch the Packers. His jaw still hurt, and his bruise had changed from purple to yellow. It was going to be challenging to come up with a story to tell his coworkers come Monday morning. He rehearsed a slip-and-fall story involving the metal staircase to his apartment and frost on the steps.

♣

David joined the Friday poker game in the breakroom. The bruise on his jaw had faded and no longer hurt unless he pressed on it. He sensed the trick card in his pocket after the first deal.

After losing ten dollars, he used the trick card to change a three of clubs, which gave him a pair of queens. The queen in the flop made it three of a kind. With a pair of sevens coming from the flop and the river, he had a full house and won twenty dollars. Endorphins coursed through his brain. He tried to hold back, but he wanted to win every hand.

"No more Friday games for you," Dubois said. "Last week, my date called me cheap and now she is *frigide* to me."

"*Tant pis*," David teased.

Artie raised an eyebrow. "You're the luckiest son-of-a-gun I've ever seen. You could go pro."

David beamed. "You think so?" The idea stuck.

Back at his desk, an extra hundred and fifty dollars in his wallet, David watched video clips of professional poker players at tournaments. The players kept their cards face-down on a glass table, although the cards were visible to the viewers and presumably the officials. Everyone would notice his trick card the instant he used it. Thoughts of taking home hundred-thousand-dollar pots faded.

Saturday morning, his car wouldn't start. He called Ed's Towing for a jump start. A teenager with a terrible case of acne arrived in a pickup and hooked up the jumper cables hanging out of the truck's front grill. "Crank it over," he called from under David's car's hood.

After the car started, David parted with fifty dollars.

"Your battery's suss," the kid said. He revved his pickup and sped off.

David stopped at an auto parts store advertising a sale on batteries. A new one cost a hundred and fifty dollars, installed. Good thing he'd won that much Friday, although he was out fifty for the jump start. In the waiting room, he read in the *Effham Falls Forum* that the Rusty Nail was sponsoring a poker tournament that weekend. He drove out to the bar, paid the entrance fee, and took a seat at one of the tables.

Two hours later, he'd progressed to the next round. His second-round opponents were a smarter class of poker player and he took pains to hide his subterfuge. While his trick card could improve his hand, it did not guarantee he would beat anyone else's hand. David folded often, but leaned on any advantage when his chances were good.

At the end of the night, they invited him back for the final round the next day. If he could hold on and win it, he'd take home enough to pay cash for a new vehicle.

The final round brought heightened levels of scrutiny. The players were seasoned pros and knew far more about the game than David. After a couple hands, he knew he'd be lucky to place in the top ten. Betting strategy, his biggest weakness, tipped off the rest of the table. Whenever he had a good hand, the rest would fold. He tried bluffing, but they caught on quickly. The trick card sometimes seemed more of a crutch than an advantage.

David eyed the three diamonds on the table, none of which were face cards. He had a five of diamonds and a three of clubs in his hand, but the trick card changed his club to an ace of diamonds for a flush. He raised a small amount, hoping someone would guess he was bluffing. The two other players who hadn't folded slid chips into the pot and called.

David flipped his cards over. "I just knew someone would have a flush," one player said. "I just wasn't lucky enough to have a pair of diamonds."

"Hey, wait a minute," another said. "I had a diamond and a heart. One was an ace." He swept up the cards he'd folded earlier and flipped them over. "Right there! Where'd you get that ace of diamonds?"

"I could ask you the same question," David said. "It was dealt to me."

"Something's fishy," the other player said. "I'm sure I saw something like this before, but my cards got picked up before I could prove it."

Norman, one of the bar's managers, came to the table. "Everyone take a break. We're going to check these cards out."

While they waited, some players watched sports shows on the bar's televisions. David stood by himself and avoided eye contact. Why hadn't he thought through the ways the trick card could go wrong? It was so obvious now.

Norman called for the players' attention. "There was a bad deck, and we apologize for that. Given the circumstances, we don't believe it's fair to continue, even with a new deck." He waved his arms for quiet. "We'll replay the final round next weekend. Same time."

As the crowd dispersed, Norman pointed to David and waved him over. He motioned to the player who also had an ace of diamonds. "Hey, Chris, you come over here, too." He tilted his head at a bouncer and indicated the office in the back. The four of them went in and the bouncer closed the door.

"This won't take long," Norman said. "Considering the money in this tournament, we are pretty careful about keeping the decks clean. I personally checked each of the decks, and this was no mistake. Someone put that ace there. I don't know which one of you two did it."

Chris started to protest, but Norman waved him quiet. "Bottom line: you two are disqualified. It's my decision, and it's final."

The bouncer opened the door and ushered David and Chris out. Chris trotted over to his friends and David endured a round of stink-eye as he walked to the exit.

Back in his apartment, David went over the tournament in his head. Why hadn't he realized the trick card could turn into a card someone else already had? Poker wasn't like blackjack where multiple decks were common, especially in casinos. It was moot now, as the card was in the office at the Rusty Nail. At his next office poker game, he'd have no advantage and would probably lose a lot of money.

When Friday came, David reluctantly joined his coworkers in the break room. They would expect him to win a lot, and he'd have to explain his luck had run out. Artie dealt the cards and David barely looked at them. A jack and some other card. He glanced at the cards in the flop and folded.

"What happened at the big tournament?" Dubois asked. "I heard there was a problem, and they kicked some players out."

"They think someone was cheating," Artie said. "They had evidence but couldn't tell who did it. It was just bad luck David got that card. Our boy is good, but he doesn't cheat. Right, David?"

David offered a weak smile. "It was an unfortunate coincidence."

The next hand held more promise for David with a pair of sevens. A seven in the flop gave him three of a kind. He raised, and two other players folded. He won the hand and pulled in ten dollars. His confidence returned. He bet on the next hand and made two more dollars.

David's luck ran out, and he was soon down twenty dollars. He brushed his hand across his pocket by habit and found the trick card. They must have shuffled the cards at the Rusty Nail. How long had the card been there? He sat up and clasped his hands together.

"Oh, he woke up," Dubois said. "What happened? Want to give me more money for my hot date this weekend?"

Artie dealt another round. David didn't have anything special, but he could bump up his chances. When the river card hit the table, he studied the possibilities. All he had to do was pull the card out of his pocket and . . .cheat. Not only cheat but steal money from his coworkers using his unfair advantage.

His stomach churned, and he stood, tossing his cards on the table. "Sorry guys, I got heartburn really bad."

Back in his cubicle, he sat with his head on the desk. It hurt his forehead, but he had more important things to think about, like how to win without fleecing his friends and coworkers. He *had* to play, somehow, somewhere.

Dave paid the Uber driver and walked into the Wet Whistle. The police had cracked down on drunk driving and he planned to have a few beers.

After the incident at the Rusty Nail, he hadn't dared join any of the poker games there. He'd heard of some clandestine games elsewhere, this bar in particular. The clientele looked rough-and-tumble, and his plan was to look like an easy mark in order to get a seat at the game. With the money he expected to win that evening, he could afford to take an Uber home at the end of the night and leave the driver a generous tip.

He caught the bartender's attention, ordered a light beer, and asked about the game in the back. The bartender laughed loudly, displaying the gaps where teeth used to be. "They'd chew you up and spit you out. You wouldn't last ten minutes."

"I've got money," David protested. "And I think I'm pretty good. Do they play that Texas Holdout game?"

The bartender stared at him for a moment. "You know, I'm going to send your skinny ass back there for entertainment." He snapped his fingers. "Then Jack'll have money to pay his damn tab. Don't go anywhere. I'll be right back."

David nursed his beer and fidgeted. He needed the thrill of slapping his winning cards on the table and raking the pot into his growing pile.

After a minute, the bartender returned. "They'd be delighted if you would join them for a friendly game of poker." He could barely say it without laughing. David left him a tip and walked to the back.

David sprinted out the back door of the Wet Whistle with several angry men in hot pursuit. The last pot had over five thousand dollars, which he had stuffed inside his jacket with his other winnings before fleeing for his life. With no moon, the night was dark, and he ran between unfamiliar buildings, praying he wouldn't trip over anything. He had a good lead, but he could hear the men behind him.

"Kill that cheating son-of-a-bitch!"

"He got my whole paycheck!"

"He got my rent money!"

David saw a pickup slowing for a four-way stop. The tailgate was missing, and he dove into the bed from behind as the truck sped up. After he caught his breath, he knocked on the back window. The driver's head whirled around as he stomped on the brakes. David slammed into the back of the cab.

The driver slid the back window open a crack. "What the hell are you doing in my truck?" he shouted.

"Sorry, I was desperate," David said. "I was at the Wet Whistle and smiled at the wrong woman."

The man's angry face changed to an expression of amusement. "You're lucky you didn't get your dumb ass killed. You look like you have an office job, not the type to hang out there. Hell, the Whistle's too rough for me anymore." He leaned over and opened the passenger door. "Hop in. I'll give you a ride."

David vaulted over the side of the truck bed and climbed in the cab.

Some of the men at the poker game worked at the mine, and David was sure they had recognized him as well. In a town this small, many of them likely knew where he lived. He wouldn't be surprised if it had been someone's girlfriend who had punched him in the alley. He'd have to grab essentials, jump into his car, and leave town in a hurry. Where to? Anywhere as long as it was out of town. "Are we close to the hardware store? I'll pay you to drop me off there."

"It's not far. Keep your money."

David patted his shirt pocket and recalled something the man who had given him the magic card had said. *Bad luck like a monkey on my back.* "Not money. I have something else for you."

DAN McKAY has had several short stories published in anthologies every year since 2016, including the *Fark Fiction Anthology*, the *Talking Stick*, and the Fargo Library's *Northern Narratives*. Dan is the winner of the 2005 Bulwer-Lytton contest, and his winning entry was featured on *Car Talk*. Dan is active in local writer's groups and lives with his family in Fargo, ND.

One Small Cloud in the Sky
Alexander Vayle

There was small comfort in admiring his trees. Though small comfort was better than none. Bill never learned what type of tree grew in his backyard, but they were gnarled and knobby old things, reaching over his junky garage and shading the sparse grass and ample thistles of his diminutive lawn. Their branches, which Bill had always likened to the arms of old people, looked like they should be in a terrible, arthritic pain that flared mercilessly each time the wind kicked up and bent them back and forth. He felt sorry for them. But what could a man do? Pour out a bottle of Tylenol around the trunk and let it dissolve down into their roots? A silly thought. Though Bill seemed to have a lot of silly thoughts these days. Not the least of which, was an idea of how to exit the life he currently lived.

His home sat on a stretch of old pavement on the east side of Effham Falls—not large enough to be called a street, too big to be called an alley. This snippet of road, only six blocks long, was an oddity in the town. A holdover from the days when the Falls was a mining community of hundreds instead of a town of thousands.

Flanked by a scattering of small, sagging houses and a weed-ridden park, this road was once known as Pascot's Way. It was named for Emerald Pascot, the daughter of a miner who disappeared into the Earth after she wandered into a mine, and whose little bones yet lay in the dark, far below.

Eventually, the name Pascot's Way was changed, though no one in town can answer the question of why. There's no record among the town authorities of when the sign changed, or who proposed the new name. The oldest members of the community will simply tell you, one day the post bore a green and white sign reading Pascot's Way, the next day the sign was changed to Harm's Way, and it has remained so ever since.

Bill grew up there and was bullied relentlessly for his address. He was called the Bum Street Kid. Hobo. He was told that he smelled like garbage, even though he'd always kept himself clean—obsessively so as he grew—in direct response to the name-calling.

By the time he left home at age seventeen, his mentality had been irreparably set to consider himself a lesser individual, not capable of what others could achieve. Certainly not deserving.

In his adult life, Bill's financial stability had always been precarious. So, when his father passed, and his mother's declining cognitive state prompted a move to Blakewood Assisted Living, he first sought to sell their home. However, the only real estate company in town informed him that, though they were willing to try, houses simply didn't sell on Harm's Way. Houses were passed down, or sometimes fell down, but they didn't sell.

With little options, Bill handed in the key for his cozy one-bedroom apartment, packed his belongings, and moved back to Harm's Way.

Of course it's raining, Bill thought. *It's ALWAYS raining. Raining shit. Raining idiots. Raining jobless friends. It's always raining, and it hasn't let up in years.*

That was the answer he wanted to give, but not to his mother. Not to his poor, senile mother who could ask ten times during a fifteen-minute phone call whether it was raining back in "The Falls". That was the odd thing. She never asked, "How's the weather?" but always, "Is it raining there?" Snow, sunshine, or massive tornadoes. None of that mattered. Only the rain. Bill had long ago given up on reminding her that she still lived in the Falls, only a mile or so from her old home.

"No Mom, it's pretty nice here. Yes, I suppose we could use some. Yes..." He wondered how much of these daily conversations she retained anymore; if by lunch she remembered breakfast, if by supper she remembered lunch. He asked himself if he was doing this out of love, habit, or guilt. The answer, he supposed, depended on the day.

After the call, Bill sat at his kitchen table, gazing out the window to his backyard and his three massive trees. "Halloween trees", his neighbor, Elmer, had called them. And not in any joking or complimentary way. "Those things need to go. They look diseased." Elmer once said, standing with his hands on his hips, belly protruding as he glared up at the branches. Bill had simply responded, "I like my trees." To which Elmer rolled his eyes and plodded off, threatening to involve the city.

Bill's small, detached garage listed a bit. Last spring, he'd propped some two-by-fours against the north side, then added a couple extra mid-summer, enough to make it look as if he might be constructing a lean-to against the side of the building. As Bill sat at his table and watched a hard autumn wind give the old garage a shove, he thought it might be time to put up a few more. Today, of all days, would be a bad time for it to fall.

Housed within the shabby-looking garage was a car likely worth half the value of the home he sat in. A black Lincoln Continental, a few years old, but well-cared for and spit shined to a nice gleam. He'd rented it a day ago and pulled it in under the cover of dark. He'd drive it out the same. Anything else would raise too many eyebrows.

Bill scanned over a list laying on the table, written on a pad advertising Coxswains Implement, which claimed to proudly serve Minnesota farmers since who-gives-a-shit-when. Written in his own scrawl were the words: car, fill tank, gun, ammo, cat, stocking caps. Each word had a single line through it.

"Okee-dokee." he told himself, surprised by the quiver in his voice. "All set."

He lit a smoke, then lit the list and dropped it into his ashtray. As he watched the paper curl and burn, he wondered; How does a guy live for fifty-two years, and then come to this?

Bill always hoped there would someday come a great crossroads; a point in his life where he would be forced to make a decision of such magnitude that—while the incorrect choice would doom him— the correct choice would cancel out all the wrong ones he had ever made. Then things would be set right. Health, love, money; it would all be drawn to him. He would become the center of gravity for all things positive.

Bill had waited for these crossroads. Decades passed. A time when he admired others for their achievements was replaced by days in which he despised those who made more money, who had beautiful wives, beautiful lives.

He assumed all along that these mighty crossroads would be easy to spot. But now he sat wondering whether or not this was it. Would money change everything? Would they even get away with it?

A scene floated through Bill's mind. The same scene that had been playing over and over since he'd first concocted the idea to commit a crime. Over the weeks of planning, the images matured from vague thoughts to near perfect clarity.

The scene always began with Bill running at night, accompanied by the hollow sound of his breath and the slap of his feet on damp pavement. Someone behind him shouted 'FREEEEEZE!'. In his panic, he continued to run. They opened fire. Not just one cop, but several. Bullets zipped through his body, spraying blood out before him. An instant before he died, he saw his reflection in the puddle he was falling into—wide-eyed with horror and the amazement of his own death.

Bill looked at the clock. Time to go. Past time in fact. He took a deep breath and ran a hand through his thinning hair. There was a weight in his gut and part of him wished he had never mentioned the Overvold family to his coworker, Greg. But he had to. After reviewing all other options, and all mounting debt, he simply had too. Besides, no one would get hurt, and it would only be this one time.

Bill took a last, long, pull from his smoke, then stood and snubbed it out. He grabbed a light coat from a hook on the wall, filled his cat's food and water to the top, and walked out of his home.

The buzzing in Greg's ears hadn't gone away. The pills were junk. Probably placebos at thirty bucks a bottle. Just to make sure, he dug two more out of his pocket, blew away the lint, and popped them into his mouth. As he up-ended his beer to wash them down, he thought *This is the last one. Shit.*

Only having two beers was worse than having none. All it did was wet his appetite. What he needed next was some whiskey.

Two shots would warm his belly. Then a good, stiff drink to sip on. His mouth watered at the thought, at the same time his teeth ground at the reality of the situation. There wasn't a drop left in the house. Of all the fucking places to rob.

"I have 'ta go pee." The little girl. It was her second time.

"Tough. Hold it."

"I HAVE TO GO PEE!"

Greg swung his gun up. She instantly screamed and buried her little face in her mommy's sweater. Greg got *that* look from Mr. Overvold again. The look that said he would bash Greg's skull in the first chance he got.

Mike Overvold was a thirty-five-ish-year-old who clung to his youth in more ways than one. For instance, the worn and stickered electric guitar leaning up against the wall, and more importantly, his physique. Mike was in good shape, probably exercised more than kids a decade his junior. If he got a chance, Greg would be dead as a doornail.

There was a baby, too. The mom, Linda, he believed, had called him "Enney". Greg had no idea what that might have been a nickname for. Likely some new-age, made-up bullshit. All he knew for sure was that the living room stunk like crap. Mom had asked to go change the baby, but that would mean going down the hall to grab a diaper. To do that, he would have to move the whole group, like he did when the little girl had to pee. It was too risky, just the kind of opportunity Mike was looking for. Anything but sitting on the couch with his brown-haired beauty of a wife, his small bladdered daughter and the shit-smelling baby. At least the baby had stopped crying.

Two long years had come and gone since Greg robbed anyone. He hadn't lost his taste for crime, not by a long shot. The last one had simply gone bad. Bullet-in-the-heart bad.

His victim's family wasn't the type to quietly grieve their loss. No, they were more the torch and pitchfork type. They posted rewards, contacted local media, and exploded onto social media. They even went so far as to post a rendering of his face from a sketch artist at every business in town. Eventually, Greg was forced to vacate his apartment in favor of crashing in his car or on the occasional couch.

A week after the killing—Greg would never in his life refer to the incident as murder—the family jacked the reward from ten grand to fifty. That was enough to make even his so-called buddies raise an eyebrow. So he moved towns, then states, and settled into a low-key life of working odd jobs under a fake name. But nothing lasts forever.

Mike and Linda were looking at him. Greg didn't see fear, more like stern questioning as to why he was still there when he'd gotten what he came for. He eyed them back for a moment, then raised the gun at arm's length and watched them squint and turn away.

Greg would never shoot a kid. He knew that. They didn't. He'd wing the wife if he had to. But Mike? He already planned that shot. If things went south, ol' Mikey would take a bullet in the neck.

He looked at his watch. 8:17 PM. Where the hell was Bill? Late by seventeen minutes. Greg stepped backward to the massive picture window and peeked behind the curtain. The driveway was empty. When you rob someone, you can't always expect things to go smoothly. But it'd be nice if the goddamn driver at least showed up on time. Especially since Bill started this whole mess the day he took Greg aside and told him about the Overvold family's dirty little secret.

The Overvolds came from old money, as their ancestors were some of the founding members of Effham Falls. However, back then they had empty pockets and a lot of ambition, whereas the current generation knew only how to fritter away their wealth in pursuit of keeping up an image. Along with a financial backslide, morals had apparently become a bit more flexible.

Bill's acquaintance, Alanzo, had done work in the Overvold home, and told Bill they'd always paid in cash, no matter the cost. And they never went to the bank to get it. "Off the books" money, Bill had called it. A good term, and a good opportunity for them. "Off the books" money wouldn't get reported. It was almost too—

Greg spotted movement out of the corner of his eye. Mike was making his move. Greg snapped his gun up to Mike's face. Oops. He'd just been handing the baby back to Mom. But Greg had let his mind wander. That could have been a pricey goof-up.

"Why don't you just take our car and leave?" Linda's voice was nasally. Tears and a runny nose still hadn't subsided.

"Why don't you just shut the hell up?"

Mike didn't eyeball Greg. Didn't give him *that* look. Maybe he wasn't going to make a move at all. Maybe he realized his family was worth more than money.

The money.

Greg reached over his shoulder and touched the backpack. The zipper was shut tight. He readjusted the straps. Money was heavier than he'd thought it'd be, and his back was getting sore. Where the hell was Bill?

⁂

The town seemed to be watching him as he drove. Of course it did. If you look for a white car, they're suddenly all over the place. If you glance at every driver you pass and every soul waltzing down the sidewalk, they all turn and look back. But they're not actually watching. Nope. They're not paying any attention at all. *I'm just a guy in a nice car,* Bill told himself.

He turned onto Seventh and headed north. The Overvolds were way out there, where the lots were practically the size of a city block. Mayor Talbot lived out this way. The McKinleys. Other families who struck it rich when the mines first opened. They'd spent obscene amounts building three-story homes that Bill found elegant but bordering on excessive. As much as he'd love an upgrade when everything was over, he wouldn't go this far. Seventh was too ritzy. Just to get off Harm's Way and back into a nice, well-maintained apartment would be enough for him. Maybe he'd do the town a favor and put a match to his house when he left. Assuming, that was, he'd soon be able to afford to do such a thing. He wondered, not for the first time, what amount of cash the Overvold family kept tucked away in their house.

His friend, whose company worked on their basement, had charged a hair over eleven grand. He'd said Mr. Overvold had counted out the money for him in neat stacks of hundred-dollar bills and told him to keep the change. He then shook Alonzo's hand and held firmly as he asked if payment methods were something Alonzo kept record of. Alonzo assured him he did not. Only that the bill had been settled.

Eleven grand, handed out like they were paying a babysitter with pocket cash. Did that mean there was a hundred thousand in the house? A million? He'd find out soon enough.

Bill continued to watch the homes as the blocks counted down, and he daydreamed about someplace new.

Greg heard a car slowing down out front. *Bill, finally.* He took a peek through the curtains. Headlights glared at the house as a car turned into the driveway. Bill would have some explaining to do, but that could be done over a steak dinner a hundred miles from here. For now, all that mattered was that he had made it. The money was in the bag.

"This is the end game, folks. All we need to do—." For an instant, all Greg's senses cranked up to full volume. He suddenly became aware of the soft, padded sound of a foot touching down on carpet, the change in the lights as a shadow sped across his peripheral vision, the *SSSSST* sound of an object moving through the air.

A wordless frustration raced through his head, condemning himself for letting down his guard at the final moment. *Pow.* A white explosion. A spinning room. The vague awareness of falling to the floor. No more.

Bill saw Greg peek out the window. All was well. Any moment he would walk out with Mrs. Overvold. She would get into the front seat, Greg in the back. They would pull a stocking cap down over her eyes. She'd be their guest for a bit; a little insurance Mr. Overvold wouldn't call the cops right away.

Bill would drive a mildly roundabout way out of town to keep them off the main streets until they hit County Road 22. Then they'd be home free. Mrs. Overvold would be dumped off, unharmed, on some dark stretch of country road. He made Greg swear on that. By the time she came upon another traveler or a lonely farmstead, they would be long gone.

Next, Bill would drive Greg to a vehicle he claimed was waiting for him in the next town. Bill would leave him there with his half of the money, to continue on to who-knows-where. Then he'd go back home like nothing had happened. Why shouldn't he? Mrs. Overvold would never see his face, never hear his voice. Besides, only guilty people run, the innocent stay put. He'd spend the night counting and recounting his money. And then...

Bill pictured himself driving up to a local watering hole in a shiny car. A two door, a young man's ride. Black? Maybe dark red? He had always liked dark red.

He'd stroll in, new clothes fresh off the rack, a new haircut—one that said he was a man who held respect. A man of means and confidence. When he ordered, he'd slide over a credit card instead of a handful of fives and ones. He would make eye contact with the bartender, tell him to let the tab ride, thank him, and tip him well. It would all come true. It *was* coming true. He waited. His fingers drummed on his thighs. He waited...

"Is he dead?" The words came muffled by the hand Linda held over her mouth.

Mike knelt next to the unconscious thief, still clutching the guitar he'd used as a club. "I don't know. I think he's breathing. I didn't mean to hit him so hard. Call the cops, Lin. Call 911."

"He broke our phones."

"Check the landline in the office."

"What about the money... and the car outside? What—"

"Just call the cops!"

The daughter—curled into a ball and sniffling—clutched herself tighter and renewed her crying at full volume. Linda got up from the couch, infant in her arms, and hurried to the flight of steps that led to their second story office.

There was no blood, but he could see a goose egg above the man's right temple. Mike set the guitar aside and put a hand on the prone man's neck, just as he had seen on TV. Unfamiliar with anatomy, he moved his fingers here and there, touching gently, until he found a slow, yet rhythmic pulse.

He turned and looked at little Meli, still crying, but she would be okay. The real worry now was the car outside. Likely another armed man. A man who expected, at any moment, that his partner would walk out with a backpack full of cash.

On the floor in front of him lay the gun which, moments ago, had been aimed at him, his wife, his *children*. He picked it up. As he did so, it occurred to him that something so small should not weigh so much. His own experience with guns was limited to the point of insignificance.

"How hard could it be? You pull the trigger. You just aim and pull the trigger."

But what about misfires? When the safety is clicked that way, does it mean it's on or off? Do I have to cock it or is it ready to go?

He looked down at the man on the floor, somehow expecting to find answers, but there were none. Mike's heart beat at a numbing speed.

Something had to be wrong. Greg was taking too much time. He *had* seen him pull up, hadn't he? That *was* Greg who looked out the window, wasn't it? He couldn't chance honking the horn, the noise would draw too much attention. Sitting in an idling car was bad enough.

8:32 PM. He would give Greg two more minutes and then...what? Go in? Bill knew Mr. Overvold to be a local politician and businessman, "a rich chump" Greg had called him. But what if these people weren't the suckers they had taken them for? What if *they* had a gun?

Two minutes. No, more like one and a half. Bill reached under the seat and took hold of a .38 snub nose. As he surveyed the house, a light came on in an upstairs room. That was wrong. There should be no reason for it. He set the gun on his lap and wiped his palms on his pant legs. One more minute. He checked to ensure his gun was loaded. Yes and no. Three rounds. All he had left. The gun hadn't been fired in years. And how old were the cartridges? Did it matter? They would still fire. They would still...kill. At that, he paused.

"Not *they*. I."

At that moment, Bill wondered if his fabled crossroads had finally come.

"The land line doesn't work. He tore the cord."

"Forget it. Just get the kids and go out back. Go to the neighbor's house and call the cops."

Linda stopped at the last step and peeked around the corner toward the picture window. The headlights had shone before, even through the closed curtains. Now they had either been shut off or the car was gone.

"Is the car still there?"

"I think so. I didn't hear it pull out. You need to go. I'm going to stay with him. Take Meli and the baby and go."

"Come with us, hon. Please."

"I have to put the money back. If the cops find it, we lose it. It'll be stuck in evidence or something. There'll be too many questions."

"But he'll tell on us anyway. Just come with—"

"So I'll split it up! At least we'll keep some of it. I don't have time to argue this shit. Just get the kids and go."

Linda stood frozen for a moment, looking at her husband and the prone man who now had a bump the size of a split tennis ball growing on the side of his head. She gave the window one final glance, then crouched and hurried to the sofa where Meli was hugging her knees to her chest. She gently shook her and whispered. "It's okay, Meli-belly, you need to get up. We're going to go to Shelly and Jason's house, okay? Get up, sweetheart."

The man on the floor groaned.

Mike scrambled to his feet and aimed the gun down at him, both hands on it now to keep it steady. Had he been familiar with guns, he would have known the safety was indeed off. Had he been accustomed to using them, he'd have realized the pressure he was putting on the trigger was nearing tolerance. Only a whisper more would have resulted in the execution of the man before him.

Their plan had somehow come undone. Greg must have lost control of the situation. Bill's breath came shallow and fast. His lips tingled, and he bit at them. His hands opened and clenched. Opened and clenched.

Perhaps Greg was taking his time because he was tying the family up. To ensure their escape, he would *have to* tie them up. Wouldn't he? Or maybe he was making the wife tie them up? Or he was locking them all in a room, or a closet, or knocking them unconscious or...worse.

"Oh God."

Greg was inherently violent. Bill had known that since the day they'd met, almost a year ago. Greg never tried to hide it. In fact, he'd bragged about his temper. Like the time he'd stabbed a man outside a bar. Another time he'd struck someone with his pickup and left them for dead. There was also the robbery he committed a couple years ago where a woman died. He had said it was an accident, but there was something in the way he told the story which made Bill think he had been satisfied with the outcome—accident or not. Maybe more than satisfied. Maybe...proud?

There was no leaving now. He had to go in. If Greg was busy tying them up, he would help, but if he was hurting them...

No more hesitation. "Do it now," Bill told himself. "Do it before your feet turn to ice."

Bill opened the car door and got out. He started forward in heavy strides. For an instant, he questioned whether or not Greg would have locked the front door after pressuring his way inside. That was never discussed in the plan. Didn't matter now. He pounded up the steps, across the porch, then swung the storm door open and reached for the knob.

Mike peeked through the curtain. The sun was long set. The windows of the car parked in his driveway only reflected the surrounding streetlights, offering no clue as to who might be inside the vehicle. He was about to turn away when the driver's door opened. The man who stepped out wore a black winter cap, pulled down low, and a brown coat. One hand was tucked inside an unzipped windbreaker, making an obvious show of hiding something. He peeked over his shoulder once, then kept his eyes low as he strode quickly—like a man on a mission—toward the house.

Mike turned to his wife who stood ready by the back door, baby strapped to her chest and Meli in hand. He silently mouthed the word "GO!" Linda slid the patio door open and hurried out as Mike faced the front entrance and leveled the gun.

The door was unlocked. It opened easily, too easily, and slammed against the inner wall. Bill turned into the room and saw a gun pointed at him.

There was a moment of confusion.

In his mind, Bill had expected the worst. Greg had gone over the edge, and there would be blood. Lots of blood, puddled on the floor beneath the bodies of the Overvold family as they lay in a motionless heap.

Instead, Mr. Overvold stood before him in a wide-legged stance, grasping a pistol. Even as Bill began to shout, "Don't shoo—", he saw the father squint and look away. A flash issued from the muzzle of Mr. Overvold's gun, and scathing pain erupted in the left side of Bill's chest.

Bill staggered back, struck the wall, and dropped his weapon. It hit the rug beneath him with a dull and terminal thud. He looked down. His hand had automatically come up to cover the wound. Blood seeped between his fingers.

Slowly, his head—which felt too large and heavy for his neck—rose and he saw Mr. Overvold, mouth agape, watching him with round eyes.

He stuttered at Bill, "God, I...I didn't...I didn't..." then cautiously stepped forward. One hand reached up with an open palm, as if asking Bill to stay calm.

Even in his agony, Bill wanted to let Mr. Overvold know he hadn't come to shoot him. That was the agreement all along. No one hurt. No one killed. He'd actually entered the house to make sure his partner wasn't reneging on their pact.

Bill tried to talk, but only coughed. Blood sprayed out far enough to make Mr. Overvold halt his approach and offer a look of disgust at the floor where the heavy drops had fallen.

Bill's knees felt watery and weak. He slid against the wall until his butt thumped to the floor. One more deep breath. One more attempt for words. He only coughed again, with less force that time. The outer edges of the room began to blur.

✦

"Don't die, man. Don't die. The ambulance is coming. Just, ah, just keep holding pressure. You're doin' good. You're doin' real good."

This wasn't supposed to happen. None of it. Now he'd shot someone. Actually *shot* someone. Mike looked at the weapon in his hand. It felt alive and wicked. He squatted and gently set the pistol on the floor, an arm's length away. He wouldn't need it. The man before him had dropped his weapon in favor of putting a hand on his wound. Now that hand had lost its strength and flopped down to the floor. By the look of his fluttering eyelids and shallow, infrequent breath, he had no fight left.

Mike crept forward. "Hey. I'm-I'm gonna touch you, okay? I'm gonna put some pressure on that gunshot." He got on his hands and knees, stretched forward a little, and reached out to the thin waterfall of blood trickling from the man's chest. "Just some pressure now. Hold still." His palm touched the slick warmth. An odd sensation. An unpleasant one. Wet and slippery with a pungent scent that made his throat feel thick. He'd never touched so much blood. His hand tried to move away, but he resisted the urge. Forward instead, against the soft flesh of the man's chest. Harder and harder until the flow was stemmed.

"I got it, okay? You're gonna be alright." Mike settled onto the floor and placed his other hand on top of the first to add more force. As he did, the man grimaced. His dull eyes opened and roved for a second, then sprang wide. Mike realized the man was looking behind him, not at him, only a fraction of a second before a spike of pain drove straight down into the top of his skull.

"How do *you* like it, asshole?" Greg stood over Mike, who'd dropped to his side like a sack of spuds after being struck with the butt of the handgun. Greg had hit him as hard as he could. As absolutely fucking hard as he could. Maybe he'd managed to fracture Mike's skull. He hoped so. It was all he could do — after he'd awoken to the sound of the gunshot—to lie still, to play dead while he concentrated on clearing the fog from his throbbing head. Then he had to rein in his hate enough to not put a bullet in the back of Mike's skull.

"Asshole." Greg repeated. His finger was tense on the trigger as he put Mike's head in his sights. Then he noticed his partner, who sat bloodied against the wall, looking at him.

Greg got down on his haunches. "Bastard got you too, huh? Should I kill him for ya?" He took aim again. He could almost taste it. The bang. The kick. The splatter.

Bill offered a small shake of his head.

"Let him go, huh? I guess. What about you?" Greg held the barrel point blank to Bill's wound. "Should I do the decent thing and just get it done?"

Bill shook his head once more, then in more exaggerated movements.

"You sure?"

Bill nodded, tried to speak, and coughed strings of blood over his bottom lip and his chin.

"You're gonna be dead by the time the ambulance shows up. You know that, right?" Bill's eyes drifted to his still-bleeding wound, but he didn't bother trying to respond.

"I'm gonna need those." Greg unhooked a set of keys fastened with a

mountaineering clip to one of Bill's belt loops. "Thanks. Time to boogie." He tucked his reclaimed weapon into his pants, retrieved the backpack, then stepped over to the front door. With one hand on the knob, he gave a backward glance at his partner. "I'll hang on to the money. If you make it, maybe I'll swing by, drop off your share. On the other hand, if you decide to squeal to the cops about me, I'll stop by that old folks home you told me your mom is rotting away in. We'll have a little visit. You want me to visit your mom?"

Bill managed a single shake of his head.

"Yeah, we'll see. Adios, pal."

Greg stepped out the front door, flipped the keys around on one finger, and even whistled a bit. If people were looking out the windows, wondering if that was a gunshot they'd heard minutes ago, their eyes might fall on him for only long enough to think, *No, if it was a gunshot he'd be running.* Then they'd look elsewhere.

However, if there were any lingering eyes, the last thing seen would have been a man known as Greg Malkost—once called Anthony Hess and soon to have a new name—casually slip into a Lincoln Continental, disappear behind a tinted window, and head on down the road.

***

Bill heard the sound of the car he had proudly selected for the night's escapade pull out and fade away. He held onto consciousness a bit longer, hoping to hear the sound of sirens replacing that of his departed rental. No such luck. He struggled for another deep breath as his left lung filled with blood, but only coughed out a crimson spray as a tearing pain slapped him awake for a moment more. The moment passed, his head nodded, and he closed his eyes.

***

Eleven days after the night of the robbery, Linda sat alone at a steel table in the county lock-up. The steel, she imagined, was intended for sterility and ease of cleaning. It didn't feel clean though. Nothing here did. She wanted to rest her arms on the table but opted instead to lay her hands in her lap.

A few long minutes ticked by, which she spent listening to other conversations between inmates and their loved ones. They talked of children, of regrets. Some fought in harsh half-whispers. She was listening with a tipped ear to a young, lustful couple tell one another what they would do when they next had the chance, when she noticed a man shuffle up to her table.

The apprehension she'd felt while driving there took another up-tic, but when she looked up, all she saw the worn face of a fifty-something man. His up-turned eyebrows showed curiosity, his hunched stance suggested weariness. There was no threat here.

"You're..." She found herself grasping for the name her friend at the police station had given her.

"Bill. You're Mrs. Overvold? The woman we robbed?" His voice, soft and tired, matched his stance.

Linda sat a little taller and emboldened her voice. "*You* didn't rob us. My husband stopped you dead in your tracks."

Bill shrugged. "The money is still gone, right?"

Her jaw fell a bit, then clapped shut when nothing came out.

Bill approached the final steps and eased himself into a chair. "Why are you here?"

"Well..." Beneath the table, Linda's hands wrestled with one another. "We're not charging you with anything."

"I know. They told me already. I'm not getting released until tomorrow because of the paperwork. That's what they say, at least. I think they're just holding me an extra day because they can."

"Oh. So you understand, we could keep you here if we wanted. We could keep you here until...until doomsday. We have certain connections in law enforcement. Some influence, I might even say."

"So, no courts?"

"No courts."

"Because you don't want people to know about the money." Bill's words came as a statement, not a question.

Linda drew a quick breath. Her eyes scanned the room for eavesdroppers. None seemed to notice. She narrowed her eyes at Bill. "Look. No charges from us. No talking from you."

"I already talked to the cops."

"Forget the cops. I told you we know the cops."

"I talked to some people at the hospital, too. I was there for over a week."

"The officers who watched you said you were drugged to the gills. No one cares what you were rambling about. Just don't say anymore and we'll let you go. That's the agreement, understand?"

"Why isn't your husband here?"

Linda froze in a glare. He wasn't supposed to question her. This discussion, in her car-ride rehearsals, had gone quick and easy. He was supposed to be thankful for his release. Thankful to her for dropping the charges.

"Michael..." Tears rimmed her bottom lids. She refused to blink and set them free. "You don't talk about Michael. You don't deserve to talk about him."

"He shot me."

"I wish he would have hit you in the heart." Linda was struck by the truth of her own words, and quickly became aware of how she was leaning in, aiming herself at him. She relaxed and tucked a few loose strands of hair behind her ear. "I'm sorry. I—"

"Don't be." Bill said. "If I was him, I'd have kept shooting."

For a moment, Linda saw a world of struggles in Bill's beaten-down posture, dissimilar, yet equally burdening as her own. "Look, Bill, this is the way it's going to be. You keep quiet, I keep you out of prison. As far as anyone needs to know, you stopped by to meet about a job. You found my husband fighting with someone who'd broken into our home. The robber shot you and ran. That's it. Understand?"

"No." Bill's eyes had fallen to the table, but his voice hardened.

"What?"

"I said no. I'm not going back to my old life. One way or another, I'm not."

"Fine. Then it's off to prison."

"No."

"Oh, good God." Linda finally dropped her elbows on the table and planted her face into her hands. She mumbled against her palms "What the hell is with you? I'm trying to do us both a favor."

Bill cleared his throat, leaned forward, and whispered, "I've had some time to think about our situation, and I came up with an idea. Listen..."

Four days later, Bill stood in his driveway, admiring his new phantom black F150. He had all his belongings packed up and tied down. When the job was said and done, and all the totes, furniture, and cardboard boxes were piled in one place, he was amazed at how much he had.

"That's a lot for one person." he said to himself. At least he thought he was talking to himself until he heard his neighbor.

"Where'd ya get the new truck?"

Bill turned to see Elmer, standing with his hands on his hips, back arched against the weight of his pot belly.

"At the dealer. I traded in my Metro."

Elmer squawked a short, ugly laugh. "Traded it for what? One of those tires?" He continued to laugh and mutter as he meandered back into his home.

Bill, unfazed by Elmer's jab, ignored the man and focused on his vehicle. To him, the truck and all its contents looked like a mound of treasure. It was all his, and he was ready to roll. For the first time in recent memory, he felt a tingle of excitement and joy about his life.

Linda had balked at his proposal, then threatened him by suggesting she could simply hire someone to stop by his house late one night. No one would be the wiser. She'd done her best to make the threat sound genuine, but the act was in her eyes. The falsity. She may have been an unlawful person, but she wasn't violent.

In the end, she had no choice but to agree. Continued payment for continued silence. The alternative, he'd quietly explained to her, was that he spill the beans to each and every source he could find. Her family's finances would then come under a microscope, and their lofty and long-standing status would suffer an abrupt drop to the rank of town pariah.

Bill wasn't a greedy man, however. He didn't want the Overvold's millions. Fifty grand up front was more than enough, and an extra five a month was a perfectly livable wage. Lush even, compared to the meager checks he pulled in.

Bill climbed into his ride, glad he had gone for a truck instead of a sports car. The elevation seemed fitting for this new life. He hung an elbow out the window, ran his palm over the textured steering wheel, and took a deep breath of the refreshing fall air.

The engine revved. The gearshift popped smoothly into reverse, but Bill hesitated a moment to look at his childhood home one last time. There were a lot of memories there. Not particularly good ones, though. Everything he wanted to keep from this abode was secured in the bed of his Ford. Still, there was a little pang as he severed the final cords to his old life. A solitary butterfly fluttering in his stomach. He bolstered his courage with a short pep talk.

"It's okay. You're doing the right thing, Bill. It's due time for a change. Not like you're blackmailing her, just..."

His conscience retorted, *of course you're blackmailing her. This is the dictionary definition of blackmail.*

Bill should have been nervous. He'd been nervous his entire life. But for some reason, he grinned at the thought. Then he chuckled and turned to his cat who sat quizzically peeking out from his travel kennel in the passenger seat. "What the hell. Right, Abe? From now on, we do what it takes. And screw 'em if they don't like it." Bill faced the open driver's window and put his nose to the air for a quick inhale. "Smells like it's time to go, old buddy. Let's get outta this town."

The nicest truck on Harm's Way backed up, then drove down the cracked pavement, never to return. As it disappeared around the bend, the first flicker of a fire could be seen in the picture window of a now-abandoned home.

ALEXANDER VAYLE grew up on the quiet shores of Long Lake in Western Minnesota. He now resides in North Dakota where he works in the medical field alongside his wife. Together, they are raising three rambunctious sons and a beautiful daughter. His first publication, a collection of supernatural suspense titled "Among the Stray" was published by *All Things That Matter Press* in June of 2021. He followed up with the short story "For Every Action" which was included in the 2022 anthology, *Tales from the Frozen North*, by the Moorhead Friends Writing Group.

Dolls

Chris Stenson

The first time Henry walked by Effham Falls' only antique store, the three porcelain dolls in the window made his hair stand on end and his mind grow fuzzy. The tilt of their heads, the glint in their painted eyes, and their malevolent grins made his heart pound. His quickened pace turned into a sprint, and he didn't stop until he was in the safety of his room.

The second time, he stopped as if summoned and stared at them. They were antique and pretty. He liked old things and they excited him, but he had a sneaking suspicion these dolls were special. That morning, after his mother left for work, he searched the house until he found her bingo winnings. He had to have the dolls at any cost.

"*Come in. We know you want to,*" they had said. "*We're ready to go home.*"

Henry unconsciously followed their order.

The man sitting behind the counter, his skin-tone the pallor of death, snored. Henry rang the bell. "Hey, mister, are you alright?"

The man flinched but didn't open his eyes. "Yes. Just tired. I haven't been sleeping well."

"I'll pay you $500 for the dolls in the window."

The man opened his bloodshot eyes. "Go away."

"*We're worth much more,*" the dolls said.

"Each." The word slipped from Henry's mouth before his brain had a chance to say no. Buying them at any price was insane. He knew in his bones that he shouldn't surrender to the whims of the dolls. He needed to use what he learned in therapy to fight his impulses.

The man smiled. "You have a deal, but there's one caveat. You can never return them. And I mean never."

Henry pulled a wad of bills out of his wallet and paid the antique dealer the agreed upon sum. The man grabbed a set of keys. "Follow me," he said. "I'm not touching them."

Henry nodded, giddy with excitement. As they approached the display case, the dolls whispered over and over inside his head, *"Slice him. Slice him. Cut his throat."*

Henry swallowed the lump in his throat and fingered the new knife in his pocket. Momma had come to his room the previous morning and handed him a small cardboard box. A gift from Momma or someone else? She didn't say. It didn't matter. He loved the weight of the blade in his hand.

Henry and the shopkeeper approached and unlocked the case. Each doll had their name pinned to their dress. The black haired and dark eyed beauty was named Amalia, the blond bombshell was Claire, and the fiery redhead was Joselyn. Nagging guilt filled Henry's conscience as he lifted them from the case and placed the trio into a stroller he had found nearby. How was he going to explain his obsession to his mother? His brain screamed run, but before he could, the dolls' mental hooks dug deep, their whispers became more urgent. He didn't stand a chance. The warden at the asylum had told him that he had a proclivity for attracting evil and the dolls were a manifestation of pure evil, weaving their spells, entrapping souls like Henry's in their darkness.

"Do you love us?" the dolls asked.

"I do."

"Kill him!" they demanded.

Henry hesitated. He had never killed anyone before.

"It's easy. We'll help."

He smiled and pulled the knife from his pocket. The blade glowed a deep crimson red.

Per their instructions, Henry slid the sharp knife into the antique collectors back several times until the man slumped to the floor. Frothy blood bubbled from the man's mouth, splattering the dolls with a fine mist of red. The dolls smiled and squealed gleefully. Henry pushed the stroller out of the store and sauntered out into sunlight, whistling a happy tune.

"We want more," the dolls whispered.

Henry pushed the stroller down the sidewalk, a bemused smile plastered on his face.

"This one," the dolls said, pointing to the house with a sagging fence and overgrown yard.
"No, not the witch's house."
"Henry, you said you loved us."
Pain erupted in Henry's temples, and blood dribbled from his nose. Henry now understood his role. If he followed orders, the dolls wouldn't scramble his gray matter. They craved pain and suffering, but blood sustained them and kept their ancient hearts beating. He would be their surrogate, nurturing them until their souls found new bodies.
Unable to resist the dolls' orders, he pushed open the gate.
The dolls, their faces still speckled with blood, grinned. "Kill her."
The door to the house opened.
"You found my girls," the woman in the doorway said.
Agnes Bagman, aka Aggie Baggie to the neighborhood, was more than just a little quirky. She was old as dirt and batshit crazy. When Henry was in middle school, he and a few friends would play kick the can or ding-dong ditch. More than once, she had come storming out, waving her shotgun loaded with rock salt, and yelling obscenities. Once or twice, she even fired at them.
Now, she gazed right through Henry, her eyes locked on the doll carriage. "Bring me my girls."
Henry snuck a peek inside Agnes' house. Dolls were everywhere. On the floor, on the couch, perched on shelves, and stuffed in glass cabinets. Hundreds of pairs of blinking eyes stared at Henry. Their whispered threats tormented him, scratching at his mind, seeing a way in. They were lost souls searching for new homes. He nervously fingered the knife in his pocket.
The dolls in the house beckoned. The three he had bought from the antique store whispered malicious things. And Agnes wanted her babies back. The medicines Henry's doctor prescribed to control his violent tendencies and quiet the voices had stopped working. His mind whirled. He was at the precipice. One small misstep would send him tumbling into the dark, endless void of insanity.
The knife came alive, once again glowing red in his hand. With a savage grunt, Henry embraced Agnes, plunged the knife

into her belly, twisted, and yanked out. He walked her into the house.

"You stupid man," she whispered.

Cold fingers of anxiety slithered up Henry's spine as he set her down on the couch. She sighed, shuddered, and her life ebbed away.

The front door slammed shut. The lights flickered. An icy, hostile presence filled the house. Familiar feelings embraced him, he couldn't pinpoint exactly where or who it reminded him of.

Agnes's body suddenly twitched. Her eyes snapped open. An evil grin spread across her face, and she staggered to her feet. An intestine slid out from the puncture wound in her abdomen, she pushed the slithery tube back in. "You made me bleed all over my rug."

Henry's stomach lurched and fear prickled his skin. He shouldn't have listened to the doll's whisperings. He shouldn't have stabbed, but the knife became alive in his hand. He was way over his head and wished for the sanity and security the asylum offered. What would his mother say?

The front door of the house swung open on its own.

Agnes limped to the entrance, once again poking the pesky intestine back into her wound. She glared at Henry, a nefarious glimmer in her eyes. "That hurt."

"Mother, we're home," Henry's dolls said in unison.

"You've been bad girls."

They giggled.

Lips and chin trembling, Henry backed away with quick, jerky steps.

"Stop. Where are you going?" Agnes asked.

"I'm going home." The urge to run and never look back dominated his thoughts.

"Get in here. All of you," Agnes said, emphasizing each syllable with a jab of her finger. "We don't need our drama playing out for all of Effham Falls to see."

Henry stared at the red splotches on his shoes, wishing the chattering dolls would quiet down. But they kept talking. "They told me to kill you."

"I know. Do you normally follow orders from dolls?" Agnus frowned and shook her head.

Henry's brain was scrambled, his mind no longer able to decipher the cryptic messages he received from outside stimuli. In reality, he knew that the dead don't wake up, that dolls can't open doors, but here they were. He needed his mother. She'd fix this. She always did.

He clasped his hands over his ears to block out all the voices. "Shut up. Please. Shut up."

"Henry, you're crazier than I am," Agnes said.

He plunged his hand into his pocket and caressed the antique knife.

"*Cut and stab. Cut and stab.*"

He shook his head. "I'm not listening to you."

Agnes laughed. "Who are you talking to?"

A headache blossomed and his anger spiked. "I'm leaving."

At the door, the three dolls clutched Henry's leg and smirked at Agnes. "We're going with him."

"You'll be back," Agnes said. But doubt clouded her eyes. "You always come back."

Henry placed the dolls into the stroller. As he pushed them down the street, whistling and singing an ancient lullaby, his pulse slowed and a warm, fuzzy feeling radiated throughout his body. He had so much to tell his mother.

Henry's words rushed out as he described his day to his mother. When he finished, her face clouded over with anger and disappointment.

"Did you forget to take your pills this morning?"

"No, they're not working." Henry rubbed the back of his neck. The last time his pills stopped working he attempted to harm himself. One of these times he would succeed.

"I'm calling your doctor."

She picked up the phone and started to dial but then changed her mind and set the receiver down. Her eyes turned black, and malevolence bloomed in her eyes. The dolls stood in front of the stroller, mischievous grins plastered over their porcelain faces.

"Henry," his mother said, her tone biting.

"Mom, we're in trouble." A chill filled the kitchen. The presence from Agnes's house must have followed him home and now it was in the kitchen with them.

"We? You are the one who continues to make bad decisions. I won't fix your problem this time."

"Momma...what? It has always been us...we. Please. Help me."

"You think I can fix this mess?" Perspiration glistened on her forehead and red blotches covered her cheeks.

Henry wiped his tears. "Yes."

"Are those mechanical dolls?"

"No. They're haunted by evil demons."

His mother rolled her eyes. "Maybe they could fix the people you stabbed."

"They did. I wish they hadn't, but they fixed Agnes."

"Go to your room, Henry James. And take those crazy dolls with you."

Even at thirty-five years old, when his mother used his middle name, he listened. He packed the girls into the stroller and pushed them to his room. "Be nice to Momma. She means well."

The dolls smiled and nodded.

After reading them a bedtime story, Henry tucked them into his bed, turned off the night, and crawled in beside them. "Sleep well, my beauties."

Henry woke from a nightmare, a scream lodged in his throat. The girls wanted his mom dead. He took a deep breath and stared at the ceiling until his heartbeat slowed. Thankfully, it was just a dream. But the dolls were gone and the door to his room was open.

Henry stepped into the hallway. The house was too quiet. He checked the kitchen. Three steak knives were missing from the butcher's block. He tilted his head, listened, and followed the whispered words.

The three dolls stood in front of his mother's bedroom door, their eyes gleaming, and knives clutched in their tiny hands. "Wakey... Wakey... Mommy. We want to play." Moonbeams pooled at the dolls' feet, illuminating them in an eerie glow. Henry watched in horror as they carved 'MOMMY WILL DIE' on the bedroom door in large childlike letters.

"Don't hurt Mommy," Henry begged, clutching his head. Their laughter echoed inside his mind.

"Agnes is crazy. Your mother is worse. She's dangerous."

"What are you talking about. Momma is a saint."

"Your mother has dark secrets. Ask her." They crossed their arms and spoke in a low voice reserved for dreadful things.

Their knives clattered to the floor, and they slumped against the wall. Henry picked up a knife just as the door to his mother's room opened. With cold, hollow eyes, his mother looked at him, at the door, then the dolls.

"Did you write that?" she snapped and stepped closer, her hands clenching and unclenching.

"Henry, kill her."

Henry shook his head and stared at his feet. Momma's eyes scared him. He picked up the other knives, his dolls, and started down the hall.

"She'll betray you."

"Henry."

"Yes, Momma."

"When I get home from work tomorrow, either those dolls are gone or you are."

He nodded and went into his room. He placed the three dolls against the wall and nervously paced the length of the room. "That was naughty. Momma is really mad."

All three dolls stared at him but kept their thoughts to themselves.

"What am I going to do with you three?" Henry ran his hands through his hair. "Do you have anything to say for yourselves?"

They gazed at him with sad eyes, their painted lips turned to frowns. "We're sorry."

Henry had an idea. Maybe if he separated them, they would have less power to influence his decisions. He grabbed his pants slung over the chair and slipped them on. He grabbed the dolls and tucked them into the stroller. The nights were getting colder, and he didn't want the dolls to get too cold. He tore three pages from his notebook and wrote the same note on each. He planned to make his mother happy and that was all he cared about.

At two a.m., the streets in his neighborhood were deserted. He stopped at the end of the block. Which way first? He took a right and headed towards Main Street. He had an extra bounce in his step because he had found a solution to his problem all by himself. Before reaching Main Street, he slipped down the alley behind the bookstore. He knew who he'd visit first.

All three dolls sat up when Henry stopped walking. He grabbed the red-headed doll, Joselyn, from the carriage and pulled one of the notes from his pocket.

"Where are you taking her?" the other two asked.

Henry ignored their questions and walked to the stairs that lead to the apartment above the used bookstore. Jill, the owner of the bookstore, likes old things and would appreciate the doll.

Joselyn squirmed in his hands. "Let me down."

"You'll like Jill. She's nice."

Henry leaned Joselyn against the door and taped the note above her. 'She's your problem', the note said.

"Be good," Henry told the doll.

Claire and Amalia stood in the baby stroller and glared at Henry as he approached.

"What did you do with Joselyn?" Claire asked.

Henry winced. Their mental claws scratched at his brain. He took a careful step before a tug at his pants stopped him. Joselyn stood next to him with her hands on her hips.

Anger percolated inside Henry. He told the dolls he loved them and he had saved them from the witch. Why were they acting like spoiled brats? Ignoring the pain the dolls inflicted inside his mind, he grabbed Joselyn and marched back up the stairs. Somewhere in the apartment, a light flickered behind the curtains. Henry took a roll of duct tape from his pocket and taped the doll's arms to the door. Joselyn started kicking.

"Knock that off," Henry said, taping her legs to the door so her kicking wouldn't wake Jill. He scurried down the steps and pushed the stroller deeper into the shadows of the alley. The girls were screaming in his head and were throwing a tantrum. He wiped a few drops of blood from his nose and decided blond-haired Claire would be next.

He took the alleyways and the darker streets, making his way farther from Main Street and his home. He stopped at a house with peeling paint and an overgrown yard. He pulled Claire from the stroller, walked quickly to the back door, and repeated the taping process. This time, he taped a piece of gray duct tape over her mouth.

Dark-haired and dark-eyed Amalia was crawling out of the stroller when Henry returned. "Where are you going?" he asked.

Amalia bit Henry's arm when he picked her up.

"Ouch. Why did you do that?"

She stared at him with angry eyes. A light in the house came on and a dog started barking. Henry pushed the stroller as fast as he could without running. He walked for fifteen minutes before he spotted the house where he'd leave Amalia. One of his classmates from Effham Falls high school lived there. She had been a cheerleader and thought she was better than him. She was one of the rich kids. Amalia kicked, punched, and tried biting him as he taped her and the note to the door. They deserved each other.

Henry whistled as he walked home.

On the other side of town, cousins Ann and Christopher stood at the top of the second-floor landing, ready to push the two three-foot-tall dolls down the stairs. They would scream as the dolls tumbled down the steps. They had done the same thing a few weeks prior and their parents were not happy. They were grounded, but it was worth seeing their parent's scared faces when they opened the door and realized that it was the dolls, not their children laying in a heap.

"Are you ready?" Christopher asked.

"Yes...." Ann's face paled and her eyes grew large.

Her doll blinked several times and tried to bite her. Christopher's doll squirmed in his arms and its head swiveled. "Hey asshole, let go of me," the doll said. "Now."

Ann and Christopher stared at each other in disbelief. "Ann, did your doll just try to bite you?"

Tears rolled down Ann's cheeks as she nodded.

"Now it's our turn," the dolls said. "Let's see how you like it."

The two dolls squirmed loose and fell to the floor. Quick and quiet as ferrets, they rammed into Ann and Christopher, knocking them off balance. The children screamed and tumbled down the stairs. They struck the door with a loud bang, silencing them. Nobody came running, but Grandma was the first to the door.

"What in God's name were you two doing?" Grandma asked. "Are you alright?"

Ann jumped to her feet, visibly shaken, and hugged her grandma. Christopher wiped blood from his nose, balled up his fists, and nodded. Other than a few scrapes and multiple bruises, they were fine. Christopher glanced at his cousin then up the stairs. The dolls were sitting on the edge of the top step. One of them waved her middle finger at him. He swallowed his rage. They wouldn't tell grandma or their parents what had happened. Nobody would believe their story. No matter how much his cousin begged him, he was done playing with dolls.

When they were sent upstairs for bed, the toy room's window was open and the dolls were gone.

A tug of panic hit Agnes as Henry and the troublesome dolls left her yard. The souls that inhabited the dolls were ancient, as well as the most aggressive in trying to find a mind and body easily manipulated, and one in which they could reside. They were one of the reasons Agnes never allowed anyone, especially children, in her house or in her yard. The inhabited dolls bombarded visitors with their mental taints and barbs, always probing for a way in, and children were especially vulnerable.

"Evil, when locked away, will start to fester, and push its way out of its prison," Raggedy Ann, one of Agnes's other dolls, said. "You knew it would happen eventually. Your biggest concern now is finding out who or what helped them."

Even though Agnes knew Raggedy Ann was right, the dolls' escape and attempt on her life felt like a betrayal. Henry wasn't intelligent enough to know he was being played. When the dolls were finished chewing him up, they would spit him out, leaving an empty shell full of hate that would strike out at the world with vengeance.

In Effham Falls, there was a thin veil between the living and the dead. Underneath the city, somewhere in a labyrinth of tunnels, the Well of Lost Souls existed. There, black hearts and evil souls could pass through this rip in time and gather. Occasionally, a soul found its way to the surface and inhabited a doll. Some were good, but most were evil. They were searching for new bodies to possess. Agnes made sure they never found a body to use.

Agnes came from a long bloodline of Nordic witches and wise women. She chased her first demon across Scandinavia and the

Atlantic to the New World. She tracked the creature who had butchered her family, losing it in the wilderness of northern Minnesota. Thereafter, she dedicated her life to protecting humans from evil spirits and helping lost souls find their way home. Versed in Runes and binding magic, she kept the souls bound to the dolls imprisoned in her home, and kept lost souls trapped in the tunnels.

That night when she crawled into bed sleep didn't come easily for Agnes. She shrieked and woke with a start, drenched in sweat. Her pulse raced, and her heart thudded loudly in her ears. The images of the nightmare remained fresh in her mind: two dolls had woken up, come alive on the safe side of town, and terrorized two unsuspecting children. This had happened numerous times in the past, this time it was concerning because the dolls had never attacked or harmed the children before.

Agnes knew something dark and dangerous had escaped from the tunnels. How, what, or when, she didn't know, but she was scared. She feared there would be more incidents on both sides of town. She would have to check the Runes carved in the walls of the tunnel under Main Street and reinforce the spells that encircled and protected the town.

The tunnel system could be accessed through a door in her basement. She winced walking down the steps. The knife wound Henry inflicted on her abdomen wasn't healing as quickly as it should. The flesh was a shade of moldy leaves and it stunk. Maybe she underestimated Henry and the threat he posed.

The stones under her feet vibrated. She flipped on her flashlight and started down the tunnel. Dank and putrid scents rose from the pooled waters below. At the first intersection, she stopped. Her flesh prickled with fear. Primeval voices whispered from the stones and an ancient power rippled through the walls. She sensed someone in Effham Falls dabbled in ancient magic. For a century, morbid fantasies and poison ran through the heart of the city. Agnes turned. In every direction she looked, red eyes reflected in the glistening walls. A coppery scent rose from the shadowy depths of the tunnels.

Drip...drip...drip.

Agnes passed her light along the walls. Rivulets of blood trickled over the strange glyphs and symbols that covered the stone walls. Those markings weren't hers. She picked up her pace and headed back the way she came. She would need to find someone to help decipher their meaning. A cold breeze buffeted her every step.

"Agnes...Agnes."

She spun around on weak legs.

"Did you forget about me?"

Agnes backed away in quick, jerky steps. "How...?" She stumbled and fell to her knees.

The creature with the glowing eyes laughed. Agnes wasn't going home.

Henry made it home before the sun rose. He hid the stroller in the shed and entered the house as quietly as possible. His mother was still asleep. He undressed and tried to filter out the terrible whispers filling his head. Maybe it was time to go back into the hospital. He didn't think he would survive freedom. He closed his eyes and fell into a restless sleep as the sun peaked through the trees.

He woke to the smell of bacon and fresh brewed coffee. In the kitchen, he poured himself a cup. "The dolls are gone," he told his mother.

She filled a plate with scrambled eggs and several slices of bacon and set it on the table. "What are you going to do about your problem?" She took a sip of coffee.

"I said they are gone." Henry jumped to his feet, causing the chair to tip and crash to the floor. He paced the kitchen.

"Not that problem." She shook her head. "The voices, the violence."

"Momma, I'm scared. I don't want to listen to the voices, but I can't stop." Henry said, pushing the eggs around on his plate. "I think I should go back to the treatment center."

"Maybe."

"Will you pray with me?"

She put her fork down and stepped away from the table. "I'll call the doctor on Monday."

"Momma?" He gasped. "You never deny...."

"Fine. And God shall smite His only begotten son."

"That isn't right." His mind scrambled to understand. His mother never misquoted scripture, "What's wrong?"
"Nothing. Time for work."
"Can I hold Grandma's cross that the Pope blessed? It always makes me feel better."
"No."
Sudden coldness filled his core. "I can't believe it. Why not?"
"Because I don't have it anymore."
"What?"
"His words and promises are nothing but empty lies," Momma said as she left.

Henry paced, sat, and paced some more. Was momma having a crisis in belief? Was it his fault? His mental issues caused his momma a lot of heartache and sleepless nights. His mind pondered the endless possibilities, but something life-changing happened while he was in treatment.

Around lunchtime, the dolls' whispers in Henry's head went silent. Even with the voices gone, his head spun from anxiety and guilt. He hadn't controlled his impulses the previous day and had stabbed two people. Every time a squad car drove by his house, he thought the vehicle would pull into his driveway. Watching late afternoon cartoons helped quiet his mind but it took some time before he was able to drift off to sleep.

"Henry." His mother shook his shoulder. "Time for supper."
He yawned and rubbed his eyes. "What time is it?"
"Supper time."
"My head is pounding. Could you save me a plate?"
His mom felt his forehead. "Are you getting sick?"
"No. Just tired."

Henry went to his room and locked the door. Standing at his bedroom window, his thoughts turned to his girls. He was having doubts about what he had done.

"Girls, are you doing alright?" He concentrated, but they didn't answer.

A sharp pain pierced his left eyeball.
Henry, help me.
It wasn't one of the girls. "Who is this?"
Agnes.
The pain spiked, like someone shoved a yard dart into his temple.
I'm in trouble.... Effham Falls is...evil.

The words sent a chill up Henry's spine. How could she possibly be in trouble?

Outside his window, shadows moved. Something was out there. The pain in his head dropped him to his knees. He pressed his face into the quilt on his bed as tears spilled down his cheeks. "Oh, God. Agnes?"

A presence, something dark and horrible, filled his mind. Sweat beaded on his forehead, and fear rippled through his body. He expected the sensation to fade, but the terror only increased. He walked towards the door and tried to scream but no sound came out. It was as though he stood outside his body and somebody else was in charge.

A noise at the window drew Henry's attention. He swiveled around, taking control of his body once again. One of his girls, there, at the window.

Pain, like exploding firecrackers, clouded his mind as the presence seized more territory inside his head, ripping and tearing the layers of his brain as it tried to gain a foothold. Dark memories that weren't his left him feeling exposed and naked. Hatred and revenge percolated inside of him.

A second face appeared in the window, then a third. His girls were home. He clung to the image of their faces and forced the dark memories out.

Henry's bedroom door rattled. "God damn it, Henry, why is the door locked. Open up right now." Momma giggled. "Are your girlfriends back?"

He wanted to answer, but no words formed. The presence disappeared from his mind, the tendrils connecting them suddenly severed. Henry screamed. "Mom!" He collapsed to the floor, gasping for breath. His body exhausted and his mind violated, he crawled from his room. "Momma." The house was too quiet. "Momma, please answer me."

After several minutes, he found the strength to stand, and he searched the house. How could his mother disappear in a matter of minutes? The front door stood ajar. Outside, a Raggedy Ann doll lay sprawled on the steps. His girls and his mother were nowhere in sight. The doll lifted its head.

"Agnes is in trouble."

"I know. What happened?" Henry asked.

"She went into the tunnels and hasn't returned." Raggedy Ann pushed herself to her feet, wobbled a few steps and fell. "Do you kill monsters?"

"Monsters?"

The doll went slack and sighed. "Pick me up. We need to hurry."

They cut through yards and stayed in the shadows. A few curtains fluttered, but most people in this part of town minded their own business. Agnes's street was dark and eerily quiet. Henry opened the back door to her house and stepped inside. Small pools of blood were scattered throughout the living room. Blood spatter covered the walls.

"Where are the other dolls?" Henry asked.

"Gone."

"Gone?"

"Your mother was here and whispered some words. They exploded, and their evil souls were released."

His mouth went dry. "When was she here?" He stepped back, and vigorously shook his head. "There's no way."

"I saw her. Right before I came to your house."

"Momma? Oh...shit." Henry doubled over. Pain spiked in his head like an ice pike was attacking him.

"We have your mother," Henry's girls said with glee.

"Don't...hurt...Momma."

A thud in the bathroom. Henry walked gingerly down the hallway and opened the door. Ice-cold air and the stench of sulfur wafted out. His mother stood in middle of the room, her skin smooth and taut, and blood seeped from her eyes.

"Henry, help me," she said, her eyes half closed, a lidded look of satisfaction. "They want me dead."

"Who wants you dead?"

Joselyn, Amalia, and Claire laughed.

Henry spun in a circle. The voices so close. His mother cackled along with his dolls. The room grew quiet. His mother spoke, but it was his father's booming voice that filled the room.

"If you help the witch, so help me God, I'll get the strap and beat you within an inch of your life."

The words cut through Henry's soul like razor wire. Memories too terrible to remember rolled through his mind. His mother grinned just like his father, a man who enjoyed the beatings he delivered way too much. Tears filled Henry's eyes. His brain felt fractured, splintering into a thousand pieces.

"Henry!" Raggedy Ann yelled.

He rushed into the living room. Blood dripped from the ceiling and a crucifix spun on the wall. Yellowed eyes stared through the bay window. The front door rattled.

"We need to get out of here," Henry said. "We need to find Agnes."

"There's an entrance to the tunnels in the basement. Agnes is down there."

Henry picked up Raggedy Ann and found the door to Agnes' basement. When he flipped on the light, it sputtered, and popped. Behind them, his mother's laughter became more hysterical.

A faint light bled through the open doorway. Henry and Raggedy Ann stepped through and came to a halt. Five stairs lead to hard-packed soil and a smaller solid wooden door with 'Effham Falls Mine #1' written above it.

The door behind them slammed shut. Henry tried the doorknob, but it was locked. They had no choice but to go forward.

Raggedy Ann turned to him. "You can kill monsters, can't you?"

Seven-year-old Samantha dug in her mother's craft room until she found the good pair of scissors her mother told her never to touch. She lined up all her dolls on the bathroom floor and took turns washing their hair.

"Spa day. I'll make you all look pretty." She wiped, dried their hair, and took them to her bedroom. Samantha had a hard time containing her excitement. She had received a Spa/Salon toy set for her birthday and wanted to pamper her friends. She placed her favorite in the pink chair, lined up the mirror and asked. "Do you want me to trim your bangs?"

"No."

"Ohhh...fun. You can talk." Samantha's eyes grew wide and she pouted. "But I want to." She gritted her teeth and cut off the doll's ponytail anyway. Holding up the mirror, she asked "Do you like?" The doll squirmed and fell. Samantha placed the doll back in the chair and shook her finger. "Be a good girl and sit still." She gripped the scissor tighter. "Or I'll pull off your head."

One after another, Samantha cut all the hair off her dolls.

The next morning, Samantha opened her eyes and didn't understand what was happening. Several of her larger dolls, including her stuffed elephant, were sitting on her chest, and her arms and legs were tied to the corners of her bed. "Mo—"

Her toy lemur shoved a sock into her mouth. Three dolls lugged a scissor up the side of her bed, and when they reached the top, they sat on her pillow. One leaned close to her ear and whispered. "Spa Day. Should I trim your bangs?"

Snip, snip

When Samantha's mother found her still tied up in the morning the dolls were gone.

Henry pulled the heavy door inward. An overwhelming stench, as if animals had

defecated in the small place, filled his senses. Even Raggedy Ann covered her nose.

His mother stood in the middle of the tunnel, her lips pulled back in a snarl, her eyes black and bottomless. "Hello, Henry."

Henry's mind swirled in confusion, but something about his mother's action brought forth knowledge he gleaned from reading about the occult. His mother was possessed by a demon! How had his mother gotten into the tunnel before him? He read that in certain instances those possessed could be in two places at once. The stench, the freezing temperatures, her appearance, and her forgetfulness concerning religion all pointed to possession.

"Who are you?"

"We are...friends."

It wasn't his mother's or his father's voice. Henry shivered. The cool air turned colder. A steady stream of bizarre and blasphemous words flew out of his mother's mouth.

"Who are you really? You're not my mother?"

"Correct. I am many things, but not your mother."

"Can I speak to my mother?"

"She's in here someplace. Her soul is writhing in agony. A guilty mind and soul are dangerous, they corrupt completely."

"What are you talking about?"

"Like Judas, your mother has betrayed those she professes to love." The creature that resembled his mother grinned. "Tell Henry your secret."

"I killed your father. I slit the son-of-a-bitch's throat and watched him die."

"What?"

His mother's voice changed again. "*La porte est ouverte.*"

Henry knew that phrase. His grandparents were French Canadian, but his mother didn't know how to speak French. Another sign of possession.

The door is open. What the hell did that mean?

A shadow rushed them. Henry slammed the door leading into the tunnel and inserted the two thick boards into their slots. Something heavy struck the door, A demented laugh echoed off the stone walls. His heart pounded and pain spiked in his head. He tried the door to the basement and found it unlocked.

Henry opened the door. A young girl stood there holding a doll, a faraway look in her eyes.

"Holy shit," Henry said. "You scared me. Isn't it a little late for you to be out? Where are your parents?"

"I can't find my parents." Large tears rolled down her face.

"What's your name?"

"Emerald. Emerald Pascot." She stopped crying and held up her doll. "This is my best friend, Bess. Did the monsters find you?"

Henry's skin prickled. "What do you mean? What monsters?"

"The darkness below is full of monsters." The doll in her arms grinned and a shimmering Emerald walked through the door and disappeared into the mine below.

Henry closed his eyes and whispered a little prayer. He was hallucinating again. He would go home and take his antipsychotics before he spun way out of control. He cradled Raggedy Ann in his arms and walked upstairs.

"Don't go outside," Raggedy Ann said. "Evil unleashed from below is patrolling the streets tonight, searching for you and me."

"Okay." Henry yawned and rubbed his eyes. His headache continued to build.

"Place me by the window," Raggedy Ann said. "I'll keep watch."

Henry placed her on the back of the couch, then he laid down and closed his eyes. Memories of his youth rushed through his mind, his father's demeaning voice filling him with self-loathing. He needed to escape his father's harsh words.

Just a momma's boy, aren't you? I'll fix that.
Are you just stupid?
If you want to cry, I'll give you something to cry about.
You're not my son.

Henry woke with a start. Raggedy Ann was shaking his shoulder.

"Are you alright? You were screaming."

"No." He searched his pockets and checked in-between and under the couch cushions. "Have you seen my knife?"

"No."

"My knife is missing, and I think the dolls have it. We need to leave."

Henry took the side streets and alleys as he rushed home. Three small, white faces with glowing red eyes were staring out the front window when Henry and Raggedy Ann approached. The moment he stepped onto the porch his dolls ducked out of sight. A sense of foreboding came over him. The dolls' mumbled whispers filled his head like a hive of agitated bees, pushing his headache to the edge. Henry and Raggedy Ann stepped into the shadows.

"Something's here," Raggedy Ann said.

Henry swallowed hard and stepped into the room. "Hello? Is someone here?"

Somewhere inside, the dolls giggled. "Come find us if you dare."

"Is Momma here?"

When they laughed Henry followed their voices down the hallway to his mother's room. He pushed open the door. A body resembling his mother's lay withered and blackened on the bed. His knife protruded from her chest. Henry collapsed to his knees, and a great sob rattled his chest. "Oh, Momma."

In the corner, hidden by shadows, an unexpected voice spoke. "Hello, son." The rotted remains of his father lurched from a chair, and dirt rained down on the floor. "I'm back."

The putrid smell of his father's breath sickened Henry. He stumbled to his feet. "Why did you kill Momma?"

Maggots oozed from the gaping wound on his father's neck. "I wish I could take credit, but those three dolls of yours killed her."

"You're lying." Henry always believed his father was to blame for the terror and misery in his and his mother's life. His rage now out of control, he yanked the knife out of his mother's chest and swung wildly at his father. The knife caught him under the chin and his father's severed head thudded to the floor. The body collapsed into itself, leaving a pile of dirt on the floor. When Henry glanced back at the bed, his mother had simply vanished.

"Joselyn, Amalia, and Claire, come here!" Henry commanded.

The three dolls' giggling grew fainter, and the front door slammed shut. Henry gave chase but wasn't quick enough. They disappeared down a wastewater drain, their mocking laughter echoing in the tunnels below.

"That dumb bastard will never catch us down here," one of them said.

Henry grasped his knife with a white-knuckle death grip. He would find them and make them pay.

"Evil is in Effham Falls, and it's wide awake," Raggedy Ann said.

Henry went around the house, making sure all the doors and windows were locked. When he bought the dolls and brought them home, what evil had he released into Effham Falls?

He paced the house, trying to formulate a plan. Logical thought was not his best attribute. In the bathroom, standing in front of the mirror, he splashed water on his face, and ran his fingers through his hair. His mother betrayed her family and God. "Momma, why?"

The lights flickered and his mother's face flashed in the mirror. "Don't believe anything or anyone. The False Prophet is the deceiver of man."

"Momma, Momma, don't go. I don't understand." Henry buried his head in his hands. He was so deep in the darkness of his mind, neither medicine nor years of counseling would make the light shine through. He had to remind himself that nothing relating to his mother was real, that everything he has witnessed was a lie, an illusion.

Maybe it was time to go deeper into the darkness and banish any doubt.

He tucked the knife into his waist band, "Raggedy Ann, I have a plan. We're going monster hunting."

"We need to hurry. More dolls are waking," she said, a certain thrill of alarm in her voice.

"Is Agnes still alive?"

"Yes, she's caught in her own nightmare." Raggedy Ann shifted in his arms. "We need to find her. The door is open and the dead are loose."

Henry swore to himself, he would find Agnes, the three dolls, and close whatever door was open.

The sun was peeking over the horizon when they arrived again at Agnes's house.

The covers shifted and something tunneled towards Lilla. She smiled. Her cat was coming to snuggle. She wriggled in anticipation. When her doll, Molly, poked its head out and crawled onto her chest, she became alarmed. "Molly...what are...?"

Molly clutched an ultra-sharpened pencil in her hand and held it against Lilla's cheek. "Scream and I'll poke your eye out. Do you understand?"

"Yes." Lilla's lips trembled, and she started whimpering.

"Open the window."

"Why?"

"We're leaving."

All of Lilla's dolls were standing, lined up in front of the window.

"No, not all of you," Lilla said. She didn't want to be all alone.

Molly gripped the collar of Lilla's pajamas and pressed the pencil point into her cheek. "Get out of bed. Now."

Lilla pushed the covers away and stood. "Molly, no. You're a good doll."

"Lilla, open the window," all of the dolls said in unison.

Lilla opened the window. Molly jumped down then helped each one of the dolls crawl out onto the yard.

Tears glistened in Lilla's eyes. "Bye."

Agnes's house was quiet when Henry and Raggedy Ann entered. Henry was on edge. In the early morning shadows, his mother had somehow followed. The temperature was freezing and frost crept up the walls.

"We need to hurry," Raggedy Ann said.

When they entered the door marked 'Effham Falls Mine #1', the dolls' whispers filled Henry's mind, but there were other voices too. The dead were calling to him as well. He turned on the flashlight and followed the voices. Condensation dripped from the walls and ceilings; dank water pooled in the low spots on the floor. The walls emitted an eerie luminescent glow.

After what seemed like hours plowing ahead in the damp and semi-darkness, an exhausted Henry and Raggedy Ann found Agnes in a giant spider's egg sac suspended from an intersection of support beams. Her gray flesh and blue lips gave her the appearance of being a cadaver, but her eyes flickered, and the sac quivered like she was dreaming.

"Kill her. Kill her. Finish the job," the dolls chanted.

Raggedy Ann's eyes flashed anger. "We need to get Agnes out of here now and destroy the sac. The little ones will be born soon, and she will be their first meal."

At the edge of Henry's light, the dolls stepped out of the darkness. "We love you, Henry. Don't let the witch live. Kill her!"

Heat radiated from his hip. He pulled the knife from his waistband. It gleamed a brilliant red. The blade filled him with anger and hatred.

"Henry," Raggedy Ann said. "Don't listen. Fight them. Like the demon inhabiting your mother, they are evil, not you or Agnes."

Henry closed his eyes and gritted his teeth. The darkness receded, but most of the negative thoughts remained.

"Do it now," the dolls commanded.

Conflicting thoughts tore Henry's mind in two. In his confusion, he swung at Agnes's head and missed. The egg sac exploded and newborn puppy-sized spiders raced everywhere. Henry partially caught Agnes before she crashed to the floor.

She gasped for breath, and groggily struggled to her feet. Raggedy Ann jumped off Henry's shoulder and ran to her side.

Instinct took over and Henry slashed at everything. The burnt smell of electricity and the wet, popping sound of exploding spiders filled the tunnel. Those who survived Henry's first offensive swarmed all over him, injecting him with their venom. The blood-covered knife flashed dark red and his mind turned blacker. "Raggedy Ann, get Agnes out of here while you can."

Agnes and Raggedy Ann ran past him and, for a split-second, Henry almost turned the knife on them. He plucked the few remaining spiders off his body and dispatched them to Hell. He pointed his light down the tunnel and caught a glimpse of Joselyn's red hair disappearing into the darkness.

In Henry's exhaustion, time slowed. His flashlight flickered and died. He found a tin of wooden matches and glass jar of clear liquid in one of the crates stacked along the wall. In the next crate, he found a couple of burlap bags. He picked up a splintered board, wrapped it with one of the burlap bags, and doused it with the clear liquid. He struck a match and the torch caught on fire. He put everything he found into the second burlap bag and continued.

Thick, rope-like webs blanketed the intersections and corners in dark grayness. Murmuring voices--the dolls, the dead, and some he didn't recognize -- filled his mind, digging in with their barbs and taunts.

A sense of dread pervaded Henry's thoughts as he traveled deeper. His sweat-drenched shirt clung to his back. He walked at a slower pace, making sure one of the dolls slipped past him to the surface to wander unattended. The accumulated spider venom was taking its toll, his body gradually shutting down. In the back of his mind, the demons were loose and his mind was slipping into darker and more dangerous territory.

He stumbled and fell forward over a rock, brushing his arm against a web. He ignored the pain, the ugly puss-filled red welts, and smiled at the sight of the dark-haired doll, Amalia, and the blond-haired doll, Claire, stuck securely in the web.

"Look what I found. What a pleasant surprise."

"Henry, help us," they begged. "The monster will come back."

"Which monsters? There are more than one. Momma, the demon, or the spiders?"

"None of those. The monster with the sharp fangs and large claws."

Henry pulled out his knife and cut through the web with ease, carefully inserting the dolls into the burlap bag with everything else. Muffled curses leaked out of the bag before he was able to close it.

"Agnes and I made it back," Raggedy Ann whispered inside Henry's head.

What was left of the web vibrated, thrumming through the walls and floors and in his chest. Out of the darkness, his father's bloated and decaying corpse ran towards him. Red tinged saliva dribbled down his father's chin. Henry stood frozen in place and waited for his father's fangs to tear out his throat. A wave of revulsion washed over him as the creature ran through him and disappeared. Henry shivered uncontrollably. Was the feverish hallucination an ominous indication of what was to come?

He slid to the floor, his reserve drained. His eyelids grew heavy, but fear kept them open. "No...I must get up." He staggered to his feet and leaned against the stone wall for support. One wobbly step later, he slipped into unconsciousness.

"Agnes is recovering just fine."

Henry's eyes flickered. Raggedy Ann's words tickled his mind.

"The Runes are back in place."

"Good," Henry mumbled, half awake.

"Effham Falls is once again safe. Henry, you can come home."

"Are you sure?"

Henry jolted awake from his dream. Rancid bile crept up this throat. He might have been awake, but he knew his nightmare was out there somewhere, alive. He had stepped over the line between sanity and insanity a long time ago. Even with directions, he would never find his way back, but he didn't want to die. The border between life and death approached fast.

Henry got up from the floor. A shadow blacker than the rest of the darkness approached the weakening light of his torch. Yellow eyes the size of softballs glared at him. A large spider blocked the tunnel. Sitting on top of the arachnid was the evil red-headed doll, Joselyn. Her green eyes glinted with malevolence. "Give me the others."

With the last of his strength, Henry bounced to his feet and pulled the knife from his back pocket. "Do you want to play?" He strode forward unafraid.

"Be careful," Joselyn said.

"Are you talking to me?"

"No. My ride. We want you dead."

The spider lunged and Henry countered, the knife slicing into one of the creature's front legs. Black blood spurted and the ground sizzled wherever a droplet hit. The spider reared back then it and the doll scampered back down the tunnel.

Before the darkness swallowed them, Joselyn called over her shoulder. "Your mother won't be happy."

"My mother is gone."

A wave of blackness invaded Henry's mind like nausea. He stumbled down the tunnel like a soul tormented in Hell and found the open door. The flickering light of his torch illuminated the dark soot-colored wood. He stepped closer and pushed open what was left of a door. Gouged into the thick planks were large claw marks. Chucks of wood were also missing from the six-by-six timbers. Had the creature found its way to the surface or was the it still down here with him?

Henry picked his way through the damage and found a mummified body leaning against the stone wall just inside the doorway. The empty eye sockets and blackened head made Henry recoil. A shiny object was clutched in the dead man's hand. Henry gently pried apart the stiff fingers and removed his mother's favorite necklace, the antique cross that had been blessed by the Pope which her grandmother had given her. She hadn't lost it. Poppa had ripped the religious icon from around her neck when she killed him.

Momma, had your love for Poppa and I been a lie?

Henry had so many questions. Had she killed Poppa before the demon possessed her? The twisted faces of the dead laughed at him. Henry wasn't a rocket scientist, but in his heart, he knew that Momma planned all this. She was the beast.

Miles below Agnes's house, Henry patched the door to the best of his abilities and closed it behind him, locking himself away from humanity. He would guard the door, keep the town's secrets hidden, and the evil buried deep.

He collapsed next to his father, slipped his mother's necklace around his neck, and held his father's hand.

"Poppa, you were a bad man. Henry smiled. "I forgive you."

From deeper in the mine, a shimmering figure approached. Blurry at first, but soon it became clear who it was.

"You won't be alone. Bess and I will keep you company," Emerald said. A serious expression clouded her face. "My body is down there someplace," she said, pointing at the way she had come. "Will you find me then bury me and Bess?"

A small smile crept to Henry's lips. "Yes."

"There are more monsters down here."

Large claws scratched at the door.

"God help Effham Falls."

The Effham Falls Gazette labeled the day and the phenomenon as The March of the Dolls. On the morning of August 23rd, hundreds of dolls were found lining the sidewalks all over town. Some were several blocks away from their child's home, and a dozen were found crossing the street. Parents, when asked, had no explanation and could only shake their heads. Some of the children smiled and shrugged. Others told outlandish tales of their dolls coming to life and sneaking out of the house. One little girl with tears in her eyes said, "You can keep mine. She opened her eyes and scared me."

The one thing everyone could agree on was that the dolls seemed to be headed in the

same direction. Where were they going? No one would say.

At a young age, CHRIS STENSON had success winning young author contests, and his love for writing continued throughout high school and into adulthood. He is the founder and leader of the Moorhead Friends Writing Group which has hosted nationally known authors as guest speakers. His short story "Two Bobbies" was selected for inclusion in the Horror Writers Network Anthology, *The Gates of Chaos*, and was published in March 2021. "Roadkill Surprise", a werewolf short story, was included in the summer print edition of the *2021 Horror Zine Magazine*. His newest short story "Planted" will be published in *2023 Fear Forges Anthology* Spring Edition.

The Meter Reader

Daniel Haynes

"I'm telling you, guys, something's wrong with Mr. Warner," Doug repeatedly insisted.

"Just listen to yourself, would you?" Pam scoffed with an exasperated sigh and roll of her eyes. Her companion and coworker, Tammy, merely shook her head in agreement.

Both women were beginning to wonder if their junior coworker, Doug Jansen, had chosen the wrong line of work. Knowing that he had aspirations of becoming a horror author someday, each of them knew of his penchant for letting his imagination run wild with him.

Hired for the vacated position of municipal utility meter reader right after his high school graduation, after passing with the highest score on the civil service exam, the young jock appeared more than capable of fulfilling his obligations. Standing at a lean and muscular five-foot, eleven inches in height, he had been a standout football star for the Effham High School Lumberjacks.

As the middle linebacker and defensive captain of the varsity squad, he had been projected to be highly recruited by several colleges in the Minnesota/Wisconsin regions. However, as Doug himself had explained, said colleges had deemed him too small to fill the same position at their level of competition. Nor was he considered fast enough to play a defensive back position, therefore he was passed on.

Crestfallen and embittered, he had briefly considered military service to be his only option of elevating himself in life. However, his English Composition teacher, Mrs. Whetstone, had had high praise for his various writing assignments. Finding that he had a natural talent for weaving tales of fiction, she encouraged him to pursue a career as an author.

Unfortunately, Doug's grades were not quite high enough to secure any form of scholarship. And while his fiction was considered to be of top quality, he could never quite grasp the technical terminology of creative composition. Oftentimes, he needed the finer points of document settings and page layouts explained to him. For whatever reason, the language just seemed to fly over his head, and he would only grow more frustrated with his efforts to make sense of it all.

Being that he and his widowed mother occupied the lower middle class of the community, college tuition was out of the question. Once again goading him to consider a military enlistment in order to aid him in his quest for educational advancement, as well as taking much of the financial burden off his beloved mother.

However, when the *Effham Gazette* posted a notification that a civil service test would be given to fill the vacancy of meter reader, left by the previous retiring gentleman who had held the position, Doug's mother suggested he try that before committing to military service. Pointing out that a civil service job held great benefits and would serve him well when he reached retirement age.

Although skeptical, Doug conceded and the rest, as they say, was history.

Pam Whitledge was an athletic thirty-year-old woman who had inherited the mantle of Senior Meter Reader upon the retirement of their previous coworker. A married woman with a twelve-year-old daughter, she was full of life and easy to get on with.

The only other remaining seasoned meter reader was a younger divorcee woman by the name of Tammy Ravenwood. Of Native American ancestry, the twenty-six-year-old was also full of life and playful sensuality. Oftentimes teasing Doug with overt sexual glances and devilish grins. All in good fun, however, as she never allowed her flirtatious nature to exceed her playful intentions.

Fortunately, both had enough common sense to realize that it was all in good fun.

As an eighteen-year-old male, Doug was enthralled, but disciplined enough to know how to receive her "attentions". Thankfully, Tammy always knew when to reel in her behavior and reiterate that she had no true intentions toward the attractive young jock, who stood at least a half foot taller than she when the expressions on his face and in his eyes warranted that she do so before things went too far.

Doug began work in June, earlier that year, and was assigned to Pam for his initial period of training. A duration that provided some of the most unusual and unique scenarios that he had never expected to experience in this line of work.

Their job often required that they enter private locations to include those of the homes of the general public, as well as those of the various businesses, in order to record the monthly readings of electric, gas, and water meters that were often located in secluded areas. Areas such as backyards, basements, and even the occasional rooftop.

In just his second week in training, he and Pam had entered through the gate of a home's privacy fence to reach an electric meter, only to be stunned to find an attractive and fully nude young woman sunning herself in the backyard. The resident having forgotten that the three-day monthly period for reading said meter had fallen within the time frame she had chosen to fully relax.

Pam, who was as tall as Doug, turned beet-red and immediately apologized, while the lady threw a towel over herself and with an embarrassed giggle, took full responsibility and apologized likewise.

Doug had temporarily frozen in place, until a flustered Pam grabbed him by the arm and forcefully swung him around, ushering him toward the gate. A huge grin was plastered to his face as he could sense the same with his mentor.

As they exited the gate, he could not help but note, "I think I'm gonna *like* this job."

"Awwww...gawwwd..." Pam retorted as she slapped his shoulder in reprimand.

That had been six months earlier. It was now December and the accumulating snow from the steadily falling heavenly dandruff had all but cloaked any evidence of that warm sunny day and the image of that beautiful young woman.

Doug was now back at the readers' station in the town municipal building, relating his latest exchange with the antique store owner, Jonathon Warner. An older middle-aged gentleman who, although appearing somewhat haggard at times, had always been fairly amicable to Doug each month he arrived requiring access to the store's gas meter in the basement of the building.

His visit earlier that morning, however, proved disturbingly different when the proprietor exhibited behavior that was in complete contrast to his usual personality.

"I'm telling ya," Doug reiterated to his two coworkers with concern. "I think he's finally lost it."

"You're just paranoid," Pam countered. "This is your first winter on the job. You're going to have to get used to the public griping about the increase in their gas bill. It's the nature of the business."

Tammy agreed. "Yeah, stud muffin. If I had a dime for every time I was accused of reading a meter wrong or estimating a reading, I'd be living in Beverly Hills by now."

Doug vigorously shook his head in denial of the explanations, insisting, "No. Not this time. I'm telling ya if you could have seen his eyes... if you had gone down into that creepy old cramped cellar and smelled what I smelled... you'd think different."

Pam sighed. "You probably just smelled a dead rat and the stench had probably finally gotten to him after he couldn't find it."

Tammy, with thick flakes of unmelted snow still spackling her long raven-black hair, smiled up at Doug and reassured, "It's a very old little building. I've gone down in that dusty old cellar many times before you were hired and assigned the 'Evil Ward' from me. Gives me the chills just thinking about it, but I've never had issues with him like that."

Doug grinned back and batted his thick black eyebrows as he replied, "Probably because you gave him that disarming seductive grin of yours, every time you had to read there."

Like Tammy, Doug's thick black hair and newly grown beard were speckled with large flakes of snow that had not yet melted, making him appear all the more like the namesake of the school's nickname. A lumberjack.

With an exaggerated giggle, Tammy playfully gave him a chastising slap on the arm in her all-too-familiar flirtatious manner. Eliciting an exaggerated groan from Pam as she rolled her eyes.

"Anyway," Doug continued, "I've never seen him behave like that before. It was eerie."

Pam countered, "You're just letting your imagination run away with you. It's all those spook stories you write. Combine those with the aura of that side of town and you're bound to experience things you'd find 'eerie.'"

"Heeyyy..." Tammy chimed in. "That'd be a great reference for your next story. Of course, you'd have to change the name of the owner and store."

Doug chuffed, "I'm already working on one that revolves around that incident I had at Old Widow Effham's place."

Tammy appeared wide-eyed as she excitedly challenged, "You mean, back in October, when you were reading the electric meter and Wilbur suddenly appeared in the window next to it and hissed at you?"

"Damn thing liked to gave me a heart attack," Doug snarled with the memory.

It had been a seasonably bleak and overcast day, just a few days prior to Halloween and Doug had felt the old familiar childhood charge of excitement for the season welling up inside him. It was his favorite time of year and other than having lost his father in a tragic car accident ten years earlier that month, it remained his favorite season.

A heavy damp breeze was blowing as he approached the side of Widow Effham's old large and weather-beaten house. The structure creaked and groaned in the wind, it had all the trappings of a traditional haunted house seen in the movies.

Doug had pulled his insulated brown uniform jacket tighter about him as an inexplicable chill seemed to seep into the marrow of his bones. A sensation that would, on occasion, affect him during atmospheric conditions such as this, although he could never figure out why.

Gripping his battery-operated palm meter used to record the readings of various utility meters, he proceeded through the overgrown and dying grass to the side of the house where the electric meter was affixed. Being his fourth month on the job and having grown familiar with his route, he knew it to be positioned beside a first-floor window.

A newer model meter, in sharp contrast to the ancient-looking house, it possessed an easy-to-read digital display in place of the older multiple dials type units. Its relatively shiny metal surface easily detectable against the bland background of the house.

Unable to shake the oppressive chill coursing through his body, Doug drew up close to the newer meter.

Just as he was reading the display, however, a small, gray, demonic-like feline face suddenly appeared through the veil of old doily-like curtains and abruptly lunged at the window. Hissing and spitting, the Widow Effham's shorthaired cat, Wilbur, unleashed an unearthly wail as it savagely swiped at the pane of glass in direction of the intruder, causing Doug to stumble backward in a combination of shock and anger.

"Damn it, Wilbur!" Doug irritably barked. "What the hell?!"

Wilbur, unfazed by the chastising, continued to release an extended whine of warning, occasionally punctuated with venomous hissing. His ears swept back and a look of deadly menace adorned his face.

His being an animal lover notwithstanding, especially for cats, Doug merely glared at the ferocious feline in response. His dark concept of writing a tale where the demonic beast actually feeds on the Widow Effham looping through his mind.

He then snorted aloud. "Probably why Old Lady Effham's never been seen."

The girls had a hearty laugh that day when he had returned to their little office and related the tale.

Today, however, was different.

Today, Doug was not injecting any sense of levity into his tale of his encounter with the antique store proprietor, Mr. Warner. If anything, the young man expressed an extremely serious countenance of concern and what might have even been interpreted as "fear".

"Alright, alright," Pam sighed. "Tell us exactly what happened."

Gathering his thoughts, Doug turned briefly from them and began, "Well, I was knocking the snow off my boots on the store doormat, when I looked up to take hold of the door handle and...*BAM!* There's Warner, standing just on the other side of the door... *glaring* at me through the glass as if I had some nerve to show up at his door."

Pam and Tammy exchanged curious glances before the former pressed, "You do anything to piss him off? I mean, you didn't take a leak in his alley, or anything, did you?"

Doug sneered, the melting snow dripping from one upturned corner of his mustache to disappear into his beard as he countered, "Oh, ha...ha...ha."

"Weelll...?" Pam threw up her hands. "You never know."

In a facetious tone, Doug replied, "No, Pam. I didn't 'take a leak' in his alley, or on his doorstep, or parked car."

"Okay, okay," Pam conceded. "Go on, then."

Shooting his ranking coworker a disapproving look of disbelief from the corner of his eye, Doug shook his head and continued, "After I got over the initial shock, I just smiled politely at him and said 'Good morning, Mr. Warner. Here to read your gas meter...?', in case he'd forgotten that it was that time of the month."

Tammy giggled and Pam, again, rolled her eyes, "Oh, gawwwd..."

Catching himself, Doug irritably countered, "You know what I mean."

Pam nodded her head and motioned with her hand for him to continue.

Taking a deep sigh, Doug added, "Well, I waited for him to back away from the door so I could enter, which he did...eventually. But, only far enough for me to squeeze through the door."

"Did his manner change, then?" Tammy pressed.

Doug arched his brow and slightly tilted his head as he replied, "Not much. He still had a look on his face that implied he wasn't very happy to have me there."

"That's strange," Tammy noted.

"You're telling me," Doug concurred.

"He'd try to keep you from the meter?" Pam queried.

Turning back to the senior reader, Doug shook his head, "No. He just said, 'Hope you're going to read it right, this month'."

Slightly taken aback, Tammy offered "That doesn't sound like him, at all."

Pam agreed, "No, it doesn't. Jonathon's always been pretty cordial, if not friendly when we come around. Wonder what's gotten into him?"

Doug shook his head. "I don't know, ladies, but now that I think about it, I got the sense that he was distracted by something. Almost like his mind wasn't totally focused on my reason for being there."

The two women briefly regarded one another before returning their attention to their coworker.

"I hope he isn't dealing with some bad news," Pam submitted.

"All I know," Doug continued, "is that he seemed extremely irritable when I asked him if there seemed to be a problem with his bill."

"What'd he say?" Tammy pressed.

"Hmph. Nothing. He just scowled at me as if I was trying to be a smartass or something," Doug replied.

Pam shook her head in disbelief. "That definitely doesn't sound like him."

Doug countered defensively, "What? You think I'm making it up?"

Pam furrowed her brow. "No. I didn't say that."

Doug grew more irritable. "No. And, I suppose, it wasn't you who tried to accuse me of provoking your friend's dog back in July when it took a bite outta my arm, either. Was it?"

Doug still carried the fang marks of a customer's dog when he got too close to a short fence in an attempt to read said customer's electric meter. The dog, understandably protective of its master's home, had jumped up and over the fence just far enough to secure Doug's forearm in its mouth and give a vicious tug. Puncturing the flesh and sending blood streaming down his arm and onto the ground.

The customer happened to be a close family friend of Pam and her husband's and, in defense of the animal, Pam had argued that it was normally such a sweet animal and challenged if Doug had done something to provoke it. An all-too-common defense pressed by almost every utility customer in defense of their pets whenever their "angelic" animals would bite a meter reader or deliveryman, *unprovoked*.

Like defensive parents, most were just unable to accept the fact that their pets were doing only what was in their nature to do and that no provocation was required. A fact that set Doug off against his senior coworker as he berated her in a furious tirade that she, of all people, would attempt such a challenge towards him.

Their working relationship had been strained since then, only recently relaxing to the point where they could occasionally joke around together. Nonetheless, each privately continued viewing the other as the cause of the rift.

Fortunately, both Pam and Tammy had come to accept him and enjoyed his presence. For Pam, it was with reservations, although she did admire his untiring work ethic.

This latest exchange, however, threatened to undo the "bridge mending" between them.

"Why are you bringing up the past?" Pam challenged.

"Why are *you* challenging what I'm telling you...again?" Doug countered.

It was at this point that Tammy stepped between them and insisted they both cease their belligerence. "Okay, you two. Simmer down, already," the raven-haired beauty instructed.

For Doug, however, such compliance was easier said than done.

Even Tammy had to admit that there seemed to be something in the air, of late, that was contributing to the increasing irritability in the general public of Effham Falls. She could sense it, herself, although she was a steady practitioner of meditation and was capable of keeping her negative emotions in check.

Turning back to Doug, Tammy encouraged, "So what happened then?"

Still glaring at Pam, Doug replied, "Warner led me to the back of the store, to the cellar door, but didn't say anything else. He opened the door, flicked on the light, then brushed past me on his way back to the front counter."

Tammy then pressed, "You said something about an 'eerie' feeling or something when you went into the cellar?"

Turning back to the shorter woman, Doug nodded. "Yeah. Really creepy. Never felt anything like it before when I've gone down there in the past. But there was just... I dunno. I suppose I'd just attributed it to my nerves after that unexpected encounter with him."

"What'd feel like?" Tammy continued to press.

Doug released an uncomfortable sigh.

"Like I wasn't alone, down there," he replied.

"Meaning...?" Tammy gently goaded.

Doug regarded both women with hesitation, before reluctantly stating, "Like there were numerous sets of tiny eyes watching me from out of the shadows."

Both women then exchanged silent glances. Glances that were not lost on their younger male counterpart.

"What?" Doug challenged as he shifted his attention between the two.

Consulting with the senior reader, Tammy inquired, "What do you think?"

Pam shrugged. "Might as well now."

Doug furrowed his brow and again shifted his attention between the two women as he pressed, "What?"

Pam sighed. "There's been a rumor floating around…more of an 'urban myth' than anything…revolving around some supposed haunted dolls, or some such thing, that are somehow, someway, supposed to be attached to the antique store."

Doug scowled. "Seriously? 'Haunted dolls'? How come I've never heard of it?"

"Probably because you were still in school when it started," Pam speculated.

"Yeah, but I'm all into that sort of thing," Doug countered. "You'd thought I would've heard some—"

"Look," Pam cut him off. "It's not like it was common knowledge. In fact, I don't even know how it started. I first heard of it when Bob and I, and a few other couples went on a couples' retreat camping trip. We were all telling campfire tales when one of the women said that she had been 'told' by an aunt who was somehow involved in collecting dolls that she had 'heard' of some 'supposedly cursed' dolls haunting Effham Falls."

The look on Doug's face was a combination of shock, disbelief, and wonder. That he may have been watched by possessed dolls in that creepy, dusty, cobwebbed cellar…

Attempting to milk Pam for all the information that she might possess, he excitedly pressed, "Did she have any specific stories about the dolls? Had she seen them, herself? I mean, did her aunt see them?"

Again, Pam merely rolled her eyes and turned away as, with exasperation in her voice, she replied, "I…don't…know. Even the woman telling the story had heard it second or third hand."

"Well, wer-were they connected to the antique store?" Doug stammered with controlled excitement.

Pam turned back to him and sighed, "Yeah. I think so. But we all thought it was just a convenient 'MacGuffin' for the story, ya know? A handy little plot device to account for their presence, here in Effham Falls. Nothing more."

Turning back to Tammy, Doug inquired, "Have you heard of these things, too?"

Tammy arched her brow and shrugged. "Only what Pam's just told you. I used to think about it a lot when I would read the gas meter at that shop, too."

Doug continued, "Did you feel eyes watching you, too?"

Tammy softly shook her head. "No, but my grandmother would tell me stories of 'bad spirits' that loved to possess dolls. So, I suppose such things are possible."

Doug suddenly fell to silent contemplation before submitting, "What if it's these dolls that's been oppressing Mr. Warner? I mean, that's generally how possession works on a person. A demonic entity starts slowly oppressing its victim, or victims until they can get no rest, and their entire personality does a complete one-eighty. That would explain his grouchy demeanor."

Pam, once again, sighed and countered, "Or maybe it's just the stress of the holiday season playing a little too heavy on his mind. Ever think about that?"

Doug responded with a dismissive look of disapproval before turning back to Tammy.

"What, exactly, did your grandmother have to say about it? Did she tell any specific stories?" he eagerly pressed.

Tammy chuckled. "I was just a little girl, Doug. I don't remember the details of all the stories she told me over the years. Except, of course, that I couldn't bring myself to sleep with *my* dolls for several months after hearing that particular story."

The wind then began to pick up outside. Blowing through the bare limbs of the trees of Effham Falls' modest little Central Park that adjoined the city's municipal building. Causing an eerie shrilling sound in the darkening snow-filled sky.

The light of the small, inner community office casting the clear reflections of the three meter readers upon the inner glass of the large window panes as the snow continued to fall outside. Giving each of the three occupants a ghostly appearance against the dark backdrop of the rapidly approaching dusk.

It was almost time to clock out for the day and each of them now had images of demonically possessed dolls fully engrained in their subconscious.

DANIEL HAYNES is an Army Vet who served as both a Helicopter (Huey) Mechanic/Crew Chief and then later as a Civil Affairs Specialist. Daniel's passion for classic horror films/monsters began when his father would buy, build, and paint monster models for him. The Wolf Man was his favorite and continues to serve as inspiration for the unique and frightening characters he creates today.

The Guest

Susette Quinn

Coffee cup in hand, Jill stood in the Monday morning sun, looking out her living room windows at Main Street and the bookstore below. Soon the shops would open, the town bustle, and the sidewalks below come to life.

Speaking of the shops below, she needed to find some shoes, and get to work. But first, she took one more big breath with her eyes closed and tipped her face to the warmth of the sunbeam.

The rumble of a car startled her out of her peace. Sheriff Sorenson rolled by in his cruiser, same as he did every day. He would swing through town and give it a once over on his way to the corner stool at the diner down the way. You could set a clock by the man.

Salem, Jill's cat, meandered out of the bedroom while she slipped on loafers.

"Ready, bud?" she asked her silky roommate while reaching for the door.

Jill's grandmother, Evelyn, known as Evie to most, had always dreamed of owning a bookstore. Grandpa Hank made her dream come true. Jill used to spend her summers with her grandparents, and helping at the store was a reward for the avid reader. After Grandpa Hank passed away, Jill came every chance she could to give Evie a break. It seemed natural that the store passed on to Jill when Evie left this Earth.

There was an apartment above the store her grandma used to rent out for extra cash, but it had needed some updating after being vacant for years. Jill decided to make the space her own. She gutted the kitchen and the bathroom. Paint, tiles, fixtures, and refurbished wood flooring brought back the building's rich beauty.

Jill started down the stairs with Salem right beside her. At the bottom, the door opened out into an alley. She turned, locked her apartment door, stepped five feet to the right, unlocked the bookstore, and walked inside. She locked the door behind her just as Evie used to. A doorbell, high on the wall, was used by the delivery drivers to alert her of their presence. She didn't bother to go out front yet. She booted up the computer, checked the calendar to see what shipments were coming that week, then checked to see if she had any orders to prep.

    The store had bookshelves, situated in such a way to make little hideaway places for customers to work or read a book, with small workstations or big chairs in them. Along the back wall, Jill set up a coffee bar with a small beverage cooler underneath. The front of the store opened up to the street with big plate glass windows that she decorated seasonally, and a central door with an old fashioned, brass bell above it. The center of the store held a counter for the cash register and behind that, the entry to the back room. The wood gleamed thanks to Jill's hard work and Evie's secret lemon oil mixture.

    A little before 9 am, Jill went out front to start a pot of coffee for her shoppers and take a cursory look around. Lately, she had been finding books on the floor and sticky notes in odd places. Sure enough, there was a pen and a pad of sticky notes on the front counter and a book on the floor in the used book corner. She giggled and said out loud to the mystery spirit, "I see you have been busy again. I'm glad reading is important in the afterlife." While tidying up, she noticed a shaky line drawn on the top of the pad. "Curious," Jill thought as she unlocked the front door, declaring The Tattered Cover open for the day.

    Jill had always known the store had a ghost. Sometimes she could feel him watching her. It was a male presence; of that she was sure. A sense of urgency or frustration often emanated from him. The smell of pipe tobacco was his too. He caused no problems, so she deemed him harmless, as Evie had.

    When she first took over the store, the books on the floor weren't a daily occurrence, but now it was a guarantee. Every day, same corner. Was it always the same book? Jill hadn't ever given it much thought. She went back over to the used book section and took it off the shelf. It was a local history book. There were sections on mining, lumber, the introduction of railroads, and even the shipping industry in Duluth and Two Harbors, MN. Was her guest somehow connected to this book??

She took the book to the front counter and tucked it on a shelf below to read later.

The bell over the front door tinkled, and Jill's day began. Weekdays were usually a steady stream of customers, deliveries, checking the sitting areas for books left out, shelving and, of course, cleaning. Books create quite a bit of dust.

Jill had cleaned up the coffee pot mid-afternoon and restocked the little cooler of water and soft drinks under the coffee station so that when 6 pm rolled around, all she had to do was lock up and head upstairs. On a whim, or maybe an intuitive nudge, she decided to take out the sticky note with the line and leave it, a pen, and the book on the front counter.

"Okay," she said to the seemingly empty room. "You have my attention. If you can, tell me what it is you need. Or your name. It would be good to know what to call you."

Jill went to the door that led to the storeroom and called for Salem. She heard a faint *meow* and found him at the back door, ready to go home too.

The week was relatively uneventful for July. Her guest had made more lines on the paper; some straight, some at a slant. It looked like the first one might be an *A* and Jill assumed the marks would eventually form a word. Every night she left the same items on the counter. No other books had been taken off the shelves, and each morning Jill tried to piece together the shaky lines.

She and Salem had just entered the back room when Jill heard the bell over the front door ring. That door should be locked! She bolted into the store to find nothing. She checked the door. Locked. However, the bell swayed ever so slightly.

"You have my attention," Jill announced to her guest. "What are you trying to tell me?"

At that moment, the pen on the main counter rolled onto the floor. Jill walked over to pick up the pen when she saw the notepad. "You did it! Holy Moly!"

Arv was written in shaky letters on the yellow pad. Arv? What did that mean? Jill noticed that the regional history book was open. Arvid Jensen! The name leapt off the page at her.

"Arv. Your name was Arvid, wasn't it? Arvid Jensen, it is nice to finally meet you." As she spoke, an odd warmth surrounded her like an invisible hug, leaving her with goosebumps all down her arms.

"Okay, Arvid. I think I need to do some reading to find out what happened and how or why you're in this book. But I also have a store to ready, so you'll have to be patient."

Jill started her morning routine with a little more verve. She wanted to read Arvid's portion of the book as soon as possible. With the coffee pot ready and the door unlocked, she went behind the counter to start reading.

This particular chapter centered around the logging industry in the late 1890's and how it struggled to take hold in certain territories due to the lack of rivers. There was ample pine, but a lack of transportation, at least until the rail came through. Unlike the areas to the northwest, which had a viable water highway westward to the Red River, the area around the Mississippi Headwaters was more of a series of connected large lakes than a river system. And while lakes were great, they needed more manpower to move the logs across. What they did provide, however, were locations for large sawmills.

The chapter went on to talk about the different camps in this region, the introduction of the rail, the boom it created around the sawmills when they had the means to move the lumber, and the settlements that sprang up around the area. By 1900, the weekly trains dumped dozens of men looking for work.

The front door opened, and Jill slipped the book below the counter. "Good morning, Aggie. How are you today?"

Just inside the door stood Agnus Bagman clutching one of the many dolls she collected. She nodded toward the doll and said, "She told me that he speaks. He wants answers, and you will provide them. The ripple you create in the fabric of time will be insignificant. It will matter little."

"Um, alright. Did you want to look for a book today?" Jill replied pleasantly. Aggie wasn't known for coloring with a full box of crayons, so if her words seemed nonsensical, so be it.

"Digging things up might make him mad. Be careful not to anger him. He is unstable."

Jill wondered if her face showed her puzzlement. "Okay, thank you. Aggie, who are you referring to?"

Aggie's head turned toward the doll as if it was speaking. She nodded and left the shop without another word.

Be careful not to anger him. Who? And why would Jill anger anyone?

What followed was a steady stream of customers and no time to contemplate the meaning of Aggie's confusing words.

The next morning started off right at nine o'clock. Jill finally picked up where she left off in the story of the early logging settlements and came upon the page that mentioned Arvid. She learned Arvid Jensen was talented, hard-working and well-spoken, considering his eighth-grade education.

The more Jill read, the more these settlements sounded a little like the Old West. Crime, drinking, women, and isolation. Everyone had heard stories of the Gold Rush, cowboys, and the drama of western towns, but Jill never realized similar situations had happened in the Midwest.

Jill continued reading and eventually came to a late March blizzard. The men were all at the saloon warming their bellies with whiskey before the wind and snow amped up. The sawmill shut down until the storm cleared, and Arvid had checked on the mill at various times as weather permitted.

The blizzard raged for two days with snow drifts twelve-feet high. It took a team of men an entire day to dig their way into the sawmill, where they found Arvid Jensen face down on the floor with an ax in the back of his skull.

Jill's jaw dropped in shock. She wasn't expecting that.

No one was ever held responsible. A few were questioned or suspected, but the storm had wiped away all traces of footprints, and the investigation was dropped.

"Arvid," Jill exclaimed in a shocked whisper to the space around her. "You were murdered. Oh, I'm so sorry. How awful."

Jill's mind was going a mile a minute. Why did he bring this to her attention? She closed up the store and left the pad on the counter with a pen. "Arvid, if you can, please tell me what you need me to do."

Over the course of the next few days, the words *'Find Killer'* were written on the pad. Jill now knew why Arvid was sticking around but wasn't sure how to find a hundred-year-old murderer. The only information she had was what she read in the book but that didn't give exact locations or the names of the other men. She needed help. That meant she was probably going to have to tell someone she was conversing with a ghost. Who could she ask to help her who wouldn't think she was crazy? Sarah!

Sarah Moore taught history at Effham Falls High School. She and Jill were about the same age and had become friends after meeting one day when they were both teens. Sarah, always researching history for fun, was a regular at the bookstore. If Jill was in town, the two girls would go to the movies and bonfires after the store closed. Their friendship blossomed over the years.

Since school was still out for another month or so, maybe Sarah would have time to talk to her about where to start the search.

Jill had a lot of work to catch up on but made time in between tasks to shoot Sarah a text asking if she had a few minutes to discuss a small research project. Sarah replied with, 'Apps and wine on the porch after work?'.

After she closed the store, Jill scooped Salem out of the front window and went upstairs. She filled Salem's dish, told him that she would be back soon, snagged a pinot grigio out of the fridge, and drove to Sarah's house.

Sarah lived on Sixth Street, a block over from some of the statelier homes in town. Sarah's home wasn't small, but it also wasn't what some would call large. It had a big porch and some very old trees that offered shelter from the sun's heat. The home itself had all of the original wood trim and even retained the cut glass windows. Sarah was stepping outside when Jill pulled up.

"Sarah! It's so good to see you. It's been too long!" she said, coming up the steps.

Laughing, Sarah answered, "It's been less than a month!"

"See? Too long." Jill smirked, handing the wine to her friend.

The girls got comfortable and caught up on the happenings in each other's lives, nibbling on cheeses and fruits while sipping wine. Eventually, the conversation turned to the reason Jill was there.

"So, tell me what you're researching? What's the project?"

Jill told her about finding the book and noticing the unsolved murder described in it. "I'm interested in finding out who did it."

Sarah cocked her head quizzically. "What aren't you telling me? You're leaving something out."

"How do you do that?"

"I'm a teacher. I'm trained to look for the half-truths. The part my students leave out is usually the most important."

Jill sighed," You're going to think I am off my rocker."

"I promise not to judge. Spill."

"Let me start with a little back story," Jill said.

She went on to tell her friend about the non-threatening spirit in the store. Jill told her what she knew about her guest, the book and his possible writing.

Sarah was leaning forward in her chair, twirling her wine glass, listening intently.

"Over the course of a few days he finally wrote *Arv* on the paper and left the book open to a page with his name on it; Arvid Jensen"

Jill described the mills, the men, the blizzard, and the murder.

"Since then, he's asked me to find the person who killed him. I don't know where to start. All I have is this book," Jill pulled the book from her bag. "Can you help?"

"Arvid Jensen. You have a ghost named Arvid Jensen. That's so cool! Of all the buildings to be haunted in this town, I wouldn't have picked the bookstore. Lottie Effham's old Victorian, maybe. I'm sure it's seen a lot, but The Tattered Cover? Who would've thought?"

"Thanks for not making me feel like I was nutters. I appreciate that."

"Oh, I don't think you're crazy. I believe you're having a conversation with this Arvid Jensen. Maybe once you find his killer, he can move on."

"I was thinking the same thing," Jill answered.

"How about you leave the book with me for a day or two? I'll give it a read. There are small county museums all over the place, along with libraries and newspapers. We should be able to find something that'll lead us in the right direction."

"I can't thank you enough. I want to help him; this just isn't my area of expertise."

"Well," Sarah added. "It's definitely mine. I'm happy to help."

As the two friends watched the sun begin to set, Jill decided it was time to call it a night. "Let me help you clean up," she said, collecting plates.

"Don't be silly." Sarah produced a large serving tray from under the table. "We'll load this up, and I'll take care of things later."

"Thanks again, for both the hospitality and the help."

"Don't mention it. That's what friends are for. Besides, I have some time to kill before I have to report for classes."

Jill gave Sarah a hug and descended the porch steps. With a wave she hopped in her car and headed home.

Four days later, Sarah all but skipped, beaming, into The Tattered Cover. "Are we alone? Or do you have customers camped out in your corners?" she asked.

Laughing, Jill said, "No customers, we're alone. Why?"

"I've been digging, and I may have found something."

"Let's go into the back, just in case I do get a customer," Jill suggested.

Sarah grabbed a soda from underneath the coffee bar and followed Jill into the back where she unloaded the papers in her bag.

Using Jill's desk, she laid out a timeline of events. "What we already know from the book is that Arvid came here with the intent of making money and he seemed good at it. He was working his way up in the ranks of the sawmills and had been given more responsibilities. How did Arvid end up in Effham Falls though? We didn't have a sawmill here. I went back over the descriptors in the book: railroad lines, lakes, the bar, and the town. I thought I may have nailed down the county, so I looked for a county historical society and found it. I was there yesterday. Now let's add these things to that timeline."

"This is Arvid Jensen." Sarah handed Jill a photo of a nicely dressed man about thirty-four years old. She held up a finger so Sarah would give her a moment. This was the man she had been conversing with. It was nice to put a face to the name. She let Sarah continue.

"His first crew was made up of these men," she said, producing another photo. "Arvid moved up quickly. Here we can find him on a different crew." Sarah brandished an additional picture and added it with the others. Continuing, she said, "And in this last photograph, Arvid is dressed differently than the other men, leading me to believe he was part of management. I looked up all of the names, or as many as I could find. From the first to the second photo, about half the men dropped away. I'm not sure how it all worked; did they go back home or to different crews? They aren't in the next picture though. Looking at the second and last photos, we can see that many of the men are the same, with the exception of three."

"Wow, Sarah! You're good at this!" Jill exclaimed.

Sarah smiled. "I did my thesis on researching the ethnic makeup of small towns and how they became Americanized after the railroads were built. This is my jam! Moving right along, I have three names: Frederick Lapointe, Seamus Callahan, and Eugene Marshall. Seamus left the area shortly before Arvid's death. From what I could tell he was here to make some quick money and had a family on the way, so he went back to Illinois. There's very little on Eugene Marshall. He did his job, didn't complain, worked hard, was quiet, and was well-liked by the other men. I don't think it's either of them."

"So you are leaning toward Fredrick?" Jill asked. "Why?"

"Well," Sarah continued with enthusiasm, "I got lucky. I found the right historical society and the woman who worked there had an entire genealogy of those camps at that time. She knew things most wouldn't, due to family letters and stories passed down. Plus, she was extremely passionate about her own family research. She knew Fredrick Lapointe was a French Canadian fur trapper in town to try his hand at making some easy money. Emphasis on easy. It seems that Fredrick had a short temper and most people avoided him, unless he was next to you at the saloon with a bottle of whiskey and that's where he was if he wasn't working. He had a blatant dislike for Arvid, along with a few others. He and Arvid had started as jobbers on the same site and Arvid quickly rose to foreman, a position Fredrick felt better suited himself. Fredrick made no bones about how he felt about Arvid. He let everyone know who he disliked, and the men avoided him. What makes Frederick look suspicious is that he left the area right after that blizzard."

"I'm a little dumbstruck," Jill said. "You found all of this in such a small amount of time."

She stood looking at the papers on her desk, trying to take it all in when the bell out front tinkled, letting her know that she had a customer. "Ope, I'll be back soon" she said as she darted to the front of the shop.

"Cindy, how are you today?" Jill asked the customer who had entered.

Cindy was a spitfire of a woman with a sharp tongue. Jill was always careful around her. Anything said around her spread through town faster than a wildfire.

"*I'm* just fine." she stated. "Your little store seems awfully empty."

Ah, there it is, Jill thought. "Just a lull in customers for the moment. You needn't worry, The Tattered Cover's just fine. Are you shopping for anything specific today?"

Jill found Cindy the latest in trashy romance novels and thanked her for stopping by. Once Cindy had pulled away from the curb, she let out a tense breath. The woman was notorious for spreading rumors and someday, Jill figured, she would be the center of one.

Sarah was typing on her phone when Jill returned. "The real question now," she said without looking up, "is how come Arvid is in Effham Falls? He wasn't from here, didn't die here, and the sawmill wasn't even in this county. Why here?"

"I wish there was a way to talk with Lottie. She has been here for eons but doesn't answer the phone or the door. If I didn't mail books to her every now and again, I wouldn't think she existed."

"Hmm, that gives me an idea. There may be someone else I can chat with." Sarah scooped up the papers and told Jill she would be in touch in a few days. She left the store, a group of teens wandered in, and Jill was back to bustling.

Before she knew it, the end of the day was nearing. She tidied up, filled the small refrigerator, and was just about ready to head upstairs when the phone rang.

She grabbed the phone on the desk in the back. "The Tattered Cover, Jill speaking. How can I help you?"

Silence.

"Hello? You've reached the bookstore. Can I help you? Hello-o?"

That's odd, but bad connections happen occasionally. Maybe they'll leave a message later or try back tomorrow.

Without another thought she hollered for Salem and went upstairs.

Jill was boiling water and steaming some broccoli to make her garlic broccoli pasta when she noticed Salem on the couch purring up a storm. "What on Earth?" It seemed as if he was being snuggled and petted. He was butting his head against something unseen.

What the..? Oh, no! Nope. Not happening.

"Arvid?" she said in an authoritative tone. "Did you come home with me? We're going to have to talk about boundaries. You don't get to spend the night up here." She sensed movement and Salem abruptly stopped purring. "Not ok."

Letters formed in the steam covering the front of the microwave above her cooktop P-R-O-T-E-C-T-U

Jill sighed. "That's not a word."

She watched as the number 2 formed in the lower corner. "Two words? Protect U. Protect me?"

A 'Y' formed in the steam. Yes?

"Protect me from what? The alley door is locked, as well as the apartment door. I'm as safe as they get. I'll be fine. You can go."

Arvid was done communicating. Jill didn't know if he'd left or was hovering in a corner somewhere. The latter unnerved her just a bit.

She went back to making her supper then took a bowl to the living room to eat in front of the TV. Her apartment was quiet, and Salem seemed to be behaving normally. Maybe Arvid had gone.

Jill cleaned up her kitchen and started the dishwasher. Grabbing a book, she curled up on the couch with Salem and finished the latest best seller from her favorite author. She checked the time as she set the book aside. It was almost 10 P.M.

Jill went to the bathroom, washed her face, changed into pajamas, and checked the deadbolt one more time. Just in case. She didn't want to admit it, but Arvid's message had spooked her a little. Also, not knowing if he was still here unsettled her. Dousing the lights, she and Salem set off to bed.

Jill woke to the bleating of her alarm. She swung an arm out, turning it off, thinking the night had been uneventful. Arvid had been wrong. She started coffee, noticed Salem in his window seat, anticipating that first ray of sunshine, and went to get dressed for work while the coffee brewed.

It was supposed to be hot and humid, and she had a light load of boxes coming. Maybe a light sundress? At that moment, a pair of jeans fell off her shelf. She looked around the room, gingerly. Coincidence? Or Arvid? She picked up the jeans and figured they'd be just as good then grabbed a sleeveless top to pair with them. After dressing, she went out to the kitchen for coffee and toast. Jill took a minute to empty the dishwasher and put her dirty dishes in before looking around for Salem.

"Ready, bud?' she asked.

Salem simply rolled over and stretched.

Jill laughed. "Not today, huh? I don't blame you. I'll see you later then."

Grabbing her keys and her phone, she unlocked the deadbolt and reached for the knob. In the space of a blink, the deadbolt relocked. Taken aback, she unlocked it again, and as fast as she did, it clicked back in place again. What was happening?

She reached for the lock one more time. "Arvid, I have a store to open. Stop it."

She flipped the lock and opened the door, not quite knowing what to expect. Nothing. Just her staircase down to the alley. With a quick neck stretch she released the tension in her shoulders and made her way down. She opened this door with no interference from Arvid. She stepped into the alley and looked around. All seemed as it should.

Jill threw the door shut, turned to lock it, and erupted in screams. Attached to the door with duct tape was the creepiest porcelain doll she'd ever seen.

The doll's other-worldly, red eyes terrified her. She couldn't stop screaming. The neighboring building's door flew open and Ole Johannson came running out.

The sixty-eight-year-old grandfather was just as startled to see the doll but spun Jill around by the shoulders, away from the doll, and wrapped his arms around her. "Shh, shh, it's ok. I got you. It's ok," he cooed.

It took a minute for Jill to stop shaking and gather her wits. Arvid had been protecting her. Did someone try to break in last night or was the purpose just to scare her? What would have happened had they been able to get in? Would he have been able to stop them? The questions running through her head only seemed to make her feel worse.

Ole continued to calm her while wondering aloud what in tarnation could be the meaning behind this. Once he felt Jill was settled a bit, he said," Honey, we need to call the sheriff."

Ole walked Jill into the back room of the Rexall store and found her a chair. He made the call, gave a quick description of the problem, and came back to sit with her.

"Sheriff Sorenson is on his way. Any idea why that doll's up there?"

Jill shook her head. "No. Aggie was in a while back and said some odd things but I wasn't concerned about it."

"That doll doesn't seem to be one that Aggie drags around. She has her favorite three. I think it's different. You didn't hear or see anything?"

"Nothing. I don't know why anyone would want to scare me like that."

Moments later, Sheriff Sorenson's car could be heard in the alley. Ole stood and held his hand out to Jill. "Ready?"

They found the sheriff standing about four feet from the doll, hands on his hips. He looked toward them as they neared and said "Well, I never. Jill, you all right?"

"I'm not harmed physically. Scared half to death. Emotionally bruised. I guess I'm as all right as I can be."

"Can you tell me what happened?"

"I was coming down the stairs on my way to work. I opened the door, and when I turned to lock it, the doll was there. Staring at me. I was so startled I screamed, maybe a lot, and Ole came running to my rescue. That's all I know."

The sheriff asked Ole the same questions and wondered out loud how Ole hadn't seen the doll on his way in. Ole pointed to where his car usually sat and said he had a doctor's appointment at 11:00, so he'd come in the front that morning.

"Jill, has anything odd happened lately?"

"Like I told Ole, Aggie was in a while ago and said something about how 'he was talking, but I wouldn't matter' and that I 'shouldn't anger him' but wouldn't tell me anymore and left. It didn't make any sense, but she rarely does, so I didn't think anything of it. Come to think of it, I had a call at closing time last night that was dead air. That doesn't happen often. Otherwise, nothing that I can think of."

"You haven't upgraded the phone system since Evie had the place, have you?"

"No. It usually works just fine."

The sheriff smiled. "You'd have caller ID if you had. You may have been able to see where the call came from. Getting telephone records requires a warrant and a bunch of red tape, and we don't know if this is related. I'll start with removing the doll and see what Jonathon knows."

"Who?" Jill asked.

"Jonathon Warner, the antique store," Ole answered. "He occasionally has these creepy things come through his shop."

"Maybe he sold this one here to someone in town?" Sheriff Sorenson added.

He walked up to Jill's door and took photos of the doll and the surrounding area with his cell phone. He started to peel back the duct tape, muttering about creepy dolls spooking good folks and how he should be thankful there isn't more crime, when he let out a yelp. He jumped back, shaking his hand as if he'd been bit.

"You ok?" Ole asked.

Sorenson looked down at the fingers on his right hand. "Damn thing burned me!"

"What?" Jill asked. "How can a doll burn someone?"

"I don't know, but look," he said, extending his hand.

Sure enough, there were two small blisters forming on reddened skin.

Ole spoke first. "We should run your hand under cold water and wrap it up. I have some cream in the store we can use."

"Yeah, ...yeah. In a minute," the sheriff said, walking back to his car. He radioed something in then added, "as soon as backup arrives."

Minutes later, a fire truck descended on the alleyway. Sheriff Sorenson moved to greet it. He was out of earshot, but Jill could see him showing his hand to the firemen and pointing to her door. There was some nodding, and they dispersed.

The sheriff returned. "Ole, let's go look at these burns. Jill, we'll be right back."

Jill stood near the police cruiser as the firemen donned protective jackets, gloves, and face shields before producing some kind of metal bucket similar to what one would find near fireplaces for ash. Judging from the body language and movements of the men, the doll was, indeed, hot. They removed the doll and placed it in the bucket, then clamped down the lid.

As they walked toward Jill, Ole and the Sheriff rejoined them in the alley.

"Sheriff," one of the firefighters said. "You were correct. This thing is hot. We have it contained in a fireproof, airtight container but we are going to have to watch it. I don't think it's a good idea to open it right away. We'll examine it later to see if there's something inside it that would make it heat up. Doesn't really make sense, does it? You can see the scorch marks and blistered paint over there." He nodded toward the building. "Thankfully, that's a fire door, but for all intents and purposes, this looks like it was supposed to have started the place on fire."

More photos were taken before the alley was cleared and Jill's building was deemed safe. Sheriff Sorenson had a look around the store before leaving to make sure everything was on the up and up and assured her that he would get to the bottom of what was going on.

Jill was shaken. She put a sign on the front door letting her customers know that she'd be closed for the day and retreated to the back room. She slunk down into her desk chair, put her head in her hands, and let the tears flow. So many questions and emotions ran through her. Who'd want to harm her or the store? Why? What would make someone want to burn down the building?

She wiped her eyes, pulling herself together a bit, and noticed a random piece of paper with a heart drawn on it. "Arvid, thank you," she whispered to the air. "You somehow knew and you did what you could to help me. I'm grateful."

※

News travels fast in a small town. By noon, Jill received text messages from people concerned about her, or wanting the latest gossip firsthand, and both her cell and the landline were ringing off the hook. She chose not to answer either.

Instead, she got to work. She ordered a new fire door to be installed and called a security company. Cameras in the alley and alarms on the doors—all of them—suddenly sounded like a good idea. It would set her back a bit, but peace of mind was more important.

Mid-afternoon, the back doorbell rang. Jill checked the peephole and found Sarah standing in the alley. When she opened the door, her friend enveloped her in a huge hug. Sarah stood back for a second and examined Jill from head to toe.

"What the hell? A doll? I saw the mark on the door. That's insane! I heard you weren't hurt, but I had to come see for myself. You look a bit angry."

With a slight huff, Jill said, "I am angry. I was sad earlier and upset that someone would harm me or the store. Now, I'm more pissed. How dare someone try to burn down my grandparents' legacy. Where do they get off?"

"Well, I'm glad to see this side of you. I was afraid I'd find you crying in a corner. Tell me what happened. I want to hear your version."

Jill recounted the past twenty-four hours, still not really able to make sense of it, then waited for Sarah's inevitable questions.

"Arvid went home with you?"

Jill stared incredulously. "That's your takeaway? Someone may have wanted to kill me!"

"I know, I know," Sarah inserted. "I'm not making light of it, but it may have been worse if Arvid wasn't helping, if he hadn't gone with you. Also, what are the chances that it's connected to him? I think they're pretty good."

"I'm not the one doing the digging. That's been you; no one's bugging you."

"That's true, but they may want to get to the source. Arvid."

"But who?" Jill exclaimed.

"I happened to be looking into that this morning when I got a text about your discovery. The only person I could think of who's been here longer than Lottie would be the Talbot family, Robert to be exact, and the McKinleys."

"The mayor's dad? Doesn't he have dementia?"

"He does," Sarah nodded, "but I didn't think it could hurt. I started by just chatting with him. He's very child-like. I asked him if he knew of Fredrick Lapointe, and he said, 'Henry was a bad man.'"

Jill looked puzzled. "Henry?"

"Right? So I asked again if he'd ever heard of Fredrick, and he said, 'Stay away from him.' After that, he seemed to get a bit agitated, so I got out some building blocks for him to play with, and he settled right down. I decided not to ask anything more. No sense in upsetting him."

"You kind of have to walk on eggshells with dementia patients. I'm glad you chose to let it go," Jill added.

"My uncle in Nevada has dementia. I have limited knowledge, but I know at least that much about the disease. Since I was already at Blakewood, I decided to go see Mrs. McKinley. She had a stroke a while back and is as pretentious as ever. I told her who I was and asked if she had a minute or two to answer a quick question. She looked down her nose at me but let me talk," Sarah said, rolling her eyes. "I told her I was working on a project that had to do with the history of Effham Falls and that I was having trouble connecting a name. I mentioned Fredrick, and she immediately looked away from me, like she was deciding whether to talk to me or not. After a beat, she turned back and told me that Fredrick was the great-grandfather of Henry Lapointe and, like all the men in that family, he was nasty and violent."

"So, who is Henry, and what's the connection? Is there a connection?"

"Unlike you, I grew up here, and I can remember a big to-do when I was a kid about a murder. The guy was deemed insane and put in a mental hospital. I Googled what little I could remember and, low and behold, the man's name was Henry Lapointe. He's out of the asylum now and lives on the other end of town with his mother."

"No way!" Jill exclaimed. "So Fredrick somehow made his way here after the murder and made this his home."

"If you need a distraction," Sarah added, "we can get online and see what we can find regarding marriage and birth records. My question is, how can we prove that Fredrick killed Arvid?

"I don't think we do," Jill said wryly. "I think we plant a seed and let someone else run with it. What do you think about calling *The Gazette*, letting them know about the Arvid Jensen cold case, how I've been researching it, and that Henry's relative may have killed Arvid? The doll on my door is still hot news; we can add the connection and have someone else solve the murder."

Smiling, Sarah nodded. "That could work and takes the pressure off of us. I like it. Who do we call? Bennie or Joe?"

"Let's see which one calls me first for the story on the doll. I'll give them the details and see what shakes out."

Two weeks passed and things had calmed down. The doll did, indeed, belong to Henry Lapointe. Joe, from *The Gazette*, finally called to let Jill know the story was on the front page and that he'd drop a copy off for her. Arvid had been pretty quiet but was still around. Jill assumed he was waiting, also.

She was going to the store early, hoping to read the paper and see what was discovered.

"Salem, bud, you ready?"

Salem stood with a big stretch before weaving to the door. At the bottom of the stairs, Jill paused. She had to steel herself a bit every day in order to open the door, even though she had cameras installed and could see that the alley was empty. She'd seen someone hang the newspaper bag on the bookstore doorknob about an hour prior and was excited to see what they found.

Arming and disarming the alarms she had installed took a second or two but made her feel more secure. Salem wandered off toward the front window and his usual perch while Jill pulled up a chair at her desk.

"Well, Arvid, this may be it," she voiced to the room as she unfolded the paper. There on the front page was an old photo of Arvid and another of the doll that had been affixed to the door. Jill proceeded to read the entire article.

Frederick Lapointe had shown up in an Effham Falls saloon roughly two weeks after that historic blizzard. He eventually got together with a barmaid named Claire, who ended up pregnant. He was forced to marry and stay in Effham Falls. He continued to trap, hunt, and frequent the bar. Claire had three children with Fredrick. She'd stopped working and kept to herself. When Fredrick passed on, she was finally free to tell people of the abuse she and the kids had suffered at his hands. Claire also let it be known that Fredrick used to brag about how he'd killed once and that she'd better watch out. Her own son had gotten into a bar fight in his thirties and killed a man. He left a wife and kids to fend for themselves when he went to jail. Turns out that if you tracked the Lapointe men, every generation had a murderer.

The article went on to say that *The Gazette* had traced Fredrick back to the same sawmill as Arvid and that it was circumstantial, but likely, that he'd killed Arvid because he was jealous. Law enforcement had officially closed the case.

The doll taped to Jill's door was Henry's and even though Henry claimed to have no knowledge of how it got there, the officers surmise that Henry was trying to warn Jill to stop investigating. Henry has a history of mental illness, violence, and once killed a man himself. The doll had been disposed of by the fire department.

Jill paused for a moment. There was still no clear-cut way Henry would have known that Arvid had been talking to her or that she had been the one to initiate the investigation. How did the doll find its way to her door?

"Arvid, it's over. The world knows Fredrick killed you." Jill spoke to the air. "Now what?"

A soft voice near her ear said, "Thank you. Going home." And with that, he was gone.

"I'll miss you," Jill whispered to the already empty room.

Born and raised in Wisconsin, SUE QUINN transplanted to North Dakota in the late 80's. She raised her two girls in Fargo and is proud to see them take wing on their own. She is a full-time bookkeeper and part-time bookseller. When not busy with friends or traveling, she can be found writing or editing. She has her first official, published short story in *Tales from the Frozen North* but has more in the works.

Heart's Desire
T.J. Fier

A stinging gust of Minnesota autumn air blew up Addison's coat as she stopped dead in the middle of the sidewalk. Why was her mom calling? She knew Addison was on the way to the bookstore.

"Yeah, Mom?"

"We have to run to urgent care." Her mother's voice poured out in a rush. "You'll have to make yourself dinner again tonight."

A thick wet cough rattled in the background, along with her father's tense voice and the jingle of car keys.

"Is Dougie okay?" Addison held her breath.

"He might have a new infection."

"Didn't he just—"

"I'm sorry, baby, but we've got to go. You understand."

"Yeah, I—"

Her mother hung up without saying goodbye. Since his cystic fibrosis diagnosis at six months of age, her little brother had been in and out of the hospital almost monthly. Once Addison hit twelve-years-old, she begged her parents to stop dragging her along. By the age of sixteen, she knew the routine. Mom gone all night, and sometimes Dad. Another dinner of macaroni and cheese, alone in front of the TV.

"Fuck my life," she muttered, shoving her phone and hands into her pockets.

Addison dipped her chin into her jacket collar and hurried toward the local bookstore, The Tattered Cover. The smell of paper, dust, and coffee filled her nose as the bell above the door tinkled. Shelves of books towered high above her head, beckoning her from every corner as she rubbed her cold hands.

"Hey, Salem."

The ebony cat dozed in the front window display of new releases squeaked, slitting open his amber eyes, and gave a ruby-tongued yawn.

"How's my favorite kitty?"

"Hey, Addy," Jill shouted from behind the front counter. A stack of paperbacks nearly hid the petite woman from Addison's view. "What's your poison today?"

"The new one from Rainbow Rowell?" She scratched beneath Salem's fuzzy chin. The cat rewarded her with a motorboat of a purr.

"Oh, shoot." Jill popped out around the counter, surveying the display at the edge of the YA section. "I just sold the last one an hour ago. I'm so sorry. You want me to put in an order?"

Addison's already tight chest constricted further. Being stuck in an empty house at night wasn't so bad with a good book. Now what was she going to do?

As if on cue, a figure blew through the front door. Addison immediately recognized the bent-backed woman dressed in black from head to toe. The scent of clove, rosemary, and cinnamon shook from the older woman's long wool jacket. No one was quite sure how old Solveig Larsen might have been, but Addison guessed at least ninety.

"Hello, Solveig. How are you?" Jill said pleasantly.

"Out enjoying the first gusts of winter." Solveig's laugh was warm and rich despite the cracks in her voice. She bobbed her head in Addison's direction. "I had a feeling this one might be here." Two bright blue eyes shone from beneath a curling thatch of sterling silver hair. The ancient lady, less than five-feet tall, stood almost a head height shorter than Addison.

Addison let out a relieved breath. "Oh my God, I'm so happy to see you."

"Same, my dear. What's gone amiss?"

Addison and Solveig were Effham Fall's most unlikely pair after bonding last summer when the ancient woman found Addison dozing between the Tattered Cover's stacks, an open *Encyclopedia of 5,000 Spells* in her lap. Addison was exhausted after waiting another night for her parents to get home from the hospital. Solveig had plucked a volume from the shelf next to her head and murmured, "Try this one instead. The spells in here actually work."

After Solveig offered to show her how to cast, they became fast friends.

Addison vibrated with a mixture of relief and anxiety. "Ya see, Mom just called, and Dougie—"

"Urgent care?" Solveig's eyes twinkled, wreathed in wrinkled, paper-thin skin. "I had a distinct feeling I would find someone in need when I decided to pick up my latest order from Jill."

"I got it right here, ready to go." Jill hurried behind the counter and placed a paper bag on the polished but worn wood surface. "I might have stolen a glance at that beautiful herbology book. The illustrations are just gorgeous. Came all the way from Norway."

"A very dear old friend of mine wrote it." Solveig tottered over to the counter and lifted the volume from the bag. She ran a loving hand over the large, leather-bound book and opened to a page of a brilliantly colored illustration of an herb fringed in pink. "See this? *Dianthus superbus*. Reminded me of frayed stars as a little girl."

"Pretty." Addison's stomach rumbled. "Sorry, I haven't eaten since breakfast."

"Oh no. Would you like a ginger snap?" Jill hurried to her small coffee bar and plunked a cookie tin open. "It's not much..."

"No, no, that's okay." Addison rubbed her yawning belly. "I'm not a big fan of ginger."

Solveig studied Addison's drawn face. "Your mother forgot to pack your lunch again, didn't she?"

"It's not her fault." Addison shivered. The woman had a way of looking deep into the pit of her and sussing out the girl's deepest truths. "Dougie is having a tough month."

"More like a tough year." Solveig pressed her narrow lips into a tight line. "I'll take you home and give you a nice, hot meal. And it's a waxing moon, so," she dropped her creaking voice to a whisper, "it's the perfect night for a certain spell I've been waiting to show you. How does that sound?"

"Wonderful." Addison's empty stomach flipped. Lately, this casting had gone from careless dabbling with herbs and oils into more complex concoctions, including chants in Norwegian and fire. Last time they had written Dougie's name on an onion bulb and buried it with a stone, shell, and feather in the older woman's yard. They had hoped it might help alleviate some of his cystic fibrosis symptoms. The spell seemed to have worked until Dougie came down with a near-fatal case of pneumonia a month later.

"Well, then, let me pay the lady, and we'll head to my house." Solveig held out a wrinkled roll of twenties to Jill. "Oh, and please give Arvid my best. He seems especially out of sorts lately."

Jill's mouth dropped open. "I'm sorry, what?"

Solveig gave Jill a mystic grin. "Don't worry, my dear. You'll figure it out. All of it."

Addison glanced between the two women. "Whose Arvid?"

Solveig tugged Addison toward the bookstore entrance while Jill stared at them in stunned silence. "Never you mind, let's get some food in you."

Solveig's cozy Cape Cod stood at the corner of 7th Street and Orange, in the shadow of the magnificent turn-of-the-century behemoths further down the street. A dense hedge surrounded her yard, which provided the woman privacy when performing various rituals on her rear patio.

Despite the cold weather, Addison couldn't wait to cast. Solveig's spells always seemed to result in something unexpected. Once, they tried a spell to rid themselves of cravings for certain sweets. The following day, Addison woke with an intense desire for sour cream potato chips. Another time, Solveig attempted a spell to help improve Addison's poor clairvoyance. Addison smelled the wind the next day, predicted rain, and was rewarded with a day-long deluge that flooded Effham Falls and swept away two houses.

Who knew what wonderful, horrible things they might conjure that evening?

"That was delicious." Addison spooned the last delicious bite of Solveig's stew while one of the older woman's many kitties dozed in her lap. "My parents barely cook anymore."

"They're busy people." Solveig puttered around the kitchen, brewing a pot of post-supper tea, and gently removing a black cat from the counter while humming softly. "But every child deserves a hot bowl of stew the first cold day of the year." Solveig pointed to the empty bowl. "Want more?"

"Nah, I'm stuffed." Addison sat back, feeling a rare moment of contentment. She surveyed the woman's cluttered kitchen full of drying herbs, stacks of stoneware casting bowls, and piles upon piles of books. Some for cooking, most for magic. "I wish I could have dinner here every night."

Solveig poured two steaming cups of tea. "Do you remember the afternoon we first met?"

"Gosh, I'm not sure." Addison ran her fingers along the orange tabby's satiny spine. "Was it a year or two ago?"

"Yes. I discovered you weeping in the farthest corner of Evie's bookstore. Er, wait, I guess it's Jill's now." Solveig added a teaspoon of honey to each cup. "Anyhoo ... I can't stand watching girls weep so—"

"You gave me your handkerchief," Addison finished, a slight grin tugging at her lips. "And told me to put several garlic cloves in a bowl, cover them in vinegar, and put it under my bed while I slept."

"And you said?"

"'Would powdered garlic work?'"

Solveig chuckled fondly. "When I looked into your sad eyes, they reminded me of when I was a girl. I was a sad girl, too, at least until my great-aunt taught me her witching ways. I've waited years to find someone to mentor. Unfortunately, children are usually a bit frightened by me. But you weren't. Were you?"

"Why would I be scared of you?" Addison shrugged. "You're the only interesting person I've met in this stupid town. Well, I guess Jill isn't so bad."

"The feeling is mutual." Solveig placed a teacup in front of Addison. "Now, this tea is a little different from the other ones. I added a bit of saffron to help get your blood flowing. And this is a green tea to help with focus. We'll need that this evening."

"Why?" Addison took a tentative sip. She nearly choked. The bitterness seemed to punch the back of her throat.

"A little more honey?" Solveig dropped in another teaspoon before Addison could answer. "I've scanned my charts, and tonight is the perfect night for a spell I've meant to do for a while. Something potent to help us get through another bitter winter."

"What kind of spell?"

The older woman's eyes crinkled. "One to bring you your heart's desire."

Addison frowned. "Like a love spell? I don't exactly have a crush on anyone. Well, I guess Alex Olson is kinda cute."

"No, not a love spell." Solveig leaned forward, her watery, yet intense, eyes boring into Addison. "What do you want more than anything else in the world?"

"I have no idea." Addison sighed. But in the next breath, she immediately knew and felt terrible about what had come to mind. She covered the quiver on her lips with a gulp of tea.

"None at all?" Solveig smirked, and also took a long drink of her tea. "Well then, more magic for me, eh? Will you still help me? My arthritis is kicking in, and we have some herbs to chop."

"Of course."

"Good. Now finish your tea, and we'll get to work. The moon is about to rise."

"Is it time?" Addison shivered, clutching a sputtering white candle between her stiff fingers. The two women weren't allowed to wear jackets while casting because the discomfort from the cold enhanced the spell's power.

"Yes, my dear. It's time." Solveig lit the last two red candles, marking north and south. She rubbed her gnarled hands together, taking in each detail of their ritual. A silver bowl filled with rosemary sprigs, a penny, a silver knitting needle, and a piece of rose quartz sat in the center of a chalk circle drawn onto the ancient woman's back patio. "Now, one more thing."

"One more?" A plume of Addison's breath poured into the cold night. Just above the tree line, a waxing moon hung round and ready for their ritual.

"This is when I need you to be brave." Solveig reached into one of her deep pockets and pulled out a white mouse. For a moment, Addison was sure the little rodent was dead -- until its tail twitched and whiskers stirred.

Addison flinched and squeaked. "Where did that come from?"

"Had to drive all the way to Bemidji." Solveig stroked the mouse's back. "I gave him a drop of valerian oil to knock him out and rubbed lemon oil on his back to mask his scent from my kitties."

"What are you—"

"Brace yourself, child. This is about to get messy."

"Messy?"

Solveig plucked the knitting needle from the bowl and plunged it into the mouse's chest without ceremony. A stream of curses rasped from Addison's lips as Solveig dripped the mouse's blood into the silver dish. The rosemary sprigs wilted. The penny tarnished, and the rose quartz turned black as onyx.

"You killed it," Addison croaked, shivering harder than before.

"I did. Here, give me your candle." She tugged the taper from Addison's quivering grip, murmured a couple indecipherable words, and blew it out. "Now take my hands." Solveig calmly wrapped her blood-stained fingers around Addison's.

Addison's chest constricted. "The mouse. Why did you do that? *Why?*"

"Potent spells always require blood." Solveig's eyes shone black in the moonlight. "Now, repeat after me: Red as blood, black as night, goddess moon, give me my heart's delight."

"I can't, I—"

"Yes, you can. I need you, your power, your words. Focus, child. Say it."

Addison's voice came out in a whistling creak, but the words still poured forth. The moon shone brighter than before, and the cold air grew warm, melting her frozen toes, fingers, and ears, questing deeper and deeper. Solveig's voice lengthened, deepened, and richened into a bell-like tone as they repeated the words. The quartz turned from black to rose again. The rosemary sprigs smoked, and a thin tendril of black smoke curled above their heads. The candle flames lengthened, burning to twice their average height.

"Now, girl. What is your heart's desire? What do you want more than anything else?"

"I don't—"

"You do. If you can't say it, then sing it in your heart. Now, before the candles burn out."

The words Addison couldn't speak rang pure in her head and thrummed deep in her thundering heart. Solveig gripped her hands so hard she wanted to cry out. Tension built into a hot knot in her chest until she let out a breath she didn't realize she held.

"Yes. Good." Solveig released Addison's hands and threw them into the air. The ancient woman whispered a slurry of words in a foreign language, turned her face to the moon, and let out a delicate, creaking laugh.

The ache in Addison's chest immediately waned. A cloud obscured the moon, and the whole world seemed to fall silent. All she could hear was the thudding of her pulse in her ears and Solveig's satisfied sigh. A brief breeze whipped through the backyard and snuffed out the candles.

The two women sat in the moonlight until Solveig whispered, "Let's get you home. Our work is done."

Addison blinked awake, half-on, half-off her bed. She was never a peaceful sleeper, so the state of her bedding didn't surprise her, nor did the fact she had sweat through her flannel pajamas. She rubbed her eyes and grabbed her phone from the bedside table. Eight-forty-five? She was fifteen minutes late for school!

Where was her dad? Even when Dougie went to the hospital, her dad always tried to see her off to school in the morning.

A faint noise stirred from the kitchen.

Someone was home, but someone who didn't know to wake her up for school? For a moment, Addison considered calling 911, then thought better of it. No need to be hysterical. Sometimes her parents were a bit groggy after a night in the hospital. This wouldn't be the first time they forgot about her and her needs. She thought she might run down to the kitchen and remind them of her existence, then figure out her tardy situation afterwards.

She found her oversized father sitting at the kitchen table, turning a coffee cup around and around and around with shaking fingers. Red rimmed his puffy eyes, and he wore yesterday's clothes—now rumpled.

Addison hesitated before saying, "Hey, I'm kinda late for school."

"Addy. Sorry I didn't see you there. I was ... do you want some breakfast?"

"I don't think I have time—"

"Don't ... don't worry about school today. You're taking the day off."

"Day off? Daddy? What's going on?"

Clears his throat. "It's Dougie."

"Dougie?"

"The doctors had him stabilized. The meds seemed to be working. Everything was looking good. Thought he might be able to go home in a day or two. But then ... then he went to sleep last night and never woke up."

A wave of dizziness drove Addison into the chair across from her father. "Is he ...?"

"Yes. He's finally at peace and in God's hands."

"At peace." Addison's breath hitched in her throat. *What's your heart's deepest desire?* The question rang through her mind over and over on repeat. Solveig had tricked her. Hadn't she? Addison never meant for her brother to die. She only wanted her parents to remember she existed, and needed love, attention, and concern just as much as her brother.

Tears dribbled down her father's face. "It's gonna be okay, Addy." He rose from his chair, reached his big arms around Addison, and pressed her against his chest. The smell of the hospital still clung to his clothes. His sour coffee breath usually caused Addison to wretch. This time was different. This time he had nowhere to be but right here, holding her, consoling his only child.

Addison buried her face into her father's broad chest. "Yes, Daddy. It's going to be okay."

※

Theatre professor by day and writer by night, T.J. FIER's other works include the short story "Kelpie" in *Nothing Short of Terror*, "The Hunt" in *Tales from the Frozen North*, "Reindeer Games" in *The Colour Out of Deathlehem*, and the "EVP Session #454"* in the September 2021 issue of *Brilliant Flash Fiction*. Her debut novel, *The Bright One*, was released by Three Little Sisters Publishing November 2022.

The Nudi Alibi
Tina Holland

Kathy patiently waited for the City Council to open the floor. Her flyers had been printed up by Joe Schmau and he had passed them out beforehand.

"We will now open the floor for New Business," Mayor Richard Talbot called out.

Kathy stood and with each step toward the center floor podium, she was one step closer to the next phase in her life.

Cindy Swanstrom brushed past her. No, pushed or rather body checked was more accurate and impressive for the 4'10" woman of no more than 125 pounds. Cindy's quick strides ate up the distance to the center stage and she was out of breath by the time she arrived. "I want to discuss Kathy Balsam's Nudist Colony." She was waving a pink piece of paper — the color of Kathy's flyers.

Kathy increased her steps, though truthfully, she wanted to sink into a vacant chair. As she forced her feet forward, she caught a glimpse of the flier in Sheriff Craig Sorenson's hand.

COME OUT OF YOUR SHELL
AT THE
NUDI ST COLONY!

"Ugh." Kathy should've double-checked Joe's work. He might be fast, but Effham Falls had more than a few errors in *The Gazette* because of Joe's lack of caring. Now she would have to explain to the entire town that she wasn't running a nudist colony. Although given the righteous indignity Cindy held at the moment, she was tempted to say there was nothing in the bylaws that said she couldn't let people run naked on her property.

All this because she wanted to start over. To run a retreat for Artists. It was because she was bored. Her son, Sam, was off in the world. Her ex-husband had left years ago with that cocktail waitress from The Rusty Nail Bar and Grill when Sam had been about ten.

And she'd written the end of her final *Susan Law* mystery series, letting Susan go off into the sunset with Detective Diego Costas. Someone should have a happy ending.

Kathy reached the alcove of the Stage, and Flynn Stewart of all people sidled up next to her. "I always knew you had a wild side, Kate."

She bristled. "Flynn, you can call me Kathy or, if you forget, Mrs. Balsam will do."

"Mrs. Balsam doesn't look like someone who would open a nudist colony." His voice was warm and teasing.

"She's not. I mean, I'm not opening a nudist colony. Joe misprinted it."

"Well, you better get to explaining that before the end of the meeting. You certainly don't want Widow Effham getting a copy of the meeting notes."

"What are you doing here, Flynn? You don't come to town meetings."

"I'm looking to sell The BarFly and that has to be approved by the council. I'm finally leaving Effin' Falls."

"You're leaving?" Kathy was too startled to come back with some witty remark. Though she had never forgiven Flynn for dumping her before college, she couldn't really picture Effham without him. Truth be told, he served as an inspiration for Diego Costas in her mysteries.

"I can't stay here anymore. I'm tired of hearing Seymour Fairfax and his cronies telling crash story after repeated crash story. I need the council to approve the sale of The BarFly because Fairfax owns the airstrip."

"Good luck." Flynn would need it. Especially since many veterans considered The BarFly the unofficial meeting place since Effham had no VFW or American Legion.

"Yeah, you too." He nodded at the podium. "You better get up there. Cindy looks as if her head might fly right off."

"And furthermore, I dug up this bit of erotic porn that Mrs. Balsam wrote under the pseudonym, Kate Pine." Cindy's voice projected across the room.

Oh no. Not her romance. Kathy moved forward, but not before Cindy continued her tirade.

"Desiree's Delectable Desire!" Cindy held the book in the air, waving it like Father O'Malley did the bible during Sunday Mass.

Kathy's feet slugged along like she was walking through a swamp, but she finally reached the podium. "I'm not opening a Nudist Colony!"

Flynn was chuckling. She recognized his infectious timbre. A smile spread at the ludicrous nature of it all.

"How do you explain this?"

"For Pete's sake, Cindy. It's a goddamn typo."

There was a collective gasp in the audience.

"Maybe just a regular typo," Flynn offered up. "I'm not sure God printed it. As a matter of fact, this looks like Joe's handiwork."

Kathy glared at him while simultaneously relieved he was on her side. "Yes. I had Joe print them up as a sample. It should say Nudi Street Colony and they were only for today's meeting. I'm nowhere near opening up."

"What is it? Some kind of mumbo jumbo commune?"

"It's going to be a retreat center."

"For nudists?" The woman reminded her of a terrier with a sock. Never surrender without a fight and a whole lot of teeth.

"No, artists and writers. There are no nudists."

"How do you explain this?" Desiree's bodice-ripping cover waived like a banner of war.

"I don't. I wrote it. It didn't sell so I moved on to the *Susan Law Mysteries*, as you all know."

There were collective nods.

"Will you have these types of authors at your retreat?"

"And what if I do?"

"Well, we shouldn't allow those sorts of people in our town."

Cindy spoke with renewed vigor, but Kathy could tell she'd lost the audience so she went for the jugular. "We can't stop tourism."

"Do you think it will bring tourists?" Prudence, the owner of the Wayside Motel, asked.

"I hope so. My plan is to convert my barn into a hall. It could also be used for local events. Then I'd like to convert my granary into a small cabin. Eventually, I'd like to run a B&B. Not right away," she assured Prudence. "And of course, any workers from out of town will need a place to stay."

The motel owner nodded.

"Are there any other concerns you have?" Kathy inwardly winced.

"What kind of permits are you looking for?" Mayor Talbot asked.

"I'm not sure. It was one of the reasons I wanted to inform the town of my plan."

"I'll send Ed out to your place."

Kathy nodded and stepped down. She hoped this would be the last she'd have to see of the place.

Who knew Kate would become a famous mystery writer? Her books were damn depressing though. All of Susan Law's love interests were either murdered in the first five pages or they were the killer. Except for this last one. In the *Law of Averages*, Susan ended up with Diego. Rumor had it this was Kate's last book. Flynn hadn't read them all, but he would have Jill order some into the Tattered Book Store. He needed to get his hands on *Desiree's Delectable Desire*. It must've been a while ago. Kate had gone by Kathy ever since Frank left.

"You're next," Sheriff Sorenson nudged him.

"I'm here seeking the town's permission to sell The BarFly."

If people thought a nudist colony caused an uproar, that was nothing compared to the sale of one of Effham's three bars. He could barely hear himself over the din of yelling.

"Kate! Wait up."

Kathy turned, figured Flynn wouldn't just let her leave. Though it didn't really matter. He e would be leaving soon enough for the both of them.

"Are you really starting up this retreat?"

"I am."

"Why?"

"I'm done writing. My agent wants me to take up another genre but I'm over it. I think my proverbial muse needs a long overdue break." It was probably more information than Flynn wanted, but too bad.

"Are you really done? You're so good at it."

She was done tiptoeing around people. "You think you know what I want...no, need better than I do?"

"Well, I— "

"Everyone thinks they know what I want. You, my agent, my publisher, Sam, and even town busybody Cindy. I've had enough. I finally get to do what I want." She'd been advancing on him until they were blocking the door to city hall.

"Oh good. You're still here." Mayor Talbot spoke to her as he opened the door. "The city council would like you to put together a class."

"Why?" Kathy and Flynn said simultaneously.

"We'd like Kathy to host a class so we might better get an idea of what we are looking at. If you could have something ready by this coming Saturday, that would be ideal."

"That's in five days!" Even she heard the panic in her voice.

"The town has faith you can do it. I'll have Ed and Chief Sorrell stop over to make sure you are good to go with the codes."

"I can check out the wiring for Don and give him a report."

"That would streamline the process. Thanks, Flynn," Mayor Talbot answered before walking away.

"You just couldn't resist putting your nose in where it doesn't belong, could you?" Kathy threw the words at Flynn.

"Hey, I'm just trying to help you out. If you want the Chief to stop by, so be it."

"No. You're right. Does Wednesday work okay?"

"I can stop by tomorrow."

"No, I have my last signing at Jill's."

"Fine. Wednesday, then."

Kathy walked into The Tattered Bookstore. Under her arm, she carried a tote filled with bookmarks, fine-tipped Sharpies, and her laptop.

Jill greeted her. "Thanks for doing this."

"No worries. We've had it scheduled for months."

"I know. But after your announcement on Monday, I'm expecting a larger turnout."

"Really?"

"Everyone knows this is the last Susan Law mystery, so I suspect we will get a larger than usual crowd."

"You'll order more though, right?"

Jill wouldn't meet her eyes.

"Is everything okay?"

"I hope so," Jill said before she walked away to greet the customers who entered the store.

Overall, the signing went pretty well.

"So, you're given up all this to run a B&B?" Chief Sorrell said as he handed Kathy his book.

"That's the plan," she answered.

"A shame really. I was beginning to like that Detective Costas character." The Chief mumbled as he walked away.

Ed Jane sidled up to the table. "Can I have one?"

Kathy grabbed a book off the stack. "How would you like it made out?" She pasted a smile on her face, wondering what odd thing Ed would request.

He put his hand to his chest before speaking. "To Ed, my friend and the inspiration for Diego. Sincerely, Kathy Balsam."

She gave him an odd look. Given his glass-covered blue eyes, pale skin, freckles, and fading red hair, his comment made no sense. "You don't look remotely like Diego Costas."

He put his hands on his waist. "You don't know. Women could crawl all over me if they thought I inspired him."

Kathy shook her head and wrote the inscription.

"Thanks."

"No problem. By the way, Flynn is coming by tomorrow to do an inspection. Do you want to drop by as well?"

He clutched the book to his chest like a small child with a bedtime story. "What time?"

"Nine."

"I'll swing through closer to ten. I'm overseeing a couple other projects."

Her book stack dwindled, the last customer gone, and the door locked behind them, Kathy breathed a sigh of relief.

"By the way, I received a few orders for *Desiree's Delectable Desire*," Jill said.

Relief was replaced by fluster. "Oh God, who?"

"I'm not at liberty to say. Bookstore/reader confidentiality." Jill smirked.

"Oh, please." Kathy waved her hand. "I won't tell you my next writing project."

"I thought you were done?" Jill asked, tilting her head slightly.

"I was but I'm feeling cozy mysteries coming on."

"That's wonderful."

Kathy leaned forward. "So, who ordered *Desiree's Delight*?"

"Well, your usual local fanbase."

"You are avoiding the question."

"Well, Flynn ordered a copy."

"Really?"

"Why does that surprise you? He's read all your books. He's usually right up front when half the town shows up after a new 'Susan Law' shows up in my shop."

"He wasn't here tonight." Not that he showed up at any of her signings.

Jill shrugged. "He already bought his copy."

"He did?"

Jill scooped up the remaining *Law of Averages* books and brought them to the front counter. "He has to be your biggest fan. When I got to the store, he was one of the first people who asked if all your books were in stock. He let me know I was running low before I set up the computer system."

Kathy didn't know what to say to that, "So you want to come up to what will be The Nudi Street Colony?"

"Isn't that just for the town council?"

"I don't think so. Besides, I could use a friendly face."

Jill scanned the books. "Okay. It's not as if I'm doing anything else."

Flynn arrived at the Balsam Farm and found Kathy waiting outside her house, coffee cup in hand and tapping her foot. He turned the key in the ignition and just watched her. He wasn't late. They hadn't actually set a time. Why did she look so impatient?

No sooner had he stepped out and she said, "Where were you?"

"We didn't set a time." He didn't bother to hide his confusion. "I thought you'd be here at nine."

He looked at his watch. "It's nine fifteen."

She pulled her phone out of her back pocket. "See, you are late."

Flynn just shook his head. "Fine, fine. Let's take a look at the space."

He walked around what was once a pole barn used to store lumber, hay, or equipment, but hadn't been used for much of anything since Frank left. He pounded on the metal. "You gonna insulate this?"

"Not before the weekend."

"I meant eventually."

"Yes. I will likely make most of the improvements recommended by you or Ed."

"Good. Just so you know, fire sprinklers are now required in places of public accommodation, but only for occupancy of three hundred people or more," he said.

"I will probably put those in any way to protect my investment," she said.

"Once you do, I would recommend annual fire inspections like the rest of Effham's businesses. It'll be just as easy to add you to the annual list."

"Sounds like that would go a long way to keeping the peace."

"If you do all that, there's no reason you couldn't host weddings and the like as well."

"And deal with bridezillas and the like? No, thank you!"

"Oh sure, leave the rest of us to suffer."

"Really? The BarFly is a mecca for weddings, is it?"

"Yes," he said without preamble.

She shook her head and mumbled, "Yeah, right."

"No, really. You know that custom where the wedding party steals the bride and groom? They either end up at The BarFly or The Rusty Nail."

"It's been so long I forgot that stupid tradition."

"Well, you guys never did it."

"We were too young."

"You were too young. Barely eighteen. Frank was older."

"Yeah, twenty-two. A college boy." She fanned herself.

"Was that the draw?" He couldn't help but ask, wondering how he lost Kate to dumb ole' Frank.

"That, and he was interested."

"I was interested."

"You were a football star. I was your study buddy. That was never going anywhere. And you only noticed me after I was smitten with someone else."

She wasn't wrong. He was more interested in chasing skirts and dreams than making any connections in this Effin' town. He had hoped to leave years ago on a scholarship, and he would've if he hadn't screwed up his knee senior year at the homecoming game. After that, he wallowed in grief and, rather than keep up his studies, he barely graduated. "I'm sorry."

Her head swiveled back to him. "What?"

"You're right. I was an ass, and I should've continued studying rather than push you away. At least I finally have a chance to make things right."

She moved closer. "How?"

"I'm selling that bar and gettin' out of Effin' Falls."

Kathy didn't know why she let herself think Flynn was talking about her. "You don't need to leave town to make a change."

"We can't all be smart and successful writers like you, Kathy Balsam."

She heard the sarcasm in his voice. "No, we can't."

Ed Jane entered her barn. "Have you already done the fire inspection?" he asked.

"Actually, the building will be fine as long as she doesn't exceed two hundred and fifty people, although Kate is planning on updating even though it isn't necessary to meet current fire code," Flynn said.

"Very good. I actually don't have anything for you either. Because your property is nearly sixty years old, I believe we'll be able to grandfather you in. Before you begin any projects just stop by townhall and we'll get you the appropriate permits."

Kathy shook Ed's hand. "Thank you."

"No problem. I'm looking forward to Saturday's class." He walked out the way he came.

"Uh, sure." Ed's comment made her think she should probably get a head count.

"You okay, Kate?" Flynn asked.

"Yeah, I'm fine. Look, are we done here?"

"I guess."

"Good, cuz I gotta get going. I have a class to get ready for."

"Do you need any help?"

"Do you want to pick up the supplies?"

"I can. Where at?"

"Rexall Drug. I called an order in. Ole has it ready. I also had stuff printed at the Gazette."

"Not Joe!"

"No, Bennett handled it."

"Can I get it and come back?"

"Can you come tomorrow? And help me set up? I have to get started on the class stuff."

"Sure. See you tomorrow."

※

Flynn arrived early the next day and Kathy was decent enough to make him some bacon and eggs to go with his coffee.

Once finished eating, he said, "I'll go grab the stuff from my car."

"Great. I'll meet you out at the barn."

Flynn walked the short distance to his car and managed to get all the papers and folders in one trip.

"I could've helped you," Kate said when she opened the red door.

"I've got it," he said over the top of the papers he carried.

"Set them here," Kate said.

They proceeded to set up some folding tables and chairs in a classroom style facing the back of the barn.

"Where'd you get all these?" Flynn asked.

"The fire hall. Donald dropped them off last night after the signing. And Ed brought over an old projector they had at city hall, but I don't think I'll need it since I've got all the slides printed out."

Flynn looked at the stack of paper he brought in from his trunk. "What now?"

Kate pulled papers and folders from the stack and set them up assembly-style on the front table. "We're going to put these folders together, so they are all nice and neat for the commission." She pulled a folder, pried it open, and began placing the three-holed papers in before adding lined paper to the back.

Flynn followed her lead. After they'd been at it awhile, he asked, "So why mysteries?"

"Are you serious?"

"Yeah. Why did you stop writing romances?"

"Besides the fact they didn't sell?"

"Yeah."

"Well, after Frank left, I admit that I wasn't feeling much like romance, so I had this idea of a female sleuth who came from a family of lawyers but never wanted to become one. Besides, there are so many weird things that happen around here."

"I hadn't noticed."

"How could you not? There was that incident at Quarters when we were kids, and all those dolls pinned to houses a while back. Nobody has ever seen the Widow Effham, but we all know about her. Like I said, weird."

"Oh, yeah. So this is the next step?"

"Yep."

"Why not take up romance again?"

"Writing, no thank you."

"What about actual romance?"

"This from Effham's eligible bachelor." She gave him a wry grin.

"I don't know how eligible."

"Oh please. That dark brown hair and eyes, those muscles. and not to mention a business and homeowner."

"My business and home are both The BarFly."

"And the bar gives you immediate access to women who probably want to cash in on your all-American good looks," she scoffed.

He moved closer to her. "You think I'm good-looking."

"I-" She tripped.

Flynn caught her. Once she was righted, he couldn't resist. He kissed her. She was as warm and soft as he imagined. His heart beat faster, and he gripped her as if she might slip through his fingers.

But her hands were pushing him away and she was stepping back. "I think you should go."

"Katie, I—"

"We're done here. Just go!" She pointed toward the door.

Not wanting to make the situation worse, Flynn walked towards the door.

Kathy wasn't certain what woke her up. It was likely the light. She could see shadows playing along her wall and thought it was car lights, but her bedroom didn't face the road.

She shot out of bed and ran to the window. Her barn was on fire! "No!" Running down the stairs and out the back door, heedless of her bare feet or state of dress, she stared. Far too long. Dashing back into the house, she grabbed her phone off the charging pad, pressed 9-1-1, and gave the operator her information.

Her efforts were in vain. The flames licked and devoured her newfound dream as she sat in helpless wait.

Flynn drove as fast as the old logging road, AKA Nudi Street, would allow. He was close. The airport and BarFly were at the bottom of the hill Nudi Street was on. The fire hall was in town, and it would take them longer to arrive. As he approached the top of Nudi Street, he saw the blaze cresting the treetops. "Dear God, I hope she's okay."

His first thought had been Kate when he heard Nudi Street on the scanner. He wasn't sure what he would do if he lost her. After yesterday, he decided he wanted, no, needed to stay in Effham Falls at least long enough to explore what lay between them.

As he rounded the last section of forest toward Balsam Landing, he saw her pole barn engulfed. He noticed the house was fine when he pulled up. However, the owner sat in her pajamas, head in her hands, her small shoulders shaking. Flynn couldn't reach her fast enough.

"Kate." He was out of breath, even for the short distance he'd just come.

Her eyes were bloodshot red. "It's all gone. Everything."

He looked to where she pointed and, sure enough, the granary was burning. So was her unused chicken coop. He was about to ask her what happened when Chief Donald Sorrell pulled up in his city-issued fire pickup truck.

"Woo-wee, that is quite a fire!" Sorrel sauntered over to where they stood.

"Jesus, Don! A little sensitivity. Kate's buildings are burning, for Pete's sake."

"Sorry." Don kicked the dirt with his toes. "Unfortunately, we are gonna have to let it burn out." He nodded at the two fire trucks arriving. "As soon as we can, we'll get these contained."

Three hours later, the rag-tag fire department had managed to contain the three structures to smoldering mounds of warped metal roofs and charred lumber. Kate's house was safe and, more importantly, so was she. She'd watched the entire event unfold in silence. Flynn was worried about her. He wanted to talk to her.

Sorrell walked over with a clipboard to where Kathy sat. "Kath, I'm real sorry about your buildings, but I think now is the best time to fill out this report."

"Don, she can stop by in the morning." God, Sorrel could be an insensitive S-O-B.

"It is morning." Kate nodded to the sun peaking just beyond the trees. "Come on in, I'll make some coffee."

"And eggs?" Sorrel asked.

"Coffee will be fine," Flynn interjected before Sorrel had Kate relegated to the kitchen.

Kate raised an eyebrow.

Sorrel nodded and followed them in. Once they were settled at the dining room table, the Chief started questioning her right away. "Did you burn last night?"

"No."

"Campfire?"

Kate shook her head.

"When was the electrical last inspected?"

She shrugged. "When Frank was around, but I'm just guessing."

"Faulty wiring then." Sorrell checked something on his paper, inhaled the last of his coffee, and stood.

"Faulty wiring? How is that possible?" she asked.

Flynn stood. "Ed was just out here yesterday. He told Kate she was grandfathered in."

Kate rolled her eyes.

"Did Ed say that?" Sorrell asked.

"He did," Kate said.

"Faulty wiring wouldn't account for all the buildings." Flynn waved his hand towards the collapsed buildings.

Kate's worry lines deepened. "He's right."

"What else can it be?" Sorrell asked.

"Arson," Kathy blurted without thinking. Not thinking, but something didn't feel right about the fire.

Both men looked at her and then turned as Sheriff Craig Sorenson entered the house.

"Craig, come in. I'm glad you're here." Kathy was relieved to see him.

"Hello, Kathy. Chief, Stewart."

"Why are you here?" Don asked as he stared hard at Craig.

"Just a formality. Wanted to make sure Kathy, er, Mrs. Balsam, was okay and investigate any possible wrongdoing."

"It was faulty wiring," Don insisted.

"Kate thinks it was arson," Flynn interjected.

"Do you?" Craig asked as he flipped out his notepad. "Why is that?"

Don threw up his hands. "I'll tell you why. Because she's written too many damn mysteries. Kath, leave this to the professionals."

Craig nodded. "I agree with Chief Sorrell. Leave the investigation to the professionals."

"I'm glad you can see sense, Sheriff." Don stood taller and puffed out his chest.

Craig put his notebook in his back jean pocket. "I'm nothing if not logical. Now let's take a look at these buildings and see what happened."

"I just told you it was faulty wiring."

"Sorrell, I don't tell you how to do your job. Let me do mine," Craig said then exited the house.

Kathy followed the men. Was she getting ahead of herself? Was it an accident?

"Nope. Definitely looks suspicious." Craig had his notebook out again and was writing.

"How so?" Flynn asked.

"See how the ground is saturated from here to the house."

"My men just hosed everything down."

Kathy nodded. They must have pumped thousands of gallons onto the fire from the hookup.

Craig took a step, lifted his foot, and stepped again. Water seeped from under his feet. "I see that, but it doesn't account for the sponginess of the soil by Kathy's home."

They walked around and, sure enough, her soaker hose was on.

"Did you turn this on, Kath?" Don asked.

"No! There's been no reason. This is one of the first days it hasn't rained."

"That's likely why the canopy didn't catch fire," Don surmised.

"Thank God," she said. She couldn't imagine the guilt if her buildings had started the forest on fire.

"Which begs the question of how the fire started and spread." Craig made more notes before flipping his notebook shut and putting it in his pocket. "I'll be in touch."

"Me too." Don gave her a two-finger salute before leaving.

Both men walked to their vehicles and drove down the road. The fire crew had left long ago. Kathy moved back to the safety of her house and sat on the porch steps. "What am I going to do now?"

"You can host down at the BarFly."

She looked at Flynn. "You wouldn't mind?"

He gave her that boyish grin she remembered from long ago. "Of course not. I'll be glad to help you set up too. We sort of fell into a rhythm yesterday."

"We did, didn't we?" The tension in her body since the fire started subsided.

"Certainly. Meet you down there." He looked her over.

She realized she was still in her Edgar Alan Poe-themed raven jammies. "Yeah. I'll see you down there."

Kathy and Flynn had finished setting up The BarFly about twenty minutes earlier. Kathy sat and looked over their handwork. It sort of looked like a PTA Meeting set up in the gym after prom.

"What are the streamers from?" she asked.

Flynn sat down next to her on the stage. "Veteran homecoming."

"Oh. That's nice."

"They are. Usually, the celebration starts out with the whole family here. If you look out front, I think you'll see that we still have some of the lawn games set up." He pointed his thumb in the direction of the road.

"That sounds wonderful for the families."

"It's one of the highlights of owning this place." He shook his head. "I wish more weekends were like that and less of all these old codgers getting lit three sheets to the wind and reminiscing about the good ole' days."

Not wanting to dwell, Kathy stood. "Well, I suppose I better head back and reprint everything for tomorrow."

"Do you need to print it?"

"I guess I could just read off my laptop. Lord knows it'll save me on ink."

He pointed to the ceiling. "Could you use the projector?"

"Yeah, yeah. I could. Does it use HDMI or what?"

Flynn walked to the side of the stage and lifted a curtain next to the stage. There was a small panel of buttons. "Not sure. The whole thing was refitted last year when that Texan, Buzz Caulfield, flew in. He paid for all of it."

Kathy watched as Flynn started randomly flipping switches. Stage lights came on and off, changed colors, and then the jukebox switched on. The song *Every Rose Has Its Thorn*, by Poison, began belting through the speakers.

They both stopped and stared. It wasn't really their song, but it was one they had both liked even though it was an odd choice for a love song. As if on cue, the light system cast red roses about the room in a dancing pattern.

Kathy was so mesmerized that she hadn't noticed Flynn tap her shoulder.

"You want to dance?"

"Are you serious?"

He offered his hand. She took it and placed her arm on his shoulder. His hand held her waist.

They began an informal waltz, but as the song continued her hands wound their way around his neck, and he cradled her waist in both of his. The song was in its last stanza, and there was barely any space between them. The music stopped, the dancing roses stopped, and silence filled the air.

Kathy wet her lips and looked up at Flynn's tousled brown hair. She heard his heart beating. Or was that hers? The way he was looking at her... Would he kiss her? She was brave enough to admit she wanted him to kiss her — again.

He lowered his head.

She stretched up on her tippy toes to meet him halfway.

"Excuse me."

They both turned to see Sheriff Sorenson in the doorway.

Kathy was relieved Flynn still held her, otherwise she might have fallen. Once she steadied her nerves, she tapped Flynn on the shoulder, letting him know she was okay.

He released her and walked toward the sheriff. "What can I do for you, Craig?"

"Came here when I didn't find Mrs. Balsam at home." He nodded at her.

She walked toward both men. "Why did you need to talk to me?"

"Well, seems you were right about the arson."

"I was?"

"Yep, turned out to be the chief."

"What?" both she and Flynn exclaimed.

Sheriff Sorenson hid his thumbs in his front pockets. "Can't say I'm surprised."

"You're not? I am." Flynn said. "I never cared for Donald, but I never thought he could burn down a structure."

"I did," Sheriff Sorenson replied. "This wasn't the first fire I suspected he started, but it was the first where he wasn't as neat."

"What do you mean?" Kathy asked.

"Well, for starters, he called your fire in before you did. That red-flagged him in my book." Craig waved his notebook. "I also suspected him of the fires near Harm's Way and one near Seventh Street."

"Why would Don do that?" Flynn asked.

"He was helping the owners collect the insurance money."

"I didn't have anything insured. I assure you I did not hire him to burn my buildings." Kathy didn't want to be accused of arson, even if she was the first to suggest it.

"I know that, Kathy. He had an entirely different motive for you."

"He did?" A cold chill went down her spine. Part of her wanted to know what Donald's motive was, but the larger part of her did not.

"It was probably why he wasn't so careful."

"What do you mean?"

Craig flipped through his notebook. "He left his fingerprint on your water spigot at the house. I have it on file, and I was pretty pleased to find a print that didn't belong to you. So, unless he's been watering your garden..."

"No! He hasn't," she assured him.

"Why did Don do it, if not for the insurance money?" Flynn asked.

"He's sweet on Kath." Sheriff Sorenson shook his head.

She threw her hands up in the air. "That makes no sense."

"I agree. When I asked, he said he hoped you go back to writing mysteries," Craig said.

"He's in custody?" Flynn asked.

"Yep, about the last thirty minutes or so. Actually, the reason I came here is I need you to come down to the station with me and fill out some paperwork."

Kathy nodded and followed him into town. Who would've guessed the fire chief was an arsonist?

※

Kathy hit the remote and clicked on the last slide in her presentation. The room was packed, and it did look as if most of the council and PTA were there. "Any questions?"

Cindy Swanstrom's hand shot up.

"Yes," Kathy said, acknowledging her.

"Is it true Chief Sorrell burned down your house?" she asked.

"Yeah, and how did he do it?" Ed Jane asked.

Kathy did the only thing she could. She surrendered the stage to Sherriff Sorenson, then she went to the back, sat at the bar, and ordered a Roscato Red.

Flynn handed her the nearly full glass. "Looks like it went well."

"I don't think they heard a word I said." She nodded at all the hands flying.

"Just do it again."

"Where? I can't keep tying up your bar."

"I won't be here much longer."

"Oh right, you're leaving." She wanted to forget that after the kiss they shared. She stared into her wine glass.

"Not right away."

She raised her eyes to meet his. "Really?"

Flynn rested his forearms on the bar across from her. "After yesterday, I thought I'd stick around for a bit."

"What about the BarFly?"

"Oh, I'm still selling it. As a matter of fact, Cindy made me an offer."

"Really?" Kathy squinched her face at the idea of having to work with that pit bull of a woman.

"Besides, I think I have something a bit more rewarding than bartending in my future."

"Yeah?" Kathy took a sip of her wine.

"Mayor Talbot offered me a position as temporary fire chief until the council votes on it next month."

"That's great. Where will you stay?"

He shrugged. "I can get a room at the Wayside."

"Why don't you stay with me?" she blurted.

"Katie! What will people say?"

She punched him in the arm. "I don't care."

He raised an eyebrow.

"I have three extra rooms."

"You're sure you don't mind?" He grabbed her spare hand.

She gave him a side-long glance. "I don't."

He kissed her hand.

"Why'd you do that?"

"Cuz I can't reach your lips over the bar."

His comment left her speechless. She got a warm tingle near her heart. She set down her glass and walked around the bar. Not even paying attention to the townspeople. Kathy walked right up to Flynn, wrapped her arms around his neck, and planted one on him. It was better than the other day. He was warm and safe. She hadn't felt that connection since high school. "I missed you, Flynn Stewart."

"I missed you too, Katie."

"You inspire me to write again."

"Yeah?"

"I'm still working on a title in my head. The Mystery of Love?"

He made a distasteful face.

"The Love of Mystery?"

He grinned. "How about the Nudi Alibi?"

"Perfect." She kissed him again.

TINA HOLLAND studied journalism at university, then went to work for a Fortune 500 company, working in logistics for over twenty years. She now writes full-time and helps her husband run his crop-dusting business in the summer months. When she's not writing she likes to travel, read, and spend time with family and friends. You can find more of Tina's work on her website, www.tinaholland.com

I Don't Know You
Silvia Villalobos

Light glistened through the frost-covered trees, sparkling like glass. The last sun rays spilled over terrain covered in snow. From behind the wheel, Emma shivered at the sight. *How could anyone live here?*

Effham Falls, the sign read. Minnesota. She'd been driving north for the past eight hours, almost to the Canadian border. A familiar ache settled in the back of her neck. Emma dug in, kneading hard. She might reach old age driving like this.

The oldest woman on earth lived in Effham Falls. Or so she'd heard. There was a connection between lower body temperature and increased longevity, some *Insights Magazine* study read. She'd bet on the stillness of time, instead. On giving the soul a chance to have a say out here, far from the world.

A line of cars slogged past in the opposite direction. Smart people, escaping winter while she headed into the frigid air.

The highway became a bumpy road, then a slush road. Emma turned into the third lane after the sign. *Leads to Main Street*, the woman on the phone had said. *Then to your right, dear, second building after the cemetery.*

Emma hung another turn, drove through the intersection and past the snow-covered graveyard. This was the very definition of being adrift, and good enough to think about laughing. Adrift in the wide-wide world. Circumstances dictated the drifting; the rest was an act of faith. Or an ailment.

There was no curing the wanderlust syndrome. Only ameliorating the symptoms. At eighteen, she'd left for Argentina on a year's worth of minimum-wage savings, controlled by urges to travel the world. In truth, it started at twelve when she'd followed a saleswoman ten blocks from home. When spotted, she'd run back confused by the frissons of thrill.

Emma had since stopped trying to be normal. Maybe the din of everyday existence had grown too loud. She longed for the simplicity of constant movement, away from San Diego, from everyone and everything she knew.

All of this is my fault, Mom had said. *I'm sorry but it is.*

To take the sting out of it, she'd half-hugged Mom, then stopped by Jenny's for sugar-filled road snacks and banter before jumping on the I-15.

The wind whooshed past, shaking the car. Emma tightened her grip on the wheel. Now that the sun had dropped in the sky, she could barely see ahead.

The Wayside Motel sign illuminated only *Ay* and *Mo*. A thin figure stood by the door, waving. Emma waved back, unsure. She stepped out of the car but stayed put.

"I'm Prudence," the figure said with too loud a voice. "You must be Emma."

The motel lady she'd spoken with on the phone. Overdoing the hospitality, wasn't she?

Even from ten feet away, Prudence emitted the potent scent of mint, pepper, and sugar, along with something acrid Emma couldn't place. Dressed in all black, she would have blended into the shadows, if not for her silver lightening eyes.

Then Prudence smiled. "Welcome." Her face lit up like a candle, keeping the darkness at bay. She motioned and hurried into the red brick building.

⁂

Emma made her way through the entrance filled with people wearing football jerseys. Men with shaggy beards, missing months of haircuts. Women far from girly-looking, with spray-painted hair. Coats sat piled on chairs like shed skin. Football playing on TV. One man, his face painted as if ready for battle, screamed at the screen.

They quieted when she brought in the cold air, first appraising then dismissive.

Emma followed Prudence to the counter, a key laying out in plain view. "Room Two, dear." She fixed Emma with eyes that looked like snow skies. "Up the stairs and to your right."

Then Prudence busied herself with paperwork, the new guest forgotten.

Small-town mysteries best left unsolved.

Emma had left home with one objective: Go someplace cold. The chain islands off the south coast of Iceland in the North Sea had a pull on her wandering spirit, but not on budget and sanity. So, Minnesota it was. Northwest Minnesota, where the oldest woman on earth lived. Where she'd heard that, Emma couldn't recall, but among memories like fleeting wisps of smoke, this one was seared into her brain.

The place smelled of sandalwood and mint. For a moment, Emma wished to hide and watch. A stranger, observing the ways of this town and its people. The TV volume pounded against the walls, far and near, the tone a tremor in the frame of the floor. She took in the mass of people and sea of faces. Everyone's attention was on the game, whether standing or sitting, silent or shouting. A varied collection of football buffs.

She panned across the room and froze into the spot. Heard something drop. The freakishly tall man leaning against the wall, steps from her. She knew him. She'd recognize him anywhere.

"Roman. What are you doing here?"

Brief silence moved through the room, followed by whispers and eye rolls.

Emma tried an apologetic smile. Small-town people were awfully polite.

Her fling from Ensenada peeled himself off the wall and stepped closer. His jet-black hair, parted to the side, fell over his eyes. Roman pushed it aside with his fist.

"Sorry." His eyes took on a sharpness, then a blank look. "You have me confused with someone else. My name is Drake." Roman tipped his head, his smile tight; no recognition in the dark eyes. He picked up the key she'd dropped and set it on the counter. With another nod he turned and sauntered away.

The morning started like all countless others when she was anywhere but home. Confusing at first. *Where in the world was this place?*

Crowded and cold, with a faint smell of mint. A sink in the corner and mirror hanging above. Fishing art hung on the wall in contradiction with the frigid air out there.

Wayside Motel in Effham Falls.

She fluffed and plumped her pillow. Sat up to look out the window at gray clouds against blue sky. With summer a distant memory, this was reflection time. Or so she'd hoped.

Last night played in Emma's mind like a film reel. Over and over, setting her new world spinning on its axis after a three-day drive.

How strange, that a man who didn't have a starring role in her life could hurt her.

Why pretend? One reason came to mind, and what shitty luck. Of all the places she could've gone, where winter made its home, she'd wandered into an old fling's lair. With her luck, Roman was the local football coach, adored and idolized, and happily married.

She sat at the edge of the bed. Outside the window, a snow-covered road sneaked past. The sky grew gray and threatening again. Winter had turned the town into a forbidden place with trees like skeletons, bereft of leaves. The cemetery, its tiny plots on mounds, looked like a snow-covered vineyard from up here. The quiet side of town.

Emma kicked the blanket aside and pulled on her jeans, shirt, and sweater. She ran through morning rituals with memorized speed. Life was too short to waste on tedium.

She applied lipstick in the mirror. Out of habit, and to cover pale skin. If her thirties brought anything unwanted, it was paleness. Emma concealed the purple circles under her eyes with a drab of foundation and added more lipstick. Something to busy her hands. She clipped her brown curls back, away from her face.

Prayed that there was coffee downstairs.

She'd hauled herself here to wander the woods, test her pain threshold to cold long enough to ask herself again: *How do people live here?* She came to get away, giving herself a half-baked reason like learn about the oldest woman on earth. But what if Roman led a quiet family life here? Should fling and family life have intersected, that could be awkward. She did not come for awkward.

"Coffee?" Prudence was already pouring, stealing glances at Emma.

"Thank you."

A soundtrack played in the background. Incidental music with a soothing piano flair. "Party's over, I see."

"That was for the game, dear." Prudence reached under the counter and produced a heart bracelet. "This fell out last night, when you dropped the key."

Her engraved bracelet, a gift from Mom. "Oh. Thanks."

"Drake found it under the table."

"Please say thank you for me."

"I thought you knew each other."

Emma fumbled through pockets, busying herself with nothing. But Prudence was patient. "Just seeing things after a long drive."

"Mm-hmm."

"If I see ... Drake, I'll thank him." Emma looked around the room. "I'm sure everyone's home with their family. Frying bacon for the kids." She sipped her coffee.

"Kids are brats, dear, and families a drag." Prudence gave Emma a long look. "Drake agrees. But in his line of work, one learns life's too short to waste on noise."

He'd never shared his line of work. She'd never asked. Tacit agreement between short-time lovers.

A group of women hobbled down the stairs, books under their arms. Pleasantries exchanged, they floated out the door as one entity of loud voices.

"Guests at Nudi Street Colony." Prudence grabbed a rag and started wiping the counter. "Writers' retreat."

What a soothing thought, a writers' retreat. Like a blanket to wrap around and luxuriate in its warmth.

"Starts tonight," Prudence said. "Kathy Balsam runs it. We form a circle, close our eyes and listen to one reader at a time, music in the background. It's balm for the soul."

From the corner of her eye, Emma caught sight of a dog padding closer, tail wagging.

"Hi there."

"That's Doozy, the retriever. Belonged to an old friend who passed on."

Doozy came to sniff, head tilted as Emma oohed and awed. Then, as if on command, the dog bolted to the farthest corner, barking at nothing. Stopped, padded in circles, barked again.

"Dogs sense more than our reality." Prudence kept polishing the wood, bent on removing the shine all together.

"A sixth sense?"

"You don't believe so."

Emma smiled, lifted her shoulders. She could think of a hundred reasons dogs barked at empty corners, none having to do with ghosts.

"Thanks for the coffee." She excused herself with a smile.

"The eatery's around the corner." Prudence said. "The antique store past the church, and if you keep going, the park." A telling look. "Men play basketball there."

No more needed to be said.

Emma buttoned her coat and stepped out into a cold that cut through layers of clothing, settling deep into her bones.

Welcome to Effham Falls. Strolling the street may render spirits identified by dogs. Or men playing basketball, an old fling among them.

The wind whipped past, scattering snow through the air. Piling it on doorsteps. Brick buildings lined the road—a post office, a general store. No cars and only a few people milled about wrapped up in winter coats and scarfs.

If she kept going, she'd find the woods on her own.

Years of traveling and solitude had succeeded in erecting a wall around Emma's heart. She didn't much care about people's take on her. No sense getting mired in opinions. *Normal* was an illness, the way she saw it. When asked about the *normal* things—marry, start a family—sarcasm proved the wrong answer. She'd wade through idle chat, change the subject, endure strange stares.

But this? A man who'd passed through her life pretending not to know her was a curiosity to satisfy. If she'd said something insulting during their week-long fling, now was the time to apologize. Clear up the air. Move about the world without leaving bad feelings behind.

The aroma of freshly baked chocolate chip cookies drifted through the cold air, bringing a fleeting sensation of warmth and comfort.

She wandered past an old train track, taken aback by the hills in the distance, peaks covered with snow. She caught a few stares that morphed into wide grins when she made eye contact. Did anyone dream of moving to the city, or were they content in slowdown small town? No wonder the grumpy looks.

Helluva thing to come to terms with, living in a town most of the state didn't know existed. Or maybe not, if that was what they'd always wanted. At least they knew what they wanted.

She walked past the church and antique store before coming upon an opening that could've been a park, a make-shift basketball court taking up the whole space. Several men were shooting around and, on the sideline, a few others high-fiving.

No Roman.

She turned behind a line of snow-laden trees and hurried along the road. In the distance, the tower of another church came into view. Small towns, she'd heard, had more churches than anything else. Except, maybe, liquor stores.

A bouncing sound came from behind. Emma whirled and faced a man in fleece jacket and beanie hat pulled down to his eyebrows, dribbling a basketball. Roman. Or Drake. On his way to join the basketball team.

"Good morning." He kept his voice quiet. "Out and about in the cold."

"You too, I see." Her breath trembled like the surface of water shuddering along a breeze. There had been nothing more than desire between them. But that was the thing with desire. It gave our bodies a mind of their own, bypassing thoughts, creating its own world. That was the awe of it—and the terror.

He gave her a look she knew well, only guarded now. "Usual 'round here, Sunday morning basketball. Good for the frozen bones."

Emma noted the day of the week. She hated tedious memory notes.

"Prudence has your bracelet." His eyes remained distant.

She choked out a nervous laugh, showed him her bracelet-decorated wrist. "I'm sorry if I said something wrong."

Silence.

"Did I make a stupid small-town joke?" She pointed around. "Whatever it was, I didn't mean it."

"I don't know you."

Words to lacerate the heart.

"I'd like to help," he said. "But I don't know you."

She stole a glance around, then lowered her voice. "August in Ensenada." She rolled her hand to drag him down memory lane. "The motel. Room Ten, after drinks at the bar across the street." She let out another nervous laugh. "Are you going to make me spell it all out?"

"Sorry." A beat of silence. "I didn't get your name."

"Emma." She stamped her foot. Caught herself and laughed.

"Emma." His eyes were dark and steady. "I'm sorry, Emma."

Roman's friends emerged from behind the line of trees, white clouds of breath floating around in the cold air.

"Enjoy your walk." He tipped his head and jogged toward his friends.

The cold sent numbing pains deep into her bones. Across the road, a short woman with red hair had stopped to gawk. When Roman left, she moved along. A car rolled past.

Emma shoved her hands deep into her pockets, ambling back toward the motel. She would not enjoy her walk. Not after this talk.

※

It wouldn't rain, that part Emma remembered well. The clouds would gather high in the sky, reflecting sunset colors, but they would not release the moisture begging to become rain.

The memory came disjointed, like a dream. Every conversation had been about rain, about clean, breathable air.

Then something happened that day. There, the dream broke into pieces, so many tiny fragments. She'd ended up sick. Mom had cried. When she didn't cry, Mom had looked ready to burst into tears. She'd walk through the house asking some invisible entity: Why?

A dream, or nightmare, only it always visited Emma during daytime. More like a memory. One associated with the bad taste of something that made her sick, with chunks of time missing, with migraines, all going back to the day when it wouldn't rain.

A knock pulled Emma from her reverie. The door opened, letting in bursts of sound.

"There is a photo-booth event in the town square." Prudence stood in the doorway, the big smile back on her face. "Live music and food if you'd like to come. Right after church."

Emma cleared her throat. Her voice had gotten used to little talking. "Thank you."

Prudence closed the door without another word. She hadn't pried since Emma's arrival. Not once. They'd hammered out her stay details over the phone. *Stopping by for a few days,* Emma had said. Prudence had asked arrival time and how she took her morning coffee. Take that, small-town-curiosity storytellers.

Emma's hand went to her heart bracelet. Why would Roman pretend not to know her? Was their weeklong fling a blip so faded on his radar it was completely gone from thought? Was that how he moved about the world—use, discard, forget?

I don't know you.

That wasn't the man she'd made love symphony with until dawn. They'd talked about keeping in touch, exchanged numbers. Back in San Diego, Emma had thought about calling once or twice. Roman had never called. With time, thoughts of him were tossed into the bin of memory, no regrets or grudges left behind.

But she hadn't forgotten.

Feigning ignorance over knowing a name he'd screamed out during sex—why?

I almost forgot how to breathe, Emma.

She pulled out her phone and hit a pre-programmed number.

Three rings later, Jenny's singsong voice came on. "Where are you, wanderer?" A chuckle.

"Minnesota. Effham Falls."

"Sounds cold."

"I have a question."

"That bad, huh?"

"Remember my Ensenada trip in August. Me talking about the guy I met there?"

Silence. Long, unsettling silence.

"Jenny?"

"You meet guys everywhere you go, Emma."

"But you remember me telling you about this one guy."

"Sure. This the part-time singer?"

"That was a long time ago. Why do you keep bringing up the singer?"

"'He had an angelic voice, and soft hands that explored every inch of my skin.' Your words. That's an unforgettable visual."

"I'm talking about Roman. There hasn't been anyone since. Sure you remember."

Silence again, then Jenny's hesitant voice. "Sure."

"Jenny."

"No, okay? I don't remember you talking about a Roman."

"You don't remember?"

"You must've taken pictures, selfies," Jenny whispered. "Remember him that way. Why is this important?"

"You're right. I'm sorry."

Something banged in the background, then a muffled voice. Jenny had company.

"Listen, I gotta go." Emma hung up.

She opened the phone camera, heart pounding. There'd be no pictures. She never memorialized moments with pictures. Kept everything in her mind's eyes, there for her recall only. The sole photo on her phone was Mom, a gesture of goodwill more than anything.

She tossed the phone across the pillow.

What drew her to Effham Falls? A pull, a want, a curiosity. What better than a small town in early winter, the perfect setting for a wandering soul?

She groaned at the sound of the alarm and reached out to grab the phone. Mom's picture flashed on the screen. A different kind of alarm.

"Hi, Mom."

A shuffling sound, then Mom's voice came on. "Oh, I was getting ready to leave a message. Is everything okay? You never answer my calls."

One day she'd stop telling Mom about her trips ahead of time. "Just fine."

"How is the town?" Mom sounded unconvinced. "People treating you well?"

"There's a nice lady managing the motel. Odd but nice."

"Odd how?"

"Do you remember me talking about a guy named Roman a couple of months ago?"

Silence fell like nightfall, all consuming. "Why are you asking? Have you had migraines again? Emma, you need to call a doctor."

"Stop. Please." She hadn't had migraines in years. Would've loved to forget that period in her life, but Mom would never let that happen, would she?

"It's gibberish talk, Emma. You have to watch out for gibberish talk, the precursor to migraines. I told you. The doctor told you."

The doctor told her people experienced changes in speech during a migraine, but only fifty percent of those studied. That was years back.

"Mom, stop. I'm thirty-one. And I'm fine."

"Why are you asking about a guy?"

If that was what it took. "I knew this guy Roman. Met him in Ensenada in August. We hung out, had a few drinks, had fun. Then we went our way and now ..."

"He's there in Minnesota?"

"Yes. Do you remember?"

"How would I? Is he bothering you?"

"Nothing like that. Just a bumping-into-an-old-acquittance thing."

"I'll call you tomorrow." Something in Mom's voice caught Emma off guard. "Please monitor your symptoms."

Symptoms she didn't have. Emma hung up, clear on one thing—she wouldn't answer the phone tomorrow or any other day.

Get out. She had to get out of this room and out of her own mind, where no one had answers.

Just then, the church bells tolled.

The man wearing a cloak danced around a bonfire. Four women near him clapped and tapped their feet to the song.

Dance like no one's watching, Emma heard it said, and the man embodied that perfectly.

Tables stacked with platters of ribs and corn and potatoes lined one side of the road. The smell of barbecue and spices permeated the air around the square.

A three-piece rock band was working through *Eye of the Tiger*.

In the town square, portable metal booths sat in the middle of the road. Giggling youth ran in and out, covering their mouths while laughing hysterically. A group of elders watched nearby.

Prudence appeared at Emma's side. "Wanna try a silly photo?"

"Thanks, no. Is this a yearly event?"

"Our Wacky Winter Fest."

She'd arrived just in time. If she rolled her eyes harder, they'd pop out of her head.

A circle of kids ran around them until Prudence shushed them away. Townsfolk milled all about. In the middle of the square, an old lady covered in blankets sat in a wheelchair playing a six stringer.

"Is it true the oldest woman in the world lives here?" Emma asked.

Prudence half-laughed. "Our claim to fame, but she lived on a farm outside of town. We all tell the story wherever we go."

Emma waited for a follow up that took forever.

"Bonny finally died last month." Prudence looked away. "The oldest woman on earth, but no one really knew how old. Story goes 124 years old."

Bonny was a story they told wherever they went. It hit Emma just then. Roman had told her the story. That was what subconsciously drew her here, to this particular winter town.

She wasn't going crazy.

When Prudence stopped to chat with someone, Emma meandered aimlessly. She came upon the dancing circle again. The dancer had gone, but the women stood by the fire.

"You must be Emma," said a round-faced woman with David Bowie hair. "I'm Kathy Balsam." She handed Emma a cup with something dark red. "It'll keep you warm."

"The Nudi St. Colony Zen master."

Kathy laughed an all-out laugh, her eyes two laser beams on Emma's face. "You can call me that. What do I call you, then?"

"Just Emma." She smelled the cup contents. Simmered wine with sugar and spices. Strong.

Kathy laughed again. Anyone with Bowie hair was okay with Emma.

"Come join us at the Colony," Kathy said. "We worship the written word. The untamed prose." Blunt laughter. "Bold and untamed." Kathy articulated the words as if she'd just invented them, birthing their meaning into the world. Rolled them in her mouth like something delicious.

"Thank you."

"Do you write?"

"I tried in college. Inspiration is fleeting nowadays."

"When the muse leaves me, I listen to people tell their stories. Like Jill, our bookstore lady and, before that, her grandmother Evie who talked to Arvid, the ghost. Oh, and Drake has got stories, too."

"Drake?"

"You've met?"

"Briefly. He ... was at Prudence's for the game last night."

"Our grave digger, Drake. Not his real job, just helps the groundskeeper." A hearty laugh. "Grave digger who gets hired out of state for odd jobs. Great stories he tells."

Emma felt disoriented, as if the ground could not hold. He'd said little outside philosophical absurdities to her. He'd mostly listened.

"Storyteller ...what kind of stories?"

The wind picked up, slamming into them. Kathy moved closer to her group. "Everyone, this is Emma."

The trio murmured their helloes in unison.

Kathy grabbed a stick and stirred the fire, Emma's question gone in the gale of wind.

People said small towns were suffocating, with everyone in your face. Not in Effham Falls, where folks played hard to get.

The women pulled Kathy into their conversation—a plot to bring back the cloak-cape dancer. Emma set the cup down and wandered in the opposite direction, away from the commotion and music.

She wanted answers. The need to know burned within her, leaving her taut and unrelenting. She ambled past the stop sign and the bench. Searched for towering figures with jet-black hair in vain.

The road twisted up ahead, leading past Main, past the cemetery. She couldn't be more than a ten-minute walk from the woods, the open skies out there, the ability to see for miles. Maybe not tonight, in the biting cold, but soon.

She picked up her pace and started jogging to warm up and calm her overthinking mind. There was peace in movement, the faster the better. Peace and time to hear herself think.

Chunks of her time with Roman faded in and out of memory. Conscious reality overwhelmed by old memories. Mind pops came and went, distorting everything, like intrusive old thoughts—a child wandering on a winding road, getting lost. Then found. Mom crying. People fussing over her. The bad taste of something that came with headaches. She'd never asked about those days. What if it was all in her mind?

At the lamp-lit crossroad, she increased her pace, immersed in the utter silence away from Main Street. Everything was silent but for the whistle of wind.

Something moved in the distance. Under the lamp, the silhouette of a man standing on the curb. Black pants, boots. Jogging created the illusion of being safe. But in reality, she was more exposed than ever.

She kept on, giving the intersection a wide berth. Considered a turn around. But the figure under the lamp could reach her in any direction. She shook the tingling feeling from her arms and ran in a semicircle, ready to head back without making it obvious.

The silhouette stepped right under the light. A man with a slight stoop, as if too tall for doorways.

In that instant, Emma saw Roman's eyes. Or eyes that looked like his. He held on to something midair, a phone maybe. Clouds of cold breath swirled, rendering him more an apparition than real. He turned and hurried into the night, toward the cemetery.

Shadows stretched in the distance, then darkness. A darkness so intense it pulled the curtain over that side of town.

Emma's breath came short, the center of her world off balance. Instinctively, she held out her arms to regain equilibrium before the absurdity hit like a two-by-four. She was standing in a world that had hardly ever made sense.

She jogged back, turning to look behind. Nothing stirred.

I don't know you.

He'd looked right at her, then turned and disappeared into the night. Like he'd disappeared from everyone's memory. Everyone's but hers.

Emma massaged her forehead, replaying Ensenada through her mind.

She had taken one of her week-long jaunts, that time to Mexico. He was there for a fishing trip. They'd met in a bar, had drinks, and ended up in her room at El Camino Motel. One night led to two, three. A whole week. They would always arrive late at night. No security cameras, she remembered that detail. But someone must've seen them together.

※

Prudence sat on a chair with Doozy at her feet. "You look like you saw a corpse."

The woman had a way of seeing right through her. Or Emma wore all the universal emotions on her face.

She tried a smile.

An unsettling silence sprung between them, punctuated only by Doozy's heavy breathing.

Music played in the background. Music with no soul this time. Just there to fill the space, the time.

They stared at each other for a moment, like in a frame of film caught in the projector.

"Why don't you sit down?" Prudence sprung to her feet. Guided Emma to the chair and pulled one for herself. "Another daze moment?"

"What?" Was it her or had someone cranked up the heat?

"I saw you earlier, in your room. You were in a halfway world, between dream and reality. The world of memories."

Emma let out a laugh-cry.

"Is there a memory, Emma, that keeps you from moving on?" Prudence flashed her bright smile and pulled the chair closer. "I can help you."

Words wouldn't come. Emma let out a moan, which may have been mistaken for agreement. At least it wasn't so hot anymore.

"If you keep an open mind, I can help. Semi-lost memories that terrorize us can be retrieved. It will help you move on."

Emma nodded, still unable to talk.

Prudence hurried to the back room and returned with a cup smelling of cabbage and sage. A combination so potent and familiar it gave Emma vertigo. She struggled to focus.

"Hold this token."

Emma did, trying not to scoff.

"Drink the tea, and I'll say the spell."

Why not? What if she had been meant to travel here for this reason?

"Now close your eyes."

She complied, half scared, half excited.

Prudence mumbled unintelligible words for some time, then said: "Go back to when you were very young. When everything changed. Think about the pain that came to you and try to feel that pain."

Emma nodded.

"You may have been in a daze ... things were not clear. Something severe may have happened. Try to dig deep, to feel it, see it."

Emma pushed herself through the steps. But she couldn't focus. The taste had left her mouth dry.

"You may have been following a winding road." Prudence's voice grew quieter, the edges softening. "Something or somewhere new. Like in a daze. And there was confusion when ... when you snapped out of it. See it? Feel it?"

Emma summoned all her will to *see* whatever Prudence insisted that she see. The images wouldn't form.

"There was someone. She hugged you, comforted you." Prudence's voice was shivering. "You had questions... but young, so young. She told you everything will be okay over and over and that buried the memories. The reassurances, the avoidance buried the memories. There was guilt and the treatment, the herbs, maybe ... no one had answers. All those questions and no one had good answers. But the reversal herbs ..." Prudence was crying.

Emma opened her eyes and set down the teacup and token. It took a moment to find her voice, to find the courage to ask. "You knew everything about me before I arrived, didn't you?"

Prudence wiped her eyes.

"What's this old memory I can't remember?" Emma scoffed. "Your spell pretense was awful."

Silence.

"Tell me, please."

Prudence looked at her with gray eyes glossy with tears. "I promised, but I can't carry on like this." Her voice faded into a shape shifting note of regret.

"Tell me, Prudence."

"It shouldn't be me who tells you."

"You already started under the pretense of some spell."

Prudence searched the room as if for an escape. But nothing saved her. She shook her head for some time, then stopped and cleared her throat.

"You just started meandering as a child. Walked out of the house and kept going. Like in a daze. Some people ... medical people said it could have been from a concussion. As a child, you may have fallen and suffered a concussion."

"What?"

"There were no answers to why you would just start wandering. Sometimes far away from home. In the absence of fact, myth took over. Some thought a possible head injury may have activated what psychologists used to call the wanderlust syndrome, meandering in a daze. A constant wandering. It continued as you got older, but more focused."

"Traveling is not a medical condition."

"It's not just traveling but an urge to drop everything and go. Look up the Jean-Albert Dadas story in 1860. He suffered a concussion and would go into places without knowing. The family would find him two towns over."

"I don't ... I didn't do that. Good God, that's a story from what, 160 years ago."

"Since nothing scientific explained or cured it, herbs were suggested, reversal herbs that could help, but ..."

But also harm.

A mixture of sage and cabbage and some root smelling herb. The potent smell she couldn't scrub off her senses. Reversal herbs.

Prudence was back in full cry mode. "I broke the trust."

Emma stood and paced. Doozy followed for a while then returned to Prudence.

"Did my mother talk to you?"

Silence for a beat. "She worries, with good reason since you drop everything and leave to places unknown for weeks at the time. She connects it all to the past. Yes, your mother called me when you mentioned Effham Falls. She's been hiring people to look after you for some time."

The floor dissipated beneath Emma. She felt herself floating in a great nothingness as the walls vanished. Soon there would be nothing but pulsing music, there to fill space and time.

She's been hiring people to look after you for some time.

In the absence of facts, myth and lies had taken over her life. Everyone was in on the lie — Mom, Jenny. The hotel receptionists, tour guides, waiters and strangers in bars.

Roman, who'd crossed the line. Oh, how he'd crossed the line.

She wanted to scream. Go to her room, lock the door and pull the covers over her head. Turn off the world. She wanted to burst like a seed pod and reclaim a different space for herself. Let the breeze blow through every fiber, cleansing it anew, and putting it back together.

Prudence gave her an out. "How about the reading at Kathy's?" Her eyes were tired and nothing more.

As if the plan all along, Prudence slipped into her coat and out the door, leaving it open. A few seconds passed and then the distant whir of a battered old car engine started in the distance. Gusts of wind whooshed through the trees.

Emma followed into the zero-degree temperature. What else was left to do but get out into the freeze and chase down a fanciful dream?

After all, life may be only a dream.

SILVIA VILLALOBOS lives immersed in the laid-back vibe of Southern California. She writes mystery novels and short stories. Her debut novel, *Stranger or Friend*, was published by Solstice Publishing in 2015. Her short stories have appeared in *The Riding Light Review* and *Red Fez*, among other publications.

The Come Hither

Donna R. Wood

1953

Alice needn't look up from the ledger. She knew Widow Effham was approaching by the sound of the shuffle of hard-soled shoes. Alice hated the shuffling. It grated on her last nerve like fingernails on a chalkboard. Why? Why couldn't the woman just pick up her feet when she walked? Honestly, it isn't that hard.

The heavy black purse landed on the counter with a thud, startling Alice. "Widow Effham, good morning. What can I get for you today?" The sight of the widow sent shivers down Alice's spine. The widow was a small woman with a skeletal frame at best. From underneath the sleeves of her bodice, her slender, bent, and knotted fingers jutted out like Swiss army knives. The widow had given up wearing gloves some years ago. If she couldn't get them on herself, she wouldn't wear them at all, and that was the end of that. No one had laid eyes on the widow's face in just as long, if not longer. The wide-brimmed black hat, covered in a sheer black veil made sure of that. Alice was quite certain that she didn't want to see what was hidden under the veil anyway.

The widow didn't make a sound. She simply pointed with her boney finger at the items she wanted from the shelf: a small bag of sugar, a bag of flour, a pound of table salt, and a can of tuna for her cat, Wilbur.

"Will that be all?" Alice asked in her kindest voice. There was a part of her that felt sorry for Widow Effham, who lived alone in the old Effham house at the end of Main Street. Alice, like everyone else, was unsure of exactly how old Widow Effham might be. It seemed as though she had just always been there. In fact, Alice remembered Widow Effham from when Alice was a child. She didn't look any different than she does now, and that was forty-three years ago come December.

Coins clanged and clattered on the counter as the widow pulled each one from her purse. Somehow, the widow always knew exactly how much the total would be. After dropping the last coin on the counter, the widow turned and shuffled her way back out the door, paying no attention to the goodbye Alice had called after her.

2022

Lottie Effham rocked back and forth as she watched the comings and goings of the townspeople from behind the curtains in the small house on the edge of town. She pulled her shawl tight around her shoulders and gave a shiver as the north wind seeped in through the window.

When Jacob was alive, Lottie would sit and rock in that same chair for hours, waiting for him to come home from the mines. Only then, there was a sense of excitement and anticipation. Now, it was just waiting. Waiting to live, to die, or become nothing at all. Wilbur climbed into her lap and curled into a ball, purring while Lottie pet him to sleep.

Lottie let her mind wander back in time to the place where she was happy, and loneliness did not fill her days. Jacob had been a fine man, a fine man indeed. Her heart had been ensnared by that strapping Scotsman ever since she had first laid eyes on him back in '03. Her ma and da didn't take a liking to him until he struck it rich here in the Iron Range of Minnesota. And that's when all the trouble started.

Ma had come from a fine, noble English family – if in fact the English had ever really been noble. But Lottie's thoughts digressed. Ma…? She liked the finer things in life. Things that

Da couldn't give her out here in the 'Devil's Domain', as Ma called it. Under the lush brush of the Minnesota hills, there was a redness that reminded Ma of the teachings about Hell. Oh, Ma was certain that every man, woman, and child on the range was destined to wake up in Hell come Judgement Day and the saints be praised, she wasn't going to be among them. Everybody else, but not her. She viewed herself as a pious and right-living woman, and it had been her righteous duty to point out the short-comings of others every chance she got. In fact, if it hadn't been for Ma there wouldn't be a church in Effham, and all would be damned for certain. That's the way Ma had seen it anyway.

The townsfolk, however, saw it in a whole different way. Ma's screechin' and preachin' didn't do anything more than put the come hither on Effham, and many believe it to be true and certain to this very day. Ma's meddlin' in the affairs of the townspeople drew a line right down the center of town. Those believin' Ma's rantings on one side, and those who thought her a raving lunatic on the other. A line never to be crossed again.

Da, on the other hand, was a simple man, who enjoyed simple things. After a hard day's work in the mines, he enjoyed a hand of poker with his whiskey down at the saloon. Ma could never understand how he could associate himself with the rabble-rousers and the ne'er-do-wells on the wrong side of town. She warned him. Oh yes, she had warned him time and time again to mend the error of his ways, or there would be Hell to pay.

Lottie crinkled her bent nose and pursed her thin, dry lips. It was Ma's fault that she had been sitting in this lonely room for so many years. It was Ma who had not only put the come hither on Effham, but on Lottie herself. Destined never to lay eyes on Jacob again, and to live until the flesh drops off her corpse and there's nothing left but bones to carry her weary soul through the world. Then after that, she would wander the streets of Effham with only faint glimpses that she was even there at all.

It had been New Year's Eve in '05 when Lottie and Jacob became Mr. and Mrs. Jacob Effham. It was supposed to be the happiest day of her life. Ma had had other ideas. In the privacy of Ma and Da's home, Ma did it. She openly and unashamedly put the come hither on Lottie, so strong and so powerful, it could never be undone. She stared Lottie straight in the eyes – soul to soul – and mustered all the anger and resentment her heart could muster, and declared with a wicked smile, "I wish you long life and good health. May you never know the comforts of death."

Some say Ma was only trying to spare Lottie the horrors of an eternity in Hell for her misdeeds. Others said Ma was overtaken by a demon from the very Hell she feared. And yet, still others said that Ma was only doing the Good Father's work. At the time, Lottie hadn't given her mother's words much thought. Lottie's love for Jacob had been strong, fierce, and blinding to any misgivings or disapprovals that her mother may have had.

Jacob had been good to Lottie, despite Ma. He had built her this fine home with his bare hands. He employed an upstairs girl, and a downstairs girl, a maid, a cook, and a butler. A small giggle escaped from Lottie's still pursed lips as she remembered the Model 36 Jacob had bought her back in '09. Ma was absolutely livid. Not as livid as she had been when Lottie took up cigarette smoking, but livid just the same.

There had been a such a ruckus in the driveway in front of the house, Lottie had run out to see what was happening. There was Jacob in the driver's seat of a Model 36, blasting the horn — Ah-ooo-gah! Ah-ooo-gah! He had it special ordered just for her and had placed a bright blue ribbon on the hood. Jacob had had such fun teaching Lottie how to drive it. They zigged and zagged up and down Main Street until finally Lottie got the hang of it. Lottie Effham was the only woman in town who knew how to drive an automobile, and she secretly enjoyed flaunting the fact. Oftentimes, Lottie would drive the car to the old general store a few doors down from her own house, just to be flashy.

Lottie's heart sank into her stomach as the wonderful memory faded to black, replaced by the greatest loss of her life – Joseph. He had been a good lad. Always minded his mother, and his manners – especially when Ma was around. Joey would tag along whenever Lottie would take Jacob his lunch at the mines. Those mines! Those unrelenting, unyielding, cursed mines that always seemed to take more than they offered in return. Her pride and joy. Her sweet and precious baby boy, taken in '11. Lottie had never been the same since. She would often linger in his room, untouched for one hundred years, just to feel close to someone...anyone. Lottie spent many a year rocking in the chair and cradling his teddy close to her heart, while trails of regret streamed down her cheeks. On occasion, she would wail into the night. It was a blood-curdling pain that manifested into the world, only rivaled by that of the Ban Sidhe.

The sound of her name being called outside interrupted Lottie's stewing and reminiscing. Lottie recognized Agnes's shrill voice as she was running up the front steps. "Lottie! Lottie!"

Agnes pushed her way inside, heaving for breath as she made her way to the sitting room. "Lottie..." Agnes gasped as she paused to heave another breath. She had practically run all the way from her bookstore on Main Street to Lottie's house. "Lottie, you're never gonna believe in a million years what I found out!" Agnes shouted.

Agnes was, as the whole of Effham agreed, as batshit crazy as they come. However, she was and would always be Lottie's oldest and closest friend. Wilbur hopped down from where he had been napping on the sofa, turned, and hissed at Agnes before trotting into the kitchen to find something to eat. He never liked Agnes. Truth be told, he never liked anyone, and sometimes not even Lottie. Wilbur minded his manners most of the time, mostly out of gratitude for when Lottie let him in out of the rain the night of the big storm back in 1923. He had made himself at home that night, and just never left, to Lottie's delight and dismay.

Agnes sat on the warm cushion that Wilbur had vacated. "Lottie, I've solved all your problems! You'll see!"

Lottie cocked her head and raised a brow. "Oh ya have, have ya now? Pray tell, which problems might those be?"

"I was watching the television in the back of the store. While flipping through the channels, I came upon this show that was on. It was all about this family who went about hunting all the likes of dark creatures and even demons! I think it was a documentary of sorts, but anyways, they went about doing all this, that, and t'other and, low and behold, the answer was right there on the television set. You got a shovel, Lottie?" Agnes sat wide-eyed and hopeful as she waited for Lottie's answer.

Lottie broke the awkward silence that filled the space between them, "A shovel? You plan to bury my problems in the garden, do ya, Agnes?"

"Oh no, Lottie. That ain't the way they showed to do it. We gotta dig up your problems, and then light them on fire, and then we gotta pour salt on 'em for good measure. Once that's done, all your problems will be solved." Agnes leaned back and crossed her arms in triumph.

Tapping her knotted finger on her chin, Lottie eyed Agnes suspiciously. "Have you lost your mind, Agnes? Digging up problems? Where? Is there a graveyard for problems that us normal folk don't know about?"

Agnes leapt up from the sofa to face Lottie. "No! No! No! You don't understand. See, we gotta go dig up your ma, and possibly your da, and burn their bones and throw salt on 'em. Then wa-la, all your problems are solved and the come hither is broken."

For all her faults and weaknesses, Agnes had always been good to Lottie. It was this that kept Lottie from tossing the nutter out into the street for even considering such a thing. Lottie had confided in Agnes years ago about what had happened on her wedding day, and even the times before that. Agnes was the only one in all Effham that knew the secrets of the Widow Effham. On some level, Lottie felt that if she told Agnes, and Agnes told anyone else, no one would believe her anyway. Lottie hadn't had a best friend since Sile' passed away in '42. As crazy as she seemed, sometimes...not often, but sometimes, Agnes was pretty smart. This, however, was not one of those times.

"And you got all this from a television show!? Aggie, none of that is real. You know that, don't ya?" Lottie was pacing back and forth. What in the world? She had told Agnes and told Agnes a hundred times over not to get one of those idiot boxes.

Agnes's eyes welled up with hurt feelings. All she wanted to do was to help Lottie, and all Lottie could do was yell at her, and make her feel stupid. Agnes's lips quivered as she spoke, barely above a whisper. "I'm sorry, Lottie. I'm just trying to help."

Lottie let out a sudden burst of laughter, which was a rare occasion indeed. "Could you imagine two old ladies such as us digging six-feet down under the full-moon? Oh, what a sight that would be." Lottie leaned on the back of the chair and steadied herself. She hadn't laughed so hard in almost a hundred years.

"But, Lottie, what if they're right? What if those folks who go hunting know something that we don't? What if that's really all there is to it and we're just too afraid to try?"

"Aggie, we've been friends for a very long time, right?" Lottie asked, a solemnness in her eyes.

"Yes. For at least fifty years now. What's that got to do with anything?" Agnes responded.

"In all the years we've been trying to solve this thing, did you ever wonder what would happen to me? I mean, you do know, right?" Lottie said, a bit more matter-of-factly than she had intended.

"You would be free, Lottie. Free to do whatever you want to do."

"No, Aggie. I wouldn't be. As it is, I am 133 years old. No one's supposed to live this long. No one should want to live this long. Once the come hither is broken, the Cù Sìth will be upon me before I knew what I was about. Afterall, it's been waiting for me all these long many years."

Tears raced down Agnes's cheeks. "No." She shook her head. "No. You can't go, Lottie. I need you." Agnes sniffled. "You're my best friend...my only real friend."

"I don't want to go neither, Aggie. But I'm not sure I want to stay either. Look at me," Lottie said, placing a hand under Agnes's chin. "There's naught but skin and bones and nary a bit of meat. It won't be long and there'll just be bones. And who knows after that. It's inevitable that I *will* be gone, one way or t'other. The question is where, where will I go?"

Agnes covered her mouth with her hands and let out an awful cry as her heart shattered in her chest. She had never thought that one day Lottie wouldn't be there anymore.

"There, there, now it isn't as bad as all that, Aggie," Lottie said. "The decision we need to make is how I take my leave. Break the come hither and be whisked away by the Cù Sìth, or just fade away into nothing? I like the idea of a Cù Sìth escort to the afterlife, rather than fading away into who knows what really. If I choose to fade away, will I just be a soul forever destined to wander the Earth, searching for a way out? At least if we find a way to break the come hither, then I know what to expect, and I have a hope of seeing my Joey again...and Jacob."

"So...you're saying we should get the shovels?" Agnes asked, with a cocked brow and a kink of a smile.

Lottie paused a moment before responding. "Yes. Yes, I suppose I am."

Agnes swiped the blackened handkerchief across her forehead, mopping away the dribbles of sweat slowly making their way into her eyes. Grave digging was hard work, and she never, ever wanted to do it again. She glanced at Lottie sitting at the edge of the deepening hole. "I sure hope this works the first time, Lottie," she called from the depths. "I don't think I got it in me to do it again."

Lottie grabbed a bottle of water from the box beside her and tossed it down to her friend. "Here, you better keep hydrated." Lottie felt terrible that her best friend was left to do most of the work herself, but what could she do? She barely had strength enough to walk these days, let alone dig six-foot holes.

There was a definitive thud when the shovel met with the coffin below. Wide-eyed and filled with terror, Agnes gazed up at Lottie. "Sounds like this is it." Agnes knelt and began brushing the dirt away. She didn't know what to expect when it came time to open the lid, but she suspected it would be horrific. After all, Lottie's mother had passed nigh on sixty years ago now. Might be just a bucket of bones, might be a bit more than that. Agnes wasn't sure she really wanted to find out.

Lottie shone the flashlight into the grave, illuminating the door she thought she had closed on her mother once and for all so many years ago. The coffin had been deep maroon – dark like her mother's soul as far as Lottie had been concerned. It was shiny, with a pristine white, satin interior. If Lottie had had her way, Ma would have been buried in an old pine box or, better yet, wrapped in an old gunny sack. Either way, Ma never deserved the ridiculous circus that had been her send off. For the love of Jesus, you would've thought she was the Queen of England herself or something. Ma had even had the nerve to hire herself a marching band to lead the funeral procession to her final resting place, right in the backyard of the Effham house where Lottie had to look at her practically every single day. If it hadn't been for the townspeople being able to see the grave from the street, Lottie had seriously considered placing a compost pile on that very site.

"Well, let's get on with it then," Lottie said.

Agnes brushed all the dirt from the top of the coffin and dug little notches in the soil so she could take hold of the latches that held the coffin shut. One by one, the snap of each latch filled the little hole. "Are you ready?" Agnes asked, looking up where Lottie sat on the edge of the earth.

"Ready as I'll ever be," Lottie said. "Open it up."

Agnes closed her eyes as tight as she could before lifting the lid at the head of the casket. The smell of death rose out of the grave as Agnes struggled to turn around and grope in the dark to open the bottom of the casket lid. Her whole body shuddered with fear. She squinted open one eye to keep watch that Lottie's ma didn't suddenly rise up and get her. Agnes had seen that happen more than once on the television and, come hell or highwater, it wasn't going to happen to her.

Lottie peered down into the depths of the grave with her gaze landing on the one person she never wanted to see again. The thought of burning Ma's bones and salting them actually felt right in the moment. As far as Lottie was concerned, there was no greater evil to have walked the Earth than that which was lying mummified in the depths below.

Ma's decomposing face was horribly disfigured with the sunken eyes and the skin taut against her bones. For all the effort Ma had put into beauty, it certainly wasn't doing her any favors now. "Here," Lottie said, throwing a large garbage bag down to Agnes. "Get her in there and I'll help you pull her up."

Agnes placed the bag over Lottie's ma's head and began pulling and stuffing until Ma was sufficiently inside the bag. Thankfully, Agnes had had the good sense to bring gloves. The foul smell wafted in the air around her, causing Agnes to choke and gag. "Get it out of here!" she shouted up to Lottie.

Lottie tugged while Agnes pushed, and finally the old bag was sitting on the ground at the top of the grave. It had only taken them all day and half the night to get to Ma. It was rather anti-climatic to have reached the point where the only thing left to do was light her up.

"Do you think we should say a few words or something?" Agnes asked in a hushed solemn tone.

Lottie glanced at her friend for a second and, for just the briefest of moments, she considered it. After all, it was her mother. "Nope. She's gotten all the nice accolades she's going to get in this world. Get the gas can, Aggie."

Agnes would never forget the smell of gas and death. It was the most atrocious odor she had ever smelled in her entire life, and she was grateful she would never have to smell it again. She turned to Lottie and hugged her ever so gently and tightly. "I'm going to miss you so much," she sobbed.

"I'm not gone yet, so save your tears for the moment it matters," Lottie said. She hadn't meant to be so cold, but she just wanted to be done with it. There was a sickening knot building in her stomach, and she just wanted it to be over and done with, one way or t'other. Lottie sucked in a deep breath and struck the match against the matchbox. She watched as the tiny flame floated down to where her mother's body was strewn out next to her grave. Before long, the whole body was engulfed in flames that danced and licked the air around them.

"I'm sending it back to you, Mother. All of it. All the hurt, the pain, the years of belittlement, beratement, and the come hither you placed on your own daughter. Why did you do it? Because you were jealous, Ma! Jealous of Jacob! Jealous of Joseph! And jealous of the love we had that you could never seem to find for yourself! I've spent 133 years in hell because of you. I hope you get to spend eternity in the hell you feared so much that in life you couldn't bring yourself to smile or laugh or God forbid, love – anyone, including Da!"

With a stubborn swipe, Lottie wiped away the tears streaming down her cheeks. That was one thing she was never giving Ma the satisfaction of again, even now in this moment. She would not cry. She would stand tall and firm.

Agnes placed a soft hand on Lottie's shoulder. "It'll be okay, Lottie." This was all she could think of to say, and she didn't really know if would be okay or not, but she had to say something.

"I don't feel any different," Lottie whispered.

Agnes took a breath and lifted the ten-pound bag of salt. "You will, Lottie. We just got to finish it. Before we do though, I just want you to know that I love you like you are my real and true sister."

"Love you too, Aggie. See you on the other side." Lottie grinned.

Agnes began pouring the salt over the flaming body. As the flames began to extinguish, Lottie started fading away. She could feel herself lifting and floating and it was peaceful and joyful and all the things she had ever hoped it would be. She was free.

Kneeling beside the shell of the woman who had been her best friend all these years, Agnes wept. She laid down beside Lottie's body and sobbed until well after dawn. When all the tears had flowed, she sat up and pushed Ma's ashes back into her coffin. Agnes spent the rest of the morning filling in the hole, just like Lottie had asked her to. Even though Ma had been Ma, Da would not want her left to the wilds like that. That's what Lottie had said.

EFFHAM, CHARLOTTE (LOTTIE) ROSE, succumbed to the comforts of death at her home on Saturday, September 19, 2022. Charlotte was an amazing woman who had lived a long and healthy life, just like her mother had wanted her to. She is preceded in death by her parents, her husband Jacob Effham, and their son, Joseph Effham. A private graveside service will be held in the family cemetery on Thursday, September 24, 2022. Instead of flowers or gifts, Lottie's last request is that donations be sent to the Effham House Foundation, which strives to preserve the history and significance of Effham Falls.

DONNA R. WOOD began her career as an author in 2011, when she published her first full-length novel, *Stick and Bones*. Since then, she has gone on to write three novels and several short stories. Donna is a certified wellbeing coach and is the owner of Butterfly Phoenix and Butterfly Phoenix Publishing. Donna is a supporter of women's rights, and LGBTQIA2S+ ally, and interfaith minister, and coffee connoisseur. She makes her home in Fargo, North Dakota, where she enjoys spending time with her children and grandchildren.

The Family Graveyard Shift
Sarah Nour

It was the only establishment with its lights still on at this hour. The building was a modest brick, sandwiched between Emma Jean's and Main Street Antiques. The logo on its glass door was a white daisy with the words Wallflower Diner.

Dalia got out of her car, legs stiff and aching from the nonstop four-hour drive from St. Paul. Her hands had been on the verge of fusing to the wheel at ten and two. She stretched her legs, flexed her hands, and checked her watch. 10:43 PM.

Being a paralegal often came with overtime hours. Dalia knew that. She'd been too good an employee to request early leave. That was why she'd sped past every town and rest stop until she'd passed the sign that read *Welcome to Effham Falls*. All things considered, she had made good time, though she wished she'd taken a moment to switch her beige pantsuit and heels for more comfortable driving clothes.

Dalia pulled open the door to Wallflower Diner, relieved to find it wasn't locked. "Hey, are you open?"

An older woman in a floral dress with a faded denim jacket stood behind the counter. She looked at Dalia through a wide set of eyeglasses.

"That depends," she said with a smile. "Do you tip well?"

"I'll tip you my life savings. I'm starving."

The woman pulled a menu out and placed it on the counter. "I'm Sylvie and I'll be your waitress. Would you like iced water?"

"Yes, please. Thank you."

Sylvie departed to the back room, presumably the kitchen. Dalia took a seat at the counter and placed her purse on the stool beside her.

True to its name, the diner had white, minimalist flowered wallpaper, and flowerpots with white plastic lilies on every table. The tables and countertop were all wooden, which gave it a humble, rustic feel.

The words on the menu swam before Dalia's eyes. She rubbed her forehead, wondering if she should have asked for coffee, as much as she disliked it.

She hadn't been sure how Effham Falls would welcome her. Leah had warned her about the casual racism of her hometown. In Dalia's own experience, small rural towns didn't take kindly to any outsiders, let alone outsiders who looked like her. Though Sylvie seemed friendly, she gave the impression of being someone's kind but not very worldly grandmother, the type to give innocent, back-handed compliments like "You don't look Middle Eastern."

Sylvie returned with a tall glass of ice water. "I can give you directions to our twenty-four-hour motel. Good place to get some rest before getting back on the road."

As much as Dalia appreciated the maternal advice, the last thing she wanted was rest. She suppressed the urge to yawn. "I should be fine."

"Well, you look like a city girl to me. I doubt this is your final destination."

Dalia wondered if Sylvie meant she didn't look white enough to be from around there. "Actually, it is."

"Effham Falls isn't exactly on the radar for most folk, don'tcha know."

"I'm searching for someone." Dalia handed back the menu. "I'll have the everything bagel, please. Toasted, with cream cheese."

"Coming up." Again, Sylvie departed to the back.

Dalia sipped some water, grateful to be woken up by the cold jolt of ice. Now more alert, she pulled out her phone and checked her messages for the umpteenth time. Still no word. Not a single reply or even a read notification for the hundreds of messages she'd sent in the past four days. Despite knowing it was pointless, she checked Leah's social media pages, just as she'd done compulsively since she stopped calling and texting. As expected, no signs of life.

Dalia's gaze shifted to the iron ring on her finger, the one Leah had given her for her birthday just two weeks prior. Then she looked back at the phone, lingering on a profile photo of her beautiful Leah. It had been taken outside the family lake cabin.

She was posing with an axe and a proud smile next to a pile of firewood she'd just chopped. The photo perfectly exemplified the country-girl gumption that made Dalia fall in love with her.

Leah said she wouldn't be gone for longer than the weekend. She was visiting her family in Effham Falls. Dalia hadn't gone with her because, while she never pressured Leah to come out to her family, she refused to be introduced to them as Leah's friend or roommate.

It was Tuesday night. Dalia hadn't heard from Leah since Friday. She feared the worst had happened: Leah came out, and they hadn't taken it well. If they'd harmed her in any way, Dalia would make them pay.

Sylvie placed a plate before Dalia, startling her. She'd been so absorbed in her phone, she'd lost all awareness of her surroundings.

"So, who is it?" Sylvie asked.

"I'm sorry, what?"

"You said you were searching for someone. Who is it?"

Dalia put her phone back in her purse. "Leah Harper. Do you know her?"

"Oof." Sylvie folded her arms. "I'm... familiar with that name, yes."

Relieved to have a lead, Dalia hastily spread the cream cheese onto her bagel. The sooner she finished eating, the sooner she could go out and find Leah. "Do you know where I can find her?"

"I suspect she's busy." Sylvie's voice now had a cold edge to it.

"With what?"

"That family of hers. They're always up to no good."

"What do you mean?" Dalia asked, wondering if she was about to hear useful information or some small-town gossip that wouldn't amount to anything.

Sylvie unfolded her arms, leaned across the counter, and looked at Dalia with narrowed eyes. "I'll give you an example. A few months ago, there was a funeral for one Mark Carlberg. Fifty-eight years old, hated by half the town. Never had a kind word for anybody. He was a handyman who overcharged for his services. His work would fall apart the next week."

If Dalia's mouth hadn't been full of bagel, she would have asked what any of this had to do with Leah. In an instant, Sylvie had gone from downhome granny to vicious busybody. She reminded Dalia unpleasantly of her middle-aged aunts when they'd gather to gossip, clucking like hens over a pot of coffee.

Sylvie continued, "Now the Harper family, they got a right collection of shovels, and a giant pick-up truck to carry them all in. Every time there's a funeral, there they are, driving that pick-up across town to the local cemetery. Of course, they always wait 'til dark to do their work."

Dalia swallowed. "Their work?"

"For weeks after the funeral, I must have talked to about eighteen people who said they saw old Mark Carlberg wandering the street at night. Not only that, a local landlady who sued him for shoddy workmanship had a pipe burst in her building. Flooded the whole floor. Then another handyman in town—he and Mark never got along—fell and broke his ankle while he was scaring off a home intruder. Then a young man who wrote a bad review of Mark's services got in a car accident and fractured his spine."

Now this was sounding like some local legend. "Well, he's dead, so it couldn't have been him causing those things."

"Oh, it certainly was," Sylvie said, wagging her finger. "And I'll tell you how: necromancy."

Dalia repeated the word to make sure she heard correctly. "Necromancy."

"You know what that means?"

"I know it's bullshit."

"No, it's blasphemous. What's worse is that our local preacher allows it. I don't know if they pay him or whatever's going on, but he allows that godforsaken family to dig up our dead and make them walk."

"That's ridiculous." Dalia began wrapping the rest of her bagel in her napkin.

"What's more, they always choose the most hated, acrimonious people to bring back from the dead, and they always go after the people that wronged them in life. Just two weeks ago, we had a murder-suicide—the mayor's oldest grandson, Edward Nordahl, his wife Lara, and both his parents. And wouldn't you know it, that spoiled, rich—"

"I'll take the rest of my meal to go."

Dalia stuffed the bagel into her purse, then pulled out some dollar bills and placed them on the counter as payment. As she walked out, Sylvie called after her, "No one here trusts the

Harpers, and for good reason. Cemetery's just down this road, left of Lawn Ranger Landscaping. Go see for yourself."

Dalia couldn't say how she ended up at the cemetery. It wasn't like she knew where anything was in Effham Falls, except the places Sylvie had mentioned. Maybe, on a subconscious level, she decided it was the better alternative over the motel. Whatever the reason, once the cemetery gate shone in her headlights, she pulled over. This was her only lead, so what could she do but follow it?

Guided by the flashlight on her phone, Dalia made her way down the path between the headstones, her mind working to manufacture excuses to avoid trespassing charges. *I'm searching for my dog. I'm a paranormal investigator. I'm doing a Gothic photoshoot. I'm trying to find the ring I dropped while visiting my great-aunt's grave.* Anything was better than "I'm looking for my missing girlfriend who, I was told, comes to this cemetery to raise the dead."

Movement to her left made Dalia whirl around, brandishing her phone like a self-defense weapon. She heard a click just before a harsh light shone in her face, blinding her.

"You're trespassing!" The voice was guttural and distinctly masculine. "Get out of here!"

"I'm not—I have permission—" Dalia tried to concentrate while shielding her eyes, squinting to see the man who seemed twice her size.

"You've got no business here! Get out!"

"What's *your* business here?" Dalia demanded, her voice coming out high-pitched. She turned off the light on her phone and stuffed the phone into her pocket as her vision adjusted to the flashlight.

The man came into focus. An aged, rounded face, beard stubble, red plaid shirt with sleeves rolled up to the elbows. "You know I could have you arrested, ma'am?"

Dalia raised her chin, willing her fight-or-flight response to set itself on fight. "What are you, a guard? What are you guarding dead people for?"

The man's hand closed around her forearm. Something glinted on his wrist—a bracelet? Dalia reacted instinctively, using her other hand to sink her nails into his arm.

The man gritted his teeth through the pain, refusing to let go. "You're leaving if I have to drag you out of here."

"You're not taking me anywhere—"

"Dad! Dad, stop!"

They both turned, the man aiming his flashlight at the new third party. A slim woman in a grimy t-shirt, dirt-smudged jeans, and heavy-duty work boots. A high ponytail and a dirt smear on her cheek. A voice Dalia would recognize anywhere. Her heart skipped a beat.

"Leah?" The name came out as a question, betraying Dalia's bewilderment.

"What are you doing here?" Leah asked, sounding almost as bewildered.

"*Me?*" Dalia's initial relief at finding Leah alive suddenly gave way to fury. "I came to find *you*! What are *you* doing here?"

The man let go of Dalia. "Leah, who is this?"

Leah turned to her father, wringing her hands in a seeming show of deference to his authority. "Dad, this is... She's... We can trust her."

Dalia's anger flared. Now that she knew her girlfriend was alive and not incapacitated in any way, it was clear that Leah had simply abandoned her. She'd ghosted her completely of her own free will.

"Well, I don't think I can trust *you*," Dalia snapped.

Leah met Dalia's eyes, her expression so apologetic that Dalia almost regretted her harsh words. Damn it, why did she have to love this woman?

"Dally, I'll tell you what's going on, just—"

"Whoa, whoa, whoa," Mr. Harper said, sounding every bit the stern father. "Now I did *not* give you permission to tell her anything. You know how important secrecy is to these operations."

"I know, but—"

"Whatever this is," Dalia interjected, holding up her phone, "it's looking pretty bad, so unless you tell me what's going on, I'll have to call the cops."

"They won't do anything," Mr. Harper said matter-of-factly. "They know why we're out here."

"Dad, please, trust me," Leah pleaded. "Could you just let us talk alone?"

Mr. Harper's brow furrowed in disapproval. He looked from Leah to Dalia and back again. "Just watch out for those claws." He held up his arm to show the nail marks. "She could put your eye out."

Leah nodded. "Could I borrow your flashlight?"

Mr. Harper handed Leah the flashlight, and she gestured for Dalia to follow her. Still fuming, Dalia walked with her past a few rows of tombstones, out of earshot from where Mr. Harper stood.

"So, this is why you haven't returned my calls? Because you're working a graveyard shift? Is that a family pastime?"

Leah stopped walking, turned to her, and sighed. "I'm sorry. I didn't tell you because you wouldn't believe me."

"Believe what?"

Leah pointed the flashlight to another side of the cemetery. "Look over there."

In the distance, Dalia saw moving figures and piles of dirt, partially illuminated by lanterns on the ground. She squinted. There were people digging. She counted three of them. Two large mounds of dirt. Two graves being excavated.

"Who are they?" Dalia demanded.

"That's my mom and my brothers," Leah replied.

"What are they doing?"

Leah hesitated. "I don't really know where to begin."

Dalia faced her girlfriend and folded her arms. "Begin anywhere. I'm listening."

Leah took a deep breath. "You know how I told you most of this town's population is of Scandinavian descent, right?"

Out of all the places Dalia expected her to begin, this wasn't it. "Um, yeah?"

"Well, in Norse folklore, there's this... this undead being called a draugr. They're basically revenants—animated corpses—and they can enter people's dreams, they can curse people, make them sick—"

"Wait. You're here because of undead monsters?"

Leah reached under her t-shirt and pulled out a chain necklace. "Iron makes them weaker, but it doesn't kill them. They're hard to take down when they're active, so our best bet is E.D.C.—excavation, decapitation, cremation. We would do it during the day, when they're weakest, but then people would see us, so we've got to take the risk of doing it at night."

Dalia's mind paged through all the undead lore she was familiar with. Somehow, she didn't remember draugr being mentioned on any episodes of *True Blood* or *The Walking Dead*.

"So, every Scandinavian person in this town becomes this... weird zombie?"

"No, not everyone. People who have enemies, people who held grudges and had grudges held against them—they're most likely to become draugr. Usually, it's easy to tell who's risen from the dead. But there was a recent murder-suicide of four people in town. This guy killed his wife and both his elderly parents, then himself. The family wasn't well-liked around here, to say the least. When we realized a draugr was roaming at night, we thought it was the murderer going after his former employees who sued him for wrongful termination. But attacks kept happening after we E.D.C.'d him. So, we did his mother next—"

"This is insane."

Dalia ran her hands through her hair, tugging at the roots a little in case she was dreaming and needed a jolt of pain to wake up. Her birthday ring caught a few hairs, resulting in more pain than anticipated. She thought back to all her times with Leah, replaying conversations they'd had, mentally combing through their history for any hint of bizarre idiosyncrasies. The closest she could recall was that Leah believed in ghosts and astrology. Not too unusual, and certainly not relationship dealbreakers. This, however, was an entirely different level.

"I was going to tell you eventually," Leah said. "We've only been together seven months. I was thinking I'd tell you on our one-year anniversary."

"You really expect me to believe any of this? I knew white people had weird customs, but not... this."

Leah gave her an amused smile. "Says the woman who believes in djinn."

"I didn't say I *believed* in djinn. I said I was open to the possibility that they exist."

"So why can't you be open to the existence of draugr?"

Dalia didn't have an answer to that. "How'd your family even get started on this anyway? Is it a tradition or something?"

"You could say that. My great-grandparents came here from Norway. They knew about draugr—they E.D.C.'d their fair share of them back home. They even had their kids marry non-Scandinavians because they were afraid their descendants would become draugr. This town is a breeding ground for them."

"So why not just leave? Why do any of you stay if it's a breeding ground for these... things?"

"Most of my relatives did leave. Only one of my brothers lives here now. The other came from out of town to help us out. Who else will take care of this? Someone has to."

Dalia rubbed her temples. "Do you know how batshit this all sounds? Actually, no, you don't, because family traditions always seem normal until you tell someone about them. Then you realize—"

She was cut off by the sound of someone shrieking. She turned toward the excavation site to see a woman—Mrs. Harper—trying to climb out of one of the open graves. Something was on her back, a dark figure trying to drag her down.

One of Leah's brothers ran and grabbed her hands to pull her out. "Jake, the cross!" he hollered to the other. "Get the cross!"

Once out of the hole, Mrs. Harper thrashed about on her hands and knees, trying to get the dark figure off her back. Jake came running with a long iron cross—*Where'd he get that?* Dalia wondered—and he brought it down hard on the... zombie? Vampire? Whatever it was, it cried out like a wild animal in pain and leapt off Mrs. Harper. Landing on all fours, it whipped its head back toward Jake. Its skull briefly flared up with a harsh white light.

Jake dropped the cross and began screaming, frantically swatting at his arms. He dropped to the ground and rolled back and forth.

Stop, drop, roll, Dalia thought. *He thinks he's on fire.*

The undead creature rapidly crawled toward Dalia and Leah. Leah thrust the flashlight into Dalia's hands and, in one swift motion, moved in front of her and pulled a dagger out of her boot—an antique one, from the look of it.

The creature stopped crawling and pulled itself to a standing position in front of Leah. It wore a torn dress that matched its gray skin, half of which had rotted away to reveal pitch-black bones. Thin strands of hair clung to the balding black skull, and its eye sockets contained glowing white orbs. The decayed flesh around its mouth revealed the full extent of an eerie, black-toothed smile.

Leah lunged forward, slashing at the thing's chest. It staggered back with a screech, bony hands clutching its torso in pain. The orbs in its eye sockets suddenly flared like the headlights of a car. Leah dropped the dagger and fell to her knees.

"Get them off me!" she screamed, clawing at her arms, her neck, her shirt. "Spiders! Get them off me! Get the spiders! Get them off!"

Dalia stared at Leah helpless on the ground, lost in delusion. The creature—the draugr—had done that to her Leah. With that realization came a fury that overpowered her shock and fear. She didn't stop to think. She tossed the flashlight aside, ran to the draugr, and aimed a punch where its nose should be. Her iron ring pressed into her finger with the impact, cutting into her skin.

The half-decayed corpse stumbled backward, orbs dimming. Dalia briefly glimpsed the axe before the draugr's head flew off its shoulders, and the rest of its body fell apart in a crumpled heap of bones and fabric, as though it had barely held together.

Mrs. Harper stood triumphant with an axe in her hands, silhouetted by the light of the lanterns behind her.

Dalia felt a mix of awe and disbelief. When she had begun the trip to Effham Falls, she never thought she'd see a middle-aged woman behead a telepathic Scandinavian zombie with an axe. It was like seeing an older version of Leah in a bizarre alternate reality.

Back at the excavation site, Jake was back on his feet, having recovered from his delusion of being on fire. He said to his brother, "Told you it was the wife! Pay up."

"Dude, that was a joke," the brother said. "I never agreed—"

"Enough!" Mrs. Harper snapped. "Dylan, get the lighter fluid. Jacob, get these bones back into the hole. I think the head landed over there. Go get it."

How odd, Dalia thought, that she could bark orders like that so easily. Like this was all routine. In a daze, she realized Mr. Harper had arrived on the scene, and had picked up the flashlight she'd tossed aside.

"Everyone alright?" he asked.

"It was the wife," Jake replied, picking up the draugr head. "Mom hacked her head off."

Dalia was suddenly startled by Leah's hand on her wrist. "Dally, baby, you're bleeding. Someone get the first-aid kit!"

Dalia whirled around, realizing she'd momentarily forgotten about Leah. She met her girlfriend's eyes and found them clear and lucid. No more delusions of spiders.

"You're okay?" Dalia asked, sounding as dazed as she felt.

Leah gently removed the ring from Dalia's finger, which was indeed bleeding. "It's not the first time I've had one of them in my head. Last time it was snakes."

"It scares me how casually you said that."

Dylan approached with a can of lighter fluid in one hand and a first-aid kit in the other. Leah took the first-aid kit with her free hand. "Come on, let's go over here. There's a place to sit down." Dalia followed her to a clearing nearby, just far enough to talk in private, but close enough for the lanterns to extend their light. No headstones, just a wooden bench underneath a single white birch tree. It occurred to Dalia this could be a romantic spot under different circumstances.

Once they were both seated, Leah opened the kit. "This wasn't how I planned to make a believer out of you."

Dalia let out a hoarse chuckle, the first laugh she'd had in days. "I blame myself," she said, extending her bleeding hand. "I had to fall for a white girl."

Leah sprayed antiseptic on Dalia's ring finger, her expression anxious. "If this is a dealbreaker, you can tell me now."

"Look, I may need time to wrap my head around the fact that those... weird, undead things exist, but do you really think I'd pass up a chance to date Buffy?"

"She killed vampires."

"You know what I mean."

Leah pressed gauze to Dalia's bleeding finger. "I'm sorry for ghosting you. I didn't know how to tell you the truth, and I didn't want to lie. I did most of the investigation around town, trying to figure out the draugr's identity based on who it was targeting. Every time you sent me a message, it was easier to just set the phone aside."

"You know there's a lady running a diner in town who thinks you're all necromancers?"

That made Leah laugh. It was good to hear her laugh again. "I'm sure that's not the worst rumor out there."

Once her finger was all bandaged up, Dalia took Leah's hand in both of hers. "I forgive you for ghosting me. But expect me to hold it over your head for the rest of your life."

"Rest of my life?" Leah sounded hopeful. "So you do see a future for us."

"Yeah, I think I do." Dalia glanced back at the scene at the open grave where Leah's parents and brothers had gathered. Dylan tossed aside the lighter fluid container. Jake lit a match and dropped it into the grave. Flames erupted, bright yet controlled, within the rectangular hole.

Turning back to Leah, Dalia asked, "So, do they know about… us?"

Leah shrugged. "I think they have their suspicions. We haven't really talked about it, but it's not like they can afford to disown me. That would be one less person taking care of the draugr problem."

"I feel like I need to impress your mother. She's kind of a badass."

Leah tucked Dalia's hair behind her ear. "I think punching a draugr is a good first impression."

Leah held Dalia's hand and led her to the gathering. Dylan and Mr. Harper were shoveling dirt back into the other open grave. Meanwhile, Mrs. Harper warmed her hands against the fire. Jake stood beside her, watching the flames. Aside from the fact that this was taking place in a cemetery, it seemed like an ordinary bonfire, minus the s'mores.

Mr. Harper paused his shoveling. "Dalia, is it? My wife told me you punched the draugr. I have no trouble believing that."

He held out his arm for emphasis, showing the scratch marks Dalia had left. She could only smile and nod. What could she possibly say in this situation?

Mrs. Harper gave her daughter a stern look. "Leah, have you been recruiting people to our mission? I thought we taught you the importance of keeping this all secret." Then she looked at Dalia with some admiration. "Though I got to say, you recruited a good one."

Leah gave Dalia's hand a squeeze. "This is Dalia El-Shami. My girlfriend."

Jake turned in Dylan's direction. "I was right! I told you she liked girls! You owe me."

"We didn't bet anything," Dylan replied, sounding exasperated. "Besides, I never said you were wrong."

Mr. Harper leaned against his shovel. "Well, I didn't see this coming, so maybe *I* owe you boys."

Mrs. Harper sighed and shook her head apologetically at Dalia. "We're giving you such a good impression, aren't we?"

Dalia laughed. "I'm sure you're not gambling addicts. Just zombie hunters, or something like it."

Jake shrugged. "Close enough."

"Well, Dalia, we're glad to have you here," Mrs. Harper said. "And I hope you're glad to be here."

"I am."

Dalia squeezed Leah's hand and looked down into the fire. Between the sparks and flashes, she glimpsed the black bones. The corroded jaw of the skull formed a silent scream as the eye sockets blazed and the flames devoured the undead evil from the inside. Somehow, she was certain that, after this night, there was nothing she and Leah couldn't face together.

SARAH NOUR is a freelance journalist who has written for the *High Plains Reader*, *Area Woman*, and other local FM publications. Her poetry and short fiction have appeared in *Northern Narratives*, *Red Weather*, *Wild Musette*, *Crow Toes Quarterly*, *Parakeet Magazine*, and other publications.

Enjoy! Barbara Bustamante

CHOICES

Barbara Bustamante

I magine, if you can, an event that changed my life. Something so intimate that no words were ever spoken. This is a story I kept secret from my family and friends until it was finally revealed during a visit to Effham Falls more than forty years later.

In the bright morning sun, with the sky decorated by soft feather-like clouds in a sea of blue and the crispness of a light breeze, I turned my car's ignition key and heard the gentle hum of the engine. I pulled out of my parking spot, excited to be finally on the road. The tree-covered hills surrounding the small lakes changed with the seasons, but the route was always the same. The sun shone through the treetops, flickering like the view of an old film. I had made this trek many times before, and the anticipation was always the same.

This trip's plan was inspired by a late afternoon gathering of friends at the county fair. Since our childhood home was on the way, I asked my brother, John, before I left if I could stop by. John agreed that it had been a long time since our last visit. In my younger years, I'd looked forward to each return. A place of safety and security. In winter, it is a place of warmth and inviting aromas. In summer, a place where the trees provided shelter from the hot sun, and for refreshment. This is where I go to restore my soul. Home.

As I drove past the lakes and valleys between hills and curves in the road, my thoughts entertained memories of past political conversations with my siblings where I always got caught between the conservative views of my brother and the liberal stand of my sister, Marie. I'd rather they would work out their differences and not involve me. I prefer to just listen.

Before long, I approached John's driveway, and the turn brought a rush of feelings. The sound and feel of the tires rolling over the gravel of the narrow tree-shaded driveway felt like an invitation for me to bask in the morning sun.

At first glance, the log home revealed the toll time had taken on its facade. The sun had faded the stain on the logs and there were other signs of damage from insects and woodpeckers. The deck and steps were neglected and needed repair. John greeted me when I slid out of the driver's side of my car. Habitually, I searched for his beloved farm dog, Max, who had died a couple of years prior. John found taking care of a dog hampered his retired lifestyle anyway. Once inside, I found comfort in familiar surroundings.

"How was your drive up here?"

"The weather was good, and the roads were clear."

"What time are you going to the fair?"

"Around four."

"By the way, would you like to go into town for lunch?"

"Sure."

"Let's go out to my garage. I have some things to show you."

Time flew by as he showed me all his projects and their progress. He was so proud of his car and treated it as a fine work of art - well cared for and maintained. As a skilled mechanic he was a wiz, but I think he learned carpentry work from Google. To show off his new car, he invited me to go for a spin on our way to lunch. The next thing I knew, we were headed down the highway to Effham Falls. We pulled into the Rusty Nail Bar & Grill's half-full parking lot on the outskirts of town and found a spot close to the door.

Inside, the low lighting was a contrast to the bright sun outside. We waited patiently; the place filled with the buzz of friendly chatter. A waitress escorted us to a comfortable booth, presented menus for our perusal, and took our drink order.

"What looks good?" John inquired.

Impressed by the large menu, I replied, "There's a lot to choose from. It may take me a while."

When the waitress returned, I opted for chicken strips, fries, and raspberry tea, and John chose a pulled pork sandwich, soup, and a Coke.

While waiting for our food, we sipped our drinks.

John abruptly commented, "You know I'm against abortion. How do you feel about it?" Startled by his private question in public, and unaware of where this was going to end up, I said "It's hard to say unless it's happened to you."

Seemingly unprepared for my reaction, he said nothing.

I took a deep breath and continued. "There was a time back in the late seventies when we were traveling out of state to one of Bob's bowling tournaments. We stopped for supper, I suddenly got very sick, and Bob took me to the hospital. I was diagnosed with a tubal pregnancy, which is where the embryo is stuck in the fallopian tube. While I lay in bed, I felt lost and didn't know what to do. Nothing made sense. I wasn't prepared for that. I realized that a life would be lost. As much as I hated to lose my baby, I felt guilty for saving my own. A deal had to be made. In the end, I promised to never forget my baby, and to live my life worthy of this decision. I have kept this promise. There isn't a day that goes by that I don't think about the baby I lost. I will always love the baby I couldn't have."

When I finished, there was silence. He had wanted a confrontation he could defend, not a first-person testimony.

John and I quietly ate our food. Our conversation moved on to something else. Later, we stopped for dessert at his daughter-in-law's shop. We continued a pleasant conversation as we headed back to his home. When we relaxed on his patio again, nothing was uttered on the subject. But I saw a different brother. His eye contact and laughter expressed a sense of love and understanding that prevailed. When I prepared to leave, we hugged and said our warm goodbyes. As I drove down the driveway to the afternoon gathering, I knew we would see each other again soon.

The gathering in Effham Falls went off as planned. When I left, I was relieved that the day was almost over. A canopy of trees passed behind me as cool breezes swirled through the car. The warmth from the setting sun surrounded me as I sailed down the highway. Grateful for the beauty of this ancient glacial lake bottom, I gazed at the vast rolling landscape of lakes, trees, and fences patrolled by an occasional hawk or crow while heading east toward an urban jungle.

The afternoon had turned into the evening when I pulled into my parking spot. Familiar shrubs and trees greeted me as I slid out the driver's side of my car. The trek to my second-floor apartment culminated in a sigh of relief after I shed my shoes and collapsed in my recliner. My mind took the opportunity to review the events of the day.

The conversation with John suggesting his conservative leaning had caught me by surprise because I wasn't prepared to defend such a personal issue, and one that few in my family knew about. But I told him my story, and it wasn't what he wanted to hear. He wanted me to support his politics, but I ended up presenting my morality. I had told him because I loved him – the same love that had brought both of us into this world.

I sat quietly, watching through the leaves of my beloved houseplants, as the last light of sunset was smothered by the eternal darkness of the night. I reflected again on that night forty-some years ago. A night much like that night....

Mile by mile went by as my husband, Bob, our two-year-old daughter, Donna, and I traveled on a weekend trip. How cozy it was riding in that old blue Datsun pickup. After driving for several hours, we decided to stop for supper. A truck stop diner was our choice because of its reputation for good food and fast service.

Once inside, we settled into a spacious comfortable booth and ordered our drinks. At first, I felt the need to pee. I asked to excuse myself, and Donna insisted on joining me. As we entered the restroom, I felt a sudden sensation of nausea and lightheadedness. With one hand, I grabbed hold of the nearest stall and pulled Donna along with the other. Inside the stall, I dropped my jeans and fell to the toilet in shock. There was blood everywhere. I asked Donna to go get Daddy for help. Later, I learned Donna had told him, "Momma wants you and she has ketchup everywhere." What felt like a lifetime later, a kind employee arrived, assuring me that she would clean up the mess. Unsteadily, I returned to our pickup truck.

Cooling breezes caressed the heat from my body as I lay in darkness on the firm bench seat of our Datsun pickup, waiting for my family to join me. Too weak to sit up, I saved my energy for the trip to the hospital. When they returned with their food, Donna sat in the middle, cradling my head in her lap while Bob drove.

At the ER entrance, I was separated from my family when the staff wheeled me inside. While Bob parked, I was examined, tested, and given IV fluids. I wanted my family. I didn't want to be alone. Little did I know I was fighting for my life. Due to hospital regulations, Bob was not allowed to bring Donna to see me, but a nurse reassured me that they could visit me the next day.

Clueless of my condition, I lay in a hospital bed comforted by pain meds. When the doctor finally came to my room, I was unaware that he had already consulted with Bob. The doctor explained that I had an ectopic pregnancy where the embryo gets stuck in the fallopian tube. The hemorrhaging was caused by my body trying to flush the embryo out of my system. If I had bled one more hour, I would have died. The embryo was alive, but it wouldn't survive. The doctor asked me to authorize the removal of the fallopian tube with the embryo inside. I asked for a chance to think it over. He left the paperwork at the nurse's station for me to sign.

Then I lay there in silence, pondering my situation ...

I am pregnant.

The joy of having another child is dashed by the reality of impossibility. I've so little time to deal with the sadness that fills my heart, so little time to gratefully commune with my baby. Facing the loss of two lives – the baby's and mine – or losing its life to save mine, the baby has no hope in either case. Nothing seems fair, but I have a responsibility as the mother to make things right. As right as it can be.

I believe that life begins at conception as I was taught. My husband and my parents aren't here to help me either. How can I do this based on the facts and my feelings? I'm between a rock and a hard place. My baby can't tell me what it wants and I sense the end is near.

"You have no name or face, but I know you," I say aloud.

I owe it to my baby to do something ... anything, but all I can do is humbly promise to make my life worthy of this sacrifice. From the heart, I know I will never forget this little one and my love for it. Sensing peace in my decision and the acceptance of my new burden, knowing it is the right thing to do, I reach for the button on my bed.

After the nurse leaves and the room darkens, I close my eyes and reach down to cuddle with my baby one last time until we drift off into slumber.

That night of restful sleep ended abruptly when a surgical team rolled me down the hall to the operating room and quickly hooked me up to the machines. I silently uttered, "Goodbye, I will see you again someday." Then the anesthesia entered my breathing mask and I was out.

I opened my eyes in recovery, met by the gentle voice of my nurse. She offered me something to drink, which I accepted since I hadn't eaten for over twelve hours. The doctor stopped by to inform me that all had gone well and I was being discharged for my trip back home. I asked him what was being done with the removed fallopian tube. He told me that it would be sent to a laboratory to be analyzed. In my grief, nothing made sense that day.

When I returned to my room, the nurse kindly brought me a light meal and a change of clean clothes that Bob had dropped off. Before I knew it, I was in a wheelchair headed for the front door where the little pickup waited for me at the curb.

Weeks later, as I recuperated at home, I finally realized how much the operation had taxed my body. Hormones were all messed up, healing of the incision was slow, and getting my energy back took months. When I did go back to work, my friends couldn't understand why it had taken me so long. I wasn't about to share my feelings.

Everything changed that night forty-some years ago. That day my baby died. If I could have switched places, I would have. It wasn't a choice. It became an obligation. Every day I'm reminded of this. Every breath I take is for my baby. My tears are for my baby. This relationship made a difference - an understanding between my baby and me. And as parents, Bob and I adjusted our expectations and found balance.

The loss of an unborn child has been a long journey of grief and loss. I made lots of mistakes while I dealt with this emotional pain. I only recognized my physical pain. I filled my mind with work and responsibilities, which was easy. I had a great work ethic. I felt the urge to fulfill the needs of those around me, but I didn't pay attention to my emotional pain. When I wanted to talk about my loss, I didn't know where to start. I didn't know who to ask or what to say. Licking my emotional wounds in silence became a way of life. Any attempt to broach the subject with my husband fell flat. Maybe that had something to do with our drifting apart. Deep down, I cared and searched for hope, but with our divorce and other changes over time, more loss sought me out. But this time I made sure things would be different.

I improved what worked for me. I became a new woman – smarter, wiser, and better equipped to take on grief.

Now as a woman in my seventies, I've seen change and lots of it. Growing up under the old system from the 1940s to the 1970s, conservative values were consistent and blended with the church, school, and home. As long as everyone was on the same page, this worked. When it didn't work, it became the subject of rumors. For example, parents taught and enforced matters involving sex. Sex education in the schools was just starting and materials involving female anatomy were only privately offered to the girls. This implied that girls were the only ones responsible enough to handle the information. Believe me, when these materials were handed out, every boy on the school bus was peeking over our shoulders to get a glimpse.

This was also about the same time I heard the phrase, "Boys will be boys." There were 'good girls' and 'bad girls'. I didn't have much of a chance to socialize with either group, but I favored those with better reputations, so I was shocked when I learned that one of my 'good girl' friends had dropped out of school because she had become pregnant. I remember my disgust. She and her family had to shoulder the shame. There was no mention of the boy involved. Abortion wasn't an option. It was illegal. Morality was set by men for families, schools, and the church. As a result, I was very pro-life. Even though women were forced to have children under difficult circumstances, love for their children was unaffected.

After high school, I went off to a religious college in a large city. There, my beliefs and values were tested. My college life was rocked by the passing of Roe vs. Wade, which made it legal to have an abortion. One of my roommates knew my stance and hid the fact that our other roommate was having an abortion. I wonder if she was using the abortion as a birth control method. Not long afterward, she got her abortion and that was my first lesson in 'Hate the sin, love the sinner.' I couldn't abandon my friendship at the cost of my values. This didn't change my stance, but I was able to view a glimpse of the bigger picture. Little did I know that I would be facing this issue head-on years later.

That night of agony in the hospital changed me---not from pro-life to pro-choice, but from human to humane. The relationship made a difference - an understanding and consideration between my baby and me. However, I had a chat with Bob about that night forty years earlier and I learned his perspective. (Oh, yes, old people can remember things from forty years ago but don't ask them where their keys are.) I admit to taking many of my rights for granted. That is my error. But I'm grateful for the right to have made the decision I did.

This last summer, the courts overturned the right to have an abortion. I think now how women and their families will be affected by this. It feels like a step backward, to a time of control and shame. Will we see homes for unwed mothers again? We have benefited from scientific and medical advancements. Babies and mothers live where decades ago they would have perished. But we continue to wage religious and political battles with each other. Whether the issue is rich or poor, conservative or liberal, mainstream or evangelical, we fight and scrap like a bunch of little kids over a bag of candy. In the meantime, overzealous egos cause people to fall between the cracks.

I still don't believe in abortion, but I'm not so quick to judge the decisions of others. My baby died, but its soul did not. If I could have switched places, I would have. It wasn't a choice. It was an obligation. Every day I'm reminded of this. Every breath I take is for my baby. My tears are for my baby. I now know that the arrangement made wasn't with my baby, but with God. My baby is in God's hands now. It's all about God's love for creation and our love for our neighbor, and God's forgiveness of our goof-ups, and the forgiveness to ourselves and our neighbor. But most of all, it's about God's grace to heal and make things right so that I can be confident that my baby is safe, secure, and loved.

What hasn't changed over the years is the nature of people. We still have love, fear, hope, and dreams. Mistakes are made and we learn from them. We wish life would deal us a better hand but, in the end, we do the best with what we have. I want to be the person who could have been there for me in my time of need. My goal is to be kind and listen more. You never know when your actions become a gift to others.

I'm an old woman reflecting on the events of my past and my visit to Effham Falls that day. I'm glad to share my thoughts and feelings about my transformation from a naive young mother to a wiser, experienced elderly woman. I've taken off the blinders of my youth to view the whole picture. Friends and family will now know but, hopefully, others will also learn from my experience.

BARBARA BUSTAMANTE is retired from the food service and education industries. She has a poem and three short stories in the Moorhead Friends Writing Group anthology, *Tales from the Frozen North*. She lives in Moorhead, MN with her cat.

It Came From The Woods
Sadie Mendenhall-Cariveau

At times, when Evangeline would drive through the streets of Effham Falls in winter months, she marveled at how magical it appeared. When snow skittered in the air, surrounding everything in a light dusting without hitting the ground, it felt more like driving in a snow globe. The holiday signs hanging from the streetlights and electric poles only added to the cliché imaginings that made her smile.

"Mom?"

"Hmm?" She looked at Taylor. Miraculously enough, she was looking at her instead of the tablet she clung to.

"Why are you smiling like that?"

"I was just thinking how Effham looks like a snow globe." She shrugged, tilted her head, and looked at Taylor. "Wouldn't that be something?"

"Oh sure, you bet." Taylor grinned. "But just think, if it was, we could be trapped. Prisoners of Krampus forced to repeat everything over and over again."

"Well, if we are prisoners, you may want to start applying yourself to school and chores more instead of worrying about your TikTok videos and gotcha characters or whatever those are. You could be our only hope of escaping. It all hinges on your report card." She looked at her daughter sitting in the passenger seat, tablet laying in her lap with some random, artsy edit. She was proud of her daughter's creativity but, in her mind, she wouldn't be a decent parent if she didn't remind her now and then that responsibility and integrity were also good characteristics to possess.

"Hey, that's not fair, Mom. My followers need me to come up with characters and stories. I am an inspiration. I could end up getting paid for this if I get enough out there."

"Right, and are your followers going to be there to catch you when you don't graduate high school?" Evangeline sighed. "Taylor, honey, you know I love your art. I just have to be a parent now and then, not just your friend."

"Fair point."

Evangeline shook her head as Taylor put her headphones on and started editing more videos and characters. How her kid did that and still managed to toggle to her chat server was amazing, but it alienated her from the world around her. Evangeline missed the days when her kids sang to the radio or read their books aloud on errand days. Since Moira left for college on the west coast, Taylor slowly disappeared into the realm of online living, boys, and cosplay.

Evangeline checked her rearview mirror. Her youngest daughter was sound asleep, her head resting on the seatbelt like it was a pillow. Evangeline smirked and looked back at the road ahead, remembering how her other kids looked after their over-the-road naps. The lines and wrinkles that would blaze on their pale skin from whatever design was on the seatbelt cover and the pressure against their cheeks.

Lost in her own imagination and memories, Evangeline continued driving, slowing on the icier parts of the roads home. Other drivers could go as fast as they wanted in the blowing snow, she'd rather play it safe. The slower pace allowed everything around her to fall away as she pictured small unicorns and other creatures on the breasts of the waves of snow causing the road to look like a scene from a story or cartoon. Things in Effham Falls were wonderous at times, or they were to her at the very least. Perhaps it was because she had never been one to accept that the ordinary was all there was to life. *Life is what you make of it. Never forget that, girl. We carry on and rise from our ashes. Held together by pins and patches, a little duct tape and grit.* Her great grandfather's words bounced in her thoughts.

Aloysius had been an odd man. Her mother thought he was crazy, but truth was that he was just an eccentric. He had come up from nothing. A boy from the wrong side of the tracks who just happened, somehow, to end up with her grandmother. Evangeline had been close to him, especially toward the end of his life. He would tell her such fantastic stories. He helped Evangeline see magic and beauty everywhere. When she was twenty-one, he passed away suddenly. When Evangeline found him, she clung to his hand, sobbing and, in a way, waiting for him to get up. He was old, older than even she knew. It wasn't until the autopsy that she discovered that the eighty-something man she loved was really over one hundred years old. Her mother was appalled when she found out that he had left everything to Evangeline. She begged Evangeline to sell it all. When Evangeline refused and instead moved in, she became a footnote in her mother's life. Her mother came from money, and if her summer break fling hadn't ended with an unplanned pregnancy, Evangeline wasn't entirely sure that she would have married her father—especially if she had known he was related to Aloysius.

The crunch of the snow beneath her tires as she pulled into the drive of the house made her smile. Aloysius had been an inspiration to her. He had somehow managed to keep the house from falling completely apart and had updated things as needed. On the outside, it looked like a small box. Inside, though, proved that appearances weren't what they seemed. Of course, the seamless appearance of all the changes and additions helped further that illusion. The homey feeling that her grandmother had described in her childhood remained.

A tap on the car window caused Evangeline to cry out a bit. Taylor's boyfriend, Devon, backed up, first looking like he might show sympathy, but then he just started laughing. She had forgotten that his dad had asked them to let Devon stay the weekend while he was away on business. Her husband, Grant, had reluctantly agreed simply because he was trying to keep his new home in one piece.

"Hey, I didn't mean to scare you."

Evangeline shook her head as she stepped out of the car. "With a face like that, it was bound to happen eventually." She turned and grabbed her travel mug from the center consul and readjusted her purse. "Taylor, hon, would you start bringing in the bags?"

"Yeah." Taylor huffed, stuffed her tablet in her pocket and went around to the back of the car. "Devon, you can help."

"Would you let the boy put his stuff in the house first before you start delegating and not participating?"

"Ouch, Mom. That hurt." Taylor gripped her chest and feigned death with theatrical ease.

"Sure, it did. I bet I really hit you in the feels." Evangeline laughed. "Just go set your bags down in the front room, Devon." She stepped around the car, trudging in the snow like a drunk ostrich. "I don't know how the turkeys make walking around in this look so easy."

"They're just better at being short than you are, Mom." Taylor's pride in her cleverness at that moment was evident in her giggle.

"Keep it up, kid. Keep it up." Evangeline opened the back passenger door and unbuckled the seatbelt. It was apparently the only thing keeping her slumbering child from faceplanting into the seat in front of her, or her own knees. "It's truly amazing how a child can sleep like this."

"Do you need help?" Devon came up beside the car and rested his hand on the door as Evangeline hoisted her daughter up and cradled her close while she backed up.

"Yeah, you can help carry things in." Taylor's usual bossy attitude was as cold as the wind blowing around them. It was always in overdrive when Devon was over.

Evangeline faced Taylor, eyebrows raised. "And you can certainly help, right?"

"Of course, Mom, someone has to make sure he does it right." She grinned.

"Mmhmm, just make sure everything makes it in safely." She watched Devon shut the door of her car. "Oh, and could you make sure she remembers to double check that nothing is left behind?" Evangeline readjusted the dead weight of her youngest child. "Damn it, she's getting heavy."

Without missing a beat or the opportunity, Taylor's voice cut through the air and the crunch of the snow as Evangeline made her way to the porch. "Or you're just getting old."

Sometimes the boundaries of their mother daughter relationship were blurred by the banter of their humor and the flinging of insults back and forth, so much so that even Evangeline had a hard time finding them. It was no wonder that other parents in her inner circle offered their advice so often. She was surprised they hadn't flat-out told her that she needed to put her foot down. Only problem was that she couldn't because the reality for her was that she was basically having conversations with herself. The two of them were so much alike it was uncanny.

"What was that, Taylor?" She struggled to keep from slipping as she made deliberate steps up to the landing. "You want me to make something extra cheesy for dinner tonight? Is that what I heard you say?"

"Nope."

"Well, don't worry, I can make that happen if you keep it up."

"Oh, c'mon, Mom," she said pouting. "It was funny. You know it was."

"Yep, ha ha, it was so funny I didn't laugh." Evangeline could feel the misguided concern in Devon's stare as he stepped in front of her to open the door. "So, how about you start bringing everything inside?"

"Whatever," Taylor mumbled.

Evangeline was certain her daughter was rolling her eyes, but she didn't have the energy to deal with the latest mood swing. "Thank you, Devon. I appreciate it." She could hear the distinct huffing and stomping in the snow as Taylor came up behind them.

"No problem. Here, lemme help." He sidestepped Evangeline and went to open the inner door, bending down to coral the dogs and thwart their excited attempts at door dashing.

"Kiss ass," Taylor grumbled behind her.

"Behave and be nice, Taylor." Evangeline smirked as she stepped into the entryway. "He is your boyfriend, after all."

"Yeah, but you and Dad invited him to stay, not me. Nobody asked me what I wanted."

"We will discuss this later. For now, just cool it." She shook her head, walked past them, and made her way through the chaos. The much quieter back of the house was a relief after the first fifteen minutes of the weekend being full of teenage angst.

All she could hear were the semi-distant sounds of the other two kids coming in and out of the house in alternation, exchanging their jokes and puppy love coos to one another as they did. She tucked her youngest into her bed in the room off of their T.V. room. She smoothed her hair back from her face and kissed her forehead. As she stood to leave, she looked out the window at the falling snow. There was no longer a trace of grass or any evidence of her back yard, save for the tips of the bricks that surrounded the firepit. The blowing snow was mesmerizing, moving this way and that and seeming to never touch the ground, though she knew that was impossible.

"Mom? What are you looking at?"

The sharp whisper from Taylor broke her gaze. "Nothing, just the snow."

"Again, with your snow globe theory?"

"No, I just like how the snow makes the woods look back there." She pointed to the tree line along their property line at the base of their hill. "Made me think of some of those holiday cards from when I was little."

Taylor shivered. "Pass. In fact, it's a hard pass." She turned and went to the living room.

"What?" Evangeline stepped out of the room and looked at her. "Taylor, honey, are you okay?"

She shrugged, shaking her head. "I don't want to talk about it."

"Well, I hate to break it to you, but I'm not giving you an 'I don't want to talk about it' option." Evangeline stood in front of her, opening up her hands in her usual gesture to let Taylor know that she was waiting for her explanation.

"What's going on?" Devon came into the living room and sat down next to Taylor. "Are you okay?" He looked at Evangeline.

Evangeline found it annoyingly endearing that he was so protective and attentive of Taylor. Still, she sometimes wished he would read the room and know when it wasn't a good time to interrupt. "She's fine, unless she decides she wants to spend the rest of the weekend helping me reorganize the pantry." She looked at Taylor, who was frowning. "No? Then start talking."

"It's dumb, okay?"

"Then where did that fear come from?"

"Wait, fear?" Devon looked at each of them in turn.

"Fine. I've been getting the feeling that someone or something has been watching me when I take the Nugget out to go to potty."

"Okay, well, that's easy enough. It's more than likely just a turkey or a deer." Evangeline started to turn around.

"No, it's not, Mom."

"Oh?"

"How do you know? Have you seen it?" Devon sounded agitated.

"No, I haven't, but I've felt it when I go to take the trash out". She started to bite her nails but seemed to think better of it. "Sometimes, there are sounds. Like I've heard things walking, but when I turn around, there's nothing. Nobody is there. No animal either. There aren't even prints."

"It's just your imagination then. Something caused because of the things that you've heard somewhere or seen on T.V.," Devon said. He leaned back, pulled his arm away from her and took out his phone. "We've all done that before."

"You think? What a relief! You are always right and so much smarter than me."

"Okay, Taylor, that's enough. He's just trying to help." Evangeline gave him a stern look, her jaw clenched. Devon had a lot to learn about social cues, and girls in general for that matter. "I want to know your experience. Devon, if you can't listen to her, then would you please go to the kitchen and preheat the oven?"

Taylor waited until Devon left the room. "It's like I've turned my head in time to see something peeking from behind the shed. Something big. I just don't know. Maybe Devon is right and I'm just being paranoid."

Evangeline gave her daughter a hug. "Taylor, never doubt yourself. You know, my great grandfather, the one that used to own this place before you were born? He used to say that there are things all around us that we can't always explain or even understand. That's why there's magic in the world. You just need to believe and be patient."

"Yeah, isn't he the guy that Grandma said was crazy?"

"Is there a difference?" She smiled. "The point I'm making is that Devon is a kid. He doesn't know everything. If it scares you, or if it's something you are experiencing, then it's real enough for me. Besides, who is he, really, to judge the reality of your experiences?"

"I'm her boyfriend."

"And you are eavesdropping." Taylor tossed a throw pillow at him. Devon knocked it into a stack of games on the table near the couch.

"No throwing things, and you be careful and watch where you smack things too." Evangeline snapped.

Taylor stuck her tongue out at him.

Evangeline shook her head. "Taylor, if it makes you feel better, I will have your dad take the trash out tonight when he gets home." She gave her a thumbs up and went to get dinner ready

The evening passed without too much of an issue. The kids helped Evangeline clean up and Devon managed to convince Taylor to go for a walk with him. Evangeline's youngest had slept through the meal, not willing to wake up for pizza. Instead, she groaned about popcorn chicken. In the end, Evangeline gave up and called her husband. Luckily, when Katie was in the mood to refuse what was offered or too tired to wake up on errand days, Evangeline could count on Grant to come to the rescue and stop somewhere to grab the food of choice. It wasn't ideal, but it helped keep Katie from going for days on end without eating.

Evangeline tapped her cell against her palm and looked around the living room. Devon was trying to ease Taylor's fears of being outside in the dark by walking her around the back yard with a flashlight. When Evangeline had told Grant about that he laughed, reminding her that they were teenagers once too. Of course, she knew that he was probably right, but she also knew that Taylor was truly scared and wasn't going to find a make-out session in creepy back yard a fun thing to do. Still, she did hope that it eased her fears, even just a little.

Deciding that there wasn't much to do but wait for Grant to get home, Evangeline grabbed her book from the table and peeked into her youngest daughter's room. Katie was still sleeping, muttering into her plush unicorn. One dog lay at her feet with its head on resting on her legs while another was on the floor next to her bed. Evangeline smiled, patted their heads. "That's right, girls, keep her safe and warm."

Evangeline was nearly through the short hall between the front and back of the house when the front door slammed shut. Taylor came storming into the front room. Devon wasn't far behind her, looking sheepish.

Evangeline clutched her book and phone against her chest then held her other hand out to keep Taylor from knocking her over. "Do you think you two could possibly slow down and shut the door like normal people?"

"Mom, please explain to Devon about the woods," she huffed.

"She's trying to say that before the snow was here, there were strange lights in the woods and that Moira had found skeletons in there."

"Skeletons, no, but she did happen across some deer heads and other various bones. Nothing fully assembled or human though." Evangeline shrugged.

"So, poachers or hunters then?" Devon looked smug.

"Well, possibly, but..."

"Poachers need weapons, idiot," Taylor snapped. "We've never heard a single shot fired and nobody has ever gone into them with a bow or spear or anything."

"Spear?" Evangeline almost laughed.

"Look, I ran out of names for hunting weapons. Don't judge me." Taylor stuck her tongue out and continued. "As for the lights, Papa Jasper used to say that the lights were faeries or spirits of ancestors or something like that. He said that Nanna Becky taught him about the woods and how to see and speak to everything. Grandma just says that Papa lied a lot and hid the truth from people, and that this place and everything around it is bad news, that the land is cursed because of Aloysius."

"Wow, really, Taylor? Papa never did anything to deserve that. Your Grandma just didn't like that they weren't like her family and that, in the end, it wasn't the happily ever after of her dreams." Evangeline crossed the room and set her book on the dining table. "I don't know why I let you spend time with her."

"Mom, I'm..."

"Enough." She held her hand up. "A lot of rumors have gone on about your grandparents and Papa's family especially. One thing always gets left out. Grandma married into the family because she was pregnant. Had her parents not tossed her out on her ass for getting knocked up she wouldn't have given those rumors a second thought."

"Okay, Mom, I'm sorry. It's just, whatever is out there, it didn't come from rumors. I know what I've heard, and I know what I've felt."

Devon ran his hand through his hair. "Taylor, I keep telling you, I didn't feel anything, see anything or hear anything when we were out there."

"Yeah, well, maybe it's because you don't believe me."

"Or it doesn't exist."

"You just don't get it, do you?"

The door leading from the entryway opened and Grant came in with a paper sack of popcorn chicken and ranch dressing. "Who doesn't get what now?"

"Devon doesn't believe that there is anything out in the woods, and Mom is mad at me because I repeated what Grandma said."

"Well, for one, you should never repeat what either of your grandmothers say." Grant chuckled. "Whether or not you believe them is up to you." He winked at Devon. "You, kid, are on your own. I've learned that you never argue with the women in this family."

"And that means what exactly?" Evangeline went over to him and took the bag of food.

"Just that you're always right, dear." He kissed her forehead and followed her over to the kitchen table.

"Mmhmm."

Taylor took Devon's hand and pulled him towards the living room. "We're going to go play video games now."

Katie came running into the room, the dogs bounding around her. She didn't say a word, just raced up to Grant and Evangeline. The dogs jumped around like it was one of the best games, with their tails wagging and tongues hanging out of their mouths. Grant leaned down, picked Katie up and hugged her tight before setting her at the table and sliding in next to her.

Evangeline placed some of the popcorn chicken onto a paper plate with a portion of the ranch dressing. "I wasn't sure you were ever going to wake up." She set the plate in front of Katie and sat down across from them.

"Mommy? Daddy?" Katie's voice was high pitched, almost sad.

"What's up, kiddo?" Grant rubbed their youngest's back then snatched a piece of the popcorn chicken from her plate.

"Is why I woke up is because I had a nightmare." Her voice sounded small.

"Oh, honey, I'm sorry. Do you want to tell us about it?" Evangeline looked at her husband, but he was so focused on their daughter that he didn't notice.

"I had a dream that there was something bad outside." She ate a few pieces and started swirling one in the ranch dressing on her plate as she yawned.

"Like what?" Grant rested his cheek on his fist and listened.

"Like something bad and mean, and it was trying to get me." Katie took another bite and pushed her plate away. "It was a monster." Evangeline knew that Katie was saying monster, but with her mouth full of chicken it sounded like she said mopster.

"Nothing is going to get you, Katie. It was all just a dream." Grant explained. "That's all a nightmare is, a dream, nothing more."

"Let her at least finish speaking. Is there anything else?"

"Just that it was from outside. It came from in the backyard and it hurted Taylor and Daddy and you and it was taking me to the trees."

The dogs started barking and running toward the back of the house.

"I'm scared!" Katie buried her head in Grant's chest and started crying.

"Shh, it's okay. It's just the dogs being idiots." He tried to reassure their daughter, but she only cried more.

"Don't let it hurt us. I don't want to have no parents and no family."

"That's not going to happen, baby." Grant wrapped her in his arms and lifted her. "Let's go check it out and see what they're doing."

Evangeline followed them into the living room. The dogs were rough housing together with one of their toys in front of the couch. Taylor lifted her head from Devon's shoulder. She stretched her legs and arms out straight in front of herself.

"Hey guys, is she okay?" Taylor asked.

"Yeah, she's fine. Just a nightmare." Grant was headed into Katie's bedroom. "Let's get you to bed."

"Will you read to me?"

"Yes, I'll read you a story."

"How about four?"

"How about two, and that's it."

"Okay."

"Evangie, babe, would you get me some water? I have a feeling these are going to be long stories." Grant winked at her.

"Yep, I'll go grab it." She snickered a little as she walked into the kitchen. She loved when Grant read to their kids when they were little. It generally meant that they would be sound asleep in no time, which made it easier during storms and blizzards. Katie was no exception. She was a Daddy's girl through and through and between her late nap, the weather, and her nightmare, Evangeline was glad that she could count on Grant to be the hero.

She turned from the island and thought she caught a glimpse of what looked like someone peeking through the window. She looked again then did her best to brush it off.

Coming back into the living room with Grant's bottle of water, she almost bumped into him. He towered over her, yet she hadn't seen him there. She stepped backwards and looked around him. "Where is Katie?"

"She's asleep." He grinned and took the bottle of water from her. "This for me?"

"Nah, it's for the other guy I'm married to." She shoved him playfully.

"C'mon, let's get some rest." He took her hand and kissed her palm before heading to their bedroom on the other side of their living room, directly across from Katie's room.

"Okay, kids, I'm headed to bed. The last thing I want to do tonight is leave you both unsupervised, but I also don't want to watch you play games either." Evangeline looked out the back window at the snow again. "I'm trusting the two of you. Don't make me regret it."

"Yes, ma'am."

Evangeline could hear the embarrassment in her daughter's voice.

"Huh? I'm lost." Devon looked up from the computer game bashfully. "What are we doing?"

"Nothing," Taylor told him.

"No, he needs to know. I'm trusting you both. I'm trusting that you will not disappoint me, Devon. That means no hanky-panky. Nothing that is rated above PG. If it's not in a Disney film, fit for Katie to watch, you two don't do it," Evangeline said as she walked into her bedroom.

"What does that even mean?" Devon asked as she was about to close the door.

Her head dropped as she turned back around. "I would say that if you don't know you should be good, but I don't think you are that naïve. It means no sex, kid." She looked past him and Taylor on the couch and out the window.

"Mom, are you okay?" Taylor moved to stand up.

She shook her head and smiled. "I'm fine." She went into her room and closed the door.

"Evangie? Hey," Grant hugged her tight. "Honey, are you okay? You look like you saw a ghost."

"I don't know that I didn't. I was talking to the kids then I saw footprints in the snow, like something had been walking around the firepit and towards the deck. Would you please go look?"

Grant stared down at her. Evangeline knew she sounded crazy, but she tried her best to explain. In the end, she wasn't sure if he believed her, or if he just thought she was in desperate need of sleep or medication or, hell, perhaps both.

"Please? What if there is something to what Taylor said, or to Katie's nightmares? Something has them spooked."

"You're right, Evangie. There is. It's all those damned stories that your mother keeps telling them. I told you not to let that woman be around them without supervision. She's not right in the head. You know this."

"Okay, but would you just go look?" She pleaded with him. "I get it, she's batshit crazy. You don't like her, and that's fine, but I need you to please look by the fire pit. Tell me I'm wrong. Tell me there are no footprints."

"Yeah, sure, I will." Grant pulled his pajama pants on and went into the living room. "I don't know if your mother told you, but it's time to go to bed."

Evangeline watched as Grant stood at the corner of the couch, just outside their room, staring out the window. He made a big show of stepping up onto the couch between the two kids then went about fixing the curtains so that they were on their hooks right and would close all the way.

"At the very least, turn the games off for the night and find a movie. Just don't turn it up too loud." Grant stepped down from the one couch and gave Taylor a hug. When he stepped back, he guided her to the other couch and threatened to tuck her in.

"No, that's okay, Dad. Really, I'm good. I can pull my covers up just fine on my own."

"Remember what you were told. Hands to yourself." He gave a stern look to Devon "And don't even think about moving to the other couch, either of you."

Devon just nodded, closed his computer, and put his head down next to Taylor.

When Grant came back into the bedroom, he closed the door and stripped down to his boxers. He crawled back into bed and lay next to Evangeline. She stared at him, waiting, but all he did was pick up the remote and start scrolling through their streaming options.

"Well? Did you see them?"

"Okay, so you were right. There are definitely footprints out there, but what do you want me to do about them? I'm not going out there right now. It's cold. Cold enough, in fact, they aren't going anywhere tonight. I'll check it in the morning, see what I can find. For now, let's get some sleep."

The next morning, Evangeline woke up late. When she emerged from her room, she was greeted by the smell of food cooking and the sound of laughter. She continued to stretch as she looked outside and saw that the sun was out. Crossing the living room, she realized that Katie was up also.

Taylor came out of the bedroom and nearly crashed into her. "Oh, hey, Mom. Sleep okay?"

"Yeah, I guess I just didn't realize how tired I was."

"Well, at least you got some sleep. Dad is making breakfast."

"I could definitely eat." Evangeline made her way to the kitchen, wrapped her arms about Grant's waist, and leaned her head against his back.

"I'm assuming it's the bacon that earned this affection?"

"Nope, I just love you, especially because you let me sleep in. Of course," she smirked and leaned around to look up at him, "the bacon is definitely an added bonus."

"Well, I'm glad you are in such a good mood."

"Oh?"

Grant asked the kids sitting at the table if they could take the dogs out. While Taylor was unhappy about the idea, Evangeline could see that she wasn't going to argue. Sometimes, the snarky attitude her daughter gave off could be controlled. She was impressed.

Once all the kids were outside, Evangeline gave Grant a piercing look.

"Look, I told you last night I would check out the footprints" he said as he handed her a plate of bacon and eggs. "So, this morning I went out there before anyone woke up."

She moved a piece of bacon as if she were coaxing him to continue.

"Well, there are footprints alright, but they make no sense. It's like they start suddenly right on the edge of the levy across from our room by the big pine and then they traverse the backyard. They go almost to the end of the house, near the garage but then they just stop. There's no back tracking, nothing. They just vanish."

She looked up at him and shook her head. "That is just..." She bit her bacon, lost in thought. "It's crazy, that's what it is. What could possibly do that?"

"I don't know." He shrugged. "I honestly don't know."

They finished their breakfast, discussing in hushed tones what the girls had said the night before. Neither one of them had an explanation for the prints. Evangeline felt a chill in her core.

"They are right about one thing." Grant took a sip of his coffee. "Whatever made the footprints came from the woods."

Since she was a child, SAIDE MENDENHALL-CARIVEAU has had a passion for writing and remembers telling teachers and family members that she wanted to be a writer. She has won awards, certificates and scholarships for her essays, short stories, and poetry since sixth grade. Sadie became more inspired and determined to see her dreams come to fruition while serving in the United States Air Force and began participating in workshops and pursuing degrees in Creative Writing. Drawing inspiration from her own life and everything she feels affected by, her writing has been published in both online and in-print journals as well as the anthology *Tales from the Frozen North*. Sadie's goal is to complete her poetry collection and her book and to never stop writing.

Final Wish

Robin Cain

The drone of the plane engine lulls me into that space between deep relaxation and sleep, but I'm jolted back to consciousness by the inconsiderate passenger sitting to my right. Not only is he a man bordering on too large for a single seat, but a restless traveler as well. His meaty arm has all but overtaken the right side of my body as his attention shuffles between a stack of newspapers, his second cocktail, and a third bag of complimentary peanuts. I sigh and squeeze closer to the window. Not what I needed for this particular trip.

I'm heading back to Effham Falls, a small town in the northern reaches of Minnesota, and a place I briefly lived once upon a time. This place that always felt like it sat in the middle of nowhere wasn't my first choice for a weekend getaway, but my trip isn't of the vacation variety. I'm returning out of duty, to honor the final wishes of a man I haven't seen in ten years.

The news of his passing reached me a couple weeks ago when I had answered the phone without first looking at the screen. A voice and a name I didn't recognize. An introduction made worse by a bad telephone connection. Just when I'd decided someone had the wrong number, the caller spoke her son's name.

Grayson.

Even now, wedged in a plane seat and in dire need of a good night's sleep, the name brings about inexplicable melancholy. I gaze out the window, press my nose against the glass, and remember what has brought me here.

Friends found Grayson laid out on his sofa, a needle still hanging from his arm. His death appeared to be an accidental overdose—until they found the suicide note.

The rest of the details distorted as I dropped to my knees in the middle of my kitchen. Though I'd always feared Grayson's weakness would take him much too soon, the reality of his having made that a conscious choice shocked me. His infrequent text messages over the years never revealed anything more than a man still trying to stay clean. I never imagined this would be how our story would end.

The pilot announces that we'll be landing soon. We've breached a thick layer of clouds and the ground is now visible. Fields plaited in perfect green squares and circles appear stitched together by unpaved roads. Splashes and tendrils of blues and greens mark the too-many-to-count lakes that give Minnesota its nickname. Farmhouses and barns dot the landscape in nearly precise intervals. Farther to the northeast, fields transform into forests, lakes multiply in numbers, and buildings start cozying up to one another. The airport, up ahead, is exactly where I left it.

Effham Falls is still a couple hours' drive, but that will give me time to collect my thoughts before I'm supposed to meet with Grayson's mother. The travel details and meeting time were all finalized with minimum discussion. Since then, I've spent the days struggling with what, exactly, we're going to discuss.

The airport is an easy in and out and, in short order, I'm making my way back to the town where I lived after college graduation. At the time, with no job and student loans to pay, living with my parents became my only option. They had assured me I would 'absolutely love' their new home in Minnesota. If only.

This drive reminds me how much I hated Effham Falls at first. Not enough good stores and too many churches, fried fish but no sushi, a one-movie theater, and a main street that rolled its sidewalks up every night. Most job openings at the time were in the tourist industry, paying minimum wage (neither fact appealing to my Political Science degree), and getting the better jobs relied on 'knowing someone'. I didn't know anyone so, within the month, it became apparent that small town living wasn't for me and I made plans to leave. That one night changed the entire trajectory of my life, a fact that is not lost on me.

"How do you expect to pay rent and your loans without a job?" The bulging vein on the side of my father's head clued me in to his frustration.

"A couple of friends from school said I could crash with them for a while. The job market is better in Chicago," I told him, though I had no proof. "Besides, I don't like it here."

My mother accused me of having a bad attitude, and I told her she needed to butt out. Big mistake. Dad yelled, Mom cried, and I took off for the Rusty Nail Bar and Grill—the only bar I had seen in my travels to date and, subsequently, the place where Grayson saddled up onto the stool next to mine.

"Well, hello there. You're the new girl in town. I'm Grayson." His matter-of-fact statement confirmed what I'd already suspected: everyone knew everyone in this small town, and the 'new girl' hadn't gone unnoticed. I scooched away from him, but he just kept talking.

That was the thing about Grayson. He had no fear of social situations or of what people might think. I'd learn that his sitting down to talk to me, a total stranger, came as second nature to him as my predisposition to avoid the same thing.

He was living a life of sobriety when we met, a fact he unapologetically shared that first night. He'd done a stint at rehab and come out the other side convinced he was a changed man. Though he didn't name his drug of choice, his consumption of soft drinks that night led me to believe alcohol was his kryptonite. His real weakness, I later learned, was far worse.

Despite his confession and what seemed to be our opposite personalities, that evening marked the start of 'us'. Something about his Ying fit well with my Yang. That's not to say our relationship depended on sex. His ability to get me to open up kept us talking for hours. He never offered any judgement, only acceptance and a sincere interest in what I had to say. Plus, he made me laugh....God, did we laugh. As an unemployed twenty-something living in a strange land with her parents, I desperately needed self-confidence and a friend. Grayson managed to provide both and feed my soul at the same time. The battle he fought didn't make itself apparent until weeks into our relationship.

The sign on the highway informs me the next exit is mine. My palms are sweating, and a knot seems to have taken up permanent residence between my shoulder blades since Grayson's mother's call. The exact details of what I'm here to do are unknown, but my history with Grayson has propelled me forward without my asking too many questions. Like everything involving my relationship with him, the Universe is telling me to trust my gut. I have twenty minutes to get to Blakewood Assisted Living Center if I'm to be on time.

I pull into the parking lot with five minutes to spare. My reflection in the rearview mirror reveals eyes filled with apprehension and sadness. I let them close for a moment and I hear Grayson's voice.

Annie, you're a beautiful soul. You can do this.

No one ever believed in me like he did.

After checking in at the automated Welcome kiosk, I'm directed by the receptionist to the elevator and the second floor where June McKinley lives. It's only three o'clock in the afternoon, but a handful of people in a room to my left appear to be enjoying some form of Happy Hour. Their boisterous conversation and laughter tell me they've likely been at it awhile. A shot of liquid courage is enticing, but I get on the elevator instead. I need my wits about me for this next thing—whatever it is.

Based on the numbering system, Mrs. McKinley's apartment should be at the end of this long hallway. Prematurely placed Halloween decorations hang in various windows. Bulletins posted on walls announce an elaborate assortment of upcoming activities. This facility has always had the reputation for being one of the better and pricier options in the area and everything from the expensive window coverings to the plush carpet testify to this. I learned shortly after moving here that Grayson's parents were one of the oldest and wealthiest families in town. They paid for his first stint in rehab. They paid for his second as well, but his mother pretty much disowned him afterwards.

"Ann? Is that you?"

Focused as I am on the hallway ahead, I didn't notice the little lounge area to my right where Mrs. McKinley is sitting in a wheelchair. Though we've never met, the gray hair and years-older body can't disguise the fact this is Grayson's mother. The round face and vibrant blue eyes are a dead giveaway.

"Mrs. McKinley?" I make my way over, ready to offer a handshake, but a stroke or something has left her right side disabled. I switch to an awkward, bent-at-the-waist hug. Her one good arm attempts to go around my shoulder but returns to her lap from the midway point. I'm unsure if it's due to lack of ability or desire.

She scans me from head to toe. "Did everything go well with your trip?"

"Yes, ma'am. No flight delays, and good weather. The car I rented seemed to know the way here."

Not even a smile. "Please be sure to keep track of all you've spent so I can reimburse you as we discussed."

"I already told—"

"There will be no argument. These are his final wishes. It's my responsibility to see them carried out as he wanted."

I'm torn between my desire to not take a dime from her and my genuine need for reimbursement. Unsure what to do, I go another route. "I want to tell you again how very sorry I am for your loss, Mrs. McKinley. The Grayson I knew loved you very much." Though this woman surely had much to do with Grayson's lifelong issues, as his mother, she deserves some empathy—and this lie.

She removes a tissue from inside the sleeve of her blouse and wipes her nose. "He must have loved you more. I suspect that's why you're here."

The words 'love' and 'Grayson', intricately entwined within my psyche, have been tucked away in a dark space I rarely, if ever, visit. Her speaking them aloud, even in this passive-aggressive manner, brings all my conflicting emotions to the surface. With no tissue hidden, I turn from her and wipe my eyes with my sleeve.

"Come now. Let's go to my room. I'm sure you're tired from your trip and anxious to check into the motel. This won't take long."

Her apartment smells of lilacs. A delicate scent unbefitting the woman I'd heard about over the years. Industrial cleaner and bleach might have been more apt. She motions for me to take a seat in the living room and asks if I'd like something to drink, but her gestures seem to come more from a sense of obligation rather than any sort of kindness. As she rolls her chair from here to there to make us tea, I give her the benefit of the doubt. I wander over to the fireplace and study the framed photographs covering her walls, looking for ones of Grayson. I'm curious what ten years of living did to his looks.

There had been five children in the McKinley family, and the various photos make it appear as though everyone went on to have their own families. Schools, sports, weddings, babies — smiling faces all captured for later. As I recall my own assortment of photos at home, I wonder how this family is doing after losing a brother, an uncle, a friend.

Then there he is. A single picture on the mantle, at the end of a line of what I assume are grandchildren. My breath involuntarily catches somewhere around my heart.

Grayson.

His blue eyes stare back at me as he reclines in what appears to be a stadium chair at a sporting event. His mouth is partially open, his head tilted back. Laughing, near as I can guess. His laugh…that right-from-his-stomach contagious laugh bounces off the walls of my brain and I find myself smiling despite what brings me here.

The picture looks like it had been taken not too terribly long after I last saw him. A few crow's feet at his eyes, a hint of thinning hair, are the only things that show some, but not too much time had passed. He looks good, even when his insides were likely being torn apart by addiction.

"I see you've found his photo." Mrs. McKinley has somehow managed to soundlessly sneak up behind me.

"When was this taken?" I grip the framed photo and take a step back from her, though doing so makes no sense. Am I afraid she'll take it from me?

"I can't recall, but that's one of the few times in his adult life he looked happy and healthy. I had it framed so everyone can remember him that way." She motions for me to sit on the sofa.

While I had been absorbed in studying pictures, she had placed two cups of tea on the coffee table, along with a manila envelope. The sight brings me back into focus. I sense the details of my duties, the exact reasons I've been summoned are in that envelope. All I know for sure is that Grayson wanted me to deal with his ashes. For more reasons I can't explain, I bring the photo of him to the sofa.

Mrs. McKinley opens the envelope, pulls out a wrinkled sheet of paper and two smaller white envelopes. One of them has my name written on it. 'Mother' is written on the other.

"Forgive me for my lack of small talk, Ann. None of this is pleasant for anyone, so I'm hoping this last step will finally bring us all some closure. The fact that Grayson made this request, even left instructions on how to get a hold of you, leads me to believe you two were still in contact." Her statement seems like a question, but I'm unsure how to answer.

"Yes...well, no, not exactly. I haven't seen him since I moved away, but I tried to stay in touch with him over the years. I wouldn't hear from him for long stretches of time, but he'd eventually reach out. His last text—"

"I seem to recall that you broke off the engagement very suddenly and moved away. Are you married with children now, Ann?" She studies me as the question leaves her lips, seemingly oblivious to the fact she cut my last answer short.

"No." The quick lie is still easier than the truth. Though I rehearsed this meeting in my mind a million times since she first called, the discussion isn't going according to plan. But there might still be time.

"The only reason I ask is because flying all this way for a man who killed himself—with illegal drugs, no less—would surely be difficult to explain to a family."

She's pushing me closer to anger, and farther from my good intentions. I think I might know now why Grayson never wanted me to meet her. I can almost hear him saying I told you so. I unclench my jaw and look directly at her. "No...I don't have to explain myself to anyone."

A whispered huff of what sounds like exasperation escapes her lips. "All right then. If you're ready." She lifts the wrinkled sheet of paper. "This is the note that Grayson left me. I'll let you read it." As she extends the paper, a tremor finds its way into her hand.

I can't bring myself to take the piece of paper, much less read what's written on it. The words, whatever they are, will make this real, and I'm not ready. Not ready to learn why Grayson left us. Not ready to break down in front of this woman who cared more about what this town thought of her than she did her own son.

Her wheelchair is so close I can hear her labored breathing. Or is it mine? I take a few shallow but steady breaths, then find the courage to take the paper from her and lay it on my lap.

"I'll give you two a moment alone," she says, wheeling herself into the next room.

Her choice of words lingers, and I glance down at Grayson's smiling face. Does he somehow know I'm here with his mother, that she's getting under my skin?

No, he wouldn't want me to let her get the best of me. I sit up and force myself to read.

> *My apologies to whoever finds me like this. I hope I don't stink too bad.*
>
> *LOL.*
>
> *I'd tell you to take the needle out of my arm for the sake of appearances before you call for help, but I'm pretty sure that wouldn't fool anyone. We all know that there's no such thing as a secret in a small town. Besides, my family knows me too well, and most everyone else will make up their own story anyway. The people in this town have never understood why or how much I've struggled, so f'em. (Effham. get it? My mother always hated that joke.)*
>
> *Whoever is reading this, please make sure the two envelopes on the table get to my mother at Blakewood. She'll figure out what to do with them. I've written her phone number below.*
>
> *There's a better world waiting for me out there somewhere. Sorry I couldn't wait any longer to get there. ~G.*

My tears stain the paper. Part of me wants to throw Grayson's photo across the room. The other part wants to clutch him to my heart. My most pressing questions haven't been answered, but now, at least, I can see that he seemed to have been coherent in his choice, and not a person completely out of his mind on drugs.

A ringing phone pulls me from my thoughts. Mrs. McKinley picks up an extension in the other room. The envelope with my name on it is still unopened. Does etiquette demand I wait for her to proceed? The decision is made when she wheels into the room, a simple wooden box resting on her lap.

"That was my daughter calling to tell me she'll be here soon. She knew of this meeting with you this afternoon."

I'm not sure which is more unsettling: being interrupted by another family member who never supported Grayson, the two envelopes laying on the table, or the newly introduced box sitting in her lap. Damn you for making all this my reality, Grayson.

The envelope with my name the more pressing issue, I point. "What about that?"

"In Grayson's note to me, he made clear his desire to be cremated. He didn't want to be left lying around my house or buried in dirt somewhere. His ashes, along with that envelope, are to be given to you. He didn't want me to read your note and I haven't. I trust he had his reasons." She lifts the wooden box with her one good arm and gestures for me to take it. "I entrust this to you now. Take this and your envelope with you when you go. My only request is that you let me know when it's all done." Her indifference, combined with her blind trust in me, is unnerving.

"What would you have done if I hadn't agreed to this?"

"That thought never really crossed my mind. The things Grayson wrote in my note convinced me that you would come. And he was right, wasn't he?" She stops to wipe her nose. "But I must tell you that my daughter is pretty upset with how I'm handling this. She believes we should oversee disposal of the ashes, and I'm guessing she's coming over early to try one last time to change my mind. I suggest you leave before she gets here." She gathers our untouched cups of tea and heads to the kitchen.

I'm in sensory overload and unable to move from the sofa. The sister's impending arrival, her intention to change the course of events, have added another plot twist. Though I want to believe that relinquishing Grayson's remains, even if he had been a disappointment to the family, couldn't have been an easy decision for his mother, I've seen no proof of this. I also don't know if her mind can be changed. What I do know is that after all these years, if nothing else, I owe it to Grayson to carry out his wishes, whatever they may be. Neither his sister, nor his mother, should be allowed to get in the way of that. It's time for me to go. I stuff the framed picture of Grayson into my backpack. His mother doesn't deserve proof of any happiness he might've ever had.

We say goodbye at her doorway. Neither of us offer a parting hug. All disingenuous pleasantries are over. I reach the end of the hallway, and the ten long years of second-guessing myself has me wondering if I should turn back around. Things just can't be left like this. I turn and start to speak, but she has already disappeared. All regrets I had prior to our meeting now make way less sense.

Inside my rental car, with Grayson and my envelope on the seat beside me, I ponder my next move. Reading a suicide note in a tiny rental car parked at an old people's home must surely break some decency law. Not that a cheap motel room is going to be any better, but my choices are limited. I opt for Plan B, but before I start the car, I move the box to the floor just to be safe. Though Grayson would no doubt find humor in his ashes dumped all over the car, the idea of scraping him off the carpet horrifies me. Now certain that won't happen, I head to the motel.

The Wayside Inn is as I remember. Nothing more than a single-story roadside building with a funky vintage sign announcing free cable tv, but I know it's clean and adequate—or at least it used to be. The desk clerk, a woman named Prudence whom I recall owned the place back in the day, stares at me with empty eyes and says nothing, even now when I'm standing right in front of her.

"Is something wrong?" I glance around the lobby, wondering if there is something I'm missing.

"No, nothing at all. You're Ann Hanson, right?" Her steely gray eyes are made more pronounced by her all-black attire.

I don't know if she recognizes me from the many times Grayson and I stayed here back in the day, or if I'm just the next name on her day's list of customers, but something doesn't feel quite right. The odd herbal aroma of mint and sugar that she's giving off isn't helping. So far, there's nothing welcoming about the Wayside Inn this time around. Maybe all those weird rumors I used to hear about part of this town being haunted hold some truth after all.

"Yes, that's me." I put my ID and credit card on the counter in hopes of moving our transaction along.

"You know..." She's lowered her voice to just above a whisper. "Lots of folks around here have been wondering if you'd actually show up."

I've been away a long time, but nothing about her remark surprises me. Like Grayson said, there's no such thing as a secret in a small town.

"And why would that be?" I could venture any number of guesses, but I really want to hear her version.

"Rumor has it the family is blaming you for everything."

The pain her words inflict has me momentarily gasp for air. The remark is proof of the ugliness of Grayson's relationships with his family, the ways of this stupid town, and the ignorance of people when it comes to the subject of addiction. I focus on controlling my breathing and sign the forms she pushes in my direction. Damn if I'll let this town get the best of me.

"I didn't say *everyone* is blaming you. Just the family. I, personally, think it's nice that you showed up. Nice guy like Grayson... it's really too bad he could never get his act together, huh?"

The phone on the counter rings. My chance to escape. I head for the exit.

"Free coffee here in the morning, Ann. Enjoy your evening," she calls after me as she picks up the receiver.

The parking lot is nearly empty. Now that the sun has nearly set, the temperature has dropped, and I'm shivering despite the angry, uncomfortable sweat I had going on in the lobby. Multiple reminders of how ill-prepared I am for this trip. I retrieve Grayson and my things from the car.

The motel room has obviously not had any renovations in my absence. North Woods fabrics, worn carpet, and a television from the dark ages, but the bathroom is clean. I fling my suitcase into a corner and set the box and envelope on the bed. The old-fashioned clock on the nightstand is making a weird ticking noise that will annoy me later when I'm trying to sleep. But I'm annoyed with everything right now. The clock marks off the minutes I fume about current events.

Time to shake off my encounter with Prudence and unseal the envelope.

Hello dear Annie-

I hear him say those words, and the tension in my neck eases.

If you're reading this, you now know why I never wanted you to meet my mother. I'm sorry. Necessary evil. I'd say I hope she wasn't awful to you, but I know better.

That aside, yes, I'm a shit and you're very angry right now. I hope, in time, you'll understand this choice of mine at some level. I'm tired of the battle, Annie. Tired of fighting these demons of mine. There's has to be something better out there than this hell that's been my life. Three strikes at rehab and I'm out, so to speak. I'm a failure and I can tell I'm about to fall off another cliff. I just can't do it again. So here I am, and I hope I've succeeded. But I have one last favor to ask you.

Remember that day we went to Eagle Mountain to celebrate my sobriety milestone? When I asked you to marry me, remember? I truly believed in the possibility of living happily ever after, that the worst lay behind me. I believed that us, together, would make me invincible. You always supported me when no one else would, and even though I managed to fuck all that up, that day up there was brilliant.

Now I want you to share a day like that with me one last time. I want you to take me up there to rest. There, where it felt like we were on top of the world, where we made plans for our forever, and threw caution to the wind. I found my smile up there, high above everything that has dragged me down since.

Spread my ashes where we made love that day—when I was sober and you loved me. I want to be in that place for all eternity.

My asking you to come back to do this after all these years is unfair, but please know that I don't think you owe me. NONE of this is your fault. It's all on me, and I'm asking you to understand. I need this last beautiful goodbye. Please do this for me, Annie. Let me go in the wind so I can find peace, and maybe a happiness I had once upon a time.

You're a beautiful soul and I trust you.

P.S. I hope you find my little Buddha. Let him look after you now.

Memories rush to the surface. I'd forgotten how hopeful we were back then, six months after his second stint in rehab. With a new job and a commitment to AA, he'd regained some of the weight the drugs had stolen from him, and he looked good. Even better, he seemed to have finally faced the truth: He was an addict. We'd had those glorious months of believing he'd turned the corner, and I believed in him enough to say I'd marry him.

It's too late in the day for the drive to Eagle Mountain. A quick text to my family to let them know I'm okay—my second lie of the day—and I curl up in a fetal position under the covers, still in my street clothes, and close my swollen eyes.

A backfiring truck wakes me. The first hints of daylight come through the still-open curtains, and the clocks says I've been asleep for twelve hours. A long day ahead demands a quick shower and, with little thought to my appearance, I dress and grab Grayson's ashes, my backpack, and head to my car. The free coffee Prudence spoke of has me pivot to the lobby. Thank God she's tied up with a customer and doesn't glance my way, but the old Golden Retriever laying in the corner raises its head and wags its tail in greeting. How come he didn't show his sweet face last night when I needed to be welcomed? I scoot out the door before I'm tempted to make friends and get covered in dog hair.

The road out of town is empty except for the occasional semi. The radio on this cheap rental car didn't include any subscriptions and reception is spotty, so there's nothing to distract me from my thoughts as the miles pile up. I'm not surprised Grayson has chosen this destination. He'd always loved it out there. Yes, a fitting choice, but I wish I'd packed warmer clothes and a heavier coat. The temperature reading on the display downtown read a crisp forty-five degrees when I left. The top of the mountain will be even colder.

Mile markers keep count of the memories flooding my brain: conversations Grayson and I had, the laughs we shared, our crazy adventures, the lies we told, the promises we broke, the pain we caused each other. These highs and the lows of dating an addict remind me how I got here. My guilt reminds me why.

"Damnit, Grayson. I loved you so much. If only we'd both been stronger."

The hours pass and the entrance to Eagle Mountain looms ahead. I glance at the box on the floor. This is it, my friend. We've arrived.

The six-mile hike to the top is taking me longer than it should. Out of shape and ten years older, lugging Grayson in my backpack, I'm sweating despite the cold air. Much of the trek is through dense forest, and the path, which is rocky and full of tree roots, demands my full attention. I should've packed more appropriate shoes. Should have. I should have done a lot of things. Better shoes hardly rank in importance. I laugh out loud at the thought. I bet Grayson might have even done the same.

The forest gives way to an opening, and Whales Lake is now visible off to my left. If memory serves, the summit should be just ahead, but I think there's a bit of a last brutal ascent to get there. With the goal so close, I push through without stopping and find the familiar flat hunk of granite at the top. I stop moving just to make sure my pounding heart won't explode. Struggling to catch my breath, I set down my backpack and take in the view. This highest point in the state, even if only a little over two thousand feet, feels like the entire world is spread out below me.

This is where Grayson and I made love that day. This is where he wants his ashes left. We made it.

A dragonfly hovers at eye-level for a moment then lands on my shoe. The sight reminds me of the first gift Grayson ever gave me. The necklace nothing more than a cloisonne insect on a simple chain, but the clerk at the antique shop in town had told Grayson how a dragonfly represents great transformation and hope. A recovering Grayson, and the only guy I ever knew who believed in more 'woo-woo' stuff than me, loved the symbolism and serendipitous nature of his find. The necklace better suited a woman, so he bought it and asked me to wear it as a reminder for him. The guilt of having lost track of that gift long ago pokes at my already festering wound.

The wind kicks up a bit, but the dragonfly remains rooted on my shoe.

Is she here to be my witness?

I hug the box of ashes closer, not quite ready to let go. But I didn't hike up here for nothing. I must carry out his final wish.

You can do this, Annie.

"But I don't want to, Grayson."

His remains are in a plastic bag inside the box. I undo the twist tie and find chalk-white ashes and tiny fragments of a human being. Massaging the bag brings a chunk of something to the surface. It's a blackened piece of metal.

Oh, dear God. It's the Buddha figurine I gave Grayson the day I left town.

How did this...? He must have...

My shoulders sag. This is what he meant in his note. His plan for me to find it brings fresh tears. And memories.

"Do you have to leave, Annie? I slipped up. It won't happen again. I'll get better. I promise."

"You disappeared for days. I thought you were dead!"

"Please, An—"

"Stop now. It's too late. I got this little Buddha for you to keep in your pocket. Maybe he can protect you from your demons. At least let him remind you that I'll always be thinking of you."

Those were my last words to him before I left town—and I didn't say the one thing I should have. But I ran from him anyway, frightened of the monster he battled, terrified of what my staying would do to all of us.

My ringing cell phone drags me from the memory. I tap the video call icon. "Gracie, what's wrong?"

"You haven't called, Mom." There is wisdom-beyond-her-years concern in her eyes.

"I'm sorry, honey. I didn't mean to scare you. I've been busy since I texted yesterday. I intended to call you and Grandma later today."

Her scowl softens. "Did you say goodbye to your friend yet?"

Oh God. My friend. The guilt rushes back.

Gracie had accepted the story I'd given her about a 'dear friend's' death and his last wishes, but my mother had disagreed with my plan since I'd shared the news. Although only one of two people in my life who even knew of Grayson (and had supported my decision ten years earlier), she used his death as an excuse to reopen the case for what she referred to as my 'history of bad decisions'.

Most people, Grayson included, believed I broke off our engagement and left Effham Falls because he'd begun using again. The truth? I didn't want him or anyone else in this town to know I was pregnant. Even after I'd left, weeks passed before I finally mustered the courage to tell him, but he never answered any of my calls. I later learned he'd been in jail. Months went by, I gave birth to Gracie and, out of the blue, I received a text from him that seemed written by a man half out of his mind on drugs. With a daughter to raise and a host of other things to worry about, I pushed thoughts of him to the background. Out of sight, out of mind.

By the time Gracie reached an age to begin asking questions, too much time had passed to try and make things right. Grayson's roller coaster behavior had already convinced me we were better off without him in our lives.

As far as Gracie knows, her father passed before she was born, and I've managed to convince myself that mine wasn't the worst lie. Her father, the man I remembered and had once loved deeply, no longer existed.

"Mom? Did you hear me?"

Her question pulls me out of my reverie, reminding me I still have a job to do.

Centering the landscape on my screen, I try to sound upbeat. "Look at this view, Gracie. My friend asked me to scatter his ashes up here."

"Why up there? Is that what he wanted?"

"Yes, we came to this place once and really liked it. He thought we could see forever from here."

"What does forever look like?"

Her literal interpretation brings bittersweetness to the moment. What *does* forever look like?

"No, he just meant that from up here you can see really, really far away. In fact, if I stand on my tippy toes, I can see all the way to you."

For the few seconds before she giggles, she is still the little girl who believes everything her mother tells her.

"Would you like to stay on the phone and help me while I do this?"

"Would he mind?" Gracie has the tender heart of her father. One day I will tell her that.

"No, I think he would really like that you're here with us."

"Okay, but what can I do?"

The dragonfly rises from my shoe and zigzags in the breeze. Its color is the same vibrant blue of Grayson's eyes—and Gracie's. I'm starting to wonder if there might really be something to this 'woo-woo' stuff.

"Well...how about if you blow him a kiss? I think that would mean a great deal to him."

Once she agrees, I grasp the bag of ashes and stand up. The dragonfly moves to the space the ashes occupied on the seat.

"Is that your friend? I mean, in that bag. Is that him?"

"It is. Are you sure you want to do this with me?"

"Yes, Mommy."

She hasn't called me that in years. My momentum hits a wall.

I'm surely going to hell. Here to honor Grayson's wishes, I also came here to finally let his family know about Gracie, but I haven't done that. I'm guessing it's too late now.

I'm so sorry, Grayson. I thought I did the right thing for all of us.

A deep breath. I aim my camera forward. Turning slow in a semi-circle, with my other arm aloft, I release Grayson's ashes into the wind. A sudden gust takes most of him up and away. The rest of him scatters into the foliage-covered downhill slope. The dragonfly has vanished.

I turn the camera around the moment Gracie finishes blowing a kiss.

"Look, he's everywhere now," she says. "Just like Grandpa."

The finality chokes me. I grasp the little burned Buddha figurine in my pocket, as if holding him will summon Grayson from the Great Beyond and end this nightmare.

Gracie moves her phone closer to her face. Her big blue eyes fill the screen. "Don't be sad. Remember what you told me about Grandpa?"

"What did I tell you?"

"You said his pain was finally gone and he was in a better place. So your friend must be in that better place now too. Right? Just like Grandpa."

Yes, I tell myself, we should all be so lucky.

In the background, my mother calls for Gracie. I don't want her to discover us on the phone, so I tell Gracie it's okay if we hang up; time to start down the mountain soon anyway. She makes me promise to call before bed. Who needs a partner when I have Gracie to worry about me?

My phone is nearly back inside my pocket when it rings. The screen displays June McKinley's number. I quickly tap the icon, albeit the wrong icon, and she starts speaking before I can hang up for real.

"Ann? Hello? Is that you?" Her accusatory tone makes me wonder what I could've possibly already done wrong.

"Yes, Mrs. McKinley. It's me. Is everything ok?"

"Yes. I'm calling to find out if you've disposed of the ashes."

Not 'Grayson'. Not 'my son'. Just 'the ashes'.

Multiple unkind responses come to mind, but I bite my tongue. "Yes. Moments ago."

"Very well then. Check with Prudence at the front desk. She'll have an envelope for you within the hour. I've generously estimated your expenses and written you a check. I believe this concludes our business."

I'm not going to thank her for her money. Nor am I going to tell her how much I loved her son. She'll never learn of her granddaughter, or that her granddaughter inherited her son's kind heart. June McKinley will never know that Grayson is resting on top of the world, in the very spot where we conceived our Gracie. Nope, neither she nor anyone else in this little town needs to know any of our secrets. As Grayson would say, F'em.

I'm certain this is his final wish.

ROBIN CAIN began her writing career as a child, penning plays for friends to perform in neighborhood garages. Since then, her publishing credits include articles for online publications, stories in various anthologies, and two novels, the latest of which is entitled, *The Secret Miss Rabbit Kept.* She currently lives in Scottsdale, AZ, and you can often find her hiking in the great outdoors. That's where all her best ideas come from.

Thank You

Thank you so much for purchasing *Welcome to Effham Falls: Small town tales*. If you enjoyed this book, please take a few moments to write a review. We appreciate it. If you'd like to read more by the Moorhead Friends Writing Group, please check out our website.

https://moorheadfriendswritinggroup.com/

Made in the USA
Monee, IL
24 October 2023